Romance and Laughter?......Guilty!

Most people wouldn't treat a letter from a friend in jail as an invitation. But that is what Samantha Wilson did.

Sam is a boomer generation gal, and with her kids now grown, a late second bloomer.

Laugh, sigh, and cry with Sam as she pursues her own dreams and story of romance and it lands her in jail !

Handsome prosecutor, Jordan Campbell, with mid-life issues of his own, and a crime ring to capture, tangles with the pretty blonde inmate.

She holds the key to all he needs and leads him on a bewildering trial of his own.

Bett Bone

Beware of Boomer Romances

Guilty Plot: A Beware of Boomer Romance (1)

An Arts & Crafts AfFair: A Beware of Boomer Romance (2)

I Do Knot! : A Beware of Boomer Romance (3)* future

National Park Road Series

Buffalo Road: A Yellowstone Park Love Story (1)

Going to the Sun Road: A Glacier Park Love Story (2)

Road to Ancient Mazama: A Crater Lake Park Love Story (3)* future

Guilty Plot

Guilty Plot

a beware of boomer romance

Bett Bone

Bett Bone

Copyright

This is a work of fiction. All the characters, organizations, and events portrayed in this novel are products of the author's imagination or are used fictitiously.

dedication

*This book is dedicated to my children
and parents, and especially in memory
of my father,*

DEAN BONE

*While he is no longer with us physically,
he lives on every day in all our hearts
and happy memories*

chapter one

The loud clang make her jump, then a hard voice called through the food delivery portal in her door.

"Inmate number #48549 come to the door."

A tray was shoved through the portal with a wad of brown paper on it.

"Mail for inmate Wilson." The portal slammed shut.

It looked more like an exploded lump of paper and twine, but spotting her mother's handwriting on a scrap of the shredded brown paper, Samantha eagerly grabbed it and took it back to her bunk. Sifting through the mess on the tray she noticed other mail underneath—more second-hand mail already read and abused before it reached her.

Mail that Sam was not sure she *dared* read.

After all, it *was* an innocent looking letter that had gotten her into this mess to start with. If only she had ignored it that night.

That miserable night ...

Stumbling through her door, Samantha had tossed the grocery bag at the couch to free a hand. Juggling briefcase and mail, she flipped the light on before rescuing her keys from the sticky lock. Slamming the door with her hip, shutting out the cold, rainy, late winter night, she locked herself into the colder, shabby, cluttered room that served as her living, dining, entry, kitchen, and home office area, all rolled into one convenient depressing space.

Dropping into the chair before her, she swore she could hear her burning feet groaning with relief. The contents of her full arms tumbled onto her lap. Too exhausted at the moment to attempt struggling out of her damp coat: Sam felt every decade of her age. Slumping, unable to move, she needed to rest her feet before getting up to fix soup for a late dinner, before making what seemed like an immense trek to her bed, all of ten feet away—fortunately the bathroom was on the way.

Resting her head against the chair back, Sam closed her eyes. Maybe she would just skip dinner, too tired to be hungry any more. Had she had lunch that day? She couldn't recall. Or care. It was already after ten, and she desperately needed sleep to wash away her exhaustion and, somehow, get up for work and start the routine again in a few short hours.

She could eat tomorrow. Trying to rise for bed, she found herself pinned down.

Shoving purse and briefcase to the floor, she paused to examine the pile of mail on her lap. As expected, they were all threatening notices that her utilities were all about to be cut off. Her life, she thought wearily, had already been cut off. At least she didn't get any of those pesky credit card offers anymore.

Could she remember the last time she'd worked less than sixty hour weeks? Yet she could not make headway on her bills, though she was hardly extravagant. She had no time, and less energy, to go spend money, Or dollars to spend, for that matter. Everything went for the necessities of survival.

And that is what it was, just survival, merely existing. Not living.

Would she ever find time to live?

Not tonight!

As survival required sleep, Sam shoved the mail to the floor to rise, but spotted one real letter amid the carnage. An actual real letter, from a real live person, with a handwritten address! How could she resist?

The letter appeared to be from a gal that had worked with her long ago. She'd become fond of the younger woman, lent an ear to her personal troubles, encouraged and mentored her at work, as much as she was able. Their lives had grown apart since – in vastly different ways. Still, she'd been like a little sister once.

The younger woman had become entangled in serious trouble a few months back, ending up in jail. This was the first contact since word of the girl's predicament spread. Concerned for her welfare coping with such an awful situation, Sam snatched it off the floor, tearing it open, relaxing as she read the first few lines.

She sounded good, positive, like she was managing well. Sam read on, learning she was at a women's correctional compound that sounded more like a college campus than prison, wearing her own clothes, even jeans, with a private sunny room. She'd discovered all kinds of benefits and programs available there, like taking advantage of a fully equipped fitness room. Also enrolling online in college courses she'd always wanted, free now as part of her rehabilitation. All her teeth, even a new crown on a broken tooth that had bothered her for years were being fixed! Obviously, she was excited with all her opportunities and the lovely surroundings on the campus where she would spend the next eighteen months.

It must have been the chill, the effects of a cold room and damp coat that finally made Sam realize she'd been sitting staring at the letter long after she finished reading. Unconsciously her tongue inventoried the inside of her mouth, seeking out the jagged edges where a filling had been lost, or an edge chipped. Sam was trying to feel sorry for the girl, while glad all was going well—for her—and failing miserably.

Resentment built like a hard bitter knot in her chest. Sam was feeling very ... well, uncharitable.

Truth was, Sam was uncharacteristically pissed right off! A thought she surprised herself thinking, and would *never* say out loud.

Sam wanted, needed, the college education she'd missed by marrying and having kids too young. She definitely needed major dental work, but could not cover the deductible to use the minimal company benefits she'd earned.

Sam *certainly* didn't have eighteen months free room, board, power and heat to look forward to!

A law abiding citizen all her life, she'd raised her children to respect that responsibility. She'd worked herself to exhaustion six to seven days a week for years on end without a vacation, clinging doggedly to honesty and integrity in a tough business world—values she'd been taught to honor. They were threatening to turn her power off next week.

Sam could not suppress her rising bitterness and anger at the unfairness of it all. Okay, she knew that honesty and integrity didn't always pay off in dollars—even seeming like a disadvantage at times—but they gave her self respect and that was more important.

Right?

Except, of course, to the power company. She tried to visualize the power company receiving a draft on her 'self-respect account'. Not funny. Besides, judging by her mood, that account was also near empty.

And crime didn't pay either—except for room, board, heat, light, dental, medical, education and fitness, and don't forget no car expenses, Sam thought cynically.

DARN IT! It was just not fair!

Her anger finally gave her the energy to rise from her chair. Mentally, she stomped off to her bedroom, fuming; her feet hurt way too much to actually be so foolish. Rebelliously, she dumped her clothes just where they fell in the tiny space at the end of her bed. She'd rolled under the covers and curled up tight, trying to warm a spot in the damp chilly sheets.

No one ever promised life would be fair, an annoying voice in her head reminded just before she muttered, "Oh, shush!" and dropped into exhausted unconsciousness.

The next morning, stepping over discarded clothes and bills carpeting the floor, Sam wondered why she had let that darn letter upset her so much?

Padding to the counter area that served as her official kitchen, she fumbled with the coffee maker, eyes still too bleary to help out. Throwing the switch, she crawled into the shower, hoping she'd put the coffee in the filter this time, instead of the water reservoir.

As the hot water beat against aching joints and sluggish eyes, Sam started to revive and waken enough to wonder what day of the week it was. And how many more she needed to drag herself through before she could sleep in for a day? Was it Wednesday? Or Thursday? Probably just Tuesday and a lot of wishful thinking. Her brain too exhausted for such heavy analysis, she knew it was a work day, so she better just get moving.

Wrapping herself in a towel, she found the Coffee God was in his heaven, granting her success this morning. Taking just a quick sip, to get her system started, Sam forced herself to straighten clothes and bed, so she could sit and enjoy the rest of her fresh cup of coffee.

Wednesday! Yes, that was it. That meant three more mornings before she could sleep in for one. Groaning, she spotted her grocery bag still on the couch; relieved, she saw nothing would have spoiled in the chilly room overnight. Bending to pick up the bills at her feet, she shoved the most urgent into her briefcase, hoping for time to open them on a work break and call to plead a delay until payday.

Picking the letter up last, Sam stared at it while she finished her coffee. She had to answer, let her friend know she cared ... but ... resentment washed over her again. How was she to write the positive cheerful note needed, when she felt this way?

Get over it. Normally even tempered, Sam did not like the way she was reacting; and anger took more energy than she had to waste. She'd write a nice note Sunday when she was rested and less depressed.

A growl from her tummy reminded Sam it still had not been fed. Getting up, she jammed a piece of bread in the toaster and went to find something clean and pressed to wear to work. Deciding on the simple navy suit she'd made from a designer pattern her last long holiday weekend off; Sam knew the beautiful cut and cleanly tailored lines would help her feel more confident and professional today. She really needed to quit pouting and get down to business.

Fortunately she liked creating beautiful clothes, the only affordable way she had of wearing them. It might be nice though if she worked somewhere they didn't matter; where she could wear jeans and flannel shirts each day. *Like in jail*, her recalcitrant mind muttered.

Enough, she'd scolded herself. Glancing at the clock, she hastily swept her fine blonde and silver-threaded hair into a knot, pinning it at her nape. Donning a slight bit of make-up to brighten her face, she brought some sparkle back to her sleepy brown eyes. Grabbing briefcase and coat, she tore out the door. If her car started, she'd still make it to work on time.

Luckily, the engine caught after just one heart-stopping cough. She forced self-pitying thoughts from her mind on the drive to work. There were a million and three things she needed to accomplish that day.

As she merged into depressingly heavy morning rush hour traffic, her stomach growled, reminding her that her dinner that night was already half prepared.

Sam's breakfast was still waiting back in the toaster.

By the time Samantha had returned to her cold dark home later that evening, her fuel-starved, exhausted brain had already settled firmly on her 'brilliant idea!'

What else was a desperate aging woman to do?

The delicious smell wafting up from her mauled package brought Sam momentarily back to her present situation—her warm, rent-free jail cell. The aromas of coconut and vanilla tantalized her starved senses. She carefully picked apart the mauled package seeking the treasure inside. As usual, her mom had wrapped it first in waxed paper, then plastic, then put it inside an old-fashioned waxed cardboard milk carton, then wrapped it in foil, with an outer mailing wrapping of brown paper—all in an attempt to get her home baked goods to her daughter fresh and intact. It just seemed to have made the guards suspect she was trying to smuggle in a disguised pipe bomb or chemical weapon. The package was hopelessly torn, mangled and what it had once held—a beautiful ring of homemade coconut pound cake—was now reduced to a huge mess of crumbs. They must have crushed and sifted through every inch to make sure they didn't miss any hidden danger. Sam could only hope they had worn gloves on their hands, as she planned to savor every delicious crumb, though she suspected more than a slice or two's worth was missing.

She hummed with pleasure as she scooped some into her mouth. No one made pound cake like her mom!

Her poor mom. And dad, poor dad. They had been so shocked and baffled. It had been so hard to tell them. That day played constantly like a sweet, sad movie in her memory.

Sam's words, tossed out so casually, fell like a bomb in the middle of the Wilson's garden, startling it to stillness.

A long legged spider paused on the shade dappled brick terrace; bees stopped, hovering over fragrant petals tumbling from urns around white iron benches. Birds, plumbing the grassy yard, raised their heads then froze, miniature statues.

"Samantha! Surely you are joking!"

"No, mom, I'm completely serious. I just wanted to warn you both first, so you'd understand. I didn't want you thinking you'd failed as parents. I thought if I explained, well, maybe you'd be less embarrassed. You do understand don't you?"

"Understand?" her father choked.

"Jail?" Both parents wailed, sure they'd misheard.

She gave her shell-shocked parents a brisk nod, turning to look away from their faces. A nosy robin was eyeing her like the worm she probably was, but she had to tell them sometime. It was not going very well. Sam gnawed her lower lip as the unnatural silence in the garden lengthened.

"But ... Samantha ... jail? That's a little extreme, isn't it dear?" Her mother asked calmly, knowing better than to argue and get her daughter's back up.

"Can't you just marry someone to protect and take care of you?" her father asked despairingly, though he'd heard the answer enough times in the past.

"Talk about a prison! I didn't say I wanted a life sentence, Dad!" Sam rolled deep brown eyes in mock horror at her well-intentioned if charmingly old-fashioned father.

"I just don't know where you get these crazy ideas! I know you don't get them from me," he muttered casting a suspicious sideways glance at her mother. She just shook her head, denying genetic responsibility. Baffled, they studied their daughter silently.

The trim figure in crisp jeans and white tailored blouse, silky blonde hair pulled into a ponytail, reminded them of the teen that had always been so bright and easy to manage growing up. It was hard to realize how much time had flown past. Fine lines crinkled the corners of brown eyes that seemed to glow clear to her soul, silver strands threaded like highlights in her hair; she was no longer young, closing in on senior discount days.

Yet still so naive in many ways, her mother sighed. Maybe hormone therapy would help, she considered a moment before asking wisely, "Sam, what do your children think of all this?"

"Oh, well, ah ... I'm sure they'll be very supportive." Her reply sounded more confident than she looked.

"You mean you haven't told them yet?" Her parents chorused.

"I will. Soon. This coming weekend, in fact ... maybe," she added less convincingly. "But don't say anything until I've spoken with them."

"Fine," her mother grinned, sure this problem would fizzle on its own. "I'm sure they'll come up with a better and more acceptable alternative for you than your father's," she added, smiling fondly at her husband, always teasing about his marriage solution to all Sam's problems. He meant well, but it was obvious that Sam needed more than that. Besides, marriage hadn't previously protected Sam – just the opposite, in fact. They'd have to quell their fears and stand behind their daughter, if it came to that.

Privately, Mrs. Wilson hoped her sensible grandchildren would be more effective at putting the skids to this particular notion of their mom's.

Sam jumped up and hugged them both, needing to escape. ""Well, love you mom and dad. I've got to get going. I'll let you know what's up. Bye."

Driving home, Sam thought about the turn the conversation had taken. Chewing her lip as she drove, she was *not* looking forward to trying to explain to her grown children what their mother was about to do.

Beneath the cake her mom had sent, there were letters on the tray from both Ronnie and her kids. She decided to fortify herself with a few more bites from her crumbled cake jumble first, before reading them. As she scooped up another handful, her fingers snagged a brief note from her mom.

Darling daughter, hope you are okay. Your father and I are so worried, but we love you. Your father went out to the airport hanger today to 'shoot the breeze' with the other old pilots. He tells me he met a younger pilot that is a really nice man, and widowed. He showed him your picture and said he was interested in meeting you some day.

Some things never change do they? But be patient dear, he just loves you. As do I. I'll try to keep him from getting you engaged before you can get out of jail and defend yourself.

Love you, Mom

"Oh, Daddy." Samantha sighed, her smile wobbly. He was such a sweet old-fashioned man. Always wanting her to have someone to protect her ...

A sob echoed in Sam's soft laughter, alone in her cell, but still loved.

chapter two

"Yes, what is it now?" The harried man growled at his secretary.

Tall, broad of shoulder, a thick head of hair, its darkness only enhanced by the lighter threads shimmering through, over eyes more silver than gray and sharp with intelligence. His lean facial features were all chiseled planes, with a strong clean-shaven jaw lacking only its normal outdoor bronze. The man was handsome as sin in a way that startled each time, though she saw him every day. Elsa watched her boss, Jordan Campbell, as his athletic body paced with the fluid grace of a sleek predator seeking a way out of its cage; looking for an opportunity to spring suddenly, from tightly bunched muscles. Only in his case, the prosecutor's taut mind sought the opening to pounce and put *another* in a cage, where he belonged permanently, safely away from society.

If only his manners were as handsome as he was, but his past ... His secretary sighed. Such a shame. Straightening from where she had paused to study his mood, she stepped through his doorframe.

"Jordan," Elsa stopped a foot into his office, "sorry to interrupt but it's your assistant prosecutor and one of the public defenders, a Ms. Airton, to see you about the Henley case. They *did* have an appointment," she responded to his scowl.

Despite his devastating good looks, like any woman that came in contact with her boss, she was a little intimidated by the tyrant that lurked beneath. He drove everyone relentlessly, but seemed to save particular venom for the ladies. Heaven forbid one of them make the mistake of trying to flirt with *this* handsome bachelor!

He had humiliatingly crushed more than one fluttery-eyed female with his scorn!

Elsa had been his secretary for many years now. Though she'd never given him cause to lash out at her for inappropriate personal behavior, she *had* felt the sting of his harsh criticisms a few times. In her first few months on the job she'd gone home to her husband in tears several times, but she'd hung in there and learned not to take his criticisms so personally. His praise of her work performance was as strong and fair as his critique. The work was interesting, challenging, and for all his stormy temper, she respected the hard working, diligent man that was her boss.

He *did* have his days though. He had definitely been getting more temperamental and harsh the last several months. Elsa heaved a sigh of relief now as he just scowled a moment before giving a curt nod to indicate she should show them in while he stacked and covered the papers he'd been working on.

"Todd," he acknowledged, nodding to the chairs facing his desk, "and Ms. ..." He pronounced 'Ms.' with a just discernible, but disdainful, hiss.

"Airton, Ms. Airton, but please call me Shelley," the young woman supplied as she seated herself, the short skirt of her suit riding high on her crossed thighs.

"Ms. Airton," he completed his greeting with a glacial nod. Jordan had met her before, of course, but always treated her as a stranger when they met again, emphasizing how beneath his notice he considered her. He had to guard his tongue whenever greeting her, as he personally thought of her as Ms. Airhead. He had only slipped a few times—quite a few. Though young, she was, he knew, a very capable public defender. She did not really deserve his derogatory title, but she sported such a fluffy, dizzy-blonde look, combined with the similar name, that he found it difficult to think of her otherwise.

If she really wanted to be taken seriously and respected for her sharp and supple mind, she should wear less make-up and more decorous clothing, he thought pompously, as he settled back behind his desk.

"Speak. Henley case. I'm busy," was his cordial opening.

Todd, his assistant prosecutor, was quite familiar with this abrupt attitude and prepared with the brief and precise statements that were all he would be allowed.

"Henley. Thirty-five year old unemployed Caucasian male, arrested for peddling drugs at the high school. Two counts sale, one count possession coke, two counts possession methamphetamines. Priors ... similar charges two years ago, attorney was Carpenter," he paused briefly at this, a raised eyebrow conveying a silent message to his boss. "Charges reduced, minimal sentence. Ms. Airton is here to discuss a plea bargain. We have him solid, no need to deal, we can convict!" Todd finished firmly, sitting back to await questions, or instructions.

Casting a considering look at Todd, Campbell asked only one question.

"Was Henley 'unemployed' when Carpenter represented him?"

"Mister Campbell," Shelley Airton jumped in impatiently, "my client is just a poor man trying to find a way to keep himself together. He knows he shouldn't ..."

"Excuse me!" Jordan brutally cut her off, not even bothering to glance her direction as he did, continuing to look steadily at Todd.

"Well?" he prompted Todd.

"No," Todd answered, "he was not legitimately employed then or since."

Turning slightly to Ms. Airton, "No deal!" Jordan said abruptly.

"But...but you haven't even considered! You haven't even listened," she stuttered in absolute frustration.

Leaning forward across his desk, his face intimidatingly close to Shelley's, he advised her roughly, "You tell your client I want his employer's name, address, description. I want the years, the hours, the dates, and the deliveries he made in his employ. I want the amount, and the means used when his boss paid Carpenter to represent him before. And I want it all in a written deposition. I do not want to hear from you. I do not want you to so much as cross my threshold until you have it in your hand, signed and notarized. Then, and only then, will I discuss any possibility of a deal with you. Period! Goodbye, Ms. Airton!" Campbell snapped.

Gaping at him, momentarily speechless with anger, she grabbed her file and briefcase, storming from the room.

"I don't know how you can work for that rude son-of-a-bitch!" Shelley complained to Elsa on her way out, through tightly clenched teeth but in a voice pitched to be heard in the inner office.

"Oh, well," Elsa replied calmly, "he is so pretty to look at, you know. Kind of like having roses at your desk to gaze at everyday." Elsa gave a dramatic sigh along with her pat response to this frequent complaint, infuriating Shelley even more.

"Roses don't have as many thorns," Shelley snarled over her shoulder, as she stomped out, slamming the outer door, thoroughly.

Jordan Campbell rocked back in his desk chair, stretching hands behind his head. Shelley's voice had been clearly heard in his office and he was pleased with himself.

"Don't give her an inch on this, Todd," he instructed. "Complete cold shoulder on the Henley case, deal with her through your secretary. If she brings you a formal deposition, then I want you to examine it for thoroughness. See if it has what we need to hang the bastard, before you even agree to approach me for a deal.

"Meanwhile, give them all the time and delays they ask for before we go to trial. I want plenty of time for Henley to sweat, and think it all over. We don't want that poor dumb bastard anyway, just his boss.

"But if Henley doesn't comply fully? Crucify him! Go for the maximum sentence in court. If we can't get the big guy, we can at least try and destroy his work force!"

"Yes, sir," Todd said with a grin. "Maybe we'll get him this time?"

"I hope so, Todd. I hope so," he replied wearily. "Keep me posted."

Will I *ever* get that bastard? Jordan wondered, turning to stare moodily out the rain drenched window, at weather that mirrored his mood.

Now this Henley thing taunted him like an elusive tease. Just to give him false hope of another chance? Would Henley be the key? Jordan's gut told him he was.

Or was he so haunted by his past failed attempts to nail Honest Abe Damon that he saw that bastard's ghost in every case that crossed his desk? Honest Abe! God, he hated that name!

Yet Todd seemed to have the same suspicions that Henley might be a link to Abraham the Liar. Or was Todd just humoring his obsession? Using it like a carrot to keep Jordan's focus on the grind of daily routine?

No. There was no mistaking the fat pitch Todd had lofted with that mention of attorney Carpenter's prior involvement. Jordan had felt his blood quicken immediately, sensing the hunt was on again.

Abraham Damon's criminal organization was made up of scores and scores of small time punks that the man used as a shield, while he paraded as a pillar of the community. A lot of the information on how the organization worked had been gleaned from those small-timers that, when pulled in, gave up only teasing pieces of the puzzle. But once a tape recorder came out, or their statement was given to them to sign ... Pouf! They zipped their lips. When pressured with harsher sentences, they all magically became the 'pro-bono' clients of a high-priced local law firm. Carpenter's.

Right. 'Pro-bono' my ass! Jordan thought.

The same law firm, coincidentally, just happened to handle all of Honest Abe's legitimate business. It was obvious that Abe was using his law firm to purchase their silence: paying their legal fees, getting them lighter sentences, paying them to do the time, assuring them a place in his organization when they got out.

Both the local law enforcement agencies and the DEA suspected Abraham's organization of being responsible for not only the bulk of the drugs in the schools, but also the force behind an area wide car theft ring. In both instances, Damon used the same corporate structure. A work force composed of youths, easily lured by the money and sense of power it gave them. And since they were minors, they were protected by law. Their sentences would be no more than short vacations with a job rewarded to them when they got out, their adult record still 'clean'. Such a deal for old Honest Abe!

Another basic source of labor appeared to be the unemployment and welfare rolls. They collected benefits while Abe paid them under the table, as his middle management. They supervised the labor force of juvenile minors on Abe's corporate ladder.

Henley, Jordan suspected, was one of those mid-level managers. Jordan needed to pin down the higher rungs of the ladder, the one's that would lead to Abe, the ones that would convict him. Possibly Henley might provide a step up that ladder.

Jordan had deliberately baited Henley's attorney. Airton was good and aggressive in defense of her clients. She'd fight harder than ever now to get a good deal for Henley, just to spite Jordan! She would see that her client got his message and delivered the goods. Perfect, just perfect.

Grabbing his briefcase, Jordan headed out of his office.

"I'll be at the law library if there is anything urgent," he informed Elsa on his way out. Maybe with enough diligence he would find some precedent he had previously missed that would give him the wedge he needed to pry open Damon's crime ring.

Elsa returned late, hot, and frustrated, after her late lunch break. Her day had turned sour.

It had been uncharacteristically hot outside, after a morning squall, for the time of year. One of those sudden record-breaking scorchers that descend out of spring rains, to tease or warn that the advent of summer was just weeks away. A reminder intended to make the school kids restless to end the term and escape. Adults looked at calendars, realizing they needed to confirm arrangements for annual vacation plans.

Elsa had been glad to escape from the incessant ringing of phone and fax, the frantic pace of a system trying to function effectively on too few resources, too little time to prepare for continual deadlines. The pace had kept all the staff at their desks for lunch most days, but today Elsa just had to escape a few minutes—or loose her sanity.

Jordan had been his usual overworked, snappish self. Even Todd seemed in danger of losing his normal sense of humor, trying to keep up. Knowing she was reaching her own patience limits, Elsa had fled for the much needed break.

One of the cafes, a short walk from the courthouse, had taken advantage of the fine day and set its summer sidewalk tables up early. Grabbing the last seat, Elsa relaxed. Though the tables and sidewalk were crowded, she could revel in the luxury of her own private thoughts a few moments, here in the warmth of the sun. She cut her pleasant lunch short a few minutes, setting off to do a quick errand at the bank on her way back to the office.

Groaning at the crowd at the cash machine as she got in line, Elsa realized she was sure to be late back to the office. It was less shielded here from the direct rays of the midday sun that had brought everyone from their offices. Elsa shifted from foot to foot, impatiently waiting her turn. The sun beat on her head and she felt the heat in the exposed concrete sidewalk through the thin soles of her heels. Her discomfort and her tension rose as the line failed to move ahead.

Checking her watch, Elsa looked to the front of the line, hoping her glare would penetrate the back of the heads of those holding things up. Her cheer in the glorious day evaporated, replaced by the renewed stress of meeting deadlines.

What were those young boys doing here, she wondered angrily, her frustration finding a target. They should be in school. Probably more local dropouts, getting younger and more numerous each day. They'll end up in our case files soon, she muttered to herself.

When she finally got through and back to the office, Todd's voice greeted her.

"Elsa! Thank goodness you decided not to play hooky after all! Pleasant lunch?" he inquired.

"No. Yes. Sorry. I'm late." Elsa filed her purse in a drawer, sitting down abruptly.

Raising an eyebrow at the terse reaction from the normally unruffled Elsa, Todd paused a moment to offer some words of kindness and appreciation.

"Hey, things have been hell here lately, I know. You've been great about all the work we throw at you. I didn't mean for my comment to come out wrong. I'm sure Jordan would agree that you deserve the whole day off, if you want."

"Thanks, Todd, you're a dear. I didn't mean to sound so grumpy. I had a wonderful lunch at Tony's. He had the tables up outside. It was the long, hot, line at the bank on my way back, that ruined my day. I was getting upset it would make me late, but it was the gang of young boys hanging out there that really wound me up. Everything we do here seems so pointless when you see some of the youth of today.

"Where are their parents?" She complained. "They drop out of school, join gangs to get attention, and because their parents don't seem to care. Then, when they end up on our caseloads, everyone is so surprised, wondering how they got that way. It just seems so futile and endless. And why are they hanging out at the bank? Because they're all selling drugs by the age of twelve? A bunch of young drug entrepreneurs? Oh, Todd, it just gets me so mad. I'd like to find all their parents and lock them up for ruining their children's futures."

Dumping her anger and frustration in Todd's ready and sympathetic ear helped.

"But," Elsa added, trying to regain her positive attitude, and a joking smile, "the good news is that Ms. Airton did not leave you or Jordan twenty phone messages while I was gone to lunch. Suppose she has given up?"

"Not likely," Todd laughed. "She's probably just been tied up," he added, heading for his office now that Elsa seemed back to her old self.

Todd shared her concern for the youth of today, but the cases of yesterday's troubled kids, now adults charged with crimes, waited on his desk.

"Five bucks says Shelley gets her twenty calls in today," was Todd's parting shot.

Elsa didn't even bother to take his bet, sure he was right; and that she would spend her afternoon trying to keep the lady at bay. Just what she needed! She wished Shelley Airton would play hooky today and leave her in peace. What she really wished was that everybody would take a few days off from committing crimes!

Late that afternoon Jordan had a call from Todd when he returned from doing his research.

"I heard something interesting, thought you might want to know. The DA's secretary mentioned that a Ms. Shelley Airton visited the DA's office today, with 'smoke pouring out of her ears'. Appears she went over your head and tried to get the DA to intervene in the Henley case. He told her to discuss it with you." Todd laughed. "The woman is in a real spot, now. He won't talk to her, and you won't talk to her unless her client comes through." Todd chuckled, "Just thought you'd like to know."

"Thank you, Todd." Jordan hung up, amused. You had to admire the girl for her guts, he thought grudgingly. However, she had made a mistake, a big mistake. He was not going to forget this.

No one played games behind the prosecutor's back and got away without paying!

"Elsa," he spoke into the intercom, "call the florist and have them send Ms. Airton a dozen dead dandelions, in an inexpensive vase, please. Be sure to sign the card with my regards."

"Yes, Mr. Campbell. I'll get right on that, sir," Elsa replied efficiently. Both of them knew that she would tactfully ignore his request. Ms. Airton would never receive any flowers from Mr. Campbell—dead or otherwise.

All afternoon Jordan had spent fruitless hours in the law library researching past cases again, seeking the avenue that would give him his chance to solidify a case on Damon. But he'd had no more luck today than he had the last time he went earlier that year. He had blamed a woman for that first time.

She had entered the library brimming with the exuberance of a friendly spring day, unaware of how her presence impacted other patrons.

A smile curving soft lips, cheeks blushed by the crisp air, brown eyes dancing with merry golden flecks, the petite blonde woman brought the fresh spring breeze into the law library with her jaunty step, her smiling glow, raising the heads of all the serious, silent readers—including Campbell's—as she passed their tables, heading for the reference desk.

"Hello," she smiled joyfully at the somber librarian, "could you direct me to the law reference section, please?" The cheerful countenance, and soft melodic voice, caused the woman at the desk to smile, in spite of herself. She actually led Sam to the proper area, instead of just nodding curtly in that direction.

"Thank you, so much," the charming voice responded gratefully, bringing a further unprecedented response from the librarian.

"If there's anything else I can help you with, don't even hesitate, just let me know. I'll be happy to help."

That exchange brought the dark head of one of the regular law library patrons up again, unable to believe his ears. Glancing over quickly, he needed to be sure it was the same person that had managed to bring such a comment from the dour Mrs. Appleberry, who ruled over this domain like a frigid tigress. And again it was that tiny disruptive blonde, noting her pert smiling face despite himself.

Hmph!

He hoped she wasn't the noisy, chatty type. He returned moodily to his note taking on the case he was studying, hoping she'd stay clear of his space and not take too much of the librarian's time. He hunched forward over his books, bringing his palms up to brace his forehead. This not only obscured the handsome and public face, but gave the impression of serious and intent study. It was one of his most effective, and often used, 'no trespassing' signs.

If he had not been so intent on establishing his no-possible-eye-contact defense, Jordan might have noticed that the pretty blonde never even looked in his direction, while he fumed patiently...

Or rather, impatiently.

Time and time again. Waiting for Mrs. Appleberry to pull the briefs he needed.

Jordan knew his way around the law library better than his own home, but searching for the obscure, unusual briefs he'd need to pin his elusive criminal down required more of the research librarian's time than usual. Yet she'd kept going off, fawning over that blonde, wasting most of his last hour that day before he'd had to return to his office.

Women! Just because the blonde had a nice smile and soft laugh—that made it seem as if she'd brought the freshness of springtime inside with her—was no reason for the librarian to ignore the other patrons. Didn't she realize how much more important his time was than that woman's?

Jordan had been so sure that day that if he'd just had more assistance then, he would have found what he needed. It was there somewhere; it had to be. He'd been running out of time to bring charges. That scoundrel couldn't get off again. Honest Abe. Damn, how he hated that man and the ludicrous nickname the man flaunted!

With a wry smile, Campbell had to admit now that he'd had no better luck today without any distractions. He probably should not keep blaming that little blonde spring beauty with the soft voice and sweet smiles and manners that had so affected... *others* ... in the library for his own failure to find a way to file those earlier charges. Frowning, he didn't know why he'd let the incident keep bugging him anyway.

Jordan slammed the file folder shut, drumming his pencil rapidly on the cover before shoving himself from his desk. Brushing strong fingers through thick, dark hair, he rose and paced the small office, growling to himself as he went. "They can't get away with this!

Not again, damn! I'm missing something." He paused to stretch taut neck muscles and roll some of the tension from broad shoulders.

Yanking at his tie, undoing another button of the crisp white shirt, Jordan rolled the sleeves up his forearms. He'd discarded the elegant vest and matching suit jacket long before. Even with his tie askew, his clothes awry, and a stubble starting to form along a hard, handsome jaw, he had an undeniable lean and casual elegance. But Elsa and the rest of the staff had long since left for home so there was no one left to admire it—or to witness him struggling to avoid failure once more.

Maybe the Henley case would turn up some of the missing pieces, though he sincerely doubted it.

Realizing his private line was ringing he reached out and snatched up the phone barking, "Office is closed."

"I knew you'd still be there," Todd laughed. "I have a bag of fish and chips takeout from the bar that I'll bring you on my way home if you'll hang in a bit longer. Trust me, I have something to tell you that won't wait 'til tomorrow. You'll want to hear this one now, boss."

chapter three

U naware of the floral tribute requested in her honor, Shelley Airton was busily drumming a pen on her legal pad, fuming and frustrated in her attempts to assist her client.

First, she had been turned out of the DA's office, now the assistant prosecutor was humiliating her. She'd always had a good working relationship with Todd in the past. Today she'd left a dozen messages for him and couldn't even get past his secretary! She had just hung up after another attempt. His secretary saying, "I'm so sorry, Ms. Airton, he's been tied up on important business all day. He suggested you just drop Henley's deposition off with me and one of us will get back with you as soon as he has had a chance to review it."

"Jerk!" She'd shouted, after hanging up. *She* was obviously *not* 'important business', and she was obviously *not* going to be speaking with *anyone*, until she followed Jordan Campbell's orders!

Todd knew she had no plans to get a deposition from an innocent-until-proven client. And what the hell did they mean by Henley's boss? What boss? They knew the guy hadn't been employed in years! He was just a poor, dumb fool that had tried to make a quick, illegal buck. Why were they playing hardball with her over Henley, of all cases?

Well, only a few options were open to her now if she wanted a plea deal, so she had better get on with them. First, she'd file for a delay and hope that someone would give her a more reasonable hearing later. Second, she'd better visit Henley, get him to sign a waiver of his right to a speedy trial, and give him the bottom line. She would have to get some kind of written statement from him, just to show she'd tried. And third, she told herself with a vicious smile, she'd find a picture of that damn prosecutor and make a dartboard out of it for her wall! Gathering up her files and tape recorder, she went to pay Henley a visit.

The pathetically hopeful look her client gave her when they brought him into the consultation room, almost made Shelley change her planned tactics. However, as cruel as it was, it would be better just to hit him as hard as the prosecutor had her, using his exact words and tone.

She was startled when instead of the expected hoot of derision as she informed him of his 'imaginary boss', Henley pulled abruptly back from the table and wrapped his arms tightly across his chest, a panic-stricken look in his eyes.

Uh-oh, she thought. Looks like we have a problem here. She read the closed body language but continued to lay out the rest of the prosecutor's positions, then waited for her client to speak.

And waited…

"You better talk to me!" She finally said angrily. All she got was a negative twitch from the closed and frozen features. Henley rose and rang to return to his cell block.

Terrific! Now her client wouldn't even talk to her!

Ms. Airton was not having a good day!

Then it got worse.

With a mixture of excitement and trepidation, Sam had waited until returning to her cell after dinner to read her other letters from the first mail she'd ever received in jail.

After shuffling them, uncertain, she picked up the already open—and most likely censored—letter from Ronnie first.

Sam's closest friend was sharp, sassy, sexy and—even in her sixties—still a stunning brunette.

Rhonda Sayles was everything Samantha was not. A successful businesswoman, strong and fiercely independent, Rhonda could tear men to pieces with a whiplash tongue and ice blue eyes, then with a wink and seductive smile have them falling at her feet. She had never had, nor required, a husband.

Of her own.

Though she never lacked for male company of any designation.

To the outside world Rhonda seemed to have a heart encased in stainless steel, but Samantha and her children held keys to the fun, caring and supportive inner woman. Without children of her own, Ronnie borrowed Sam's at every chance, proudly calling herself their "Honorary Aunt".

The two had been almost lifelong best friends despite their opposing personalities and lifestyles—or perhaps because of them.

Sam picked up the precious letter, and then just stared at it, her mind wandering back.

After months of making sure of her resolve, with business and bills only getting worse, Sam had been positive that she knew what she wanted and why she wanted it. It made perfect sense to her, and she had been eager and ready to start planning her incarceration. But based on the horrified look on her father's face, after she had told her parents, well ... maybe she hadn't explained herself well enough. She needed help from her closest friend and advisor. Not wanting to wait for another Sunday to talk to Rhonda, Sam had turned her car around and headed over to drop in at Ronnie's condo.

"Whatever it is, no way!" Rhonda greeted her firmly, but with a hug.

"But..."

"You're biting your lip again, Sam," Ronnie frowned. "And doing that squinchy thing with your eyes. You only get that kind of guilty look on your face when you've done something crazy and want me to fix it with your kids, and I don't do insanity. Whatever it is you will have to face the music yourself." Then reaching to pat Sam's hand and pull her inside, she softened her tone. "But I'm sure whatever it is we can straighten out. Stay overnight and explain what's going on. We haven't had a good girl chat in the longest time."

"Well ..ah," Sam grimaced, glancing at the trail of men's clothing strewn across the middle of the living room—clearly discarded in the heat of passion. "I'm not sure that would be a good idea," she finished lamely, wishing she had called ahead instead of just dropping in.

"Why on earth not?" Rhonda asked, calmly sitting on her sofa in her black silk robe, her hair dripping wet. Motioning Sam to come have a seat, she seemed totally unaware of the clothes between them, or the sounds emanating from the still running shower.

He certainly can't sing!

Sam stifled a giggle, knowing singing obviously wouldn't have been his main attraction.

"Listen, Ronnie, I've come at a bad time," Sam said hurriedly. "How about if..."

"Don't be ridiculous," Rhonda interrupted. "Why don't you go make us some coffee while I throw some clothes on. We'll sit down and have a good talk. There's no way I'm going to let you dance in here and then run for cover without explaining!"

Rhonda swooped up the clothes in a bundle as Sam headed for the kitchen. She heard her friend stop to toss the clothes into the bathroom, commanding, "Harold, go home. Now! And get some practice before you return."

My goodness! Sam chuckled to herself, hoping Ronnie was referring to his singing.

Moving about the familiar kitchen preparing coffee, Sam found the tin of pecan shortbread cookies Rhonda always kept in the small shuttered pantry.

Sam had always loved this room. It was light and bright and spacious without losing its coziness. A sunny seating bay, with windows facing south, overlooked a lush green park and gathered in sunlight all day. The vase of white and yellow daisies mixed with blue cornflowers and ferns sat in the middle of the table, keeping the nook bright even on rainy days. Rhonda's cleaning woman not only kept the light room sparkling and uncluttered, but also saw to it that the cozy nook had fresh flowers year round.

Sam had just settled with the coffee and cookies when Rhonda breezed through the shuttered door. Casually elegant in slim cobalt silk pants and tunic, her damp, dark hair sleekly twisted behind her head in a knot that emphasized the sculpted contours of Rhonda's cheekbones and brow—an elegant Vogue cover profile. Bringing the linen napkins over, Rhonda seated herself. Pursing lush red lips, she observed Sam carefully. This nook had been the scene of many a fun and happy chat between the two. This visit, however, looked more serious in nature. After listening for a few moments, in her normal style, Ronnie went abruptly to the point.

"What's this nonsense? Something about having to go to jail, being desperate, and looking forward to the free rent and a little R &

R? What on earth has happened? Do you really think you'll end in jail? That's nuts! And you want me to tell the kids?" Rhonda interrogated her with a voice as sharp as the blue eyes that searched Sam's face. "What's really up? I'm not buying this! Where are you really going, Sam? Why the subterfuge? Are you in some kind of other trouble? Oh, Sam…you're not pregnant, or something, are you? Do you need to hide for nine months? And how the hell could you get pregnant? You seem to have forgotten how to have sex! Not to mention you're too old. Are you sick?"

Rhonda was ruthless, suspecting Sam wasn't giving the full story, but relieved to see the amused, negative shake of Sam's head to her last questions. She paused to give Sam a chance to respond. After mere moments, unable to contain herself, Rhonda ventured another hopeful, but doubtful, guess.

"You're running off with a totally unsuitable man, and you don't want the kids to have a chance to check him out first !"

Another silent, amused shake of Sam's ponytail.

"No? Hmmm." Rhonda gathered her short supply of patience and huge reservoir of curiosity and fell silent again, watching the crown of the golden head bowed quietly over the floral centerpiece.

When Sam looked up, the amusement was gone. Her soft brown eyes glowed huge in the elfin face. Rhonda had always envied Sam's soft and expressive eyes. But now, as she studied her over the rim of her cup, she noted that while the face retained most of its youthfulness, it seemed to have lost some roundness. It looked leaner, lending gravity to the luminous eyes.

"I'm serious, Rhonda." Sam spoke softly, yet firmly. "I'm going to jail. That's a fact. I have to. I need your help."

Choking, from an inappropriately timed sip of coffee, Rhonda finally recovered her voice to insist, "You were kidding! Joking, right?"

"No. I know it sounds a little odd, but…"

"Odd? A little odd ?" Rhonda whispered, stunned to realize Sam just might be serious. "Oh darling, what could you have done to be sent to jail?"

"Well, I haven't done anything yet," Sam admitted earnestly. "I was hoping you might have some good ideas."

"You haven't done anything about getting an attorney yet? Don't worry Sam, I know just the one. The best attorney in town! You have to let me do that much for you."

"No…no. You don't understand. I haven't done anything. Anything! I'm not in trouble. I don't need an attorney…yet. Well, I guess I don't need one anyway," Sam explained.

Rhonda shook her head to clear it, setting down her cup, she leaned closer. "You're right, I don't understand. Haven't you a court date yet? Is that why you don't need an attorney? " Struggling to understand, Rhonda tried to get the facts straight, and in businesslike order, ticking the questions off her fingers.

"Okay, let's start at the beginning. One. When were you arrested? Two. What were you arrested for? Three. When is your hearing? Four. Outline the circumstances."

"I've never been arrested. I haven't done anything," Sam replied, brown eyes wide and innocent. "I just want to go to jail," she finished calmly, catching Rhonda with her mouth very inelegantly agape, and still holding three fingers in the air.

Sam took a sip of coffee, waiting for her words to sink in. Realizing it might be a slow recovery, she tried another approach. Thoughtfully fingering the silky fresh daisy petals, she spoke quietly, gazing down at the flowers.

"Remember when you told me that you never thought it was a waste of money to have fresh flowers brought in every few days year round?"

"*Flowers?*"

"Fresh flowers, yes," Sam looked up momentarily, her voice and eyes soft and sad. "You said to me, ' Why should I work so hard, if it's not to have the things in life that I enjoy most?'."

"Why…yes.," Rhonda nodded, confused but waiting for Sam to work up to whatever was on her mind.

Though the words were spoken softly, once Sam started, her frustration poured forth.

"I work and work and never get beyond the bills. I've been on a treadmill for years that won't ever stop or slowdown, but I'm not getting anywhere! Just running in place until I'm totally exhausted. I…I feel like one of those pet hamsters that the kids had. It would get on that wheel and just run, and run, and run, and finally get off to sleep and eat a little… then get right back on that stupid wheel and run fifty more miles getting nowhere! Poor thing. I always wanted to let them loose outside, but … I was afraid the cat would eat it." Sighing softly, she stared quietly out the window a moment before continuing, "I have no concept of living, Ronnie, just surviving. And I can't see the end in sight. It's getting worse, not better, or easier, and... I'm just getting older and older."

"Whew! You are depressed! I didn't realize, Sam. Well, come to think of it, I hardly see you anymore. You're always at work or... or dead tired. I should have realized, but you've always seemed such a survivor. Oh hell! Sorry. Poor choice of words. I just...," Rhonda stumbled to a halt, realizing everything she was saying proved that she should have known. She felt miserable. She should have been there for her dear friend.

"Hey, don't you feel bad," Sam patted her arm reassuringly. "You couldn't have known. It never did get me down before, not when I was working for the kids, because then I was doing it for what mattered most to me!

"Now . . . now it's just work! There are a few things I want to do just for myself but I can't get off the treadmill to pursue them. I think that's why I'm so tired of it all." Sam turned to stare blankly out the window, then shrugged her shoulders and looked down at the table. "I get so disgusted with myself for wallowing in this self-pity. Then I give myself a lecture on positive thinking. Make lists of personal goals I want to reach to reenergize myself. Next thing, it's three months later, and... well, not only have I been too busy to start the list, but I can't even find the darn thing! What's wrong with me, Ronnie? I'm just so burned out! Desperate to get away from it all, to get my time back for myself. Is that horribly whining and selfish?"

"Of course not, honey, you're due. Let me help. You should have said something sooner. I'd love to help you. Tell me, honestly, how much do you need to take a few months off and take a decent vacation?"

Seeing Sam shaking her head in protest, Rhonda rushed on. "Call it a loan then, whatever makes you happy, but please Sam, don't be stubborn now. I have tons of money just sitting in the bank rusting away!"

"Rusting?" Sam arched skeptical brows before shaking her head with a very wry smile. "No. No thank you, Rhonda. I appreciate the generous offer, really I do, but...*rusting?*" She gave a half-hearted laugh. "Only you could come up with rusty money!"

"You know what I mean. I'd rather have you putting it to good use than my bank using it. After all, you know how banks are! They probably loaned my money to some third world country that's using it to buy arms to start another civil war and destabilize the world!

And…why you would be doing the whole world a favor by accepting my "rusty" money and keeping it out of the hands of drugs or arms dealers . . . or even worse—sub-prime mortgage scammers!" Rhonda finished triumphantly, quite pleased with her irresistible logic, and the joyous laugh it coaxed from Sam.

"Oh, Ronnie, you always cheer me up," Sam smiled fondly, "but, I can't take your loan, seriously. If I had a job that paid decently and by the hour, instead of only commissions, with some way of knowing if and when I could pay you back, but…I don't. Besides, there's more to it than that."

"Then come stay here if you won't take a loan. You'd have your own bedroom, your own bathroom, and besides, it would be fun to be roommates! Don't you think?" Rhonda asked eagerly.

Pausing to pour fresh coffee to give herself time to think of a graceful way to decline Rhonda's latest offer, Sam finally decided it would be best to just be direct.

"I've decided on the solution, actually. I mentioned it earlier. I've decided to on a go-to-jail-free card for about a year or so." Sam tried to sound casual, but averted her eyes, finding she had a sudden desire to study the lush parkland outside the window.

As the stunned silence lengthened, Sam tried a different approach. "Ronnie, do you remember Watergate?"

"Watergate?" Rhonda croaked, bewildered, clenching both hands around her coffee cup.

"You know, when all those government officials went to jail, and ended up making a fortune ..."

"You're not going to rob a political campaign!" Rhonda reared back in her chair, horrified. "Are you, Sam?" Then unable to help herself, she leaned forward asking eagerly, "Which one? No," she jerked back again, "forget I said that. It's not the point. Besides, they do that by hacking these days, and you are so tech averse you probably don't know that's done with a computer instead of a saw."

Her friend fell so still and silent just shaking her head sadly, that the sound of the refrigerator could be heard humming quietly in the background.

But Rhonda understood now.

Her best friend was having a nervous breakdown! She'd never seen anyone having a breakdown, and it was eerie how calm Sam seemed. Rhonda would have expected her to be, well….nervous.

It was obvious though. Rhonda should have seen it coming. Sam was exhausted, depressed, feeling out of control of her life, her finances, her future. She was under stress and not very coherent, to put it kindly. Watergate? Wasn't that about forty, or so, years ago? Alzheimer's? Isn't that when you think the distant past is recent? Rhonda didn't know if that was right, she better check her facts. At any rate, Sam was not making any sense. Her judgement was clearly wacko. She needed help, she needed a mental checkup. She needed a psychiatrist, not a lawyer!

But how to deal with it? How to help her poor friend? Just listen. Be very calm and supportive, Rhonda decided, until she could call a hotline, or something, and get advice. She sure hoped this would be the right way to handle this! Poor dear Sam!

"Ye-e-e-s," she said slowly and carefully, "I remember Watergate. What was it you wanted to tell me about it?" Rhonda encouraged gently, leaning closer to Sam and trying to put her most earnest, sympathetic look on her face.

"It's a little embarrassing actually," Sam confessed shyly.

"No need to be embarrassed, dear," Rhonda inserted hurriedly, with a comforting little pat on Sam's hand.

"Well, it's always a little embarrassing when you have a secret desire that you've never confessed." Sam pulled her hand under the table before Ronnie bruised it.

Bracing herself, Rhonda pasted what she hoped was an empathetic smile on her face, nodding for Sam to continue.

"I mean, at first, I felt silly even admitting to myself that it was what I wanted to do. Seriously, I mean. You know, like when you're young and you realize you have a crush on a guy? You're embarrassed to admit it to yourself even, at first. And to tell someone else your guilty secret? Well, You'd die first, right?"

Actually, Rhonda did not know what that was like. She'd always been able to boldly commandeer any guy she wanted. If anyone was blushing about it, it was certainly the guy! However, she did understand what Sam was talking about, she'd read it in books, seen movies… the important thing was that she knew *Sam* was shy and sensitive like that. Especially now. Now she needed understanding nods of encouragement.

Except that last question!

Had she said die first? No wait. Rhonda hastily shook her head to that, terrified of responding wrong to Sam's obviously fragile mental state. Should I just keep a sincere smile on my face, Rhonda wondered. Or a more serious demeanor? Definitely no nodding, one way or the other, that was getting tricky. Dear, dear Sam needed a real professional's help.

Unaware of her friend's deep distress, Sam continued, "Well, it's the same kind of feeling anyway. I guess it's been a few years since I realized and admitted to myself that I was serious and ready to start pursuing my objective..."

Objective? Plus jail...oh my God! Was Sam going to rob a bank, not a campaign? Rhonda clenched her lips and tried to stay calm and, yes, smile serenely as she listened – without nodding.

"...and I never really confessed it before to other people. To anyone! I don't know if it's because I was afraid they'd laugh at me... or tell me I was crazy!"

Rhonda quickly stifled a guilty look.

"...or if what I was really afraid of was that they'd smile and nod..."

Rhonda quit smiling and remembered not to nod at all!

". . . and pretend to take me seriously... but..."

Now what could she do? Rhonda wondered desperately.

"But really be privately thinking that I was completely nuts," Sam glanced up to see if Ronnie understood, but her friend's face was buried in her coffee cup. "Are you okay, Ronnie?"

What sounded like "uh-huh" came from deep inside the mug.

Concerned, Sam rose to get a glass of water for her, cutting her explanation short.

"...So anyway, I'm sure it's what I want to do now. I'm committed to going ahead, no matter what people think. I'm going to do it!" Sam finished firmly, offering the glass of water to her friend. "That's what I meant about jail and Watergate, and fresh flowers, of course."

"Of course," Rhonda responded weakly. "Ah, do? Do what?" She asked warily, reaching for the glass.

Patiently, as if it was obvious, Sam told her.

But failed to catch the glass that Ronnie dropped.

Shaken by word she had received at the end of her working day, Shelley Airton escaped from her office. Finding herself at the pub next to the courthouse, she wasn't sure why she had come. She just knew she needed to go somewhere else, where she could just sit down and think, before having to fight the traffic home. She was on her second ginger ale, still just staring off into space, when her chair was jostled by a man trying to work his way into the crowded bar.

"Todd!"

He turned with a ready smile, until he recognized who had called out to him. "Oh, Shelley …hi." Reversing direction, as if he had just been leaving instead of entering the bar, he pinned a grin back on his face. "Gee, I'd love to stay and chat, but," with an expressive shrug, "my wife will kill me if I'm late for dinner!"

"Sit down." Shelley ordered. "I've just been fired by Henley, so you don't have to run away from me anymore."

"Really?" Todd dropped immediately into the chair across from her. "You're kidding. Why?"

"You know I can't tell you details, that's confidential. I can tell you this though," Shelley looked directly at him. "You now have to discuss the deposition you want with his new attorney. I believe you know the firm? Carpenter, Taylor & Croft?

"Well, I'll be damned…"

"You should be." Shelley erupted angrily. "And take that miserable boss with you when you visit those eternal fires down under." She snapped. Then shaking her head abruptly, she apologized immediately. "Hey, I'm sorry. I didn't really mean that. I'm just depressed."

Concerned to see such a spirited lady so low, Todd signaled for a couple of drinks, and encouraged, "Do you want to tell me about it?"

"Maybe I should. Maybe you can talk some sense into me. I'm thinking of resigning." Todd's serious and patient gaze prodded her to continue.

"My job is to defend anyone who needs me. To crusade for the little guy," bitter self-mockery evident in her voice, "but, it seems like I'm the one being taken for a ride more often than I'm really helping someone who's really poor and defenseless. There's some game going on and I'm the only sucker that doesn't understand the rules. Then I find myself hating *you* guys. Your job is to protect the public also. All of them. Society. I don't know, I'm probably not making any sense, but something is wrong with my current scenario. It just doesn't feel right anymore."

Embarrassed that she was coming across too maudlin, Shelley tried to joke, to lighten the self-pity she heard in her words.

"I *should* hate your boss, the prosecutor, because he's arrogant and treats women like crap. Right?" she asked flippantly, with a feeble attempt at a smile. "I should not hate him because he is trying to defend the public!"

"What do you want?" Todd asked the saddened woman, softly.

"I don't know. I don't know, I guess I want absolution or something. Hey, forget I even said any of this. Okay? Probably just a mood. I better go home and get some rest. Thanks for the drink, Todd. Sorry to cry on your shoulder like that."

Todd stared thoughtfully after the departing Shelley as he finished his drink. So, poor defenseless Henley was now a client, *again*, of the highly exclusive, expensive firm of Carpenter, Taylor & Croft? Interesting, and Henley's former attorney was depressed and felt like she might be angry at the wrong side? He would have to stop back at the office tonight and tell Jordan about this without delay.

chapter four

"Absolution? Is that really what she said?" Jordan questioned Todd after hearing the recap of his conversation.

"That was her word."

"Hmmm. You know, Todd, I promised myself I was going to pay back that woman for going over my head. And I am!" Jordan's flashing handsome grin had a wry ironic twist, his eyes glinted silver. "Though not at all in the way I had planned. I am going to do something she may hate even more than my planned revenge. I am going to *hire* her! I want her on my staff immediately, Todd. Talk to human resources and handle it."

"O-okay, I mean, yes sir!" Todd was more than a little surprised, though he was personally pleased. Shelley was good, intelligent, and aggressive. She would be a perfect addition to the prosecutor's office. "Ah... Excuse me for saying this, but you aren't doing this to get an inside track on Henley?" he ventured hesitantly. "She will not break confidentiality..."

"Of course not! That's one of the reasons I want her; I like her values."

As Todd left, Jordan swiveled to stare out his window. He finished the thought, under his breath, "...and I understand that desire for absolution."

Though in his own case, it went beyond his former job. It was a haunting need he'd struggled toward without being sure whether it was something he needed to receive, or give—or both—to dispel the bitterness.

Reaching into the bottom drawer of his desk, Jordan pulled out hinged picture frames. He opened them to reveal the brass-

41

framed photographs of his parents. The pictures were taken over a decade ago, years before the couple perished in an automobile accident returning from one of their frequent country-club cocktail parties. He stood them up before him, balancing them in the center of his desk. He tipped back in his chair, staring thoughtfully at them, unaware of the frown that creased his forehead.

There was a time they sat proudly on the corner of his former desk, when he was in private practice. Now they remained in his drawer. He told himself he needed the additional desktop area, though when Elsa had suggested he mount them on his wall; he mumbled something about getting around to that some other day, leaving them in the dark of his drawer.

The truth of the matter was that he didn't like glancing up, seeing them staring at him as he worked at a job they would have disapproved. They were safer in the drawer where he wasn't tempted to toss the frames in the trash in a fit of anger.

An only child, Jordan's wealthy parents had focused all their own hopes, need, and pride on him fulfilling their vision of the perfect son for the perfect couple. They instilled in him the vital importance of social position and standing as the cornerstones of a correct and successful business and personal life. *Their* idea of correct, *their* idea of success, *their* egos at stake.

Jordan had been more than happy to enjoy his privileged life, the values he was raised with, and follow his parents' guidance to what should be a brilliant future. Attending only the most prestigious schools and universities, he remained in the same cocoon of peers, and social values, that his parents had declared the right and ruling class. Graduating from law school, he took his place in an elite law firm, as his parents had ordained and used their influence to help him obtain.

He selected his own wife—unaware of his mother's manipulations herding him to her choice. He saw her beauty, her social graces, her family position and connections, and no further. Questions of character or integrity were redundant. He desired her, his parents encouraged, and were even overjoyed that he was marrying the daughter of one of their connections. They knew her history. They approved. He saw her surface, what she wanted him to see, and he wanted what he saw. She would be the perfect wife for a young, ambitious attorney. They married and would be the perfect couple.

Until he caught a flu bug and came home from the office early one day.

Until he found her in bed with one of his best friends.

Until he found out she had betrayed him with *all* his best friends.

It was not until the brutal lesson of her unfaithfulness that Jordan began to realize the shallowness of his standards. Only to find himself later ostracized by his family and peers for taking the unacceptable step of divorcing his wife. *That perfect wife that had not been stolen; just a little good-natured borrowing among friends. She had not, they claimed, outraged, dabbled outside her social class after all! And no one else need know.*

To create such a scandal, publicly severing the relationship, was so crudely unnecessary and socially damaging, they just could not understand why he couldn't just retain her as his wife, and satisfy himself in a more discreetly acceptable way.

Jordan had actually been ashamed for a time that his hurt pride, and demand for honesty and integrity in his marriage, had made him incapable of handling the situation differently. He had failed to be "tough enough", as his father claimed, letting his emotions and bourgeois values rule him.

Jordan isolated himself from his mocking friends and disapproving family at that time. Slowly, he began to revisit earlier issues—gray areas of discomfort with his upbringing and lifestyle—redefining his values, choosing his own belief system to match the person he was becoming now that he saw a wider world through his own lens. He began to shed that early training, scorning it and himself, for the hypocrisy he hated.

Throwing himself into his work, Jordan built a wall around his private feelings. Shielding himself in a cold, ruthless outer shell, he pretended until it became reality that nothing but work consumed his soul. Changing his line of work, as his values ran into increasing conflicts, trying to find balance, much as Shelley was now.

Then, while he was still estranged from the life he had known, his parents had died in the accident.

Had he wanted their absolution? Had he wanted to absolve them? Or did he just need to absolve himself? He did not know. He felt trapped in a prison, where he might never find the answer; never heal the wounds, never ease the bitterness, now that they were gone.

Suddenly a stab of anger shot through him as he reminded himself that his mother and father had been the cause of their own drunken death, and shared a role in the wreck of his own dreams, wiping out any sadness and pity he had been feeling. Abruptly tossing the frames back into his drawer, he forced his mind back to work.

"You are a raving lunatic!" Ronnie had shouted at her after almost fainting when Sam had confessed her secret desire.

"And I did *not* almost faint, Samantha," she'd protested later. "I never faint, though," smoothing a hand over her sleek dark hair, 'I may have almost elegantly *swooned*."

Dear Raving Lunatic...

Rhonda had addressed her first letter to Sam in jail, telling how much she missed her friend and that her regret for helping in her crazy scheme was making Ronnie as nuts as Sam. And sentimental. And maudlin. And warning Sam not to be surprised if it drove her to using those juvenile smiley faces on her letters in future, because she was so distraught. Making Sam laugh, as she knew it would.

When Sam had told her friend her plan, she had *finally* gotten Rhonda to agree.

Not to the sanity of her plan. And not to help her explain it to Sam's children.

But Ronnie had agreed to keep her secret—for now.

And only after Sam had promised to reconsider her alternatives and decision seriously again, before going ahead with telling her kids.

"No need for them to ever know their mother went completely looney-tunes if you change your mind."

Sam had dutifully gone out to the State Park to think it all over again. In her pocket was the list that Rhonda had given her. Both Sam and Rhonda were great list makers. Sam's were more wishful to do lists that always seemed to get lost or used for scratch paper when a thought struck her. Rhonda's lists had bullets, which shot each concise line with command. Commands for items for Sam to reconsider.

Pulling into a deserted parking area on that slightly overcast day, Sam was pleased to see that the beach belonged just to her and the seagulls that afternoon. Whenever she had a difficult decision to wrestle with she always immersed herself in the breeze off the sea and the lapping of the tides. It was one of the few ways she could soothe her mind, untangle all the knots, think deeply and clearly. The sharp cries of the gulls helped call her mind away from the everyday rattle in her head.

Hands thrust in soft corduroy pants, she strolled across the grassy picnic area and stepped up onto a broad weathered log. Standing still a moment, chin tilted up, eyes half closed, she breathed deeply of the fresh, tangy sea breeze that gently lifted silken tendrils of hair to stream behind her head. A smile curved her lips. Tension flowed from her, exhaled on her first breath, as if she could just blow her troubles away in this lovely spot.

With a lighter spirit, Sam playfully walked the log, one foot carefully placed in front of the next. Losing her balance as the end narrowed, she jumped lightly to the sand.

Keeping to the dry, deeper sand on the upper beach, she slogged along. Enjoying each sinking step that buried half her foot, reminding her that the simple pleasure of walking on the beach was not to be rushed. Nature had its own pace—its own plan.

She spotted the bright coral of a crab's claw in the darkening green tangle of sea plankton, tossed across the beach like a rippling fence line that divided the dry upper beach from the wet tide washed sands. Colorful tidbits hid in the line. White sparkled from fragments of tiny crushed shells. Pearl gray washed a weathered wooden chip. Bottle green pebbles shaped from ancient glass were tossed beside the garnet reds of still wet, iron-rich rocks, completing the jewel toned bracelet strung along the tide line.

A scowl darkened Sam's face when she saw the glittering colors of something the sea would never be able to smooth or soften and make its own. She reached for the offensive aluminum pop can and crushed it, tucking it into a pocket. Stepping out onto firmer wet sands, she set off briskly toward her favorite spot.

Down the beach, a huge gnarly tree root stump rose in starkly defined relief against the sand and sky. It had been there as long as she could recall, the casualty of some long ago and violent storm. Braced with the long shaft of the trunk buried deeply in the sand, the massive root base, with its tangle of huge roots grasping only sky, stood at least eight feet high. With the higher tides lapping close to this natural sculpture, it looked to Sam like the wrist and hand of some giant underworld god reaching out from the land to grasp and claw at the sea and sky.

Sam had been irresistibly drawn toward this desperate, dramatic image the first time she saw it. Drawing closer, its immense size still awed her but the goose bumps it inspired in the past were now replaced by tingles of pleasure as she clasped a finger-like root and climbed up. The smooth weathering of the softly silvered wood held a warmth that invited her to climb into the hollowed out palm. She nestled now in its wise, weathered clasp, her own special, secret place.

Perched so high and secure in the driftwood palm, her arms wrapped around a gnarled finger, Sam loved to rest and gaze out to sea. The waves washing eternally on the beach washed her brain of the last of its clamor and clutter, until it was totally quiet; she was totally at peace.

Out of this sense of serenity, understanding rose slowly, like a wave gathering deep at sea, to roll steadily in and lay an answer at her feet. Even when she hadn't found the whole answer she'd needed in the past, she'd always gained greater clarity of what mattered most, to help make her decisions.

Hope it works now, Sam had thought, climbing up to snuggle in the comforting wooden hand. Hugging a finger to her cheek, she let her eyes half close, let her focus narrow. She rested against the weathered, wooden flesh, while the breeze tangled her hair playfully across her cheek.

A gull circled overhead, cocking a bright, beady eye on the slight form so in harmony with the natural habitat. It glided down to land on the sand, tucking its wings to march a little closer, inspecting this new companion.

Sam smiled. You were right, Ronnie, I needed this! She laughed out loud, just for joy, startling the seagull. It ran a few steps, turned its back, giving an indignant wing flap, then stilled to peek cautiously over a shoulder at her. The aloof attempt was spoiled by the gull's natural curiosity. Finally, her gull friend sat gingerly in the sand, its back to her, alertly defending its human find, like a self-appointed bodyguard.

Like Rhonda, her other protector, determined to defend her from her own "impulsive idiocies and raving lunacies". Sam couldn't blame her friend for thinking she was cracking up. Maybe she was.

Guilty Plot

After the tone deaf Harold had been ordered out avoiding an embarrassing, for Samantha at least, encounter, Sam had finally coherently described at length and with convincing passion her long time desire and compulsion. She spoke clearly to her friend of the frustrating lack of time, the emotions, the impact the letter from the girl in jail had triggered; Rhonda had understood better. She even agreed to delay having Sam committed. It was clear, though, Ronnie believed the preferred institution to lock Sam up in was a mental hospital, not a jail!

But, a true friend, Rhonda had offered her honest if blunt advice. Advice that sounded suspiciously like orders! Orders *in writing*. Sam patted the list in her pocket.

Rhonda also made it clear that Sam had to face her children and explain by herself.

"If this is the course of action you insist on, I'll help you all you'll let me. I will not, however, talk to your kids for you. If you can't rationally justify this madness, both to yourself, and to your kids, if you're not committed enough to this project and confident what you are doing is right; then you have no right to do it. Period!"

So was Sam sure? She had better be, before she faced her kids.

Looking for her feathered friend, she found the gull had sidled much closer. Progress. Opening Rhonda's list, Sam focused on her task.

Ronnie had demanded that Sam ask herself why she felt she had to go to jail, giving up her freedom and time with her family and friends and ability to visit her favorite places, just to pursue a dream when other alternatives were at hand. Scanning the bulleted queries again, Sam answered them in her head.

She knew *why*. The need had been there for as long as she could remember, though she found it hard to confess and even more difficult to explain how important it was to her. Truly, she felt the real concerns—for Ronnie at least—were the *how* and *where*. Ironically, they touched on some of the main reasons for her decision. She needed strict discipline. Sam needed a regimented routine, and that was the clincher. She needed to be totally focused on her goal, isolated and locked away from distractions, even work, family and friends and most especially bills! Sam needed jail. Ronnie would be furious to find her challenge had helped tip the balance confirming Sam's resolve.

Relaxed now, confident her choice made the best sense for her own situation. Sam curled down letting her mind float like the gulls, on the tangy ocean drafts. She dozed to the gentle swoosh and hissing sounds as waves tumbled endlessly ashore, then pulled back, dragging tiny pebbles with their retreat.

The seagull, flew up to a perch on the highest driftwood finger, efficiently tucked legs and neck into its body, and settled in for a silent vigil.

Sam had woken from her driftwood nap to a harsh "Aarack" warning from her gull friend and a drop of moisture on her head. She laughed to see the bird had taken up station above her, until she thought to check her head for bird dew.

"As if!" the gull seemed to huff, insulted, as it had flown off into stunning sunset skies now darkening with rain clouds.

Smiling at the funny bird, Sam scrambled down and headed back to her car to meet Ronnie for a late dinner that night before heading up the coast to see her kids the next day.

This meeting should go much better than the last one when Sam had been unprepared.

"So. Just what kind of crime... Just what kind of crime are you going to commit?" Rhonda had arched quizzical dark brows, pinning Sam with stern blue eyes. "Well, have you thought of that?"

Well, ah, no. Sam hadn't. Her eyes had searched the ceiling, looking desperately for an answer there to satisfy her interrogator.

"Well....," Sam had said softly, still searching, a rosy fingertip to her lips to help concentrate. "I don't want to do anything that will hurt anyone, and…it can't be anything really bad," Sam had worked through the possibilities. "And I don't want to have to tell a really big lie….What?" she'd cried defensively seeing the expressive eye roll as Rhonda had shaken her head in disgust.

"Boy, are you ever the big, bad criminal! You want to commit a crime, be tossed in jail, for the hardened criminal that you are, but, heaven forbid, you might have to tell a lie about it!" Pretending disgust at Sam's naïve approach, Rhonda couldn't help but admire her friend's integrity. "Samantha, darling," she drawled, "while I know that telling a lie is a horrendous crime in your eyes, unfortunately they don't put people in jail for it, or that would solve your problem right there."

"There must be some way to do this honorably," Sam insisted. "I know! Can you end up in jail for not paying a parking ticket?" She turned hopeful brown eyes to Rhonda only to be met again with the stern icy-blue stare.

"Not unless you plan to live in your car, in a restricted handicapped zone, for a long, and defiant number of weeks," was the dry response.

"Huh. Don't you have any helpful ideas?"

"And become an accessory?" Rhonda cried in mock horror. "Okay, okay, let me think. "

"Why don't you murder that macho jerk that always hangs out at the Sailing Inn Pub. The one that harasses all the women. You know, the one that always sidles up to every fresh pigeon that comes in with that boozy breathed, 'Hey baby, what's your sign' line? Just think, you'd not only be achieving your goal, but you would be ridding the community of a menace. You'd be a heroine!"

This time it was Rhonda's turn to receive a very stern, reproving look.

"No? Okay, well, you're the one with the wild imagination, think up something crazy," Rhonda had challenged. "Crazier," she quickly amended.

After that conversation, Sam realized she'd need to squeeze in a trip to the library for research to find a crime; something reasonably harmless and honest, that could still get her a "go-to-jail-free card".

She'd felt guilty taking an hour long lunch break. The rest of the staff was used to her only taking a few hastily grabbed minutes from work, in the lunch room, leaving more time for their luncheons. They'd had to scramble to juggle schedules to cover the store.

Sam had decided to do her research at the law library near the courthouse. Feeling like a truant, she'd taken deep breaths of crisp spring air, and headed off at a brisk pace for downtown, deciding to leave her wheezy old car in the lot for the short trip, rather than risk breaking one of its last dying legs. She had smiled thinking that if things worked out right she wouldn't need it were she was going.

The sun and exercise worked their magic, her step lightening with her mood. She smiled at total strangers wishing them a lovely day with a sparkling warmth that had startled some and had others turning to watch her pass. Sam laughed at herself, thinking how funny it was to be so looking forward to a chance to go to jail.

So Sam was ready now for whatever Ronnie had to throw at her. She was convinced of her reasoning and she had done her research.

The sun had been casting its last shimmering rays across the bay, after the brief shower, when Sam pulled up at the popular waterfront pub. The Sailing Inn Pub was one of Sam and Rhonda's favorite nightspots—or had been. Sam paused for a moment before entering to admire the view.

The early evening was so calm now that the bay was a stunning mirror-like sheet of burnished gold and coral. Sea birds scampered along the water's edge, crisp black silhouettes against the shimmering backdrop.

"Gorgeous, isn't it?" Rhonda's contralto voice spoke at her shoulder. "How can you give all this up?"

Turning to follow inside, Sam responded with a question of her own. "Remember when we were here last?"

"Oh, let me see, it was just…no. Come to think of it…It's been almost a year! Hasn't it?"

"That's right," Sam grimaced. "I had to finish my twelve month work sentence first."

"Your what? Oh, I get it. Very clever." Rhonda realized the time for argument was over as she watched her friend head off to the ladies room.

Rhonda had promised to support whatever decision Sam made, so she held her tongue. Knowing Sam as well as she did, Rhonda thought the wiser tactic might be to just sit back and watch Sam struggle with her own conscience. The plan might never come to pass for lack of a 'good and harmless' crime. Well, she could only hope. Besides, Sam still had the hurdle of her kids to jump. Surely they would put a stop to this. She knew that Sam's parents were counting on their grandkids to talk some sense into their mother.

Sam used the well-appointed restroom to repair the damage to her wind-tossed hair and to freshen her lipstick. Startled by the luxury of a full-length mirror, she took a quick inventory, then thought maybe it was better the mirror in her cottage was so tiny.

Everything about her shape looked wider than she remembered, but then she was many years older than the last time she had really scrutinized it. She knew she wasn't really any heavier, but her upper arms and middle seemed a little thicker. So where was she thinner?

Probably in the brain.

She needed more walking exercise, less diet by being over stressed. At least her face had lost a little of its sallow tint. The day at the beach had brightened her cheeks. It had certainly brightened her mood! She chuckled again at the funny bird, her "gull friend" as she went to join her girlfriend.

Rhonda beckoned her over to a corner where she had managed to grab the last window table. There they could catch the closing scenes of the glorious sunset they had been admiring outside.

"Oh, I wish Paul were here!" Sighing, Sam stared dreamily out the window.

Rhonda responded heartily, "So do I!" The mention of Sam's son reinforced her recent thoughts.

"He would be able to capture this perfectly, " Sam continued, unaware of anything but the exquisite scene.

"Yes, he would," Rhonda relaxed and agreed cheerfully. "You know, I've often thought Paul should make his photography more than just a hobby. He really has an excellent eye, and an incredible talent. The pictures he's taken that you enlarged and framed are marvelous. I love that other beach scene he gave you. I can practically hear the bird cries and feel and smell the breeze each time I look at it!"

The tender smile that spread across Sam's face told of a mom's deep pride and affection for her son. Both Sam's children held center stage in their mother's affections. Her pride in their talents was immense and well-deserved. Her greatest happiness came from their development into such caring and considerate young adults. Their self-confidence and strong sense of balance allowed them to give generously to those around them. Young or old, friend or stranger, they would always give a friendly smile, kind words, always thoughtful of others.

Rhonda knew this as well. She had been the recipient of many of those kindnesses.

"What?" Sam asked now, catching the changing emotions that had been crossing Rhonda's face.

"Oh, I was just thinking how smart, and wonderful your kids are."

"Our kids," Sam responded generously. "You have no idea how much you contributed," she thanked Rhonda, seeing the pleased sparkle in her eyes though the head shook in denial.

"A toast, then, to 'our' kids," Rhonda suggested, lifting her water glass in tribute. "Where is that lousy waiter when you need him?" she growled, shielding, as always, her emotions.

"Good evening, ladies," the fresh faced waiter appeared, late for his cue. "What can I do for you this evening."

"Remember we're alive?" Rhonda asked with a sarcastic smile.

"Never mind her," Sam laughed, relieving the intimidated young man. "I'll have a Bloody Mary, please, and....I'm starving! I think I'd like a basket of fish and chips. Ronnie?"

"Tell me something, handsome," Rhonda drawled, pinning the nervous waiter with cool blue eyes, "What kind of fish would that be?"

"Cod, ma'am," he replied briskly, pleased to have the answer.

"What kind of cod?" Rhonda persisted, keeping him on the hook.

"Ah-h-h," the poor youth gulped nervously, unsure if this was a trick question. "Fresh?"

"Is that a question?"

"No. No, ma'am. I meant it is fresh cod, ma'am." he stated definitively.

"Well, I should certainly hope so," Rhonda replied dryly. "But what kind of cod is it?" she continued to grill the waiter. "Is it Rock Cod? Is it Ling Cod?..."

"Oh, give him a break, Rhonda!" Sam turned to the waiter, who thought she had the most compassionate brown eyes, the most angelic face, he had ever seen. "She'll have the same, thank you," she released him with a smile.

After the young man rushed to fill the order, Sam turned chastising eyes on Rhonda. "You can be so mean, sometimes, my friend."

"What?" Rhonda asked, wide-eyed with mock innocence. "What did I say that was so mean?"

"It wasn't what you said, it was the way you said it," Sam scolded gently. "Poor kid. He looked at you like a mouse hypnotized by a cobra!"

"Okay, I'll behave," Rhonda agreed reluctantly, "But they're so fun to toy with at that age!"

"I haven't ever noticed you showing men mercy, at any age!"

"Mercy isn't what they usually beg me for, darling," Rhonda quipped with a wicked grin and naughty wink.

Blushing, Sam laughed and quickly changed the subject. "So...I went to the library and took all kinds of research notes yesterday. After we eat, we'll have to sort through it all, and figure out a perfect plan."

"Oh, goody, I can hardly wait."

"Rhonda..."

"I know, I promised. I'll behave and be a good little partner in crime."

"Good. Start now, here comes our meal. Remember, not one word, not one wicked look."

"Can I give him a slap on his cute little tush?" Rhonda asked sweetly.

"NO!"

"I don't know why not," Rhonda grumbled under her breath," they always do it to the female waiters."

"Try and set a good example!" Sam whispered back primly.

"Haul out your notes then," Ronnie sighed, "before I come to my senses and decide not to be an accessory to crime. Where is that waiter? Oh, there you are. Yes, I'd like another drink young man. Make this one a double!"

"Drinks for both of you ladies?" he inquired timidly, but determined to get the order correct.

Rhonda turned to smile sweetly at him, answering for them both, much to Sam's dismay. "My friend here never, ever, has more than one drink. That's her rule," she explained patiently. "She only has one drink with dinner, and never more than one cigarette after sex."

"Rhonda!" Sam sputtered, scandalized. "I don't have sss...I mean...I don't smoke!"

After the embarrassed waiter hurried away, she turned on Rhonda. "I can't believe you said that!"

"What? I was being nice, I even smiled at him."

"But..."

"Well, he won't think very highly of you when he hears you've been thrown in the slammer, anyway." Rhonda effectively stilled Sam's protest. "Which reminds me…"

"Yes." Sam pulled out her sheaf of notes.

Rhonda settled back with her fresh drink watching Sam busily sorting through her papers. This should be entertaining, she thought wryly, adding a silent prayer that Sam would be unable to come up with anything usable.

Rhonda had forgotten that letting Sam loose in a library was like letting a compulsive shopper loose in a super mall. There wasn't anything that Sam wouldn't want to browse, try on, or gather up, when it came to information or books.

"Actually, the research was quite fascinating. I confess, I was having fun digging through all the materials," Sam chatted happily. "I kept getting sidetracked and forgetting what I was there for. Did you know that a French sociologist had a theory that crime is normal and somehow necessary in society to define the limits of acceptable behavior?

"Oh, and the insanity defense," Sam continued excited, "I guess I thought that was a rather recent phenomenon. Did you know the standard for determining mental responsibility is called the M'Naghten Rule, after the 1843 English court case?"

"I'm glad you found that one intriguing," Rhonda inserted, "I do hope you researched *that one* very carefully."

Unruffled by Rhonda's sarcasm, Sam leaned forward, "Seriously, Ronnie, back to the subject. I think I've come up with the plan. Here's what I want to do."

chapter five

It was Jordan Campbell's responsibility to bring criminals to justice, to lock them away from the community they raped to feed their own greed. One of the worst offenders was almost in his grasp, if he could just close his fist.

This offender used a network of underlings to spread pain and suffering, from the very old, to the very young and helpless. Jordan knew the man was guilty. He had known for a long time, but unless he could find the way and proof to nail him—and he would someday—the offender would remain free and unblemished and a respected citizen in the community.

But Abraham Damon was a real used car dealer if there ever was one. Only Honest Abe liked *some* of his used cars to be relatively new, always luxurious, and hand picked—*without* the permission of their owners!

Jordan could not bear to watch the sneering face of Damon's high-priced defense attorney as he sacrificed another underling to jail on a lesser offense, just to save Damon's criminal organization. And that is what would happen again unless Jordan could present a justifiable case for trial so that the current perp would turn against his secret boss, this time. But his time was up tomorrow, they couldn't delay any longer hoping to file charges on the higher ups in the chain.

"Damn!"

Glancing at his watch, he rubbed a hand across burning eyes. Taking one last look at the papers on his desk, he swore again, grabbed his jacket, and called it quits for the night. As disgusted as he was with himself, he knew he wouldn't make any further progress tonight. Close to midnight now, he needed some sleep. A clearer mind might find a last minute miracle in the morning.

As he drove home, he hardly noticed the clear starry night, his mind still immersed in his dilemma, ticking over points in his head. The way it stood now, he definitely couldn't bring a broader case to trial. He only had solid evidence to prove a lesser charge. And when it came to witnesses … hah!

He'd been certain he had the case to include Damon this time. The witnesses had been forthcoming when first questioned, but when called in for their depositions, forget it! Or, 'forgot it', would be more apt! They all mysteriously lost their memories.

Even more worrisome was a detective who had somehow lost some of his notes of the initial questioning of some of those same witnesses, the most useful ones, of course. Internal Affairs was investigating the suspended detective now, but couldn't lock down any wrong doing, so far. What a hell of a deal!

Well, that's what justice was all about, right? Laws were designed to protect the innocent. If the law said that you couldn't legally mention this … and legally couldn't do that, then legally the man was innocent based on the limited evidence left that was presentable. His job was to follow the law. He should just quit agonizing, he thought tiredly, and do what was legal … let the crook go! How could that be called justice?

It wouldn't have bothered him much early in his career. He had started as a defense attorney with an elite firm. Using every technique, every loophole, everything he could 'legally' manipulate to get his well-heeled clients off, guilty or not, that was the job. Winning cases equaled advancement. Clients got their defense rights but the firm made huge fees. It had started to bother him.

Jordan had changed sides long ago to prosecuting, seeking a renewal of the dream of the young college man that had such shiny expectations of carrying the torch of justice. God, It hurt to think of his naiveté.

Now in his early sixties he admitted a small portion of that dream still flickered hopefully, if feebly, beneath his years of experience and cynicism. He had resolved just over a year ago to commit himself anew, to try in every way to pursue real justice, not just law.

Maybe, he thought in despair, it was a job too big for him. Or maybe he was just too damn mad and tired to deal with it that night. He'd sleep and try again tomorrow, before court. That was his immediate goal.

The prosecutor left his office, the next evening, only shortly after the rest of his staff had gone home for the weekend. It was extremely rare for him to leave so early, but then he was rarely so extremely depressed.

The afternoon papers had not helped.

GUILTY VERDICT FOR DRUG DEALER
Campbell's Record as Prosecutor Remains Flawless

Tough on crime prosecutor, Jordan Campbell had only a brief, modest comment after today's victory in court when asked about his perfect conviction record. "I'm always grateful when I can help to protect our community. It is what I was hired to do."

Even worse was the gushy article in the Society column from a female reporter that wanted his attention—in a very *un*-journalistic way.

Handsome Crusader Rides Again

He's intelligent, wealthy, and handsome in a dark and dangerous way, yet Jordan Campbell is no bad boy. Proving again today that he is the most successful prosecutor and crusader for justice to ever hold office in our fair city

But the article that caused the Prosecutor extreme rage and anguish was accompanied by a large photograph.

Prominent Businessman and Philanthropist Makes Significant Donation to Local Charity

Hell, there he was. Good 'Ole Honest Abe presenting an ostentatious six foot by three foot cardboard check to a local Youth Center, with a shit-eating grin.

The proof that Jordan Campbell had failed. He had failed his community, and he had failed himself.

Very rarely throughout his career, first as an attorney, then as a prosecutor, had he failed to present a winning case. He was still just as methodical, relentless, ruthless, and precise in detail as ever, but his conscience now played a role. He wanted justice done now, not just another win scored. He didn't glory in crucifying the little guy just because he could. He wanted the corruptors, the ones that hid behind respectable masks and victimized others. He had almost had one, he thought, and he had lost. He had failed. And one more little guy was sacrificed.

For the past year Jordan had promised himself that someday together again, today. The failure was demoralizing. All day long it gnawed at him that the *someday* he hoped for might never come.

And all that news crap about his small time win in court just made it worse—even torturous—because he could not endanger any future case or get slapped with a charge of slander, or false accusation. So he had to stay mum, and felt like a fake.

He had failed but it was not a *public* failure—could *not* be public knowledge—and he felt like a hypocrite, and a failure at giving the community true security and justice.

Campbell's parents, if they still lived, and if they knew all the public and private facts, would say he was a brilliant success, to quit whining. They would probably insist on throwing a party at the country club for all to celebrate their son's victory in court, and get literally drunk on pride. They would have never seen or understood—or tolerated—his pain and bitterness, because only the superficial public appearances ever mattered to them.

And the way Damon played to that hypocrisy, showing a public face that hid the ugliness and evil inside him, while publicly thumbing his nose at the prosecutor, sickened Jordan. He hadn't realized before that his obsession with getting the real Honest Abe in the spotlight, for his crimes against youth, might actually be a very personal crusade against social mores like his parents. But, regardless of his own unresolved issues, the community would not be safe from a dangerous predator until Damon could be brought to trial and exposed.

Confidence broken, his bitterness and pain uncontrollable, Jordan escaped the scene of his failure, running home to hide for the weekend and lick his wounds in private.

No comforting welcome greeted him when he reached his darkened house. He was a stranger here, merely passing through to catch a few hours sleep, a change of clothes, escaping the empty house for the office, his real home.

Now he felt doubly rejected as he moved through the unused rooms, bumping, in the dark, into furniture that he would be hard pressed to describe. He sought the kitchen, pulling open the door of the refrigerator. Light glanced off tier on tier of naked steel wire shelving. Slamming the door, Jordan's hand groped along the wall. He finally found a light switch, illuminating a circle on the bar counter with a single spot of light. Pulling the phone over, he dialed a pizza parlor for delivery before seeking a warming shower.

Later, perched uncomfortably on a bar stool, Jordan sat down to enjoy his dinner. Biting into the crisp pizza crust, the crunching sound as he chewed seemed to reverberate in the empty room. He took a sip of beer to wash away the offending sound, only to hear himself swallowing. Holding himself self-consciously motionless for a moment, he was aware of the humming sounds of the single light fixture and his empty fridge in the solitary silence.

Jumping up, Jordan returned with the small portable television from his bathroom. Placing it beside him on the counter, he turned it to a movie channel with a companionable level of sound—but no news. Staring at the screen, he was aware only that he could blink now without having to hear the clash of his eyelashes as they met.

The lights went out suddenly. Only the eerie glow of security lights outside her cell remained. Samantha Wilson, aka #49549, had been trying to decide whether to read the letters from her kids, Penny and Paul, or to hoard them longer, when the decision was taken from her.

Like so many others, now.

Though, to be honest with herself, the circumstances of her prior life were just—if not more—limiting. And the power company *had* made it clear then that they planned to permanently turn off her heat, power, and lights. Which is why Sam had made this brilliant choice.

She remembered how excited she had been when the transport van had delivered her. *I'm here at last!* As she got her first look around, Sam realized she had not actually *seen* a real prison before. Her new home was not *quite* what she had expected. She told herself the little chill that ran up her spine was . . . just *nerves*.

Sam entered her new home with a bright, brave smile on her face

No one smiled back.

But there *was* a welcoming committee.

"Everything out of your pockets. Everything off."

"Pardon me?" Sam flushed scarlet.

Strip searched e-v-e-r-y-w-h-e-r-e!

It had been a shocking and sobering experience to actually go through the rituals of formal incarceration. She had so looked forward to this: being put in jail, freed at last from a constant struggle just to get by, free to pursue her plans. But Sam hadn't given any thought to what it would actually be like being processed through a dehumanizing system that was locking her away from a society that needed protection.

She was stripped, booked, printed, catalogued with a picture and a number, then put in a cage. She had never appreciated fully her rights as a citizen—as a person—until now when she had lost them. Her individuality was also stripped, when she was numbered, tagged, and uniformed. Now officially a second-class citizen, she could expect no respect for her status; she had none.

Sam had to admit that she'd had some incredibly naïve idea of jail not being much worse than being sent to her room...for a year!

Even the next month seemed endless now.

She'd been informed that no visitors were allowed for the first month, to allow new prisoners to settle into the rules and routines. Sam personally suspected it was so the newly incarcerated could get over the shock and humiliation before they saw anyone that knew them.

A month stretched before she would see any of those close to her, with only pre-abused and censored mail to sustain her until then. It was little wonder she spent so much time wallowing in memories of the last times she had seen her loved ones.

Reaching out in the dark, she groped for the table to set down the letters from her children, still clutched and crumpled in her hand, to save for another time. Laying back on her cot, she pulled the scratchy blanket over her and cuddled up with her memories of her last trip to visit her kids.

It had been time to face the music. The irony occurred to Sam that she had been much more afraid of facing her kids with her plan, than the prospect of going off to jail.

They both lived only an hour further up the coast, but she usually stayed overnight on the weekends she visited, valuing the extra time for private talks.

That night, they all had a date for dinner at her kids' favorite Mexican restaurant. There would be five for dinner: Sam, her children, Penny and Paul, and their partners. She would tell them all her plans at dinner. She had considered just talking with her kids, but she respected the close, committed relationships between Penny and her wonderful guy, Aaron, and Paul and his lovely lady, Brittany. It would be wrong not to involve them; they were an integral part of her children's lives and would be impacted by her decision.

As she drove along the stunning coastal highway, Sam kept trying to drag her thoughts from her worries and concentrate on the road ahead with its breathtaking scenery. Flipping on the radio, she hoped the music would distract her from the monotonous tune the tires seemed to be playing in her head. "What will they say? What will they say? What will .."

Enough! Spotting a rest area ahead with beach access, she decided to pull off the road and calm her thoughts before going further. The waves and water always helped. Or, she thought, dryly, it would be a good place to make a U-turn and face them another time!

Pulling into the turnout, she climbed down to walk on the beach. Kicking up clumps of sand and shells with her toe, she circled back and forth on the small open area, her pacing a reflection of the thoughts whirling through her mind. A mind focused on a different horizon than the one reflected in the serious eyes. She was alone, but for a single seagull on a nearby pier post, sitting motionless except for its head that turned in jerky animation, trying to keep one bright eye on the curious human that kept pacing by.

As with any serious decision, one that will change the direction of lives and shatter the status quo, once made but before put into motion, a huge wall of doubt, uncertainty, and fear rises to slam one in the face.

Sam hit that wall, suddenly realizing her next step would be to climb a wall that seemed ten miles high! Her fears loomed immense and solid. Her life suddenly seemed amazingly safe and desirable compared to what may lie ahead. The fear that paralyzed her was of her belief in herself.

"What if...," she whispered to herself, "what if I can't do it? What if after I cause my loved ones pain and embarrassment, I can't do it? After making an idiot out of myself, a branded criminal, I find out...I can't? What if I sacrifice then fail miserably?"

The gull, eyeing her warily, refused to answer any questions.

Realizing she'd been talking aloud, and getting no help, she continued her soul search silently.

A crushing failure would be humiliating, especially after making such a big issue of it. Wouldn't she be happier if she didn't try? That gave her a built-in excuse of never having to finish, never having to look at the results of her efforts and admit failure. Why did I ever think I could do this? Her mind fed on her insecurities.

Sitting suddenly on a log by the water, chewing her lip, she gathered a handful of pebbles, tossing them one at a time in the water. Unconsciously hoping to toss away all her self-doubts and fears. Why must I do this? Why does it matter so much to me? Does it matter?

Yes, a tiny voice in her head said first timidly, then louder.

It did matter! It had always mattered to her.

And she had always promised herself that she would.

Someday. How many hundreds of times had she said that?

When, Sam wondered was "someday"? Such a convenient time. Not today. Not tomorrow. It was just...someday. At what point was she going to schedule "someday" so that it wasn't . . ."never"? She had passed her sixtieth birthday, how long would she wait for that future day she had always dreamed of?

"Now!" she told herself firmly, standing abruptly to throw the remaining rocks into the water.

"Someday is Now!" She announced loudly, startling the gull from its perch. Sam would go for it. Succeed or fail, at least she would have had the guts to chase her dream. If she failed . . .? Well, then she wouldn't spend the rest of her life whining about missed chances, nurturing regrets. That if only... She would have... She could have. Excuses, for not doing anything. She'd try it! No. Sam would do it! Period!

Sam had to grab hold of her chance *now*! And spend that go-to-jail-free card. Grinning, she added, *and quit passing go and just endlessly circling the darn board.* She'd never won that game playing by the normal rules, but she could not let anything stop her now.

She leaped the low wall between the shore and her car, just as she had leaped her wall of fear, eager now to get on the road and see her kids.

A loud splatter of rain dashed against his glass door, snapping Jordan to attention.

When had it started raining? He had no idea how long he'd been sitting perched on his kitchen stool, elbows braced on the counter beside the cold, crusty remains of his dinner. Reaching automatically for his sole allotted beer for the evening, he grimaced at the warm, flat taste of dregs from the can.

He must have been staring at the television screen for hours. The flickering images hypnotic, without ever penetrating to his brain. His mind was empty, defeated, no longer capable of thought or feeling. Numb.

The late news weatherman was cheerfully assuring anyone still awake, that the brief coastal rain squall would move east to the Rockies before morning. He promised a bright, sunny weekend of fun for all.

Jordan grunted in response. Tomorrow was Saturday. He dreaded it. He didn't know what to do with a free day. He usually worked. Not this time though. No point.

He wished it would rain all weekend. He wanted to wallow in it, hide in it, an excuse and companion for his misery. Somehow, he'd have to find the will and desire to return on Monday, to continue his fruitless chase. Sighing heavily, he pushed himself up, turning off the set.

Surely someone would come up with an interesting crime to help him forget what a waste it had all been.

He shuffled off to a cold, empty bed. The rain slowed and stopped, deserting him.

chapter six

Penny's front door had flown open the moment her mom's car pulled into her driveway. She ran out to throw her arms around her mom, or would have, if the "grandkids" hadn't gotten there first. The two chocolate labs greeted Sam with an enthusiasm that would have knocked her flat if she hadn't stumbled back against the car for support.

Sam laughed and crooned to the dogs and tried to avoid their wet kisses while promising they would go for their traditional beach W-A-L-K later, not daring to do more than spell the word, as they were already overexcited. Aaron came out and corralled the dogs and Sam's bag so she could get to her daughter for a hug.

"It's about time you got up here for a visit!" Penny squeezed the air out of her mom's lungs with her hug, grinning, "It's been so long I thought the dogs would forget you, but I guess not." She laughed and stepped back so Aaron could hug her. "You'd think we never take them for walks the way they greet you. I know you spoil them."

"I wouldn't dream of it!" Sam protested happily, fooling no one.

When Sam started up the walk to follow Penny and Paul into the house, the dogs ran ahead of her but veered toward the beach trail. They stopped, checked back grinning, tails flopping back and forth, eyes eager and pleading as if to say "Come on, Grandma, let's go have fun!"

"Well, maybe a little..," Sam laughed, calling out "later" to the pets so she could spend some time chatting to her daughter first. Sam was relaxed and happy knowing she could wait to share her big news until later when they met Paul and his girlfriend for dinner.

Jordan stood at the sliding glass kitchen door staring out at his back yard. He was wearing old, soft gray sweatpants, and a T-shirt, his hair un-showered or combed, stubble unshaven. Barefoot, he held his fifth mug of coffee in his hands.

He'd slept badly and grabbed the Saturday paper the minute he heard it land on the steps shortly after dawn. He'd read every single word in the paper, including the ads—except for any news recaps of his own 'great victory'. He'd eaten frozen waffles and mostly frozen juice for breakfast. He'd done the crossword and every other puzzle the paper offered. Now Jordan had no idea what to do with himself next.

The rain had passed through. It was a bright, glistening morning. Sliding the door open, he stepped onto the deck. The boards were cool beneath his naked feet. A lawnmower droned from a distant neighbor's house. It had the friendly sound of normal life, a normal spring weekend. It made Jordan want to mow a lawn.

He didn't have a lawnmower. His lawn didn't need him anyway. The yard had a good sized deck and small patches of groomed lawn curved around islands of bark sparsely planted with shrubs and a few artful trees. No flowers. A company came and mowed, weeded, and edged the yard. He never saw them, just mailed the checks. The yard was always neat whenever he had noticed it in daylight.

Neat and sterile, he realized now. It looked like a stranger's yard, or a low maintenance plan pictured in a landscape book. A boring picture, Jordan thought, taking a sip of coffee. He didn't see any of those trees or shrubs that burst into flowers in the spring. He'd seen them everywhere he drove, so it was past time for blooms. He just didn't seem to have any. He checked out his deck. It was a nice, stained, big, empty deck.

Jordan padded into the kitchen to grab a chair, but set his coffee down instead. He went and peeked out his front door. Nope, no blooms on his trees or shrubs there either.

Disappointed, he went back to the kitchen and dragged the chair outside to the middle of his big empty deck. Retrieving his coffee, he sat down with it in his lap, crossed an ankle over his knee, sipped, and stared.

This seemed the thing to do on a Saturday. Contemplate life, enjoy your back yard...but he didn't really like what he saw. He needed something in his life, he wasn't sure what. He was sure for starters; it was not a big empty deck and colorless, joyless yard.

Jordan tipped the last of his coffee into his mouth, the dregs bitter on his tongue. Going inside, he found the last of the coffee had burned on the bottom of the pot. Turning the machine off, he headed decisively to the bedroom.

Lifting his arm, he sniffed at his armpits. Seemed okay. Shedding his sweats, he pulled on a clean shirt and pair of jeans, adding a dab of deodorant, just to be safe. Rough combing his hair with a hand, he brushed his teeth and decided that was enough. Grabbing socks, he dug his running shoes from the very back of the closet. He felt almost wanton with the freedom of preparing to leave the house without having first showered, shaved, and cinched his neck into a tie. While it was a Saturday, he was still uncomfortable, after decades of conditioning.

He headed for a home and hardware store. He picked outdoor furniture first, finding a suitable table with an umbrella and four chairs. He didn't have a clue who the other three people might be, but that's how they sold the set, so that's what he bought. He added a matching lounge chair, then a side table for his coffee or beer.

Next to the outdoor furniture was a display of every type of barbeque grill imaginable, from the very simple and portable to the massive and hi-tech. Jordan could not resist the allure of the stainless steel hi-tech model that had a rotisserie, and could grill, smoke, or do anything else, digitally timed to perfection, which a man could desire but rarely need. He was tired of delivery pizza. He could picture himself eating a mouth watering BBQ steak.

They promised the grill could be delivered later that afternoon, with the furniture, and they would give him a set of BBQ tools free. Jordan readily handed over his credit card.

Studying the brochure of his furniture, he eyed the setting in the display picture before stuffing it in his pocket. Big pots of flowers and shrubs completed the scene. Okay. He headed for an exit that went through the indoor/outdoor plant and garden displays.

He passed some massive cobalt blue pottery containers on sale. He liked blue, two of those.

Wandering down the next aisle he stopped, hands on hips, to study the choice of flowering trees. His lean, rough good looks immediately drew a female employee to assist him.

"Looking for a cherry tree?" she asked brightly.

"Which one is that?"

She motioned to a six-foot tree, heavily sprouted with bright pink blossoms.

Jordan eyed the blooms. He didn't really need any cherries, and he didn't see himself as a pink yard kind of guy. "No pink. Do you have blue trees?"

"Well, no, not trees really, maybe a hydrangea shrub? Wait, they can turn pink, depending on the PH balance in your soil...no pink... How about yellow or white flowered trees?"

"Show me the yellow."

She took him around to the other side of the aisle and pointed out a tree covered in star shaped bright yellow blossoms.

"What do you call those?"

"Forsythia, they bloom very early in the spring, sometimes they even get snowed on. When the blossoms drop, they send out lots of shoots of oval-pointed leaves. It's a very fast growing tree."

"No fruit?"

"No, I'm sorry..."

"Great, I don't want fruit. Okay, two of those." One in front and one in back, Jordan thought. "Oh, and two of those blue pots," he pointed, "and shrubs to go in them that will still have flowers in summer, what have you got? No pink. Maybe white?"

Jordan completed his selections, arranged to have it all delivered with the furnishings later that day, along with a shovel and some potting soil, then left and headed for the grocery store.

Thinking of his empty fridge shelves, suspecting his cupboard shelves matched, Jordan grabbed a large grocery cart before heading into the store. He worked on a list of priorities in his head. Big thick steaks for his new grill, maybe a freezer pack of burgers, corn on the cob, and potatoes. He'd get aluminum foil so he could grill those. Butter, steak sauce, a few bottles of beer and, what else ... ?

Maybe he should just go down each aisle. That way he wouldn't forget anything. He was probably out of everything and had hours to kill anyway, before his new back yard was delivered.

By the time Jordan had worked his way over to the last aisles, his cart was nearly unmanageable. Every space was jammed; his methodical packing allowed him to stack purchases a good two feet over the cart, with bread and bananas carefully balanced on top.

He almost skipped the last aisle, out of room, and it just looked like magazines. He thought of the foot high stack of trade journals he still needed to review at his office. No more magazines. Just before turning away, he spotted a colorful display part way down the aisle.

Books!

If Jordan had a weakness, it was books. He had started reading before pre-school, had his own library card shortly after. Every summer in his grade school years, he won the local library reading contest, with the most gold stars by his name for the most books read over the summer.

He loved to read about places near and far, people high and low. Science and space, even romance—as long as someone else was doing it—geopolitics and ancient history, crime, passion, mystery, almost any kind of book—except self-help or cookbooks—was his kind of book.

When was the last time he'd treated himself? The last time he had been able to sit and read a novel? His last airplane flight? Probably.

Leaving the cart, he jogged down the aisle to the paperback display. New releases, a quick glance showed, were shelved according to the bestseller list. Jordan picked up #1, and then checked the cover of #2; a quick glance at his watch showed it was nearly time for his delivery. He worked his way down the line, until he had all the top ten books clutched under his arm.

Retrieving the cart, he awkwardly maneuvered it one-handed over to the checkout, blocking a box of doughnuts that tried to skid off the top with his hip, on the way.

He was going to go home, sit in his new lounge chair, pop open a beer, throw a steak on the grill, and read to his heart's content. Or until Monday, anyway. He'd wait to plant the trees. He deserved to read the new spy thriller by a favorite author first, then he'd plant before he started the next book by that funny lady.

He was having fun! It surprised him. He grinned to himself at the check out counter, admiring all his new food, all his new books, as they went into bags. Yes, he felt good, kind of weird, but good. Normal. Happy, even. Maybe.

Then he looked up and noticed two young punks leaving the store, slouching along, baseball caps reversed. Their jeans wadded around their ankles, their waistbands slung so low they barely covered their crotches.

They're looking for trouble, he frowned, he knew the look, and he knew those two. They heisted cars for Abraham's chop shops and overseas shipping operations. He *suspected*. He had put them individually in jail repeatedly on theft charges, but hadn't nailed their boss, his nemesis. Yet.

The simple joy the day had given him turned sour. His recent failure burned like acid in his stomach.

Someday, he promised himself silently.

Jordan arrived home and unpacked his groceries, needing to decide where to put things for the first time as he did. He had owned the house for years but hadn't realized he had only camped there, never before had he fully stocked the shelves and fridge as if he lived there.

"Well, they're full now," he growled to himself as he shut the last cupboard door, not needing another reminder of his failures.

Leaving the box of aluminum foil, a potato, and a cob of corn on the counter, and a thick steak on a plate in the fridge for his dinner, Jordan grabbed up the sack of books to select the one he would start while waiting for the delivery of the grill and furniture.

He was deeply into a novel when the phone rang hours later to apologetically inform him that, due to his additional purchases, they did not have space or time availability and his delivery had been delayed but was guaranteed to arrive complete the next afternoon, even though it was Sunday. Managing to keep from taking his frustration out on the messenger, Jordan went for a long run instead to work off the steam.

Slapping together a sandwich for his dinner, Jordan took his book into his office to read there until it was time for bed. He had tried reading on the couch in the living room earlier. He found the room too foreign seeming to sit in alone. Tipped back in his leather office chair, feet on the desk, surrounded by the hum and lights of his electronic office equipment, he felt more at ease. Maybe later he'd figure out how to work the washer and dryer and do some laundry. No sense spending money on the cleaners. He had plenty of time to kill this weekend anyway, he thought wryly, as he paged through to find the chapter where he'd left off.

By the time Sam's party had all arrived at the Casa lo Hermosa, the earlier dinner rush was over. They had their choice of seating and the attentions of the waiter to themselves. A large corner banquet area looked inviting and private. They slid into the high-backed semi-circular bench, settling with Sam enclosed between the two couples.

The important business of selecting drinks ensued, with much discussion of the merits of raspberry, over banana daiquiris, or salted versus unsalted margaritas. The waiter relaxed and no longer rushed, not only waiting patiently, but also joining in the fun, suggesting even more fruitful, exotic possibilities. Inevitably, with each drink considered, humorous stories of past indulgence were bandied about, as the close group teased each other.

"Remember the first time I had margaritas?" Penny asked," and I didn't think they were having any effect on me? Then all of a sudden..."

Paul jumped in laughing. "Boy, do I ever! All of a sudden I had to carry you out and throw you in the back seat of the car!"

"Yeah!" Penny continued, teasing her brother. "Nice guy! He throws me in the car to pass out in the back, and goes back in to party and just leaves me there!"

"Well, of course," he grinned. "I was just getting to know a cute blonde. I couldn't leave then just because my sister was having her first tequila lesson!"

"Don't even say that word," Penny groaned. "Which reminds me. I'm the designated driver tonight, make my drink a double ginger ale straight in a tall glass."

Sam chuckled at the affectionate teasing between the two. She could see by the amused expressions on their mate's faces that the fun and teasing was just beginning.

"Ah-hah! Pen, 'fess up. I don't remember hearing that tequila story ever," her boyfriend laughed, at the same time that Paul's girlfriend arched her brows asking pointedly, "What blonde was that, hon?"

They all dissolved laughing, including the two with flushed faces, who now had to tell all. The waiter was laughing also, enjoying this cheerful group. When the decisions were finally made, he left with their drink orders, reluctant to miss all the fun.

Trying to settle down to get their dinner order in before the kitchen closed, they finally completed negotiations amongst themselves on who would order which dish, so they could all have a chance to try practically everything on the menu. The waiter thoughtfully provided extra straws and plates, unasked, as it was obvious this group shared everything!

Everything, that was, except the bill when he finally brought it. They all fought cheerfully, each wanting to claim the whole tab for themselves. When the waiter helpfully suggested he could make separate bills, they all paused to look at him scandalized; he obviously didn't understand this family custom, at all! Resuming the playful battle, Paul finally claimed the prize, with the surprise declaration that he had just received a raise, and therefore, it was his by right. The others conceded, and unimpeded conversation could begin at last.

Encouraging Paul to fill them in on the details of his work, and how he had earned his raise, Sam settled quietly with her coffee and listened to the conversation flowing around her.

She had such a deep sense of happiness and satisfaction just watching the interplay between the four young adults. She smiled with pleasure seeing her children so happy in their relationships, and the harmony of the four together.

Her children had always been close. It was rare and wonderful that as they had grown up and finally found the special one for each of them, that it had strengthened, rather than weakened that bond. Sam was fortunate to count them all as her friends now, and she respected and enjoyed each one individually. She said a silent prayer of thanks for how blessed she had been in her parents, and children and those they loved.

"You're sure quiet tonight, mom."

"Oh, I'm just sitting here enjoying listening to you guys. How are things going for you at work, Penny?" Sam deflected attention away from herself; she wanted a little more time and courage before telling of her plans.

Before long, attention came right back to her, though. "So, mom, how's your work going?"

"Oh, fine. You haven't told me how your 'kids' are," Sam countered. This term was the family joke for all the pets her children had. Anyone overhearing the ensuing conversation would have thought that Paul and Penny were talking about the exploits of their own children, but the pets were Sam's grandkids.

"Come on, mom, it's your turn now. How are things going for you?" she was asked persistently.

"Fine, just fine!" Sam answered, reluctant to break the good mood. She looked to the ceiling, trying to find the right way, the right words to start with to break her news.

Paul immediately cast a sideways glance at his sister. Penny met his eyes with a worried look of her own. They knew that expression! When their mom started scanning the ceiling like that, something was up. Something she didn't want to talk about!

A slight nod from her brother indicated that Penny was to try first to get their mom to talk.

"Grandma called last week, mom."

Sam's eyes snapped down, startled and intent on Penny, waiting to see what she would say. Yes, Penny thought to herself, something is definitely up and grandma must know what it is, though she hadn't said much to Penny.

"Grandma asked if you had been up to visit yet. She seemed a little surprised we hadn't seen you...," Penny left her sentence hanging suggestively, hoping her mother would take the bait.

"Oh," was Sam's soft response, as her eyes sought the sky again.

"Mom...," Penny's voice warned, "Come on, what's up?"

Looking down to see four pair of eyes focused on her, Sam took a deep, shaky breath, then tried to smile.

chapter seven

Sundays seemed meant for barbeques.

Though ideal results and conditions were never guaranteed. There were Nature's caprices that needed to be accommodated. And there was always, of course, the greatest danger, the uncertainty posed by the human elements.

Jordan's delayed barbeque wasn't quite the fun he had planned.

He had gotten all his groceries stuffed away the day before and read most of one of his bestsellers while he'd waited for the delivery that had never arrived.

Today he had thoroughly consumed the Sunday paper, tentatively done a load of laundry, finished his book, and then had been at loose ends again. The delivery truck still hadn't arrived so he grabbed another new book, a another thriller by one of his favorite authors, and began eagerly devouring it while he waited.

That was his second mistake.

When the truck did come, they delivered box, after box, after box to his back deck, followed by trees, shrubs, and bags of soil. He had the deliverymen position the two heavy pots on either side of his deck, then they handed him the manifest to sign, stuffed his arms full of manuals, warranties, spare part ordering catalogs, and assembly instructions, and left.

Nothing came assembled!

Somehow, Jordan had missed that factor in the heat of his shopping spree. He should have asked. He should have checked if he could just pay more to have it delivered pre-assembled. He would have paid, gladly. Too late now, the truck was gone. His mistake.

He pondered the stacks of boxes, glanced longingly at his book. Swearing softly, he headed for his garage, unsure what, if any, tools he had to use.

Coward! That was the first thing Samantha Wilson thought on wakening the Sunday she'd been at her daughter's house.

When her kids had pinned her down the prior evening at the restaurant, Sam had just smiled, and arched her eyebrows. "What's up?" she'd repeated Penny's question. "What's up is that I think they'd like to clear our table and close this place, and," Sam had yawned, hugely, "I was having so much fun I didn't want to confess...," *Was that ever the truth!* "But your poor old mom is exhausted and half asleep. Please take me home. We'll have plenty of time to talk tomorrow."

And mom *had* fallen asleep in the car on the drive home, so that had been truthful also, though Sam was sure her utter exhaustion had come from the stress of facing her kids. Having a delay in confessing her plans had been such a relief , Sam was certain she'd collapsed from that alone. So far, Sam had been truthful with her children—just not the *full* truth.

Sam rose much earlier than she had anticipated after the late night at the restaurant. Though she had expected to be so relieved because she had finally gotten her announcement made, and that was why she would sleep half the morning. It had not turned out quite like she had pictured. And it was all her own fault.

The rest of the house still seemed quiet as she padded into the washroom, planning to return to bed for a few more luxurious minutes of sleep—or to at least hide a while longer. Then going to the kitchen for a glass of water first, she caught a view out the windows.

The new day had an eye-opening freshness and sparkle that she just couldn't turn her back on. Quietly, she unlatched the French doors, slipped onto the herringbone brick terrace, and breathed deeply of the morning fragrance. All the greenery glistened in the crisp early sun with lush color, the dewy moisture releasing rich, earthy scents. The sky was a quiet, pristine blue, uncluttered by the noise of the day to come. A single gull's cry emphasized the silence, as it spread snow white and gray wings to soar joyfully above. The bay was full with the deep sapphire waters of high tide, full of rippling, sparkling energy.

"You're up early, mom."

"Oh, hi honey. Isn't it gorgeous today? I just got up for a moment, but your view is so stunning! I couldn't resist coming out to enjoy it. I didn't wake you, did I?"

"No, I was awake." Penny wouldn't tell her mother she had hardly slept at all, worrying about her.

"How about if I make a pot of coffee and we have it out here? It's too nice to be inside." Sam offered.

Spring had come with a dazzle of color. The charming brick patio that looked out over the lawn to the sparkling bay was surrounded by the bright colors of sunny daffodils, and a rainbow of tulips, already cheerfully in bloom. A rectangular glass topped iron table, flanked by old-fashioned scrolled iron and cedar slatted benches, sat invitingly on the aged brick, in the circle of flowers.

Though the air was still a little crisp, the yard was private enough so they could curl up on the benches in their heavy terry robes.

The slight briskness just made their steaming mugs of coffee more aromatic, as they clasped them to let the fragrant steam warm and tickle their noses. The warming sun bathed their shoulders. It was pleasant just to sit, sip, and enjoy the glorious morning quietly, content to be sharing it with each other.

Usually, the weekend mornings the mother and daughter were able to spend together had a special tradition of their own. They'd laze around with their coffee, catch up on all the things they saved to share with each other. Their bonds reconnected as only long and close friends do, closing the gap in time since they had last been together as if it were just yesterday.

"I brought the patterns you wanted."

"Thanks," Penny responded without her normal enthusiasm.

"You know that Pendleton wool I got on clearance last summer?" Sam tried to engage Penny in one of their favorite topics. "That beautiful tweed?"

"Yeah."

"Well, I just haven't had the time to make it up. I hate to let it sit around. How about if I give it to you, with that jacket pattern I got for it?" Seeing no sign of real interest in her silent daughter, she tried to tease a smile out of her, "See, that way, I'll just sit back and let you do all the work and then I'll swoop down the minute it's finished and borrow it!"

"I guess so," Penny replied flatly without even a twitch of a smile to turn up her mouth.

Sam gave up, surrendering to the uncomfortable silence.

After a long pause, with only the twittering birds, hopping busily about the yard, filling the air, Penny stood, saying, "Well, I have a lot to do to get ready for the barbeque today." Leaving her mother alone with her silence.

Sam shook her head. She'd seen Penny roll her eyes after her mom claimed her only problem was tiredness. Her daughter had not been fooled; they were too close for that. And Penny had shown her resentment this morning. Sam could not blame her.

Well, that went well, Sam thought, sighing and cradling her coffee, still faced with the problem of talking to her kids when they were all together again later this afternoon.

Sam had always been honest with her kids before.

As a single parent, Sam had struggled and fought hard to bring them up properly to be upstanding, responsible citizens. Yet here mom was, ready to break the law! Not a big plus for her parenting techniques.

She'd never followed the parental "do-as-I-say-not-as-I-do" practice, but it sure would come in handy about now! Like her own upbringing, she'd always felt the most effective guidance a parent could give their kids was to set a good example, a standard for them to meet.

Or, better yet, surpass, she corrected, thinking of all her flaws, all the mistakes she'd made. She'd always hoped her "learning errors", as she preferred to think of them, had not hurt her kids. Had demonstrated, rather, that not even adults were perfect, just human.

Sam just wished she hadn't been so human! Well, too late to worry about the past. Somehow, miraculously, they had managed to grow up just fine in spite of her.

Recalling the task ahead, she focused her concerns on the immediate future. Would she lose the respect of her grown children by changing tactics? Would they indulge her a few insane acts in her old age? How was she going to explain this?

Not explain?

Sam had chickened out, big time. She was a first class coward! Worse, she was starting to ask herself why she needed her kid's permission. Did criminals normally check with their families first to see if it was okay to go to jail? Sam seriously doubted it.

And she knew the first thing her kids would ask.

"WHY?"

And Sam was not sure she was ready to share her fragile hopes and dreams with her kids yet. Especially when she knew they would reject her method of achieving her plan. She was also afraid they might think that raising them had held her back from her goals, which was not true and she would *never* have them thinking so. *Ever!*

She just needed a new future for herself, now that they did not need her. And she had old dreams to bring true. Youth always had the world before them; they could not really understand the desperation that could come when age and time and responsibilities seemed to be stealing chances and choice away—time that somehow sped by faster and faster every year.

Sam needed a time out, a place to gather herself and plan and start to find *her* future, before all her time on earth slipped by in a blur.

Her plan had seemed very rational and valid *before* she needed to explain it to anyone. Maybe that was her problem. Not why she needed to *do* this, but why she felt she needed to *justify* and explain herself to all her loved ones?

Afraid her kids would block their mother's attempt to "do her own thing" as they used to say, Sam realized she would need to do something she had never done before. Something her generation had learned from watching their elected politicians on the national news. She would tell a carefully worded, less than fully accurate version of what would ultimately become the truth. Not something she would ever be proud of, but it would save outright lying to her kids—or so she convinced herself. Feeling an urgent need for a shower, she went in to prepare for the day.

"Oh, Aaron, that smells wonderful!" Sam entered the kitchen as he took a steaming fresh-baked apple pie from the oven. "I hope that is for today," grinning when he nodded. "Where is Penny?"

"Out helping her brother start the charcoal, I believe."

Sam turned to see the two heads deep in conversation out on the terrace, her sunny smile turning to a worried frown. She suspected it was not lighter fluid the two were talking about so earnestly. Her daughter was probably telling her brother that she had not gotten any more information out of their mom. Yet.

"Hey, where's that big strong guy of mine?" Brittany breezed in. "I have a car full of groceries to unload." Seeing Paul outside, she tapped on the glass, waved and pointed at the bag in her arms.

"Just in time, Brit." Aaron poured her a cup of coffee."

"Thank you, Chef Aaron. I wished I had been here earlier today. You always make the most fantastic breakfasts!"

"That's just what I told him," Sam laughed. "We'll have to get him a chef's hat if we keep this up, to hide his swollen head! I just hope I'll have room for one of Paul's great B-B-Qs."

"I know, but these guys can sure cook, can't they? It's kind of nice having a little man around the house," Brit teased mischievously, winking at Sam.

Aaron laughed good-naturedly. "Tell Pen that! And while you're at it, ask her to help 'the little man' and set the table on the terrace, will you?"

"Sure," Brit laughed, leaning out the door to call, "Pen your sweetie needs some help in the kitchen!"

The weather, the food, the company was all spectacular, but once they had finished the pie and were all sitting around full and mellowed, all eyes turned to Sam. She squared her shoulders, acknowledging that the time had come.

"I wanted to get together to tell you...to ask, ahhh...to discuss...," Pulling in another deep breath, Sam started over more firmly.

"I have made a decision. It is a personal decision, but the effects of how I plan to implement that decision will... Well, it could have an impact on all of you. I just can't proceed until I've discus... er, mentioned it to you...'

"You're getting married!" her son guessed, jumping in before Sam could continue.

She stared open-mouthed, momentarily thrown off, before quipping dryly, "Are you related to your grandfather? Anyway, as I was saying.."

"Mom!" Penny cried, amazed, "I didn't even know you had a boyfriend!"

"Wait. Wait!" Sam threw her hands up to regain order.

"NO! I am not getting married. I do not have a boyfriend. That is not what I am talking about. Please. Just let me explain. Now, where was I?"

"You made a decision." They prompted in unison.

"Yes," looking up finally from her tensely knotted hands, liquid brown eyes beseeched them not to laugh while she confessed. "Actually," she spoke carefully, "I'm afraid the decision *will* be ... required of me ... by others. My choice, at *that* time *will* be limited. And *that* decision is something I've decided not to fight." Sam finished in a rush and with a sigh of relief.

If she had not been so concerned with what she still had to say, Sam might have enjoyed the silent comic tableau before her. Four intent young faces watched her in unison, with four sets of eyebrows drawing down in confusion. Four sets of lips pursed, in simultaneous thought, then four hands reached for a drink, as if to quench their befuddled minds.

Chewing hard on her lower lip, Sam nervously decided to just blurt the rest out.

"I'm afraid I'm probably going to be going to jail."

Bad timing! Mid-swallow on their drinks, four kids started choking and coughing.

Paul was the first to recover. As he helpfully patted Brittany's back, he teased Sam, "Right, mom, and I've decided to win the lottery! Seriously, what's up?"

Warily eyeing the group, to make sure no one had a drink in hand, Sam tried again. "I'm serious." "And I have decided to take my medicine and go to jail...."

Trying to sound as logical as possible, she said calmly, "I have considered this carefully, don't think I haven't. But I've come to the conclusion that this is the only right thing to do. But...It does have one big draw back, which is why I wanted to ask...to discuss..."er, inform you first. It could have an impact on all of you. You'd be embarrassed, people might think, well...it could affect your careers, maybe your reputations...social standing..." Sam's voice trailed off.

Still believing she was joking, and would soon get to the point, Paul played along with her. "No problem, mom. I've always told everyone I have a cute, slightly crazy mom, anyway. Don't you tell everyone that too, Penny?"

"Sure," Penny laughed, "I tell all my friends she is nuts. It doesn't bother them."

"That's right!" Aaron joined in the joke, "I remember that's the first thing you told me about your mom. It explained where you got it from!" Carrying the joke a little too far earned him a playful jab in the ribs from Penny.

Sam laughed, enjoyed the teasing, deeply relieved. They were taking it very well. She didn't know why she had been so worried. "Oh good, I should have known I could count on you guys. I'm glad that's settled."

"What's settled?"

"That I can go ahead without hurting you.."

"Wait just a minute…"

"Oh, you want to know the crime?" Sam asked innocently.

"CRIME!"

"What? What crime!"

Samantha's relief might have been premature.

"But, I thought you understood. I am going to jail…just for awhile…"

"You. Have. Got. To. Be. Out of your mind!"

"But…I thought you liked me crazy?" Sam attempted, but failed to coax any smiles from the stern, forbidding faces confronting her.

"Crazy is one thing, mom," Penny said pointedly, "but Completely Mental, is another!"

"Mom, tell us you're kidding," Penny begged. "You're making us nervous. You sound way too serious!"

Sam had explained the wrong way, again.

What was the right way to broach such a subject? She had bungled telling Rhonda and now with the kids, even with this very abbreviated explanation, everyone thought she was crazy!

Well, *serious* crazy, that is, not just her normal mode.

Must be the surprise.

Sam, herself, had decided after a lot of thought, after all, weighing the pros and cons, so naturally it seemed reasonable to her. The shock, of course, made everyone react this way. And she probably shouldn't use the word 'cons'; that pun might disturb them more.

Should have gone to jail first, she mused, and explained after she got out. No, bad plan. Very bad. She was discussing it with her loved ones because she didn't want them hurt by scandal. It wasn't fair to go ahead without their consent, or.., warning them, at least.

"Penny, honey, I am serious. I've shocked you. Sorry. Just throwing it at you without explaining better , but as I always told you kids, being an adult is more than just getting to do whatever you want. It means responsibilities also, and taking responsibility for the circumstances and results of your actions..."

"Mom, no! You can't do this, I will not let you!"

"Let her go to jail if she wants, Pen!" Paul vented his shock in anger.

"You don't mean that!" Penny snapped at her brother.

"I don't know what I mean, but," he turned to scold his mother. "This whole idea is ridiculous, and you know it!"

"Maybe Brit and I should, ahh...," Penny's boyfriend started to rise uncomfortably.

"No, please Aaron," Sam reached out a hand to forestall him. "I did want all of you here when we discussed this. It will impact you, also, and I wanted you both to hear everything." Sam had almost added, *No secrets,* but caught that lie before it escaped her lips.

Sam included Brittany, with a gentle smile. "Your feelings are a part of this also, and if it causes either of you problems, please, speak up."

"W-e-e-l-l, I'm comfortable supporting any decision Pen makes," Aaron replied diplomatically.

"I feel the same with Paul's decision," Brittany added. "We do appreciate being included though," she finished politely, huddling back against the bench to leave a clear line of fire between Paul and his mother.

Paul quit jabbing the ice in his glass with a straw, and made an effort to temper his words. "Listen, mom, I can understand that it's really important to you to do the right thing, as you see it, but—

"Does Ronnie know?" Penny was suspicious.

"Yes, I did tell her..."

"You told Ronnie you wanted to go to jail and she didn't stop you?" Penny was incredulous. "I can't believe that!"

"Call her," Sam suggested.

"Oh, you can bet we'll call her," Paul growled.

"What did she say, mom?" Penny asked.

"Well," Sam couldn't help but chuckle at the memory. "I gather she thought I was having a nervous breakdown. Just nodded, humored me at first, so she wouldn't crush my tender psyche. Then, well you know Ronnie, she'd never do anything as weak and helplessly female as fainting, but…"

"No! She didn't!"

"No, but she did have a moment of shock, decided to lie down for awhile. Poor Rhonda. It was quite funny, actually… "

"She agreed?" Flat disbelief.

"Well, grudgingly," Sam admitted honestly. "She did threaten to commit me to a mental hospital, but I talked her out of it."

"Then we should commit both of you!" Penny muttered.

"It must be catching!" Paul nodded. "Wait a few days Pen, and we'll catch it too. Then this will all seem perfectly sane and we'll even start agreeing with her!"

Well, Paul's temper was cooling, at least, his mom thought, his sense of humor was returning, until he announced *his* decision.

"Don't worry Pen, we will get mom the best attorney around. I guarantee she won't spend one minute in jail."

Exactly what Sam had been afraid of.

With a great deal of cursing, and more than a few banged up fingers and scrapped knuckles, Jordan had finally managed to knock together his reading lounge, ignoring the dining set until later, and skipped the side table. He was in a hurry. He would set his beer on the deck and eat in the kitchen, for now.

Then he bolted the basic structure of the B-B-Q grill together, ignoring extras, reading just enough of the manual to connect and turn it on. He didn't bother to read the rest of the manual's operating instructions.

His fiction book was so fascinating, he urgently wanted to get back to it. He did not plan on spending the whole day reading a damn manual! Especially since every time he put it down, to find one of the referenced parts, he lost his place and had to dig through Spanish, French, and Chinese, to get back to where he had left off in English!

Grabbing his aged and prime steak, he dashed some salt and pepper on it then slapped it on the grill.

Okay! He plunked down in his shaky lounge chair, he'd tighten the bolts more later, and grabbed his book.

Totally immersed in his page-turning thriller, too impatient to have studied the digital timer, Jordan didn't at first distinguish the smell. Deeply into the sights and sounds of the terrorist bomb that had just gone off in his story, he could easily picture the charred timbers, smell the burning fires, the... he quickly turned the page, glancing up.

Fire!

Real fire!

Jordan dropped the book too late.

His steak was more than charred. It was hard to distinguish it from the other lumps of charcoal used to cook it. A rumble of thunder indicated there would not be any second chances that day.

After the delicious barbeque with her kids, despite the intense emotions, the capricious spring weather turned again late Sunday afternoon. With dark storm clouds massing off the coast to sweep inland, Sam reluctantly packed up, and kissed the kids a hurried goodbye. She made it almost all the way home, before the rains came slashing down.

Huddled on her porch, as she fumbled to get her key in the lock, she could hear the phone ringing over the thunder rolling overhead.

"Yes, I just got back." She tried to shrug off her wet coat, with one arm.

"The weekend? It went fine." She toed off damp shoes. "Aren't they wonderful kids?" Sam asked, with the affection and wonder that was always in her voice when she asked that question.

"Fine? R-e-a-l-l-y?" Rhonda's voiced dripped sarcasm.

Sam hadn't expected Rhonda to swallow her breezy explanation of the weekend with the kids, especially as she suspected they had called her, but she was still too emotionally drained to rehash it all now. "Well, we had a lot of discussion..."

"I can imagine."

"And...," Sam grabbed a paper towel to rub her wet hair, "they understand my position ..."

"Un -huh..."

"They don't want me to go to jail, but..."

"Why not? Doesn't every child want to grow up to have a famously insane jailbird for a mommy?"

"Apparently not. So... well, I reminded them that it is my decision. I'm the parent, not the child...," Sam sighed. "I'm still miserable about it Rhonda, so I don't want to talk about it right now. Just let me say this; I don't want to hurt you, or my kids, or my parents, but there comes a time when a person has to be faithful to their own chosen path, and the people that love them have to release them to follow it."

Sam's gentle, but firm, words completely stilled Rhonda's sarcastic teasing. In that moment, Rhonda recognized again the inner strength and wisdom that lay hidden behind the deceptive exterior of her friend; the forces that had helped her raise two children on her own. So Rhonda respectfully, and wisely, shut up—for the moment.

Though the call from Sam's kids *had* raised some suspicions about just *what* they had, or had *not*, been told.

chapter eight

"Good morning, Jordan," Elsa greeted him cheerily. "How was your rare weekend you got to spend at home?"

A dark scowl and a deep growl was the only response she received as her boss stalked past her into his office, though she swore she heard him snarl under his breath something about, "Rare or even damn medium-rare is not what I would call it." And he closed his office door behind him this morning—firmly.

Dear me, Elsa thought, apparently time off was *not* beneficial to the health of *that* workaholic.

Todd stepped out of his office, asking Elsa, "Was that Jordan that just came in?" Noticing the closed door to Campbell's office, he said, "Guess not."

"Oh, he's here. But he is in there growling, scowling and prowling, I suspect. Best let him settle down a bit first unless you have an emergency."

"I have Jordan's new hire on the phone, she wants to know when she is supposed to start and has a few other questions."

"I'll talk to her. What line is she on, Todd?"

"Hello, Elsa? This is Shelley Airton. I just wanted to confirm when I'm to start work there. Tomorrow morning, right?"

"Correct. We have you scheduled to come in at nine a.m. on your first morning with an orientation meeting with Jordan at 9:45. If there is a problem, I'm sure they would let you reschedule. We didn't give you much time between jobs," Elsa added helpfully—hoping the beast in the next office would be tame by tomorrow morning.

"No, no problem. It's just ... Oh Elsa, it is embarrassing to ask this, but are you absolutely *sure* Mr. Campbell knows who he hired?"

Elsa's burst of laughter was followed by the reassurance, "I'm sorry, I wasn't laughing at you, Ms. Airton. It's just that I can understand your concern perfectly. He hasn't exactly *ever* been pleasant or welcoming in the past, has he?" Elsa sympathized.

"But I can assure you he is expecting the blonde lady lawyer from the defender's office that last stomped out of here calling him a 'rude-son-of-a-bitch'. Then went directly over his head to complain to the DA. He heard all that, he knows all that, and he hired you!"

"He knows that?" Shelley gasped. "But then…"

"Yes, he thought you were rather gutsy, I gather," Elsa chuckled, leaving out the dead dandelion bouquet delivery, that she had never actually ordered. The gal was edgy enough.

"Really? Well, thanks so much Elsa, you've really soothed my butterflies. Any other helpful info?"

"Well…I wouldn't say this if you hadn't asked, but…"

"Please, Elsa, just spit it out and help me out."

"Ah, maybe a little more conservative style of dress would make you look as capable and professional as we know you are," Elsa cautioned, hesitantly.

This time it was Shelley's turn to laugh. "Thanks, I appreciate your honesty. You know I haven't paid any attention to my appearance for so long that last week, when I had time to take inventory, I changed my whole look. New hairstyle, clothes, the works, into a more mature style. So let me know if you like the change. See you soon. And Elsa…thanks!"

Some *rare* weekend! His barbeque had been a total failure——another failure. Jordan imagined he'd be able to have a good laugh over it all, even his charred steak—maybe, eventually. After all, who was to blame except himself?

He'd had to satisfy his hunger pangs with a peanut butter and jelly sandwich from his newly stocked cupboards.

But he had needed his book, more than the steak. Needed the escape it offered; needed to experience a different world where all the problems were fictional, all the solutions the responsibility of someone else. Especially after seeing those punks in the store, the reminders of his personal failure.

Even so, he'd only been able to keep reality at bay for a while.

He'd put off the chores he had created with his weekend purchases. He'd spent the rest of Sunday with his book, finishing just before falling asleep last night. This morning, reality and its reminders had returned.

It hadn't helped that when he looked out his kitchen window, before leaving for work, he saw the results of his negligence.

The rain had returned in force later Sunday evening. Spring, ever unpredictable, had changed coats again, with rain and windstorms overnight. His deck was littered with sodden, torn cardboard cartons, tipped over shrubs with dumped out dark soil re-staining his previously light colored deck.

The trees he hadn't planted were also tipped over. One had a broken limb, and many of the bright yellow blossoms had been torn off by the wind.

He had covered his grill, but not tied it down. The cover had almost blown away, but a ragged staple, from one of the cartons, had snagged it, and held it by the hole it had torn. Fortunately, he hadn't unpacked the umbrella yet, or who knew what county it would have sailed to! However, the heavy blue pots had held their ground.

He had brought his bad mood to work with him this Monday. When he entered his office, it still seemed to carry the odor of last week's failure.

Campbell paced off his frustrations, then shook off his moodiness, trying to gain some discipline over himself. It was a new week, time to start over.

And he had a new, much needed, skilled attorney joining his office tomorrow.

Shelley Airton—aka Ms. *Airhead* to Mr. Campbell—had always enjoyed her job as a public defender. She had been proud seeing herself as a crusader and defender of the poor and unprotected. But so much had changed in the last few weeks. Had her values changed? Was it the repeat offenders? The customers that came back, year after year, for the same offenses, using her to plea-bargain away their time, so they could continue to commit the same crimes?

She suspected there may have been many things that she had repressed over the years, including a growing sense that many of the defenseless were the public, not her former clients. There could be no other logical reason for her drastic reaction to Henley, her need to absolve her conscience. It had been building for some time; Shelley had just rationalized it away, just buried herself in long hours, until it finally broke free.

She had quit, throwing away her career, at a moment's notice!

As stunned as she was at her own impulsive action, it was nothing to the shock of receiving an offer from the prosecutor's office, just one day later!

She had asked Todd repeatedly if Campbell knew he was offering her the job. He told her that Jordan was the one that had asked for her. Incredible! The prosecutor had never been anything but rude, abrupt, and even brutal, in his dealings with her.

Shelley was just as surprised, when she accepted!

She still didn't know if she had taken the job on rebound from the shock, or as a challenge, or out of spite to get even with Campbell! Her disbelief, and overwhelming curiosity to know why he wanted her, had consumed her during the week she had taken off between jobs. Each time her phone rang last week, she had expected to hear Todd's voice apologizing, explaining there had been some mistake, canceling her starting work this week. Tomorrow!

This morning, as she peered into the mirror, carefully checking her new hair style, Shelley had panicked, realizing that maybe Jordan had gotten the name wrong! What if when she showed up today and he saw her face-to-face and recognized her, he started shouting?

"No! Not you! It's a mistake! I'd *NEVER* hire you!"

The image was so vivid in her mind that her face blanched in the mirror, nausea tightening her stomach. She could not face that! She might have to call in sick her first day! No, she couldn't do that, she had to face him, but…nervously she had dialed the prosecutor's office, catching them in early.

Elsa's reassurances helped, but Shelley still faced her new career with an unsettling mix of excitement and trepidation.

"48549. Come to the door."

Sam rose from her cot and went to the cell door to retrieve the breakfast tray shoved through the slot, then returned to her cot.

"Hmm. Orange juice, bran muffins, and... what is that?" She looked at the perfectly round patty that looked like some kind of egg pancake.

Deciding to read while she ate so she wouldn't have to look too closely at that yellow thing, Sam reached over and picked up the letters from her kids again, that she had read many times already over the last few weeks. She had read them, cried on them, smoothed her hands over them so many times that she had nearly recycled them into soft tissues. But she had the faded words memorized, long ago. And she still hadn't found the words to respond.

They had been very, *very* upset with her new career as a jailbird—a vast understatement.

Paul had been incensed. His letter ran along the angry lines of... "What kind of two bit lawyer does Aunt Ronnie have that he can't..."

Penny's was full of heartbreak and feeling betrayed. "How could you sneak into jail like that without even telling us when your trial was? We would have been there, been character witnesses..."

Sam had not wanted them any more tarnished by her choice than they were from a distance. And she didn't want to take a chance they would somehow block her plans. But it was breaking her heart to hurt and upset them like this.

And Sam couldn't explain anything yet, it was too soon, but she needed to write them. She recalled the letter she had received. The one she had treated like an invitation to jail. Maybe she could send them something upbeat, like...

"Not to worry, everything is fine here. Today they even brought me breakfast in bed, though not every day is that luxurious."

Sam decided to give the matter more thought. Every time she thought of writing she got so lost in her memories of their last time together. And of what a terrible coward she had been.

Even Ronnie had called her a coward, and worse, when she grilled Sam the day after she returned. But she had been there for her in the end.

"So what exactly did you tell the kids?"

"I told them that I probably was going to jail."

"Probably?" Ronnie pounced on the word. "Does this mean that you have changed your mind about jail, Sam?"

"Not exactly."

Ronnie's eyes narrowed and she gave an impatient huff of breath before asking, "Meaning? Exactly?"

Sam chewed her lip a moment then gave a sigh of her own. "Okay, meaning I misspoke." Her friend waited her out, dark eyebrows arched. "Exactly not, is what I meant."

"Listen, Sam. You want my help you better start communicating with me. I got the distinct impression from the phone call I got that you did not tell your kids everything that you told me. Fortunately for you, I didn't comment much except to agree each time Penny said you were a lunatic. But I'm not comfortable with this to start with, and if I don't know what you said, *exactly*, I can't back you up and keep our stories straight."

"I know. Well," Sam noticed that there wasn't a single speck of dust or cobwebs on top of Ronnie's kitchen cabinets or ceiling light fixtures. She had a great housekeeper. "I might have given them the impression that I had already committed a crime. Which was why I would... well, you know, go to jail."

"Samantha, look me in the eyes!"

Sam tried, but flinched at the twin cobalt lasers that sliced at her. She opened her mouth to speak, but Rhonda pointed her finger at her and interrupted.

"And do not give me any more probably or might haves, and quit gazing at the ceiling. I know that trick."

Chastised, Sam admitted, "They seemed to be under the impression that I already had a reason to go to jail."

"And you did not correct that and tell them you were plotting how to go to jail."

"Exactly," Sam said with a little smirk, then sobered when Ronnie narrowed her eyes again. "I just can't yet, Ronnie. This way only you and I know why. What if I fail? Please keep my secret for now."

"They are really worried about you, Sam."

"I know. They wanted to get me an attorney to keep me out of jail. I told them your attorney was going to handle everything for me."

"I bet that relieved them. Wait until they find out what you *did* ask him to handle for you."

Everything *except* keeping Sam from her goal—spelled gaol.

The woman that entered the office to take up her new position was a more subtle, more sophisticated version of her former self. The exuberant welcome from Todd and Elsa helped to ease Shelley Airton's nerves, as they complimented her on her new look.

Elsa took the box of her personal items off Shelley's hands and led her down the hall to her new office.

"Oh, how lovely!" Shelley took a deep breath of the vase of fresh white carnations that greeted her from the sturdy credenza behind the desk.

Setting Shelley's box down, Elsa smiled. "Just a little welcome from our office staff."

"It's not necessary, but deeply appreciated," she smiled back. Reaching into her box, Shelley first pulled out her simple brass nameplate and set it on the front of her desk.

"Claiming your new turf right off?"

"Oh, well, I guess," Shelley flushed. "The truth is, your boss seems to be a little, ah... challenged with remembering my name. I thought..."

Shelley broke off when she was interrupted by a gust of delighted laughter from Elsa.

"Oh, that's priceless, wait until I tell Todd. But, I think that problem is resolved. You're on our team now. But I do like the idea of giving Jordan a little jab by having to see that every day. We are *all* glad to have you here. I'll leave you to settle in. Todd will come get you when they are ready.

"Your new look is fantastic!" Todd exclaimed, when he came to usher her into the prosecutor's office for her orientation. "Did you do that so Jordan wouldn't recognize you?" he teased.

Shelley was able to laugh with Todd, asking, "How could I make such a drastic change of philosophy inside, without marking the event by changing the outside?"

"Good point!" He agreed, gesturing her into Jordan's office with him for their meeting.

Jordan had actually risen, and come forward to greet her! With her real name! He was polite, brief, quickly telling her that they were glad to have her on their team. He said she would be an asset to the department, he respected her ability, and he outlined the departmental objectives and his expectations, before sending her off with Todd for further indoctrination. As brief as the meeting had been, compared to his usual rudeness, it was equal to an overwhelming welcome, in Shelley's mind.

After her cheering welcome from Todd and Elsa, then a brief and surprisingly pleasant interview with the prosecutor, Shelley Airton was settling in at her new desk for her first day of work, on the side of the prosecution.

There was little to distinguish her new office from the one she had vacated a few floors below in the Public Defender's office. It had the same government issue office equipment, same paint, same tight cramped space, only her nameplate had changed slightly, to indicate her new position.

Many of the cases would be the same ones she had left behind, though, as the prosecutor had just verified, she would not be working on any of those files, only new cases, so no possible conflict of interest could arise.

As Shelley organized her desk, setting out all the personal items she had brought with her in the same familiar patterns, she turned her thoughts to the business at hand, and the terrific opportunity she now had to serve the public.

Despite her feelings for him personally, she had always respected and admired the work of the current prosecutor. As she waited for new cases to develop that she could assist with, Shelley had been given permission to indoctrinate herself by going over recent closed case files, so she could get a feel for how the office handled them. She wanted to earn the respect she had been shown and learn from the office records.

One of the files Shelley reviewed from earlier that month had her frowning, puzzled. It concerned a bail hearing and arraignment for one Samantha Wilson on a first offense charge. One of her former associates in the public defender's office was listed as the assigned attorney of record. But there was no note of a plea bargain request being entered. *That's odd.*

Quickly scanning the one page police report, she confirmed that it was a first offense with no priors. She knew Carl always tried to lessen the charges for his clients, especially on a case like this. A post-it note said "closed, see computer". Whatever had happened must not have been copied to the hard copy case file yet.

Curious, and aware the office had been short staffed, Shelley placed the folder in her Follow-up basket. When she had a chance she would look it up and make the update copy for the folder. Reaching for the next case file, she paused to look up and smile and appreciate starting on her new career.

Time had run out for Samantha Wilson after that last weekend with her kids.

Not just because of her overdue bills and rent, but because she had let them believe she had already committed her crime. Believe there was already a reason for their mom to face jail time, rather than just mom's own selfish desires. Sam needed to act before they discovered that fact. Though she felt like a delinquent sneaking around behind their backs.

Going to work that following Monday had been more a relief than chore. Able to lose herself in routine, she'd let her job be the force that guided and controlled her actions for a few hours.

The strain of the last few weeks, when she had grabbed hold of her own life, wrestled with it, decided to be the force that moved and shaped it, turning it in the direction she wanted it to go had exhausted her.

Small wonder, Sam thought, realizing how few times she had actively stepped in to turn her life's course, rather than just letting it carry her along in its wake. It had been a relief just to relax with work, just react mentally and physically to the situations presented. It was lazily seductive; inaction was *too* seductive. Sam could not let it lull her back along a discarded path.

Not after such a painful weekend. She'd had to steel herself, time and again, to keep from giving in, seeing the hurt and unhappiness and, yes, anger, in her kids eyes, caused by her own selfish desires.

But these were precisely the thoughts she needed to set aside now. The decision had been made, the pain given, procrastination over. The time had come.

The end of the week would mark her course, irreversibly. Sam would be committed, no longer able to be lulled back into the same lazy comfort zone—or discomfort zone, in reality—of that same well-beaten, fruitless path.

Then all the steps should go smoothly. Sam had worked out the main details of the crime with Ronnie's help, and the courts and justice system should be a snap since she would plead guilty. They would be thrilled to toss her in jail, racking up more points on their conviction rates. That was all those prosecutors really cared about.

Yes. Once Sam committed her crime everything would go just perfectly. And she'd sighed happily at the thought, already picturing herself isolated, free from bills and cares, embarked on her vacation in jail.

When the fateful day arrived Sam was excited, scared, determined, and totally unaware of just how much pain she was about to suffer from her best friend's hands.

Though hired to work in Prosecutor Campbell's department, Shelley Airton would also be filling in on other prosecution assignments for a few months, as all departments were chronically understaffed. Due to her recent stint at the Public Defender's office, Shelley would only be working new cases for the time being. There was too much potential for conflict of interest issues on the backlogged files.

Today the juvenile court system was thrilled to have an extra assistant prosecutor to help out. She'd been asked to sit in on a police interview with a young offender, her function primarily to act as witness and legal counsel for the police. She would write a brief report for the juvenile department office, then they would follow up on any future action on the case. But instead of the usual parent by his side and public defender, this kid had an expensive private practice attorney at his side, so the police had requested someone there to represent and cover them. It was easy work for Shelley. She just sat, listened, and advised. Once her report was written, her work on the case would be finished.

Her incident notes indicated that three young minor men were hanging out, horsing around, and creating a disturbance for business customers on private business property. Loitering, creating a nuisance, possibly panhandling, blocking access and safety of consumers, then they started "mock" fighting, pushing, shoving, being rowdy young men, knocking into the customers waiting in line at an automated teller machine.

Police were called to break it up and remove them from the property. They had been using the area as their hangout corner several times and the bank that occupied the property had lost patience. One of the youths had car prowls and other violations as a juvenile. He was taken in instead of just getting a 'warn and release'. This would be a second interview, based on something in his possession when he was first brought in.

The police interviewer asked the lanky youth a few questions about his prior offenses, just to let the cocky kid know they had his number. Then he pulled out a clear evidence bag and waved it in front of the kid's face. Inside the bag was a small black object that at first looked like a hide-a-key. It had a magnet on one side, was basically rectangular in shape, but on other sides of the case were smoked glass covers, set at a slight angle. After swinging the evidence in front of the sixteen year old, the detective set it on the table in front of him.

"Tell us what this is, Chuck."

Cocky Chuck just smirked, sitting back and folding his arms.

"You tell me, you're the man." He earned a disgusted scowl from his attorney, who clearly thought his client watched too many movies.

"Well, Chuck, our people think this little device is some kind of miniature video device."

Silence from the defendant, who appeared to be concentrating on a snappy comeback.

"Now this came out of *your* pocket, Chuck, so why don't you tell me what you use this little gadget for?"

Chuck looked a little off balance, then grinned slyly. Leaning forward to place his elbows on the table, he confided slowly, as if he was making a story up as he spoke.

"Well you see, officer, you take this little gadget here and you stick it to the wall under the toilet paper rolls in the stall in the ladies room...," he flashed a leer at Shelley, "and get yourself a little porno movie of a lot of nice, hot..."

"Enough, Chuck!" His attorney stopped him before he could finish. But the nasty grin and gleam in his client's eyes finished the sentence.

The officer wasn't taken in or distracted by the kid's attempt. He just leaned closer, smiled happily, and replied softly, "That's very naughty, Chuck, and though I don't believe that's the truth, hey, who am I to argue with you? Especially since you just confessed to another crime in front of witnesses? Better think that over, Chucky, pal."

"Shut up, Chuck, don't say another word! This interview is over!" The angry attorney stated, rising. He didn't enjoy having an idiot for a client.

Finishing sooner than she had expected, Shelley wrote her brief report, filed it with the secretary in juvenile, and headed back to her office. With the extra time, she decided to ask Elsa out for lunch.

Shelley wanted to buy lunch to show her appreciation for the way Elsa had smoothed the way for her, and calmed Shelley's nerves that first day at her new job. She had gained great respect and affection for Elsa in just the last few days, and already they were becoming friends.

Because it was a clear, warm day, they decided to try the tiny outdoor terrace at the Quiche Shoppe. The tiny café had an excellent reputation for good food. The wait staff, however, while courteous and efficient, was a little exotic.

Shelley smothered a smile at the look on Elsa's face as the young waitress sporting a maxi mini-skirt, eyebrow piercing, exposed belly—pierced, of course—and lime-green spiked hair stepped out to take their order.

"I must be getting old." Elsa shook her head after the waitress left, "The kids these days…"

The comment sparked conversation about their own youthful times, current cultures, conditions, and woes. Neither of them could fathom the trend of young men stumbling along with their pants falling off their butts. They decided it was an underwear manufacturer's conspiracy to charge more for previously anonymous designer briefs and boxers.

Then Elsa related her concerns about irresponsible parents, letting the kids run wild and delinquent from school. She told Shelley about her experience and thoughts while waiting at the bank machine a month past.

Needing to keep her morning session confidential, Shelley could only nod sympathetically, but curious if it was the same incident, she asked casually, "What bank were you at?"

"The Main street branch." Elsa replied.

"Oh," Shelley thought to herself, not the same one, must not have been Chuck and his pals, but a lot of kids didn't respect private property these days.

Soon the talk turned to early summer blooms and plantings. On the walk back to the courthouse, Elsa promised to bring Shelley some of the iris bulbs she had just divided, to brighten Shelley's condo balcony next spring.

"By the way," Elsa added, "Jordan's going to be gone all day tomorrow. He asked me to give you a list of the new case files he would like you to review and start researching. I have his list, and notes on the cases he wants you to research, back on my desk. Remind me to give it to you when we get back."

Since they were talking about flowers, and Jordan, Elsa was also reminded of the time Jordan had asked her to send Shelley the bouquet of dead dandelions. She was tempted to tell her about that now, but decided to wait a while longer, let Shelley feel more secure. Then they could both have a good laugh about it sometime in the future.

"I have been reviewing some of the recent closed cases to acclimate myself," Shelley was saying, as they headed back into the building. "I've earmarked a few that reference the computer files. If you don't mind giving me a few minutes to guide me in accessing the computer archive system, I'll print out the hard copy updates for you before I file the case folders. But once you show me the system, I'll do Jordan's list first, of course."

Placing her hand over her heart, Elsa grinned. "Oh I am going to love having you around, girl!"

chapter nine

*D*ear Ronnie,

  Well, I'm here at last,

Starting on my new career!

I have been relieved of my

rights, freedom, personality,

individuality, and no one touches me.

I am a label - GUILTY And a number #48549

I can't have visitors for the first thirty days.

Please write again soon.

Love, Sam

p.s. I've started my journal

"No one touches me..." Rhonda whispered as the tears started rolling down her face.

"Oh you poor, sweet, innocent, idiot! How could I let you talk me into this?" The tightness in her throat grew more painful, until she feared she'd burst into huge racking sobs. Poor Sam, no one touches her!

God, how could she have let this happen to her best friend?

Finally, the tears—that Rhonda would claim she had never shed—slowed, without easing the painful regret. She blew her nose a final time, before noticing one phrase she'd missed before. "Journal" was a code for Sam's project planning.

Well, at least there was that! But at what cost?

Whatever had come over her a few weeks ago to actually *help* poor Sam into this mess?

Groaning, she remembered how she had treated it like a great prank at the time.

"Well, Miss Prim, for once you are going to have some fun before I let you run off to jail." Ronnie's wicked smile had Sam blushing and frantically looking around.

"You don't have one of your ... ah, *friends* here do you?"

Rhonda laughed. "No, not *that* wild and wicked, though you're more than overdue for some of that kind of fun. And now that you mention it, I could call ... "

"Don't even think it," Sam threatened, her face scarlet. "Let's just get this over with."

They had chosen a weekday night, when there would be less traffic. They had been fortunate that it had been a rainy, concealing night.

Meeting at Rhonda's apartment, they had inventoried their clothing to be sure they had not forgotten anything or left any detail unattended. Earlier in the week, Rhonda had purchased matching tan London Fog raincoats, matching wool plaid scarves, matching kid leather gloves, matching wool fedoras, and two pair of matching leather boots.

"Ronnie, this must have cost a fortune!" Sam exclaimed in dismay. "Couldn't you have just found something cheaper, or gone to a second hand store? We are going to be the most expensively dressed criminals around!"

"Now Sam, I refuse to wear anything tacky, just because I'm helping you make an idiot out of yourself. Besides, except for the boots, everything is the same size. I'll have plenty of rain gear to last me until you get out of jail."

Unperturbed, Rhonda arranged bottles of gin, rum, vodka, Kailua, and various mixers. Sam's brown eyes goggled in horror when Rhonda reached for another box to unload, pulling out tequila, amaretto, fancy cocktail napkins, shot glasses, more liqueurs...

"Did you have to buy out the whole liquor store?" Sam gasped. "No, Ronnie, listen, just a beer or two. I don't drink much, so..."

"Don't even start with me Sam. You wanted my help; you are getting it. My way! Moreover, I plan to thoroughly enjoy myself while I'm at it. Look at this darling bar tending book I found. Now first I want you to get into your costume and get that trench coat on."

"Now? What if I spill something on it?"

"That *is* the point, isn't it? Besides, I don't want to try and dress you later when you're limp as a rag doll. You can start with this glass of wine while I heat a brandy for you. That should keep you busy while I study some of these recipes."

Sam stuffed her feet into the elegant leather boots, shrugging on the trench coat and plopping on a hat that completely covered her blond hair. Warily climbing onto the barstool, Sam was quite sure her best friend had every intention of committing torture. Gleefully, if Rhonda's excited grin as she flipped through the pages of her little recipe book was any indication.

"After Eight? No, these won't work, they're all coffee drinks," Rhonda muttered to herself turning a few more pages.

"I love coffee," Sam ventured only to receive a scowl and told to shut up and drink up, quickly. She gulped the rest of her wine and reached for the warm brandy snifter. It smelled of peaches and Sam really didn't like the smell of peaches, but when Rhonda glanced up to check on her, Sam delicately pinched her nose closed with two fingers, tipped up the glass and gulped it down, only to find another concoction waiting.

This one looked like a tall tan creamy milkshake on ice. Sam pulled it towards her and frowned. "Don't I get any of those thingies on it?"

"Thingies?"

"You know cherries, umbrellas, whipped cream, the top stuff?"

"On a Bulldog?"

"Yeah, why not? I'm trying to get in the spirit here, Ronnie, but I demand thingies!"

Rhonda hoped Sam wasn't going to turn out to be one of those obnoxious drunks. She gave an exasperated sigh, squirted whipped cream in Sam's glass and tossed a cherry on top. "Sorry, fresh out of umbrellas, kid. Now drink up!"

As Rhonda whipped up a succession of drinks—a Margarita, a Chi Chi, Collins, Mai Tai—Sam collected her "thingies" in a napkin in her lap. Saving one of the plastic swords, Sam speared a pineapple/cherry combo, lemon and lime wedges, and another sword of stuffed green olives, then laid her little shish-ka-bobs in the trough of a big leafy celery stick she saved from a Bloody Marie. Bundling it up in her napkin, she stuffed it all in the pocket of her trench coat. Rhonda hadn't allowed her much dinner, afraid it would absorb too much of the alcohol; at least she'd get her fruit and veggies, Sam thought, with a little giggle that ended in a series of hiccups.

She was just started to gulp down a tall cream filled drink when she heard Ronnie say something about not having any clam juice to make a Caesar. Cream and clam juice? Sam gagged, then hiccupped, clamping a hand over her mouth, suddenly very nauseous and dizzy.

Hearing a strangled moan, Rhonda turned and surveyed her friend.

Sam's skin had a nice green clammy sheen to it. Her cheeks were flushed, her eyes unfocused. She had a severe case of the hiccups, her head bobbled on her neck, and she had a cute blob of whipped cream on the tip of her nose. Rhonda grinned and dusted her hands together, congratulating herself on a job well done.

With Sam properly primed for her part, Rhonda wrestled her into the front passenger seat of Sam's car. Taking her place in the driver's seat, she made a final check.

"Car keys? Check! Bank card? Check!"

"I sink you're 'joying dis too mush," Sam noted blearily, her head lolled onto her shoulder. She used it to support her head as she tried to direct her focus on her friend.

"Oh, I am! I am!" Rhonda laughed. "Slobbering drunk? Check! Starting engines, check… and we're off!" She said gaily, heading for the center of town.

On reaching the bank parking lot, she turned to tell Sam to duck down. Finding her friend slumped on the front seat; she realized she didn't need to worry. Pulling into a shadowy space, on the side of the lot nearest to the police station across the street, Rhonda unscrewed the dome light, before quietly releasing the door catch to slip out of the car. Leaning low over Sam's prone figure, she realized she might have overdone the preparation.

"Sam," she whispered, shaking her shoulder roughly. "Sam, come on, it's time!" Rhonda breathed a sigh of relief, when Sam stirred and showed signs of life. "Come on now, scoot over here. That's right. Now, the car is running, Sam, Sam! Okay, now see the clock? When it gets here," Rhonda pointed as if teaching a child," then what do you do?"

"Slam?"

"That's right. Slam the car door shut, then…?"

"S-s-sleep… horn."

"Good girl! Sit up, slam the car door, lay over the wheel on the horn, then you can go back to sleep. Okay?"

"'Kay," Sam muttered, now staring desperately at the clock, where Ronnie had placed Sam's index finger. All she had to do was hold her finger there until the clock had lots of zeros, do a couple of things, then she could sleep. *Should be easy*, Sam tried to control her rolling eyes a few minutes more.

Stepping back and standing up straight, Rhonda Sayles, in her matching outfit, shut the car door and walked slowly across the lighted parking area to the automated bank machine. She inserted her card and waited for the cash she would need to bail Sam out the next morning. Taking advantage of the slight privacy enclosure, she reversed her coat to the dark side, stuffing the hat and vivid scarf in the pocket. Taking her cash, she hugged the dark walkway and made her way stealthily around the corner of the bank, to where her car waited.

Rhonda was a little surprised to see another car parked on the far side of the building. The older white "muscle" car's dome light was on. It looked like four young men were having a little party inside. She could hear a bass beat rumbling from the car and see the glint of hoisted beer cans in the smoky interior. Hopefully, they wouldn't hear anything inside the closed car over that booming stereo.

She quickly glided over to her car behind the darkened Laundromat, slipped inside, and rolled down her window. Listening anxiously, she thought she made out a faint sound, then shortly after, the distinct, continuous sound of a car horn.

"Good girl," Rhonda whispered. Glancing over at the party car, she didn't see any indication they had noticed either her, or the car horn. She quietly started her car and rolled off down the back alley. She headed home, her fingers crossed, hoping Sam's plan worked out safely.

It had taken awhile before the sound registered in the mind of the young officer, busily trying to catch up on his paperwork, on that slow night at the police station. Was it a fire alarm, he wondered? Sounded like a car horn, probably one of those burglar alarm devices, the kind that could annoyingly be set off by a gust of wind. Waiting awhile to see if the owner would go shut it off, he finally pushed his papers aside, then stepped out the front of the station to see if he could figure out where the sound was coming from.

Across the street from the front of the station, he could see a car in the bank parking lot, headlights capturing the falling rain, exhaust seeping from the rear, and horn blasting away.

"What the...? Hey, Stevens, come check this out," he called to an officer still dressed for the outside.

When Stevens finally returned, he brought the car, and a very cute, but very drunken, driver with him. Sam had to be carried into the station and laid on a bench, while the police officers tried to decide how to handle this unconscious criminal that had practically delivered herself to their front door!

Breakfast in the county drunk tank was served at six in the morning.

When she woke, Sam didn't think it was possible to feel any more miserable – until she pried her sandblasted eyes open and gazed nauseously at her meal. The pastry twist looked and felt like paper-mache, painted with glistening lacquer, like they used for displays in stores. Sam was sure it would taste similar, after lifting and dropping it back on the plate with what seemed like a horribly loud clatter to her painfully sensitive head. She opted instead for the tiny styrofoam cup of oily coffee, but she was desperately thirsty, so just closed her eyes and swallowed. She had barely moistened her furry mouth, and the cup was empty, coffee gone.

Turning to the other occupant of the cell, she asked, "How do you get another cup of coffee?"

"You don't."

"Surely you're kidding? I'd trade them all of my doughnuts and cereal for one more cup of coffee."

"Sorry kid, it's another three hours before we get another tiny cup of coffee with two of those king-sized doughnuts."

"Oh, carb city, huh? Do you know if it's like this in real jail, too?

"Say what?"

"Sorry, never mind," Sam sighed. Her head was throbbing so wildly, even the simplest conversation was too tiring to maintain. Trying to pull her thoughts together, amidst all the clatter, she worked out a solution to her most urgent need. Water!

Clasping her empty cup in hand, she stumbled from the cot to make a beeline for the sink in the corner. Her poisoned body, however, refused to comply. She managed to keep her head pointed on target towards the intended goal, but her wobbling legs kept roaming decidedly off course! Finally, all of her managed to negotiate the full eight-foot trek and arrive at roughly the same time at the sink. She dropped her elbows to the rim to brace herself, as she filled and drank cup after cup of water. Stopping to gasp for air, thinking she would feel much better now, Sam stood straight up to return.

Uh-oh, she thought, grasping for a hold on the sink. This does not feel so hot. Waiting a few minutes for her head to spin more slowly, she attempted a cautious crossing to her distant cot, aware with each step of the sound of loud splashing, crashing waves coming from the area of her tummy.

Jail might be a snap, if she could just survive this hangover! Sam groaned, crumpled to her cot, and promptly passed out.

"Okay ladies, time to see the judge!" The cheerful bellow snapped Sam awake, momentarily disoriented, she almost shushed the noisy woman before she realized it was a guard, and this was a cell, not her bedroom.

"Hustle up, follow me, and if you smile real pretty, maybe the old fart will let you out on bail!" Came another exuberant bellow.

Several floors below, Rhonda waited anxiously in the small courtroom, worrying about her friend. Rhonda had been suffering from waves of remorse and guilt ever since driving off last night, leaving Sam in a drunken stupor. When she arrived home and saw the wide array of opened liquor bottles, the dirty glasses with ice still sitting unmelted in the bottom, she began to realize what she must have done to Sam.

Oh my God! Rhonda worried. What if I killed her from alcohol poisoning? In an admittedly sadistic glee, she had mixed every type of drink that she could think of, and poured them all down poor Samantha's throat. forgetting what the sudden influx of toxins could do to someone who never had more than one drink. Rhonda panicked, wondering seriously if she had endangered her friends' life.

Sam had insisted that Rhonda had to remain completely sober, as she had to drive. But after she returned, and saw the damage she'd wrought, Rhonda poured herself one stiff drink after another. It seemed appropriate she drown her guilt and share at least some of the misery she had inflicted on her friend.

Except for a slight headache this morning, Rhonda felt fine, a veteran of many a business cocktail party and martini luncheon. As the female inmates entered the courtroom to join their male counterparts, Rhonda was relieved to see her friend, but saw that Sam had not fared as well, her guilt returning. But Rhonda saw only the unsteady gait, the sickly green pallor of Sam's face, tinted as if to match the shapeless green drab prison uniform. If she had known why the prisoners had been delayed arriving in the courtroom, her remorse would have doubled.

As Sam had followed the guard down the first flight of stairs to the courtroom, the results of the water she'd so injudiciously gulped, came back to haunt her. Her stomach began to churn again and a cold, clammy sweat broke out across her forehead and cheeks. As weakened as her legs felt, spying a restroom at the base of the stairs, Sam sprinted in desperation, her hand clamped tightly over her mouth, dragging the guard and other female inmates with her.

Chained together, by procedural orders, they were forced to stand beside Sam, at the open door of the stall, as she heaved all the poisons from her stomach. They stood mute, eyes averted, jaws clenched, trying to retain their own breakfasts, as Sam so publicly, and noisily, lost hers. Finally, they pulled her racked body from her knees, washed her face with cold towels, and half-dragged her between them down the remaining flights of stairs.

At the courtroom entrance, they stood her up to make her way in, on her own two feet, however unsteady they might be.

Rhonda watched her friend being led to the benches up front without having any idea just how 'green' her buddy Sam really was!

chapter ten

D istinguished by their tailored suits, a group of attorneys, and someone from the prosecutor's office, huddled at the front of the courtroom, carrying incredible armloads of files. They wrangled in whispers, taking turns exchanging negative head shakes, until both parties nodded in unison, then scribbled in matching files, pulled the next from the stacks, then the silent tableau began again. Occasionally, one of the defenders would turn to crouch in front of one of their green clad clients, lined up in the front two rows, to whisper, get a nod, then give the prosecution a nod, more scribbles in files, and another's fate was hurriedly negotiated and settled in the moments before the arraignment judge arrived.

"All rise. This court is now in session. The Honorable…" the familiar litany was announced. The morning session was under way. Case after case was rapidly dispatched with either the standard 'not guilty' plea, or a quick confirmation of the pre-arranged terms of the deal. Monotonously, the stacks of files grew shorter.

"Case #89347, The County vs. Samantha Wilson," came the official voice, calling out the next case, droning through the routine reading of the charges, and coming quickly to the question…

"How do you plead?"

"Guilty," the public defender said guiltily. Catching the surprise from the prosecution side, he just shrugged helplessly.

Even the judge stared a few moments, surprised, before turning a questioning brow to the prosecution side, to see yet another silent puzzled shrug.

"Ah, we would however," Carl, Sam's public defender, hastily added, "like to beg the court's indulgence and request bail until a sentencing hearing, within the next two weeks."

Checking for a prosecution nod, the judge said, "Granted. Bail to be set at one thousand dollars, please see the clerk to arrange the hearing date. Next case…"

Both the prosecution representative and the judge assumed that Carl had slipped up, or forgotten something, changing his client's plea before the hearing. Which is why they agreed to the unusual request for interim bail, delaying sentencing.

Carl had not discussed that file before court, so it was assumed he just forgot, but wondered why he hadn't just plead her 'not guilty' in the first place, to give himself time? Obviously a goof, to be sorted out later.

Samantha Wilson was just happy to have it over! She'd seen Ronnie wave to her in the courtroom. She would be arranging her release now. Sam wondered how long it would take. She had missed the nine o'clock cup of coffee while she was in court. She hoped she'd be free soon.

What Sam desperately hoped was that Rhonda had brought a cup—or a pot—of coffee with the bail money. She needed caffeine *now!* to start to feel human again. They better have more coffee in *real* jail.

What was Carl thinking? Shelley had wondered when she had first reviewed the closed case file. She was even more startled when she finally had an opportunity to pull up the complete computer case file on Samantha Wilson.

"He hates women!" Rhonda announced despairingly as soon as she returned home later that week.

Sam had settled her affairs, stored her possessions, and moved in with Rhonda temporarily, awaiting her sentencing hearing.

"I'm sorry." Sam wrapped a consoling arm around her friend, leading her over to the couch.

Rhonda's eyes, distraught when she had entered, flashed a puzzled blue at her new roommate.

"Is it the guy you've been seeing?" Sam asked sympathetically. She patted Rhonda's arm comfortingly.

"What's he done to make you look so sad?"

"What? Me? Sad over a man?" Rhonda snorted. "Don't be ridiculous! I'm talking about you," she explained. Concern softened Rhonda's face. "I found out about the prosecutor that will be handling your case."

"But, I thought that other one... "

"The one at the bail hearing? I thought so too, but no, that was just an assistant that stands in at those preliminary hearings. *His highness* can't stoop to handling those petty little details himself!" she snarled bitterly.

Surprised at Ronnie's vehemence, Sam tried to calm her. "Well, really, what difference does it make? I'm pleading guilty, anyway."

Rhonda was not to be so easily calmed or deterred.

"I have a friend that works as a courtroom clerk. I gave her a call to see if she was free for lunch. We haven't gotten together in ages, so I thought I could kill two birds with one stone; catch up on her family and pick her brains a little about procedure. It's a good thing I did! On the way to collect Linda, I saw the upcoming court calendar and the name posted for your case. A man was listed for the prosecution, so I noted his name and asked Linda about him at lunch. Did I get an earful!

"Apparently he's a brilliant, skilled, highly successful prosecutor. Famous for never losing a case, she said, until the last year or so that is. His highness, that's her term, not mine, has been slipping lately, lost a few either cases, or the opportunity to bring cases. I'm a little unsure about which, but she said he had no sense of humor about being teased about those problems either!

"She warned me not to ever get in trouble because he hates women – especially beautiful women! She says he's a total hunk, but bat at eye at him and he's ruthless. God's gift to women can't stand the silly witless creatures, apparently. The rumor goes that when he was a young, top law school grad, he married the proper type of ivy-league attorney's wife. She was rich, with a disgusting east-coast social pedigree, and gorgeous, of course. While he was working his way to a partnership in a top defense firm, the perfect wife was screwing her way through their country club. Everyone else knew what was going on, but Mr. Perfect never dreamed she'd want anyone but him. He was furious when he found out that she'd been humiliating him behind his back since almost the moment they'd married! His peers not only knew, and never told him, but were placing bets on when she'd get around to each of them again, before he caught on!" Rhonda laughed gleefully.

"How horrible!" Sam gasped.

"Oh, come on Sam, the jerk deserved it!" Rhonda snapped.

"Well, I'm sure it doesn't really matter to me," Sam sighed, before Rhonda interrupted angrily.

"God, Sam, don't you see what this could mean? Can't you understand that this guy is going to crucify you? You're everything that he hates, a silly, drunken woman that's unfortunately too beautiful for her own good!"

"Well Ronnie, I'm hardly beautiful," Sam protested with a self-conscious smile, gesturing to her casual jean and sweatshirt attire. She was feeling distinctly old and ugly without makeup on to cover the wrinkles and crinkles in the corner of her eyes, her tousled blonde hair tossed into a hasty ponytail.

Rhonda knew there wasn't any point arguing. Sam didn't realize she looked adorable in the snug fitting jeans that showed off a great, if petite, figure. The elfin face looked sweet and fresh without makeup, framed by a few loose wisps of curls, made more attractive by the smile lines that showed her brown eyes usually danced with laughter.

"The point is, Sam," Rhonda continued forcefully, "the man is ruthless and willing and capable of getting you a much longer, harsher sentence. Don't you realize that? We thought you would probably get a light sentence as a first time offender, but this guy could hit you with the book and go for the maximum time he can get under the law. This isn't funny anymore, Sam. You have to back out somehow…"

"No!" Sam said firmly. "No, I appreciate your concern Ronnie, but I'm going through with it."

"But…"

"PERIOD!" Sam stated with the strength and determination that had always surprised Rhonda when it surfaced, rarely as it did. It was that same strength that had carried Sam through years of hard work and single parenthood. The determination she pursued her current goals with, though the obstacles seemed too high. Rhonda knew when to back off, as she did now.

"Okay, okay, friend. I've done my duty and warned you. You've made your decision, and I respect that. So what can I do to help you, you lunatic?" she asked, trying to laugh away the worries she still carried, and disguise the tightness in her throat. Damn, Rhonda thought, feeling threatening moisture in her eyes. *If I start crying, Sam will kill me!* Rhonda jumped up and turned away.

"I'm buying dinner," she announced. "Come," she ordered and charged out the door.

I hope I haven't hurt her feelings by not taking her well meant advice, Sam worried, as she grabbed her coat and purse and followed her friend out the door. She was sorry to hear about the prosecutor's betrayal by his former wife – poor man. But Sam didn't see how it could impact any of her plans.

CASE # 89347

SENTENCING HEARING:

COUNTY vs. SAMANTHA WILSON

The judge looked down at the case file notes and asked, without raising his head, "Counsel, do you wish to change your plea?"

"Your honor, sir."

Glancing up in surprise when a soft, clear, feminine voice responded, instead of the attorney's deep bass, the judge met the earnest, gold-flecked brown eyes of the defendant.

"Your honor, I wish to speak for, to represent, myself. Sir? I mean, your honor, sir?"

"I see your attorney of record is here with you. Is there some reason you don't wish him to speak on your behalf?" the judge queried patiently.

"Yes." Sam replied firmly, without elaboration or any more honorifics.

Checking his notes from the earlier bail hearing, seeing the question mark placed by the unexpected guilty plea, the judge guessed the defendant felt her attorney had let her down. He advised Sam accordingly.

"Ms. Wilson, you should know that you still have the right to enter a plea of 'not guilty' and be assigned a new attorney if you are dissatisfied and feel you have not been fairly represented. This hearing can be delayed or canceled to allow a new attorney to prepare your case."

Motioning to Carl, who sat red faced beside her, the defendant protested, "Your honor, my only disagreement with this attorney is that he is trying to get me to let him reduce the charges!" she claimed indignantly, looking to the judge expecting to see his outrage at this heinous offense.

Even the prosecutor, none other than the heartless Jordan Campbell himself, had to choke back a startled laugh as he watched the judge blink, then gaze in astonishment at the petite, but angry, woman before him, as if she had just descended from Mars.

"Ahhh....I see," said the judge finally. "Ah, counsel could you please approach the bench. No! Not you, ma'am. How about just letting me talk to your old attorney for a moment, okay?"

Carl and Jordan went forward to join the judge in a quick whispered conference.

"Carl, is she nuts? There's always the insanity defense, you know."

"Yes," Carl empathized, "crossed my mind, too! But she had the pre-sentencing review, and you can see yourself from the report, they think she's not only sound, but intelligent. A sane woman with no apparent drinking problem except for this one-night binge when she was picked up."

"Little do they know," inserted Jordan, highly amused.

"Hmm, well, thanks gentlemen. I'll see what I can do," the judge dismissed them and tried again.

"Now, Ms. Wilson, sorry for the interruption, your record shows that it's clean except for this one offense. Were you aware," he asked with great diplomacy, "that in such cases it is perfectly legal to request a reduction in charges?"

"But it's wrong your honor!" the shocked defendant insisted. "Just because I've only done it one time doesn't make me any less guilty. What if, in my careless thoughtlessness I had caused an accident? What if ..., what if I had killed someone?" Samantha's huge golden-brown eyes expressed her horror. "You don't know how lucky I am your honor! I didn't get a chance, thank God, to hurt anyone else before I passed out. It would be a horrible injustice to let me off lightly, and, and just think," Sam finished passionately, "what a terrible example it would be to others!"

Another stunned silence blanketed the courtroom as the judge and prosecutor looked helplessly at each other, before turning to stare at Sam.

What the hell were you supposed to do when the defendant argued the winning case for the prosecution, the prosecutor wondered? And so eloquently, also, Jordan mentally added. Finally pulling his admiring gaze from the sweetly earnest face of the petite, blonde, self-proclaimed criminal, Jordan tried to pull himself together. Totally entranced while she had been speaking, it was only now that some faint memory of that face, that voice, a hint of the fresh scent of springtime teased at his mind. Unable to pin it down, aware the judge was awaiting his comments, he dismissed the thought from his mind.

"Your honor, in light of the defendant's obvious remorse, the prosecution asks that the minimum mandatory sentence allowed be granted, and..."

"How long is the maximum sentence?" Sam interrupted Prosecutor Campbell anxiously.

"Twelve months," the judge replied regretfully.

"Oh, well... that will be enough, I guess," replied the defendant, doubtfully. "Okay," Sam decided, "that will have to do. I'll take that maximum one."

Totally baffled, feeling as much a bystander now as the attorney and prosecutor, the judge said nothing, just banging his gavel on the defendant's decision. It seemed totally redundant for him to order her sentence. She had neatly handled that herself! So be it.

Quickly calling a recess, the judge escaped to his chambers. He wanted a fresh start on the next case on the calendar.

The prosecutor, feeling slightly dazed—even routed—was also relieved to have a chance to escape. It had just been a fluke he had handled this minor case anyway, but his assistants already had full calendars this morning. He had assigned himself to this hearing to avoid a delay. Hopefully, they would be available now to handle the afternoon session, so he could get back to his own work—and a little sanity.

As Jordan turned to leave the courtroom, he could not resist casting one last glance back at the petite, but forceful defendant. She was being tearfully hugged by a dark, sophisticated looking brunette, as the guard waited patiently to lead her away.

Incredibly, the tiny blonde had a huge and happy smile that lit up her face—as if she had just won!

Jordan shook his head, trying to shake off the enchantment of that smile. He wanted to dismiss her affect on him, though he couldn't dismiss the way her words, her values, had pierced him to the core.

Too late he felt he should have done something more. Unsure what. He checked the folder again as he strode down the hall. *Samantha Wilson* he confirmed, *pretty, principled... but probably pleasantly insane.*

She must have been beautiful.

Or batted her eyes at Campbell.

That was the only reason Shelley Airton could see, after she reviewed the rest of the Samantha Wilson transcripts, for why Jordan Campbell would let a first offender suffer such a harsh sentence. The least he could have done is move to have her serve her time in a mental health unit.

Shelley never would have suspected that her hard-hearted boss might have been too dazed to react.

chapter eleven

"**O**kay, so what's the story on the County Bank job, Todd?"

"I'll try to make this as brief as I can, but... well, we have a little old lady. Widow. Husband always handled finances, but he passed away years ago. She is totally at sea. In steps the nephew to help her out. He gets things sorted out for her, gets her accounts set up on his computer. Approximately quarterly, he picks up all her bank statements, updates all the records, gives her back a quarterly report printout, budget comparisons, the works, in an easy to read report that, by the way, she doesn't read."

"Why is he so interested in keeping track of her money? Is she well off?"

"Fairly. I wondered about his motive also, but for starters, he's much better off than she is. The reports say he is crazy about the aunt, always helped her in any way he could since his teens. Also appears there were promises to his uncle and mom that if anything happened, he'd step in and help his aunt out. They checked all this with various family members; they all confirm this is straight 'goodness-of-the-heart' stuff. No doubts before, no doubts now, no apparent ulterior motive. And, of course, the aunt herself says, and I quote the report, 'My nephew is just 'the sweetest, most considerate and helpful young pup there ever was!' End quote. By the way, the 'young pup' is forty-seven!"

"So he's not a suspect?"

"Well, the police don't suspect him, but that doesn't mean they aren't scrutinizing his whole life since before his uncle died. But, no, he seems clean as a whistle and is terribly concerned for his aunt.

He's the one that first brought the discrepancy in his aunt's account to the attention of the bank officers.

"So, on June twelfth, a Wednesday, the account shows two automatic bank machine withdrawals. One is ten times the amount of the first one. The aunt was leaving for a Mediterranean cruise with friends. She's gone about ten days, gives all her statements to the nephew the end of the month. Nephew is busy, finally enters records, sees big cash withdrawals, picks up phone, calls aunt. 'Did you take a large amount of money out of the bank on June twelve?' Answer, 'yes, needed money for trip' . 'Fine', he says, no further conversation. He thinks rather expensive cruise, but won't pry further. He's pleased aunt is having fun, getting to travel, using money to enjoy life, as his uncle would have wanted.

"Now, week later, family dinner, show slides of cruise, and aunt mentions what a great deal she got on the package tour, off-season, etc., etc. Nephew realizes she hadn't spent that much cash on the trip. He questions her more. She had paid for the actual cruise package earlier by credit card, through a travel agent. Turns out she only made one withdrawal, the smaller one, from that bank that evening, which, in her mind, was the large amount of cash he had meant. She never withdrew the much larger sum that day, or any other. Since she never opens her statements, just hands them over, she didn't know that much had been withdrawn.

"So," Todd paused to draw a breath, "nephew takes her to the bank to report it. Bank investigates for error. Machine glitch, multiplied withdrawal? No.

Glitch on multiple withdrawals from that machine on other accounts that day? No, but they are going to have an officer investigate and personally verify each discretely with their clients. The withdrawal has her correct account number and her private pin code was entered to access the second withdrawal which was just a few hours later. Same transaction, no flags, as earlier withdrawal. There is no bank machine error, so bank calls in the police. Somehow, someone stole the large sum from that account late the night of June twelfth, by using the cash machine. Doesn't seem possible, but it happened.

"That's all we know at this point, but the Chief asked if you'd stop by, and he'll update you on the progress of the investigation. The bank, needless to say, is trying to keep this quiet until they know how it was done. That's why there is nothing in the media, so far."

"So far, is right, " Jordan muttered. "Well, I wish them luck! I'll drop in on the chief. Thanks for the summary, Todd."

"Hey, Campbell, glad you're here. We were just talking about the bank job. Have a seat and listen in. My detective was just going to give me an update.

"Go ahead, Mallory," the Chief prompted.

"The witness said she had gone to see if it was still raining outside, before she went to bed. She has a window that looks out toward the bank from one of those upstairs apartments over the adjacent retail shops. She said she saw a car running in the bank lot, and a woman walking from the car, across to the corner where the cash machine is located. That parking area is well lit in the center, so the woman showed up well. She was wearing a light trench coat, red plaid scarf, and one of those low brimmed dark hats, and boots, dressy leather type boots.

"Since the cash machine is used twenty-four hours a day, that's pretty common, so she didn't pay any more attention, looking off to the north instead. Then some motion, out of the corner of her eye, caught her attention, and she looked back just in time to see a darkly dressed figure sneaking around the far corner at the back of the bank. Moments later she could dimly make out a dark figure slipping into a car behind the Laundromat. She can't see right behind the bank, but figures it was the same person. The light didn't come on in the car when the person opened the door, so she couldn't tell if it was a man, or woman, or anything else about them. It was just too dark back on that side. The car was dark in color also, and she had the impression, though she's not sure at all, that it was a 'rich' car, as she called it, a SAAB or BMW type maybe. She was watching the car, waiting for it to pull out so she could maybe get a better look, and tell what it was, when she hears this car horn going off loud and steady.

"She turns, looks back at the front of the bank. It's that idling car parked there still. She can see the trench coat lady with the hat and scarf is back in the car, but it's not moving, and the lady doesn't seem to be moving, and the horn is just blasting away. She said she waited and watched a bit, started to get really worried. She was wondering if after the lady had gotten cash out of the machine, that other person might have cracked her on the head, stolen her money, then escaped around the bank. Just then she sees a policeman come across from the station and go to the car.

"Relieved that whatever was going on, an official was now in charge, and she wouldn't have to get involved, she closed the curtain and went off to bed. It still bothered her some the next day, so she checked the police reports in the local paper, found out the lady at the bank was just a drunk driver, no mention of a robbery, so she just dropped the whole thing from her mind."

"It wasn't until another detective was going around a month later, questioning all the people in that building, that she thought of it again. Apparently, he mentioned that the night he was inquiring about was the same night that a car horn woke a lot of people, it jogged her memory. She told about the suspicious figure she'd seen sneaking off at the same time, and her suspicions about what might have happened.

"Now there weren't any bumps or bruises on the lady that was the drunk driver, she was just plain passed out from alcohol. We know that for a fact, because the report says that they had her checked over pretty carefully when she came in because she was unconscious. They were worried about her. They had a doctor examine her thoroughly and file a report.

"So, as odd as it seems, the two don't seen to be connected. As far as we can tell right now in the investigation, it was just pure coincidence. We thought about questioning the D.U.I. about if she remembered seeing this suspicious character, but the shape she was in, they don't think she was even able to work the cash machine. There wasn't any cash, or a receipt tucked into her purse when her possessions were booked in. So..."

"So you think it's just a coincidence, dead end lead?"

All Jordan received as an answer was an expressive shrug from the baffled detective.

"Where is this D.U.I. lady now?"

"The Western State Women's Correctional Campus"

"Hmm. I have some business out there in the next week or so. Think I'll pay her a little visit, though it doesn't sound like it will be any help. Meanwhile, I'd like to be updated on any progress on following up any witness leads, okay?"

"You'll get copied on everything as we get it," the Chief assured Jordan.

Jordan returned late to his office. The corridors were deserted, Elsa had left for the evening. Leaving his door open to the empty outer office, Jordan sat at his desk to make a few notes on his meeting with the detectives, along with a reminder on his calendar about visiting the Women's Campus. He'd have Elsa pull the file on the D.U.I. lady for him to take with him when he went next week.

A slight sound drew his eyes to the open doorway where a hesitant looking Shelley Airton stood.

"Oh, hello. You're working late I see," Jordan commented.

His friendly tone encouraged Shelley to speak up.

"Actually, I would have been gone by now but I have a question on a case I'm handling. I was hoping Todd might drop back by and I could get his help. I'd just given up waiting on him when I saw the light. I didn't mean to disturb you; I thought he might..."

"You're not disturbing me at all, Shelley. Please come in. Is it a question I can answer for you?"

"Well," she replied, a little flustered. Shelley would have much preferred to ask Todd; Jordan made her nervous. She had a momentary vision of Jordan yelling at her for asking a dumb question before swallowing, and courageously stepping forward. "Ah, yes. If you wouldn't mind?"

She placed her file on his desk, careful of his other papers. "I made a note of what I needed, so if you prefer, Todd could give me his answer tomorrow."

"So," Jordan quickly scanned the note attached to the front of the file, "You want a decision between these two plea bargain options?"

"Yes."

Jordan looked back down at the file but just stared at it thoughtfully, without opening it to study the particulars.

"You know this case Shelley, what's your judgment?" he asked quietly.

"I'd stick to the hard line. This is a repeat offender and he was given a big break before to no effect." She answered decisively.

She felt Jordan's steely eyes assessing her before he nodded, "Do it." Scratching 'approved' and his initials on her note, he handed the file back to her, asking, "Anything else?"

He seemed so much friendlier, more approachable tonight that, hesitating just a moment, Shelley asked the question that had been nagging at her for some time.

"Well, yes. I've been wondering why you hired me?"

Jordan was surprised, but hearing the tentative timbre in her voice, gave her a serious, if brief answer.

"Because you're gutsy, competent, dedicated, and I respect your values and your judgment."

Shelley was warmed by the sincere words, but she saw the shutters closing behind his eyes, withholding some part of his response. Thanking him for his assistance and his compliment, she said a quiet good night. Heading for the elevators, Shelley silently muttered to herself with a wry smile *and you trust me not to go after your body, don't you handsome?*

As cold as Jordan could be on a personal level, Shelley knew he had meant his kind words to her as a professional. She didn't really understand him all the time, he had a scary and abrasive temper, but she had to admit that since coming to work for him, her respect had increased. Todd and Elsa thought the sun rose and set in him, and they had been with him for a long time. She was beginning to understand why he had the loyalty of the staff closest to him. Punching the down button, Shelley closed the door on the elevator, and the questions about her new boss.

Jordan couldn't answer Shelley's question fully without revealing too much of his personal turmoil, the reasons he had identified with her need to seek a change in the course of her career, in a life. He rationalized that it would be inappropriate to share his personal feelings with his office subordinates, too unprofessional. Of course, there wasn't really anyone that Jordan did consider it appropriate to share himself with.

He was a very private man. He liked to keep his personal feelings and thoughts to himself where they could be safely ignored and buried. He had been raised to the ideal of the strong, silent type of man. Then the rules had changed.

A massive cultural wave had changed the roles of men and women, the workplace, and social values. Government was called to account, scrutinized and challenged as never before, but so were men. As new freedoms and rights were gained by women, legitimately, in Jordan's view; new pressures were placed on men, unfairly, he felt, to open up, be more sensitive, more sharing, less of what they had been raised to be. Jordan didn't have a problem with the generational rules changing, he just had a problem with them changing in the middle of his damn life. He often felt like he had been bucked off a horse mid-stream, and didn't belong on either shore.

Oh, he had opened up once, left himself vulnerable, when he had believed himself deeply in love with his new wife. Even his mother had betrayed him after the divorce. Disdaining his "archaic" values, shunning him for placing honesty and fidelity over the social scandal he had caused her because he'd insisted on a divorce—a very public and messy divorce, as it had turned out. His mother had scorned him, then turned her back on him and poured herself another cocktail.

Somehow, over the years, he had come to realize that not every woman was guilty for the behavior of those two. His anger had lessened, but by then, his attitude had become a habit that he was unwilling to break.

Of course, sometimes he felt lonely in his self-imposed fortress. He was safe, though, and that mattered more. Didn't it? Sometimes when he was around friends and their spouses, they seemed fairly happy. It caused a momentary ache, a longing in him....

Jordan jumped up and shrugged on his coat, eager to run away from the traitorous thought.

"I'm obviously too tired!" he muttered out loud, "I better get home and sleep," he excused his mental state to the room. He turned out the lights, and slammed the door on the silently mocking office.

chapter twelve

*D*ear Ronnie,

As you can see, I have a few more privileges now, so I could go to the library and use a computer (but not the internet).

Yes, you are right. You are the only person I can talk to about how it feels to be in jail, but I hate that you are blaming yourself. You know this is all on me. I will tell you how I'm feeling, I need to, but promise you will not blame yourself, or I won't feel comfortable sharing my experiences with you. Okay?

And yes, I was soooo naive.

So here goes.

For all intents and purposes, I am now guilty in the eyes of the world. The surprising result of that 'guilty' label is something I had not fully understood or anticipated. It pre-determines my perceived character. I am one of the 'bad guys'. No matter what I say or do— even my smiles, my whole personality—are now suspect, judged to be false and fake as only lies and manipulation to hide the true evil person I really am. The element of trust, the chance to be given the benefit of the doubt, are gone, past. In fact, not just gone, but those same elements now work in reverse. I am guilty now, until proven innocent. From now on, any indication of innocence, any hint I am an honest and steadfast character will be discarded as a front, a manipulation. No one is going to let themselves be conned by a con!

The hard, serious faces of the guards and administration that deal with me, crush my spirit most by their complete void of human interaction, all emotions withheld. That seems almost worse, somehow, than if they beat or yelled at me. At least then I could have some response, some reaction that proves I still exist. But I am *untouched, unhurt, un...unconnected to anything that I have known before in life. This is what I wanted, I'll remind us both. This is what I want, the chance to be left alone, to turn inward, untouched by the intrusiveness of daily life, any demands of society, friends, family, work, and...Well, I wanted to be ignored to focus on my own plans.*

So I have my wish. And I'm not whining. But you asked for the truth, and it has been quite an adjustment. But don't even think about releasing that document!

And I will continue to give those here with me the benefit of the doubt, as that is part of me that they can not take away. Though I confess I was terrified of them all at first, but they are just like me, with their own problems that brought them here.

Less than two weeks now and I can see you all!

Love, Sam

She had barely set her letter to be posted than Samantha's bold claims were tested

Sam noticed the woman sitting all alone in the last chair at the last table in the prison cafeteria, closest to the far back corner of the room. Her dull blonde hair was evenly divided by a precise white line at the exact center of a heavy brow and pulled through a rubber band at a solid nape, gathered loosely enough to modestly cover unadorned ears. She sat with her chair edged across the corner of the table, as if it was the only place left to squeeze in at an overcrowded family dinner, though no one else shared her long, narrow, formica table. The woman hunched in the awkward location, sitting on a tail of hair that had never known scissors. A foot planted solidly on either side of the corner leg, she leaned further than necessary over the pointed corner, so each time she dipped into her meal tray it pressed harder into her breastbone. Her back was protected by the walls meeting behind her in the corner. She had a view of the whole cafeteria, all approaches before her constantly swept back and forth, as regularly as a searchlight, by eyes over-magnified behind thick, heavy lenses.

She made Sam very uneasy.

Noticing that the eyes were returning to sweep back to the left, Sam steeled herself not to duck as they transited her position, unable to control a shiver after they were safely past. She wanted to shrink. Leaning forward, she lowered her head over the chicken drumstick in her hand, trying to seem immersed in her meal; to be unaware, as if it would somehow protect her from the creepy staring scan.

Sam choked her meal down quickly, finally flicking a glance up, before collecting her tray to leave the table. The distant chair was vacant. She glanced uneasily around, not spotting its former occupant. Whew! She would be sure to sit on the other side of the table, her back turned, at her next meal.

Or, not! The prickling sensation in her spine objected, changing her mind. That would be worse!

Sam wondered if this was a good place for her to have chosen with her overactive imagination. She'd try to find a sweater when she returned to her cell. She'd been chilled and covered with goose bumps since she arrived – and she doubted it was all caused by the temperature.

In her cell, Sam crawled into her bunk, settling for a blanket to wrap closely around herself. She let the warmth begin to relax her body and soul, then she closed her eyes to find the place where her dreams resided.

"Oh! My goodness!"

It had been a long, long time since Samantha had been able to enjoy the luxury of reading a good book—or reading anything.

Too long, apparently, Sam thought, rereading the paragraph she'd just finished to be sure it said what she'd thought.

"Ohh. My!" she gasped, still shocked, but couldn't resist a naughty snicker.

Books had clearly not been in her budget for ages, or the time to get by her local library during the hours they were open. It would have been a waste, regardless. She was always too exhausted when off work to manage anything but chores and sleep. And it was one thing to fall asleep with her face planted in one of her own paperbacks, shaking the crushed pages out of the bedding in the morning. She could never treat a library book like that.

So when she had received her privileges to use the prison library, she had gathered up as many paperbacks by best selling authors as they would allow.

Now she had nothing but time!

Wonderful stretches of time to immerse herself in stories and adventures, distant lands and times, and even the lives and romances of others that she would never experience on her own.

She'd certainly never experienced *that!* What she had just read in a current best selling historical romance.

My goodness!

Did the prison *know* they had this in their library? They must not have ever read it.

Sam had a copy of the printout of rules and regulations that every inmate received on arrival. It clearly outlined what was and was not allowed for inmates to have, receive in the mail, or from visitors. Sam scooted over and found her copy and double checked. Yes, there it was... No Pornography.

She immediately tucked her book under her blanket and blushing, looked nervously around to make sure no one had seen.

There were warnings about what could happen to anyone caught with prohibited items, confiscation or worse. And Sam was intrigued. She hoped to at least *finish* the book first before they confiscated it. Then maybe she could sneak it back into their library and no one would be the wiser when it finally was found out.

It wasn't until she read the second book from her stack that Sam realized she could quit trying to hide her books under her mattress as nowadays the definition of what was pornography and what was just everyday fiction had drastically changed from her younger days.

She should have been more aware, she'd seen commercials for television shows that she had been shocked to see on regular broadcast vs adult channels.

Granted, Sam *was* naive. And a *bit* prim. According to her friend Ronnie, who had more than once claimed that Sam was the only born-again virgin that had two kids that she knew.. Laughing when she always caused Sam to flinch and blush when she said words like "virgin" and "sex"—and *worse*—above a whisper. But then Samantha had never been a flower child, though she'd ironed her long hair to look like Cher. Ronnie had been a bra-burner from the start and never had *any* 'fear of flying".

Sam knew she wasn't exactly a . . . well, a free spirit. But when Sam was young they watched TV shows like Ozzie & Harriet and Father Knows Best on their new black and white TVs, and the parents in those show were even required to have twin beds, things were so proper and restricted. In fact when Sam was younger she figured her parents just had one bed in *their* room because it was so small that two wouldn't fit. And she just couldn't see her parents with stacking bunk beds.

When Sam was in high school she had read her mom's collection of Emily Loring romance novels written in the 1930s - 1950s that clearly defined romance more like the black and white movies of the time as dating, picnicking and dancing with well-mannered, upstanding citizens with high-morals, broad shoulders, strong chins and characters, that with wit and a sense of humor, tender touches and words, mesmerized one with their clear, shining eyes on enchanted evenings. They were also known for rescuing damsels in distress much like a shining knight of old.

Rather than ravishing them repeatedly as "romance" in the current era seemed to be defined.

And *now*! Now anything seemed to be on television. And everything! And books were vastly different ... even shocking to someone her age.

But vastly educational!

Until she had read it in her book, Sam had no idea that she even *had* a button that could be pushed (in an intimate area) that men could use to excite her! Her ex-husband clearly hadn't known either. Yet Sam was sure her friend Ronnie knew *all about* such things! Though Sam would die of embarrassment before asking. And the way her dear friend Ronnie liked to torment her with her scandalous exploits, all Sam really needed to do was stay silent and turn bright red, and she would probably learn it all eventually.

Though....

It had been so long, Sam could barely remember what a passionate kiss actually felt like...

Or what it felt like, and smelled like, and did to her nerves and pulse to have a strong male body hold her close ...

The more Sam considered it, she realized she'd *never* experienced being undressed just by a pair of seductive eyes!

She definitely needed to add some interpersonal experiences to her future project planning list.

Immersed in her reading 'research', time flew for inmate #48549 and before she knew it, it was Saturday.

The Saturday. She would see her kids today.

Sam could hardly contain herself. Her thirty day waiting period for visitors had ended mid-week. She'd seen her parents then.

Now, Paul and Brittany, Penny and Aaron, and Rhonda were all there when she was ushered into the visiting lounge. The kids had convinced the officials that they were all family, so "Aunt Ronnie" had not had to wait for a later turn.

They had all ganged up on her, all tried to hug her at once. The guards were concerned they might have to enforce a no-contact rule—to protect the tiny inmate—instead of the visitors. A very muffled, "I love you guys! I missed you so much!" could be indistinctly heard from a small, teary voice located at roughly the center of five encircling pairs of arms. When the owner of the voice emerged from the huddle, the guards could see that the petite blond inmate seemed rumpled, but basically unhurt, from the exuberant tangle.

"Are you okay?"

"Has it been rough?"

"You look so pale. Are you sure you're fine?"

The questions flew from all sides.

"I'm fine. No. And yes," Sam laughed, trying to respond in order. "Let's sit down and I'll tell you everything, but please, one at a time."

"What's it been like?" Penny asked first.

Rhonda had been wise enough not to show the kids the first two letters she had received from Sam. All Sam's letters to her kids had been cheery, positive, but they still needed to sit her down, look in her eyes, and reassure themselves.

"It's been a real change of pace, that's for sure! You know what's the strangest? I never really thought about how much time I used to spend getting up, deciding what to wear, dressing up, doing my face and hair, driving to work each day. There's such freedom not having to do that, I was amazed! No wonder people can hardly wait to retire. It's not the work routine, but the getting there that's the stinker.

"It's taking me a while to settle down and get used to the schedule. I have work to do here too, you know, it just seems easier. This first month, I've also had to spend most of my free time in classes. That drinking charge means a mandatory treatment program here. The first thirty days are most intense, so now I'll just have classes and AA meetings a few times a week, so I'll have more free time. And," Sam grinned, "I've been getting time to read books again."

"We know how much you love that!"

"How about friends?" Ronnie, of course, was asking. "Have you made any friends yet?"

"Fine friends she'd meet here, Ronnie!" Paul snorted his disgust.

"Hey, wait a minute, pal, my best friend is an inmate here!" Ronnie threw back.

"Oh, yeah, right, but that's different!" Paul insisted.

"Wait!" Sam interceded, forestalling the two "No, I haven't made friends here yet," bringing a relieved sigh from her son. "But it's because we're more separated in the first thirty days. It's important you understand, though," Sam continued, "that that *is* the reason. Not because I don't think there are good people here, that could make good friends, Paul." She finished with a warning look to stop her son from pushing the matter.

Her own sensitivity on the subject was part of the reason she didn't want further discussion. She'd convinced herself, at first, that she was a special case. Paul's attitude reminded her of that embarrassment. She'd judged those around her, just as he was now. She was ashamed of her timidity associating with the other inmates. It was true that she hadn't had a lot of communal time, but part of it *had been* plain and simple fear.

Sam was trying to overcome her prejudices. The same prejudice that she had found so hurtful applied to herself when she had first arrived. Paul had just spotlighted her own lack of progress, and hypocrisy, in that direction. Whether trying to convince herself, or him, she was determined to start backing her words up with actions to match now that she would have more freedom with other inmates.

How many times, over the years, had her desire to set a good example for the kids been the catalyst to looking more honestly at, and demanding more of, herself? Was that how all parents grew, by striving to live up to the expectations they set for their children?

Maybe the kids raise us?

Sam's thoughts made her smile.

"Well, you seem happy anyway," Penny had noted the smile. "But do you really think you can last another eleven months, mom?"

"Yes, I will have to won't I? I'll do fine."

Rhonda sat back, content to have a chance to listen and observe Sam, as they visited. Sam would put on a cheery front for them, but she couldn't detect any cause for immediate concern. The kids wouldn't be the only ones watching closely in the coming months.

Maybe, Rhonda thought, it might turn out okay. Not normally one to try to turn back the clock on a poorly made decision, futilely wishing it hadn't been made, Rhonda had still deeply regretted letting Sam do this – the worst decision she ever made! But now she'd try to chalk it up as a grave error, use the experience to be wiser in the future. But she had helped her friend when asked, and it was hard to regret that choice. Her only control now was to monitor Sam closely, pull the plug if she was endangered in any way. Never, ever, again, would Sam talk her into harebrained schemes! Thirty days and counting, Rhonda thought, as she tuned back in.

"...and I can hardly wait to start learning more about my fellow inmates, and what brought them here." Sam was continuing to put on a good show for her kids. "It's funny how you look at someone here in prison uniform, then try to gauge how they dressed on the outside, and what kind of life they led. We use a person's style of clothing so much for clues to who they are. I find myself watching people, creating imaginary lives for them, the way it might be.

"There is one woman I've been watching. My first impression of her was that she was a very plain, simple type, kind of old-fashioned. Maybe a farmer's wife from the mid-west. I picture her wearing an older style calico shirtdress, an apron tied around her middle, shuffling around the kitchen in slippers, baking bread and pies all day. I see flour up to her elbows, a placid, sturdy, farm wife stereotype. She'd only get dressed up in her Sunday best once a week for church. It seems so crazy to stereotype someone like that, in this day of women's lib, but I confess, I can't think of her any other way!"

"So why would she be here?" Aaron asked practically.

"Well, I figured something traumatic happened in the life she led that would have caused her to act completely against her nature. Maybe there was a drought, after years of trying to save the family farm, they went under, their whole way of life was foreclosed. Suddenly, they were out of control of a life that they were born into, expected to die in, their children carrying on down through future generations. It destroyed the farmer's pride; he took to drinking to ease the pain of failure. Not just a personal failure, mind you, but he'd feel like he had failed all the past and future generations, also!" Sam was an enthusiastic and natural born storyteller, and they all nodded now, totally caught up in this fairy tale.

"So, in his pain and anger, he needed to lash out, strike back. Unable to strike at the real cause, he struck his poor wife. Beat her repeatedly, until one day, she fights back, brains him with a copper pot. He has to be taken to the hospital with a severe concussion, stitches for a scalp wound. The police press charges for assault and put her in jail! Which, of course isn't fair, but, hey, the men stick together in this small town. Her husband probably wants to take advantage of the chance to play around, build his ego back up, you know?"

"Mom, your female chauvinist piggy side is showing," Paul teased.

Sam agreed with a grin, but it was her story after all.

"Anyway, it must have been something like that because, well, because she seems so very wary, on watch, like she's expecting more blows to come her way."

Trying to overcome her own doubts, Sam created a plausible story for the woman that sat far in the back corner. The one she privately called "The Searchlight". Trying to convince herself that only her own over-active imagination caused the fear she'd felt since that first sweep of the chilling gaze. Even after telling the story to the kids, she still couldn't keep from shivering, picturing those searchlight eyes!

The others interpreted Sam's shudder as sympathy for the poor woman she described.

"Well, let us know her real story." Brittany was as caught up as the rest in the mystery of this woman's past.

Sam finally encouraged the kids to fill her in on their own lives, after they had examined her thoroughly on the details of her strange new life. They told her all the escapades of their dogs and cats, the pets they referred to as her 'grandkids'.

The cheerful chatter was finally broken up when the guards came to indicate time was almost up. The brave smiles they gave each other held the glitter of eyes desperately trying to hold tears back. Goodbyes were choked past tight throats, as they remembered they were sentenced to be separated for eleven more painful months. It seemed to stretch into the future like eleven long years.

"I love you kids, thanks so much for coming all the way out here to see me. But, if you don't mind I need just a few minutes with Ronnie alone."

"I hope it's to tell her to get her attorney off his ass and get you out of here," Paul frowned at his dear 'aunt' and looked at his mom.

She just gave him a thin smile and waited.

"Okay. We love you, mom. Come on guys, let's all go. Ronnie has her own car here anyway." Paul surrendered graciously.

Once the kids were out of the lounge, with a look of concern, Ronnie asked, "What happened to your jaw? I didn't want to mention it in front of the kids, but it looks like it's swollen. Has someone hit you, Sam?"

Sam laughed, then cupped her jaw, at the discomfort. "Oh sure, all the time, at least twice a day," she teased. "No, it's just a toothache, and, good news, the dentist comes this afternoon. I'm scheduled for him to fix it. Isn't that terrific?"

"Well, that is great. So you saw your parents? How are they?"

Sam restrained herself to a fond, if lumpy, smile this time. "They were here earlier this week on my first visiting day."

"Your dad?" Rhonda was still wondering what had made Sam request a private talk.

"Oh, Dad, he's such a dear. He just never gives up, you know? He was telling me all about how he went out to the airfield last weekend. It was a clear, crisp, sunny day—perfect for flying. He took a buddy up to fly out over the islands, then down over Mount St. Helen's to see how the landscape is recovering from the last ash and gas explosion. He didn't see any smoke this time, though there are two lava domes now growing in the crater.

"Then Dad went to the Pilothouse Restaurant for lunch, and to 'shoot the breeze' as he calls it. Which is guy talk for gossiping, I'm sure. He started going over the merits of all the pilots he spoke with up there, and I realized he was probably interviewing them with an eye to finding me a potential husband!"

They both had a good laugh over that, Sam's dad was up to his old tricks, for sure.

"Ahhh, but he's a sweetheart. I've sure missed him," Sam added softly, her eyes glistening with moisture. "It was good to see him."

"And your mom?" Rhonda prompted, "Did she come too?"

"Of course! And bearing baked gifts, no less!" Sam grinned.

"Do they allow that?"

"Not really. She bribed them!" Sam's eyes widened, mock scandalized, before laughing and telling Rhonda the story.

Sam had been nurtured from childhood on home baked goods. Even the bread her school lunch sandwiches were made from was homemade from scratch. The pickles home grown and canned by her mom. She'd constantly had to protect her lunch from her friends as no one could resist her mom's baked goods, especially her chocolate chip cookies and home made cocoanut pound cake.

Sam had written her mom about how the cake her mom mailed—though still delicious—had been reduced to crumbs by the guards looking for weapons. So her mom brought carefully sliced portions of her cake to the jail instead when she came to visit Sam. Only to *still* be denied entrance of this 'essential nutrient for her poor child'. The guards were concerned she might have secreted something in the scrumptious cake.

Angered at this denial of 'basic human rights', Sam's mother had torn the cake into shreds on the plate right in front of the guard's face. Her dad had reached out and grabbed a chunk, popping it into his mouth, closing his eyes, sighing with gusto.

The poor guard was already drooling from the aroma of vanilla and cocoanut rising from the moist shredded chunks under her nose, surrendering quickly when Sam's mom suggested she test it also.

A deal was struck.

In return for paying half the cake crumbles as a bribe to the helpless guard, the rest of the battered cake was allowed in for Sam. Even in crumbs, with a sore tooth, Sam had thought it was heavenly.

Relieved Sam's folks were fine, but still confused and agitated that she might run out of visiting time, Rhonda pushed, "But Sam, what was it you needed a private talk about?"

Sam's delight vanished, her face became troubled, earnest brown eyes pleaded with Rhonda.

"I have a big problem. I really need your help, Ronnie."

"Anything, Sam. What?"

Sam glanced down at hands twisted in her lap, hesitant at first, then with pink tinged cheeks, leaned over to confess her problem to her long time best friend.

Checking to see no one was near, Sam demanded in a desperate whisper, "Ronnie, I *need* a man."

"Now?" Ronnie made the word sound like a howl. "You need a man, *now?*

Samantha shushed her.

"For what?" Ronnie demanded.

Sam rolled her eyes, whispering and gesturing, "For..., well *you* know!"

If the wink hadn't clued her, Sam's bright red face, certainly did. But this *was* Miss Prim, so Rhonda wanted confirmation.

"For sex?" She asked, with clear disbelief.

"Shush!" But Sam added a quick nod.

Rhonda just gaped at her, silent for a moment

"Can't you *wait*?" Ronnie asked, incredulous.

chapter thirteen

The Searchlight was in her solitary post, as usual, sweeping the room with her gaze.

Today Sam hesitated, then squaring her shoulders, walked past her usual table with her tray, headed toward that distant corner. She didn't know if it was the searchlight eyes that stopped, reversing quickly to lock in on her, or the heads that snapped around at the tables on either side, as she headed toward the back, that froze her before she crossed into the territory holding row after row of empty tables. Losing her nerve, Sam turned abruptly to settle hastily in the middle of a crowded group.

No one welcomed Sam. She was assessed silently a few moments, then a short nod indicated temporary permission for inclusion at the table. They returned to their meals. Sam had learned to consume her meals quietly, unobtrusively, and rapidly, keeping her eyes incuriously on her plate. Still, most of the group had finished and left the table before she started to push back from the table. A wiry hand reached out to clamp her wrist, keeping her in place. The hand was attached to a woman still seated across the table, watching her with hard cynical eyes.

"Listen, Blondie," she spoke hoarsely, but with a weary kindness in her voice, "you look like a sweet innocent kid. I bet you thought you'd be kind, be a friend, and go sit with that one, huh?" She jerked her head toward The Searchlight, without glancing in her direction.

"Well, yes…" Sam's voice, like her nerves, a little shaky.

"You're a nice lady, but stay away from her. She doesn't want you, and you don't want to know her." It was a statement of fact, closer to an order than a suggestion.

"I don't?"

Rising, as if all had already been said, the woman gave a last hard, "No, you don't. Trust me."

"Wait!" Sam's request stalled her.

"Why?"

Still standing, the woman responded without expression or emotion. "She's one of God's Fallen Angels. He sent her here to seek out evil and destroy it. She was raised in a strict religious cult that must not of been pure enough for her. She chopped up her grandmother, parents, and six brothers and sisters with a butcher knife, but she won't cut her hair because it's a sin." The flat matter-of-fact monotone the information was delivered in, intensified its horror. "So you don't want to be her friend."

"By the way," as she departed, she cast one last warning over her shoulder, "then she ate them."

Sam lunged from the bench, realizing she was alone at the empty table, already feeling the laser-like eyes slicing across her back, dicing her into appetizers.

Oh. My. God!

Sam collapsed on the bunk in her cell, still feeling a bit queasy from the shock and burst of adrenaline that had raced through her system at the awful news. After a few moments, as she caught her breath, she had calmed down a little, and began to think it over. Maybe, she began to wonder—or desperately hope—it was just some kind of prison joke. An initiate-the-new-woman—*scare the crap out of her!*—kind of thing?

No.

She didn't think so.

Now that she thought back she realized that she had never seen The Searchlight woman mixing with any of the other prison population, only at meals, when she sat far from anyone else. She recalled the guards had seemed to become more alert, to tense, when Sam had started to cross into the area of empty tables. Some kind of no man's land, probably. Or "No woman's land", she corrected herself mentally.

Her gut told her the story she'd been told was true. *Listen to your instincts from now on!* There are dangerous people here, not everyone was innocent she reminded herself. She better pay more attention to her fears, some of them might be legitimate, it *was* a jail after all!

Bett Bone

Sam thought of the story she had told her kids. They would expect a follow-up on the flour-covered farmer's wife story. Just the thought made Sam feel like she might just throw up.

Can't you wait?
Already embarrassed, the way Ronnie asked had made Sam feel like a kid on a car trip asking for one too many restroom stops. But before she had a chance to speak, her friend threw up her arms, complaining.

"Jeez, Sam! This is a *women's* prison! You can't just smuggle men in like cocoanut pound cake!"

As an afterthought, Ronnie murmured, "Though that could create an interesting bribe for the guard... As long as you get the *best* half on that split..."

"Well...," Sam, ignoring that last comment, head lowered, chewing her bottom lip, was still only intent on her own concerns.

"I suppose I *could*. Wait, that is. Just a little while, but..." Looking back up, she asked curiously, "Why not now? That would be best." Sam waited hopefully.

Rhonda did not know *what* to think. Maybe she should have brought the lawyer with her after all.

He was a man. He could probably do sex. But where?

"Here?"

"Why not here?" Sam glanced around, "It's private enough."

Rhonda was shocked!

She liked men and sex, and wasn't especially—or even close to being—shy. But this was *way* over the line, even for Rhonda. And Sam? Prim little Sam? What had she been hiding behind that innocent facade all these years? Or was this just a progression of her recent signs of lunacy?

Sam was reclining, staring up at the bright lights on the ceiling, feeling a little dazed. Maybe it was the anesthetic starting to work. She'd been left in the dental chair, waiting for her mouth to numb sufficiently. They said they would give her some gas also, when they started to work on her mouth.

Sam turned her head to glance around the sterile room, trying to blink the bright red spots out of her eyes. As her eyes wandered, her mind began to wander, also. She thought about her visit with Rhonda that morning.

Sam was shocked.

She would never have imagined that Rhonda would have gone into such a panic just because Sam wanted a private talk. And to accuse Sam of being a closet nymphomaniac! Where on earth could she have gotten such an idea? Sam couldn't even remember the last time she'd had sex! That was the problem. How could Rhonda have been so far off base?

Well, maybe Sam had forgotten at first to mention that it was an *imaginary* man she needed—*imaginary* sex.

You would think Ronnie would have realized that she didn't mean the real thing! But her friend had seemed a little stressed out; she didn't seem to be handling the jail sentence too well.

It was a good thing Sam was the one in jail.

At any rate, they had gotten all the confusion sorted out and Sam had gotten over her initial embarrassment—at least until Rhonda enthusiastically decided to help by describing more numerous and graphic sex acts than Sam *really* felt she needed to hear.

Sam was trying to plan for a future full of romance. But her memory had failed her so she needed some confidential and detailed help. She winced to think of some of the steamier notes she had taken down. But, that *was* why she had asked Ronnie's help; her friend specialized in steamy sex.

Real steamy sex. Sam wouldn't know steamy sex if it bit her, which she understood from Ronnie was also considered steamy. Hence the need for research with her friend.

And Ronnie's best parting advice for Sam's imaginary male was hardly surprising; it should have been obvious. Ronnie told Sam she needed to put her overactive imagination to work and visualize herself being intimate with each male she saw.

She assigned Sam the job of mentally undressing and visualizing just what each man she saw would be like when he was in a sexy mood. She knew Sam never really looked at men as sex objects, so she wanted her to practice the concept.

And despite the fact that Sam had been thinking more along the lines of good old fashioned romance—well, mostly—she'd be lying to say she wasn't *somewhat* stimulated by some of her friend's suggestions.

Of course, Sam was in a women's prison with mainly women for guards, which didn't leave her with anyone much to undress. Ronnie suggested using magazines or television, picturing how those men might smell, and feel, and ... taste....

So she had dutifully tried to start her assignment. She had started with the television, doing shameful things to the poor Maytag repair ad man. However, Sam didn't manage to feel any tingles of her own. Then she'd leafed through some magazines, waiting for the dentist. But she refused to subject any of the men in a parenting magazine to her rapacious eye, finding a sporting magazine a much more sporting choice.

Sam would have to keep looking for targets to practice on, she wasn't feeling very steamy about the whole project so far.

The door opened and the dentist, a male—*another potential subject*—stepped into the room.

It might not have gone so badly if they hadn't given Sam the laughing gas.

As the bald, rotund dentist gently cupped her chin, tipping her face up, slowly lowering his face to her open, waiting lips ...

Sam had an intimate view of the hairs sprouting in his nose. Her giggles turned into gurgles when he finally slipped his tool in her ... and began to drill.

Sam moaned—but *not* with passion.

The prosecutor had been tied up with on going court trials for the last few weeks; too busy to get out to the prison as he had originally planned. But the inmates weren't going anywhere.

As Jordan was finally to leave his office for the afternoon to head there now, Elsa came in and dropped a case file on his desk.

"What's this? If it's urgent, have Todd—"

"I thought you requested the file for Detective Mallory's D.U.I. lady that the witness saw the night that bank was robbed?"

"Oh, right. She's at the prison, also. Thanks for keeping me organized, Elsa. You just saved me a second trip." He smiled at her, dropping the folder in his briefcase without looking at it. "I'll check my emails this evening. If there is anything urgent..."

"Give it to Todd," she finished for him, as he grabbed his coat and left the office.

When Jordan pulled the file out at the prison to give the guard the name and number so he could have her brought to an interview room, he finally saw the D.U.I. lady's name. One Samantha Wilson—a name that set bells ringing in his head.

When he'd been filled in by the Chief and Detective Mallory about the witness statement from the night of the bank robbery, the date had not registered. He had forgotten he had covered the sentencing of a D.U.I. charge on a lady from that same date—of a woman that Jordan had *not* forgotten.

She faced him across the cold steel table, in a sterile room set aside for lawyer's to meet with their clients. She wondered a little fearfully what the man's intentions were.

Why? Why had the prosecutor come to see her now when she was already successfully and safely behind bars? Was this normal? What need did he have to see her? Sam fretted, waiting, hoping it wouldn't take too long. She'd been in the middle of something when ....

"Ms. Samantha Wilson." He stated in his hard prosecutorial tone.

She glanced up in surprise at the nasty hiss he used to pronounce the 'Ms.', more like 'Mizzz'. Her soft brown eyes rose questioningly only to be lashed by steely gray ones full of disdain. Though he hadn't made it sound like a question, she nodded nervously to acknowledge her name.

She had never seen his face so directly, so closely, before. While nervous of his hard accusing stare, she was stunned at how handsome the hard bronzed planes, straight nose, and hard, clean jaw were. Dark patrician brows arched firmly above the thickly lashed, but brittle gray eyes. His hair was clipped short, in a clean cut style that looked very masculine with his thick hair, instead of the boyish look that it gave some men.

Tiny silver tufts at his temples, contrasted sharply with the bronze cheeks, the dark hair, giving him a distinguished look, without portraying age. He was a hard, lean man in his prime, at the peak of his strength and power. Up close, he was devastatingly handsome, Sam realized. *And he was male.*

Sam stared at him, feeling her heart startle and jump. Feeling her breath catch in her throat. She'd read about these feelings in her romance books, but she hadn't really believed it happened after one's high school crushes. Certainly not to women her age. But she was starting to feel a little steamy, herself. Well, a lot. Yet Sam did not dare to attempt to undress *him* with her eyes! This man was much too dangerous.

So she just locked on those firm, strong sensual lips hypnotically, waiting to hear him speak.

Oh, yes, Jordan remembered Samantha Wilson. He hadn't needed to check her file to confirm that he was the prosecutor in the courtroom that day. But *this* time he planned to be in control from the start. It was a different game they were playing now, and he wanted her off-balance and he was not above a little intimidation. He'd only needed one harsh lesson in trusting the surface impression when it came to females. The pretty ones could be the most deceptive liars.

In court, as a prosecutor he saw hundreds of people there, for a few minutes only. The faces seldom registered, or remained in his memory, though most of the crimes did.

But *this* face... this *woman*... still registered, remained, haunted.

There was a softness in the brown eyes that gazed up at him, almost an innocence…

He recalled a voice passionately declaring her desire to take responsibility for her actions. This was the woman that had refused the lawyer. At the time she had caught not only his attention, but also his grudging respect, though he had a long standing intolerance with drinking drivers, thanks to his parents' legacy.

And there was that other faint memory of her also, a memory of her smiling and smelling of spring. A vague impression that he'd never been able to place—and he had tried, it haunted him.

Frowning now, he wondered just why she had been so damn eager to accept her punishment at her trial. Why such a hurry to plead guilty? Was it because there was something else she didn't want revealed at the time? Some link to a more serious crime? It could hardly be coincidence that she had been at the same location when another crime took place there.

"Who was with you at the bank the night you were arrested?" He fired the question at her suddenly, catching the startled widening of her eyes, before she lowered them quickly.

"No one! The police will tell you. I was alone!"

"Why were you at the bank at that time of night?" Another hard question flew at her.

"Ah," she dropped her head a little further, silken blonde strands brushing over her cheeks giving her a protective screen as she thought desperately. She tried to stall, "I was, well, my memory is kind of fuzzy. The state I was in, you know."

Buying time with her apparent embarrassed confusion, she wondered what kind of records the bank kept. What would be a safe answer?

"I think," she ventured, "I think I had gone to drop off a check reorder form, but...I don't really recall," she finished doubtfully. Hoping that would cover her bases, she flicked a quick glance up at his face, to see how her response had been received.

The still face gave away nothing of what the prosecutor was thinking. When she dared to look directly into his eyes, their intensity was a shock. Trapped in his gaze, she finally pulled her eyes free, before he could read her physical response to him there.

Sam felt a light flush on her cheeks, lowering her eyes to stare at a safer spot on his chin. Her eyes tracked the firm, hard line of his jaw to the silkier, softer, more vulnerable skin of his throat. She gazed in rapt attention at the pulse beating steadily beneath the warm flesh. She wanted to plant a soft kiss there, at the hollow of that bronzed throat, where it was nakedly exposed by the crisp white collar, the tie he'd loosened. Look at that broad, masculine chest!

Forgetting her earlier fears, not even conscious of following a plan of action, Sam could see herself slowly undoing that row of buttons, peeling the crisp white back from a tanned expanse of muscle. She wanted to nuzzle it; slip her hands inside to roam beneath his shirt. Her fingers widespread, she'd glide her palms over his chest, nibble his nipples, curl her fingers in the dark hairs that narrowed as they marched down his hard belly...

Oh, dear! Sam snapped her mind back, she was out of control. She had been trying that visualization thing, but not with him, not for real. This was insane, this was not like her! She was getting way too caught up in her fantasies, if they happened by accident. She hoped he hadn't noticed that she had been staring at his chest, lips parted, her breath coming softly through her open mouth. What had he said?. She wondered desperately, as her eyes jumped guiltily back to his flinty gray.

"What?" She touched a finger to the corner of her lips, relieved that at least she hadn't been drooling. What had come over her?

He mistook her startled confusion as an attempt to feign innocence. His mouth tightened into a hard, angry line.

"You heard me," he snarled," and don't try and play innocent with me." He jerked at his collar, loosening his tie more, exposing more of that throat.

"No, I wouldn't," Sam gulped, hurriedly. "I'm definitely guilty!"

She was trying to convince him of her crime—the last thing she needed was to seem innocent—and she truly felt guilty for her sinful thoughts. She'd just started mentally ravishing him, after all. Surely that was a crime!

Sam couldn't control an amused twitch that curled her lips in a brief flicker of a smile. Ronnie would be so proud of her! Now.. where was she? Chest or throat?

"And don't play coy and cute with me, either!" he snapped. "It's not at all funny, and if you think…" abruptly halting, he brushed his hand harshly across his jaw. Rising suddenly, he turned and paced over to an interior mirrored window, his hard back turned to her.

Think? Could he tell what she was thinking? Uh-ohh! Well, she did have that blushing problem, she must be lobster red with all the fun she was having. Could he tell she'd just been thinking about biting him? He seemed extremely angry. She just wanted a little nip. He had been staring suspiciously at her lips.

Jordan swore silently to himself. God, she had lips that were just too damn distracting. He was angry at himself, and at her, for the way he responded to her. He had completely lost his train of thought.

He'd been watching her soft, mobile lips change from softly, innocently parted, provocative, to tilt suddenly in a dimpled smile, before dropping innocently open again, as he railed at her.

When her tongue flickered over that lower lip, moistening it nervously, he felt like he'd had an electrical shock from the unconscious seductiveness of her action. Or was it unconscious on her part? Of course not!

Jordan was a mature man. Hadn't he learned to steel himself against manipulative women yet? Modern woman played hardball. They didn't bother trying to hook a man with sweet, fluttery ways. They just parted full lips, slid a moist pink tongue out, and went straight for a man's crotch!

It worked too, dammit, and the witch probably knew it and was laughing silently behind his back! He continued to stare hard at the glass, not sure whether he was angrier at her, or his own body that had betrayed his icy control.

"Guard," he called, his harsh voice cold as an artic draft, "take her away. I don't have time to waste on an uncooperative female! Prisoner!," he corrected quickly, damn his betraying thoughts. He waited for the sound of the door clanging shut, before feeling safe to turn, grab his briefcase, and hasten from the jail.

So, what was *that* all about?

The more Sam thought about the prosecutor's visit, the less she could understand why he had come. Surely not just for her to practice on!

Why did he have to question her now? What was the point? And why was he so hostile? Well, that one she could answer anyway, remembering what she'd heard of his lack of fondness for women.

There wasn't any point worrying about it.

Sam just couldn't believe a guy could still be so hostile towards women, just because he had one bad experience years ago. Broken relationships happened, people went on with their lives. Why was it such a problem for this guy?

Because women visually raped him all the time? That was probably annoying, for him. He'd only let her get half-way down his body. Oh well, the prosecutor's personal problems were not her problem.

Sam's problem was to figure out what it was she had been thinking of before she had been interrupted. Darn! She'd come to jail just to get away from unexpected interruptions that destroyed her chain of thought. She wanted a nice, regular schedule she could count on without all those annoying distractions, Sam thought indignantly.

And it was really annoying to be stopped half-way through a distraction!

So, she'd been thinking about.. what? Maybe if she backtracked, she would remember what triggered her idea in the first place. She pictured herself entering the interview room, the idea was fresh in her mind then, so if she just thought back from there..

Okay, she was thinkingggg... how incredibly handsome he was! How his up close masculinity felt like a physical force, shorting out all her senses. The smell of him, a scent that made her want to lick something, slowly.

Sam responded to the sensuality that radiated from him, but it scared her. She never noticed men, not having room to include one in her life. It seemed she must have saved up all that awareness to spend on this one. Was he ever worth spending it on!

Stop! Wrong direction, Sam. She was supposed to be backing up to remember her lost thoughts, not getting lost in thoughts of that man. Right?

But why would any woman who had a guy like that dump him for others? That's what she couldn't understand. Maybe his nasty temper. What had Rhonda said? That when he was newly married his wife had been screwing around with all his friends? Well, that *would* tend to make a guy pretty ill tempered. Did all his hostility come from his ego being hurt because it was his pals? Didn't seem like enough for such a long grudge. Besides, he should hate all men, not all women.

But what if he had really loved his wife? If he was one of those guys that fell totally in love just once in their lives, and then he was destroyed? Did they still make men like that? Probably only by special order in a test tube.

How awful, poor guy! He was probably only hostile now in self-defense, as a shield so he couldn't get so badly wounded again. That's all it was, Sam decided.

But why had he come to see her today?

She still didn't get that, unless, unless ... Rhonda had something to do with it? Sam didn't believe Ronnie would betray her trust. She did believe, however, that Ronnie wasn't beyond doing a little matchmaking by putting a handsome man on her trail. There was no doubt the prosecutor was one of the handsomest, most desirable around. Ronnie sure could pick them! But she wouldn't do something like that. Would she? Besides, Ronnie knew better, Sam was never distracted by men.

Sure! That's why she wasn't giving him a moment's thought, wasn't it? Might as well admit, she was attracted, she wanted to finish nibbling the man. But why this one? Why now, of all times?

Must be one of those weird psychological things. Too bad Freud was gone, he'd have a good reason. Some perverse instinct that, because she was locked up in jail in enforced celibacy, made her intensely want something she couldn't have, and usually didn't even think about. Or maybe it was the safety of fantasizing, while unable to implement the fantasy, protecting her from the fear of rejection. That sounded reasonable.

Or maybe, because the prosecutor was an authority figure and he had her under his control.. Mmm, that sounded really good, but off the point. Okay, so her reaction to her lack of control was to regain control of the man by sexually molesting him? With her secret thoughts?

Hah, forget psychology. Sam did not think that, authority figure or not, she would be having these erotic thoughts about Mr. Campbell if he was ugly and unappealing, instead of being so damn handsome and sensual!"

She closed her eyes dreamily, recalling the images as her eyes had wandered across his body, imagining undressing him. She breathed in deeply, remembering his masculine scent, imagining the touch, the taste of bronzed skin. What would it feel like to have those strong lean arms pulling her up close? His lips brushing, burning her skin? Eyes locked on hers, as he took her mouth? Oh my, she wanted him! Who needed Freud? She understood this herself. Sam was deeply in lust!

Maybe Sam should send Ronnie a note thanking her for sending her a man. One that had a really nice, tight butt!

Sam had *accidentally* checked it out when he turned his back on her.

chapter fourteen

Prosecutor Campbell opened the Henley case file. He had only planned to stop at his office to pick it up on the way home and work on it over the weekend. However he had returned earlier than expected. His last meeting at the prison had been brief and fruitless. It had also become frustrating and foolish—and he appeared to be the unfortunate fool. For a skilled attorney and public speaker, Jordan could not seem to maintain the upper hand verbally whenever he was around the woman, not faring much better this time than the last.

What he intended to be an interrogation, controlled by him, stumbled to a halt when the interrogator lost track of the end of his own sentences! And it shamed him to admit that he had let his physical and emotional reaction to the woman so influence him and interfere with his work, even as he had been sure she had lied to him. Of all the people he would have sworn would never be able to get under his hardened skin, he would have claimed that a lovely woman that was also a drunk and a liar scored the jackpot.

Still shaken after the long drive back, he did not want to be home alone with his thoughts. He needed the comfort of his office, the control and respect of his position, and the discipline of his work to regain his normal sensibility and balance. He left his office door wide open while he worked at his desk just to ensure he kept his nose to the grindstone and did not dare indulge in any distracted thoughts and staring off into space.

Jordan had plenty of time now to spend all night reading the Henley file again, cover to cover. Something he had done a dozen times before, but he wanted to make certain he knew it backwards and forwards before—after months of delays—it finally came to trial.

Secretly, he was hoping to find something new, something missed after so many reviews. Not likely! Nevertheless, he'd start at the beginning again and concentrate on every slightest detail.

When he reached the police report inventorying the personal items on Henley at arrest, his eyes were burning. He forced himself to focus on each word, regardless. He read again of the drugs, the amount of cash Henley had, even the less interesting items in his jean pockets. Listed as: wallet, key ring (car, misc) , Swiss army knife (3" red handle), key ring (postal box keys), matchbook (Owl Lounge), condom… Well, at least he believed in safe sex, he noted wryly.

Jordan's mind turned rebelliously to soft lips and gold-flecked brown eyes, pink tongue, and soft moist lips... Hell! He caught his breath at the remembered image, totally uncomfortable with the sensation, feeling desire at the thought of a woman's face.

And a criminal! He cautioned himself, but as much as he tried to pin that thought in his mind, he couldn't cancel out the earlier images of a sweet, innocent looking face demanding justice. She'd seemed so fragile facing the judge, but even more delicate today, her pixie-like features contrasting the coarse, ungainly prison garb. He could hardly make out the trim lines of the slim figure in that sack!

Shocked, Jordan realized his mind had imprinted every single detail of Ms. Wilson's court appearance that long ago day. The clothing, the circumstances he'd last seen her in, hadn't tarnished it in his memory. If anything, when she had first turned those eyes directly on him, he felt she had reached out and grabbed him. Momentarily he'd forgotten where he was, and why.

The more she had gotten to his senses today, the harsher he had become, shielding himself from her by using bitterness and anger. Did he fool her? Or had he just fooled himself into believing he had? His body hadn't been fooled; that was for sure!

He'd needed to get up, move away and turn away from her, thrusting his hands into his pockets, jingling his keys, to hide his…'keys'!

Turning back quickly to Henley's file, Jordan checked it again. Yes, two key rings! Why two? Because the second ring held post office box keys. Not a single key that a person would just add to their car key ring, but 'keys'. Now why would Henley have a second ring that held only postal keys?

"Elsa!" Jordan barked over the intercom. "There was some report from the Attorney General's office a while back about mail fraud and local post office boxes. Find it and get the Postmaster for me on the phone."

Jordan had already flipped off the intercom before his secretary could respond.

Todd and Shelley had been standing near Elsa's desk, discussing a case with her when the disembodied voice hurled itself into the room, causing all three to jump.

"What was that?" Shelley laughed, startled.

"I don't know," Elsa replied, already dialing the number for the post office, "But my guess is it's another of his brilliant brainstorms," she smiled happily. "Yes, the postmaster please, this is the prosecutor's office calling..."

Meanwhile, Jordan paced restlessly in his office, anxious to check out his suspicion. All thoughts of Sam had been rudely and abruptly displaced, but not forgotten.

Sam had her suspicions. She'd asked Rhonda to visit her alone, first, the next weekend visiting session.

"Okay, Ronnie, spill it! I know what you're up to, I'm just not sure I understand why."

"Well, hi. Nice to see you too. But what is it I'm supposed to be up to? I swear I'm in the dark."

"You know what I mean. The prosecutor!"

"The prosecutor?" Rhonda repeated, totally baffled. "You mean THE prosecutor, that tall, dark, gorgeous one? Is that what you mean?" Her cobalt eyes widened in excited interest momentarily, before clouding in a worried frown, wondering what the prosecutor had to do with anything. Trial over, sentencing done and being served, so...

"He's out of it," Rhonda reasoned out loud.

"Well, he is not out of it, apparently! And well, I'm sorry Ronnie, I guess I was wrong. I thought you put him onto me," Sam confessed a little sheepishly.

"Sam, nasty as I think his attitude to women is, the guy is delicious! With you safely locked away and out of competition, I guarantee you that if I had any influence with the man it would be myself I'd put him onto!" Ronnie gave a wicked leer, then remembered herself.

"Hey, sorry Sam, but I find devastatingly handsome men so-o-o distracting! Don't you? Oh, I take it that friendly glare means 'No.' So what is the deal? Has the prosecutor's office been in touch with you?" Rhonda returned to the subject seeing Sam was too agitated to be cheered today by any juicy jokes about men.

"Not his office, *him*! He came here and had them drag me away into a room where he could question me."

"When?"

"Yesterday."

"Why?"

"I don't know why. I got the distinct impression he thinks I'm not telling the truth." Sam paused a moment, chewing her lip, then added, "He asked if I was alone at the bank."

"Uh-ohh…"

"I told him I was all alone, the police could prove it. That seemed to satisfy him, I think. On that question, anyway."

"Was my lawyer, any lawyer, here when he questioned you?"

"No. We were alone."

Ronnie gasped. "You were locked up in a room alone with that hunk?"

"Ronnie, would you please get your mind out of the gutter and help me out here?" No need for both their minds to be in the gutter, Sam thought. She had decided not to impress her friend with her undressing experiment yet. Especially not while she was stuck only half-way down the body in question. Besides, sounded like her friend had other plans for the rest of him. She'd keep her own attraction to herself

"Sorry, Sam. What would you like me to do?"

"Think! I don't know, do something, think of something. Why can't he just leave me alone?"

Why would you want him to, Rhonda wondered, but kept the thought to herself this time. She tried to apply her mind to the problem, to figure why the prosecutor was involved. She planted her elbow on the table, cupping her chin in her hand, unconsciously mirroring Sam as they both concentrated silently on what to do about this new, unexpected problem.

"I can't think of anything," Rhonda confessed after a long silence.

"Me either," Sam agreed.

"So what else did he say about why he was here?"

"He asked me if I was alone at bank. Then he asked me why *I* was at the bank at that time of night."

"And you said?"

"You know, drunk, fuzzy memory, think I was dropping off a check reorder form, but don't really recall."

Ronnie rolled her finger motioning for Sam to keep talking.

"And then I lost track of what he was saying for a while, and when I asked him, he got really angry and said I had heard him and not to try to play innocent. So I said I wasn't, that I was definitely guilty! Which I guess made me smile a bit, and he got really angry and left."

"That's all?"

Sam nodded. "It didn't make any sense to me so I thought you might have sent him."

"How weird."

"Exactly."

"He must have had some reason. You're the one with the great imagination, Sam, can't you come up with one?"

"While I appreciate your confidence in me, I'm a great dreamer Ronnie, but I'm not so hot on real life. Besides, my imagination doesn't work when I'm worrying." Sam sighed in frustration. "It's not fair. I came here to be alone."

"Yes, it does seem unfair that anyone who goes to such lengths to be left alone, shouldn't get a little peace and quiet."

Sam glanced sideways quickly to see if Ronnie was being facetious, but for once her face was innocently bland.

"Well, our time is up if I want to spend some with the kids. Thanks for coming to see me again, Ronnie," Sam said softly. "See if you can figure out if something is up, okay?"

"I'll try, honey. You try not to let it worry you, and get on with your plans. Until next week, then. Now smile, dammit, so I can send in your kids."

"Oh, Paul, it's gorgeous!"

Tears glistened in Sam's eyes as she gazed at the enlarged photograph Paul had given her. She recognized the location immediately. Sam realized her son had made the long drive just to capture her favorite beach at sunset and bring it to her here. It made her throat ache, as she studied the picture through watery eyes.

Touched by her pleasure, slightly embarrassed by the emotions so clear in his mother's voice and eyes, Paul tried to conceal his own feelings behind a bantering tone.

"Hey, you think that looks nice, you should have seen it framed. I can't believe they made me dismantle it before I could bring it in here for you! Anyway, this room doesn't have much of a view. I thought you could pretend it was your window. The frame even looked like window panes." He shrugged it off. "I'll try to smuggle some more shots in for you next time. But only if you promise not to get all watery-eyed and drip on them."

"Yeah, mom, knock it off," Penny complained, teasing, "you're going to have us all crying soon." She quickly brushed a palm across her cheek to wipe away the evidence.

Trying to control the emotional flood, Sam forced laughter back into her voice as she chided back, "Hey, don't blame me! Can I help it if your brother takes such heartbreaking pictures?"

It was hard for her children to see her here. Sam tried to keep her attitude light, gay, and cheerful when they came, make it all just a fun game. She couldn't let them see her sad, frightened, or lonely, though she'd been all those. They would hurt too much, worry over her too much. It was not fair when they'd had no choice in this but to suffer with her.

She'd admit all after she was back home with them. She'd tell the truth—the full truth this time—and that their mom had been naïve and foolish to think it was a lark. But not now, not yet. Now she had to be strong.

"This is perfect Paul. It's just what I needed!" Sam exclaimed happily. Thank you, honey, this will help so much, means so much!"

Sam's cheery reassurance was just what the kids longed to hear, needed to hear, each time they came to visit. They hoped it would be okay as they marked every day left on her sentence off their calendars, praying for it to end.

Back in her cell after the visit, Sam slumped in her bed, all need for pretense gone. Alone now, no longer guarding her emotions, she gazed at the photograph and let it take hold of her.

The waning sun trailed golden fingertips of light across the waters of the bay, as if gently calming and stroking it to sleep, as night fell. The sky had softened to blush-colored drifting clouds, flattened from their prior white billows, then settling into rippling scarves of soft lavender. The dark formation of islands on the distant horizon had hazed into a deeper shimmering lavender, and by the trick of last light, looked like a mirror image of the cloudy scarves above, reflected on the sea with only a golden swath of light between.

Rising in harsh contrast in the foreground of the gilded pastel fantasy, was her gnarled tree stump. The water lapping at the trunk base broke into a ruffled white spray, like a cuff of lace around the buried wrist. Rising up to the blackened silhouette of the claw-like roots, sinister, skeletal fingers that reached up desperately, grotesquely, for a last grasp at sea and sky.

A masterpiece of color and imagery, Paul seemed to have captured the contrast between heaven and hell, in this one stunning photograph.

Her beach.

Sam swallowed, feeling the dam of emotions breaking free deep inside. Moisture began to trickle, then roll down her checks as she silently mourned for the sights, sounds, and salt-laden smells of her time there. For the wind calmed to a soft kiss, felt brushing her face. For waves lapping a murmur, a sad song, as she grieved. Her driftwood hand had cupped and sheltered her; yet now it looked so sinister, so forbidding. She'd known the feel of that sun-warmed wood hugged to her skin, like a long, faithful friend, and now felt the pain of abandonment.

But her true misery lay in the agony she'd given to those she loved. The beach, mere surrogate, for pain too bitter to examine, blame hers to own. And that knowledge splintered her soul. Heart torn by her own betrayal, all she'd held tight inside burst in private in aching, throat burning grief.

Awakening later, empty from spent emotion, Sam rose and splashed icy water on her face. She held a damp washcloth against her swollen eyelids to cool them and tighten the puffy skin. It would be time for supper in the hall soon.

With renewed resolve, Sam silently commanded the woman in the mirror to make it all matter. She'd never make it worth the cost, but she couldn't waste the payment.

She'd return from supper tonight and focus on her project and planning Then she would rest more easily. She had come here to find the isolation and discipline she felt she needed. Now she was driven by a stronger force. She owed it not only to herself, but more than ever to her kids to complete her goals.

The Monday morning meeting had just commenced. A knock on the door announced the arrival of the police property clerk.

"Good, thanks, here they are Jim," Jordan signed the receipt, offering the keys to the Postmaster.

"These look like ours. Let me get these numbers down so we can check it out."

"Are those the box numbers? Do any of them match up with the AG's complaint circular?" He waved the copy in his hand eagerly, then stilled his questions momentarily, realizing the Postmaster was still trying to record the numbers.

"Sorry. What was that, Jordan? The post box numbers? No." Jim explained, "The keys have an identification number that is recorded against a box number when the box is rented. That way, if someone just has a key, they won't know which box it opens, unless they are authorized to use it. It also insures they can't open a box they are no longer renting, just by keeping the key. Since I knew this was urgent, I instructed my assistant to stand by at the computer. Let me give her a call and we'll get the post office box numbers and names registered to these keys. Beyond that you'll need warrants. Mind if I use this?"

"No, please!" Jordan pushed his phone across, aware of the stress in his voice. He jumped from his chair and strode out to his outer office. Finding Elsa busy on the phone, he went off to find Todd himself.

After having had to wait over the whole weekend to follow up this lead, Jordan was having trouble containing his impatience. Well, at least he'd gotten all his trees and plants dug in, and made another trip to the garden center for more to plant. His yard was shaping up at least, he thought wryly, hopefully the case would also.

"Todd, come sit in on this," he called, before rushing back to his own office. The Postmaster was just finishing his call.

Jordan grabbed a legal pad from the credenza behind his desk. The minute the phone was cradled, pen poised, he asked, "Well?"

"She'll call back with the answers. Shouldn't take long, Campbell, no more than five to ten minutes."

"Oh," disappointed, Jordan leaned back in his chair, the steel points of his eyes, locking on the phone. The Postmaster pushed his list across the desk, so Jordan could enter the first set of numbers for the boxes while he waited.

"Todd, good, have a seat. You know Jim..." Catching the flashing light out of the corner of his eye, Jordan was pushing the phone and list back to Jim before Elsa's voice even came over the intercom.

Jordan had to force himself not to rap his pen against his desk, to subdue his tension and impatience, while the Postmaster completed his call and finished noting down all the details his assistant had drawn from the records.

"Okay, these numbers correspond to two different branches, within twenty miles. I think it would be easier if we call the first seven-digit number Box A and the second, Box B.

"Let's start with box A," the Postmaster read out the ID number, then the box number and branch location.

"Box A is the longest standing rental, it goes back eight years, was assigned two keys, the name on the registration is listed as 'Henley Enterprises'. Here is the other key identification number assigned to box A," he shoved a note across to Jordan.

"It isn't one of the keys we have here, but no secondary name was ever noted. That's not that unusual. Many times patron's will pay for an additional postal key deposit without designating an individual. They might give it to a friend or employee temporarily, so they can run down and get the mail, pick it up while on vacation, whatever. We have no way of knowing who has it. If at the end of the rental period, it's not returned, we don't return the deposit.

"Box B has joint names on the registration, though the rental is only signed by Henley. The second name, and a second key, is registered to this guy. It was rented just over five years ago." Jim pushed across another note labeled 'B' with a new number and the second name on the registration.

"Unless there's any thing else I can help with? Okay then, well I guess we'll be waiting to assist further if you guys issue search warrants on these boxes. By the way, a computer search shows that there aren't any other boxes current or past, in our district, under

Henley's name." Jim rose, gathered his papers, shook hands and accepted the thanks from Jordan and Todd as he left.

Jordan swiveled his chair to Todd,

"First, I'll call the Federal Prosecutor, he's a good guy, we'll work well together. I'd like to meet here, as soon as he can make it. You coordinate the others based on his availability. I want the police chief and detectives on the Henley case. Call them the details on the second box holder," Jordan paused his rapid fire instructions momentarily to check, "on B box, immediately, so they can get started on him now. Maybe they'll have something before we meet. Then get the typists started on search warrants with the numbers and info we have here. When we meet with the feds and the detectives, we can fine tune any changes and, hopefully, print them right out. I want you to personally walk them straight upstairs, get a judge to sign them, so we can send the detectives away with them in hand to start executing."

Jordan reached for his phone, his normal way of saying 'we're done, get out of my office', and was barking instructions at Elsa before Todd could even finish his notes and scramble from his chair.

He was relieved to see that the temporarily kinder, gentler Jordan was gone, and excited that his boss was back on the warpath.

chapter fifteen

It had been a week of emotional excess. Now Sam tried to push her feelings aside and discipline herself to focus on serious concerns. She still didn't understand why she'd been interviewed by the prosecutor—at this late date. She could not let it all unravel now. The reason for the visit worried her. Sam needed to understand why.

It was obvious that Rhonda had nothing to do with his visit. The confession letter had not been used; it seemed secure for now. To think Sam had suspected her pal of trying to use it to match-make?

Clearly, Rhonda had him pegged for a match of her own!

Sam was careful not to let slip her own feelings about the man, but she'd been unable to help a tinge of jealousy thinking of herself locked up with Ronnie free to chase the only man that ever made Sam's throat go dry just thinking of him. Her friend had no idea *how* 'distracting' that particular man was for Sam.

Get on with your plan, Ronnie said when she left. Oh, sure. Easy for her to say.

Sam had hoped a few good nights of sleep were all she'd need to regain her normal common sense—and get Jordan Campbell out of her head. *Wrong*. The problem was trying to sleep when images of him kept her tossing and turning all night! Sam cursed her vivid imagination.

Sam finally resorted to her faithful habit of making a 'pros and cons' list, to try to solve her problem logically.

She didn't even know Jordan; she wasn't in a good spot to get to know him, either.

He didn't even know her, but didn't seem to like her, anyway. He didn't even like women, period. She was a criminal; his job would make him hate criminals. So, even if she weren't a female, Jordan would probably hate her just on principle.

And Sam's thoughts were hardly the platonic type, so she wasn't looking for another friend.

Insurmountable 'cons' seemed everywhere she looked. Therefore, it was completely illogical for Samantha to waste any more time thinking about him—except as a potential adversary.

There that was settled!

But ... he was the only man to grab her attention like this. Why? And along that line, she wished he'd leave her attention alone, and just grab her directly! Stay focused, Sam, no getting physical right now, we're thinking, she reminded herself firmly.

Okay. Why did she persist in thinking that his hostility toward women was nothing that an understanding and loyal woman couldn't cure? And why did she, after just one brief and stormy personal meeting, want to be that cure?

Yes, she did have to confess to that.

Despite her lusty thoughts, it was not *one* wildly sensual night she wanted. It was much more. Sam wanted romance with her lust. She'd been picturing what it would be like being with, spending time with an intelligent and sensual man like him. Time spent with not just any man, only Jordan.

Crazy thoughts! But somehow she felt a bond; felt she'd always known him on the inside, though he was a virtual stranger on the outside. She didn't believe in reincarnation, yet couldn't explain why she felt so drawn, so close, to this stranger. As if she already knew him from some other life, or other time. Crazy, for sure!

"Probably just massive hormonal imbalance." Sam muttered to herself.

Or was Ronnie right all along?

Was Sam in the wrong institution?

How did you know if and when you'd lost your mind if it was still there thinking your thoughts? Whoa, that was a scary one, and totally unproductive.

Fortunately, it was time for Sam's daily exercise. A little body over mind was just what she needed now—or earlier—and she knew just whose body ...

She had to stop reading those naughty novels!

Shelley hauled a stack of case files down the hall to Elsa's desk in time to see the last of a string of top law enforcement officials being ushered into Jordan's office; Todd closed the door firmly behind them.

Blowing out an exasperated sigh, Shelley shifted the files to her hip, turning to Elsa with a questioning look.

"What? Having a big party and I'm not invited?"

Shelley pretended to pout, easing the heavy files down to brace them on Elsa's desk. "I've been trying for days to grab a minute with Jordan or Todd to go over these case summaries I've completed. All I've gotten is a cold shoulder and doors closed in my face. What's going on? Is it something I've done?" She looked seriously concerned.

"No, not at all, hon," Elsa reassured. "But don't even think of leaving that stack of files on my desk!" She laughed to take the sting from her words.

"Huh," Shelley shifted the burden back up in her arms, "rejected by you, too? Well, at least I know it's not just a guy thing. What should I do? What's up?"

"I've got to make a quick call for Jordan, he's waiting. Why don't you haul that stack of files back down to your own office while I do. Then come back, we'll talk. Plus, I have more files for you," Elsa threatened, punching in her phone numbers.

When Shelley returned, Elsa hoisted another stack of new files, almost as high as the ones Shelley had finished, from the floor behind her desk.

"Thank goodness! Todd left these last night, knowing better than to put them on my desk. But I haven't been able to roll my chair back all morning, or had a minute to get them down to your office, either. Big meeting to coordinate, but the gang's all there now," she motioned to the closed door of Jordan's office. "And they'll be at it for hours, so you might as well get started on this new stack. It may be another day before you can get a sit down with either of them to go over the reviews.

"Jordan said to tell you if there is any case that can't wait for a decision, to just go ahead, act on your own best judgment. So he is not unhappy with your work, honey, that's for sure. They need you to pick up the slack for awhile, but that is not why you aren't invited to the party. One word. Henley. So don't get your feelings hurt. Sorry, but my time is tied up on it also, so we'll have to visit later," Elsa dismissed her kindly, but firmly.

Shelley understood now, turning back to go hole up down in her own office, giving Elsa the privacy she needed to assist Jordan. She couldn't be anywhere near anything to do with her prior defense client. It was clear something had broken on the case. It was hard to suppress her curiosity, wondering what was going on in Jordan's office; anymore than she could repress the resentment caused by Henley's name. She had changed her life, her career over that name. But maybe that was for the best. She silently wished Jordan good luck as she settled at her desk. Shelley would deal with her share of the office's burdens, and eventually, along with the rest of the public, find out what was up on Henley's case.

Jordan's meeting finally broke up, successfully, many hours later as the working day ended, with a lot of ground covered. Search warrants for all the postal boxes were completed, signed by the judge, and handed to the officers that would execute them tomorrow.

Another promising lead had come from the jointly held box. A background search showed the second man had a sheet, and even better, a current pending charge. The detectives would follow up on that also, to see if they could find some leverage there.

Unfortunately, neither of the boxes was on the Attorney General's list, but the second box had been opened in the same timeframe; Jordan kept his suspicions there might still be a link. Whether any of the evidence they discovered would set him on Damon's trail, or even compromise Henley further, remained to be seen. Yet it *was* new territory, and they'd wring every bit of information out of it they could.

The Prosecutor was thrilled just to have a few new strings to pull on, to see what would unravel. As Jordan ushered his last guest out of his office, the police chief turned back, recalling a message.

"By the way, Campbell, almost forgot. My detective Mallory said he had a few things he wanted to discuss with you on the County Bank job. He'd like to meet with you. I cleared it. Told him to work with you direct on this. So whenever you have a chance, please give him a call."

"Sure, I'll connect with him tomorrow morning, while I wait to see what the search warrants produce. Tell him to come by around nine, I'll need the distraction," he grinned.

"Just be gentle with him, Campbell. He's one of my best. I know what a bear you can be when you're impatient for results," the chief cautioned.

"Deal," Jordan smiled, knowing he deserved the reminder. "I'll even have doughnuts here."

"She's holding something back. Can't really tell you why I think that. Just something I can't put my finger on. Maybe you can help."

Detective Mallory, in charge of the County Bank investigation, was in the prosecutor's office filling Jordan and Todd in on the progress of the investigation to date. He had tracked down and interviewed all the customers known to have used the bank machine in the twenty-four hour period either side of the robbery.

Jordan, true to his word, had provided doughnuts and coffee, and was trying to listen quietly, if not calmly. Mallory was reporting on his interview, yesterday, with one of those regular bank customers, one Rhonda Sayles.

"When I first went to interview her, she seemed very wary. Guarded. Thought maybe I had my man. Excuse me, woman. How could I make a mistake like that?" Mallory chided himself, with a humorous roll of his eyes, blowing an appreciative whistle to indicate the enormity of the error.

"Definitely woman with a capital 'W'!" he chuckled.

"Anyway," spotting Jordan's clenched jaw, Mallory resumed a professional demeanor, "when I explained we were interested in anyone she may have seen at, or around the bank machine, she said 'no' before I even had a chance to tell her the *date* I was inquiring about.

"That struck me as strange, but then she seemed to relax and was more open and believable. She said that being a single woman, she was always alert and aware of her surroundings when she 'was in a dark area at night'. Said she never used that machine at night if anyone else was at the machine. Then she repeated that, no, she didn't recall anyone around. And seemed believable, but, of course, I ran checks on her anyway.

"The bank wouldn't release any of her account records without her permission, or a court order, but they could assure me that she had no need for anyone else's money. I gather she is a very successful businesswoman that's had both personal and business accounts at that bank for years. It was indicated to me that she saves way more than she spends. She owns her condo, car, and the building her business is located in free and clear. No major debts.

"I just can't see any motive or reason why she'd be involved in a case like this, risking everything she's built up, unless she did it for the thrill. She just doesn't fit as a suspect otherwise," Mallory shrugged. "But I still have this gut feeling that there was some undercurrent, she was hiding something. When I went over her exact words again later, it just reinforced that feeling. I'm old enough to remember Watergate hearings. I always get worried when someone answers a direct question and qualifies it with an 'I don't recall'. And while her *exact* words might have been true, I felt like they weren't the whole truth. I sensed she said 'never at night' to cover her earlier error saying 'no' too soon before I told her the date. She's a sharp one, but again, maybe I'm just the suspicious type—or it could be I never did mention it was night time, either.

"I told her we'd be in touch if we had further questions. I even hinted the prosecutor's office might need her assistance, or contact her about testifying, hoping to shake her and worry her into some confession or reaction. And boy, did that *ever* get a reaction, just not what I was expecting!"

"Well?" Jordan prompted, his patience starting to shred.

"Well, sir, it's a little embarrassing to tell you what she said. I'll use her exact words. Ms. Sayles said, 'The prosecutor, do you mean that Mr. Campbell?' When I said yes, her eyes lit up and she gave me a very big smile and said, 'Well, you tell that handsome prosecutor of yours that I'm not only ready, but willing, to give him *anything* he wants!' Then she winked at me, sir." The flustered detective flushed at having been the unwelcome purveyor of such a blatant message.

"Sorry, sir, but I had to tell you. Maybe you could get further with her. Umm ... , I mean ..."

"I'm sure he could!" Todd interrupted with a hoot of laughter, unable to contain himself any longer. Mallory broke into a nervous grin which he squelched quickly when he saw the look on Jordan's face. The prosecutor's love of femme fatales was as well known in the precincts, as around the courthouse.

"You go see her, Todd," was Jordan's curt response. Then remembering his manners, "Oh, and thanks, Detective Mallory. Please let us know if anything else develops. Todd will update you on our end." He dismissed both men from his office.

"Women!" Jordan cursed, pulling over the data from the Attorney General's office that he wanted to study before his next meeting.

Todd managed to stifle a smile at the obvious disappointment on the face of the stunning brunette that opened the door at his first ring. He saw her blue eyes searching over his shoulder. Elsa had scheduled the appointment with Rhonda Sayles for the 'prosecutor's office' to visit, deliberately, at Todd's request, not informing her that it would not be with Mr. Campbell. Despite his happily married status, Todd couldn't help but appreciate the tall, slender and sensuous lines accented by the elegant black silk jumpsuit, of the woman before him.

"I'm Todd Blake, with the prosecutor's office, Ms. Sayles. Thank you for agreeing to see me so soon."

"Please, come in Todd, and call me Rhonda," she invited gracefully, immediately using his first name in the way of women confident with men. "Can I get you some coffee, anything to drink?"

"No, thank you. I don't want to take up too much of your time. We appreciate your offer of assistance to our office," he stated smoothly, successfully hiding all hint of a smirk.

"If I could just ask you a few questions?"

"Certainly. Please have a seat." Graciously, she hid her disappointment.

Rhonda had been very disturbed when the detective had interviewed her, but had decided instantly not to jeopardize Sam. She had carefully answered the detective's questions in hopes of shielding Sam, while learning why and what they were investigating.

She was determined to continue being helpful, while trying to distract or stall, and learn more than she offered the prosecutor—well, when it came to information anyway.

"I understand that your interest is in who may have used the cash machine around the same time I did." Rhonda immediately took control of the conversation. "I saw no one. But, if you think I can help, please ask away. Maybe if you were more specific about *what* crime you are investigating, I could be of more specific help," she offered with a pleasant smile.

"I reviewed your interview with Detective Mallory, I'll try not to cover the same ground. Ms. Sayles, do you know..."

"Rhonda."

"Yes, Rhonda. Do you know a Mr. Abe Damon, or have you had any business dealings with him?" Todd asked, closely watching Rhonda for any reaction, any change of posture or expression.

"No, the name is not familiar. I do business with a lot of people, however, and I confess that I can't always recall every name," Rhonda replied calmly. "What does Mr. Damon do?"

Rhonda expressed only the curiously blank look of someone hearing the unfamiliar, Todd noted. "Maybe you would be more familiar with his nickname, Honest Abe?"

Still no flicker of the eye, no reaction except a slight turning down of the corners of her mouth, as she shook her head.

"Honest Abe? He runs a car dealership here in town?" Todd prompted.

"No, sorry," she replied coolly. "Does he sell BMWs?"

"Not usually."

"I drive a BMW Todd, and I would never buy a car from anyone who called himself 'Honest-Anything'. I can assure you of that," Rhonda told the young man disdainfully.

Todd studied her thoughtfully for a moment. She seemed calm and at ease with the questioning. Mallory was usually very perceptive, so there must be something that would trigger a reaction.

"Were you driving your BMW that night?" he asked next.

"Yes," she replied firmly.

"What color is your car?"

"Dark huntress green." She smiled at her little joke.

"Do you usually use the cash machine that late at night, Rhonda?"

"I usually use the cash machine whenever I want cash, Todd. I don't waste time going inside, so time of day doesn't regulate my trips to the bank." Rhonda answered breezily, and Todd noted, without ever really answering his question.

"What did you need cash for that late at night?"

Arching dark winged eyebrows at this impertinence, Rhonda replied coolly, "I really don't recall." Quickly lightening her tone, she added, "I probably was out of cash and had a busy morning scheduled the next day. Didn't want to run short if I took a client to lunch. I just hate people who invite you to lunch and then forget their wallet, don't you, Todd?"

There it was again. She didn't really answer his question, but tried to divert him with humor. She was a very controlled lady, but like Mallory, he sensed there was something she was avoiding discussing. And she still never questioned the night references.

"So you drew your cash from your business account then?"

"Ahhh, no, my personal account, I believe."

"But you do have your business account at the same bank, is that right?"

"Yes."

"With an ATM card?"

"Yes."

"Wouldn't it have been logical to draw the funds from your business account, if it was for a client?"

"Not necessarily. Besides," Rhonda said, barely recalling in time that they were only discussing a *hypothetical* reason for her withdrawal. "As I mentioned before, I don't really recall if that was why I wanted some cash on hand."

Did she sound a little defensive, or was Todd just imagining that?

Using an old interrogation technique, he just nodded, gave a thoughtful 'hmmm', then wrote at great length in his notebook. Glancing up after a few minutes, he noticed the increased tension in Rhonda's posture. She had edged forward on her chair and was gazing fixedly at his notebook.

Rhonda wondered if the car party of teens, that she'd seen *behind* the bank that night, had anything to do with whatever the police were investigating. She was uncomfortable withholding that information, and safe as they had not asked about the back of the bank specifically. Plus she couldn't figure out how to offer the information without explaining why *she* had gone behind the bank. Rhonda had not expected to be interviewed again so quickly. She just wished she knew what the hell it was they were after. "Oh, sorry?"

Todd repeated his question. "So there wasn't another car parked in the space in front of the bank machine, or just leaving that space, when you arrived?"

"No."

"You're sure?"

"Positive."

"But you're not positive why you needed cash that night?"

"No, not sure."

"I see," he replied, though his expression indicated otherwise.

"Ms. Sayles, Rhonda, would you object to signing a release so the bank can give us your transaction records on your accounts? We'd like to clock all the cash machine traffic, verify deposits for people who used the machine that date, and in the days just before and after. Just to search for electronic errors, of course."

"I'd be happy to provide you a release if you will limit access to it to your office," Rhonda said without a moment of hesitation. "Anything to help solve your case quickly, as long as the privacy of my accounts is protected, of course. I'll have my attorney contact your office to draw up the appropriate paperwork today."

"Why, thank you, we appreciate your assistance, and will insure the access is strictly limited."

Her immediate willingness to open her financial records to them had taken Todd by surprise. Especially after her evasive response to his questions about her cash withdrawal.

"Well, I guess that's all for now. Can I call on you again if I have more questions?"

"Anytime. But tell your boss that I'd be more than happy to drop into your office, if that would be more convenient for him," Rhonda offered as she showed him out.

"I'm sure he'd be pleased to hear that," Todd responded with a straight face.

Getting into his car, Todd sat for a moment sorting out his impressions.

Mallory was right. It was illusive, but there was something bothering Ms. Sayles, though he wasn't sure it had anything to do with their case. Rhonda's parting comment indicated Mallory was also right about her avid interest in his boss.

Maybe Jordan could get to the bottom of this? Todd couldn't help but grin at the thought.

chapter sixteen

"All right!" Jordan growled, "I'll see her. But not at her home! Bring her in here. And Todd, schedule yourself for the meeting also and I swear if you leave me alone with that woman for even one-half of one second, I'll fire you!"

"Sure, Boss," Todd grinned. "I always did want to try voyeurism," he teased, ducking out the door in time to avoid an airborne legal pad.

"Elsa, our boss is dying to meet a gorgeous brunette. Would you call and make an appointment. He's a little shy, so make it for here at the office, when I'm available to chaperone."

"Certainly, Mr. Blake," Elsa played along. "What's the lady's name?"

"Ms. Rhonda Sayles." Todd described a curvaceous figure in the air, with a teasing leer.

"And just how long of a 'date' do you think you three will need?"

"Oh," Todd considered, "I think Jordan can survive about a half of an hour … max. But make sure it's not late in the day. He fades."

"Got it. I'll make it for thirty minutes in the morning, but I want ten dollars on fifteen minutes maximum."

"What are you two betting on?" Shelley asked, joining the conversation.

"I'm glad you asked that. Can you imagine, Shelley? Our loyal Elsa here," Todd dramatized, "doesn't think our beloved leader can last a whole thirty minute appointment with a sassy brunette!"

"What's your bet again, Elsa? Did I hear ten dollars on fifteen minutes? Well, I'll put twenty dollars down that he pisses her off with that rude charm of his and she storms out of here in five minutes flat. That guy needs to grow up when it comes to women! He needs to quit whining about something that happened twenty years ago." Shelley stated vehemently as she turned to head back to her own office.

"Oh ... Mr. Campbell, sir ...," she stopped cold.

Jordan pushed himself off the doorframe of his office, walking silently past Shelley to stop at Elsa's desk. Still without sound or expression, he pulled his wallet out removing a one-hundred-dollar bill and dropped it on the desk.

"Ah ... so, what's your bet, Boss?" Todd ventured nervously, trying to lighten the tense, frozen silence.

Jordan returned to the door of his office before turning and fixing Shelley with his steely gray eyes.

"I bet...Ms. Airton," he enunciated her name carefully, "that you are probably right. I have behaved as less than a perfect gentleman at times, haven't I?"

There was no way that Shelley was going to take a chance and answer *that* question.

"The money is a fine," Jordan continued, his voice flat, but controlled. "Treat yourselves to lunch on me. If the three of you fine me each time I treat women with my...'rude charm'... maybe I will 'grow up' before you are all millionaires." And with that, he entered his office and quietly closed his door.

It seemed like the wall clock had ticked off an hour before anyone moved, before they all turned to stare at each other, wondering if they had heard correctly.

The hundred dollar bill lay in the center of Elsa's desk. Physical evidence.

All three turned to go silently back to their business, still stunned.

Search warrants on the Henley postal boxes had been executed and Jordan and the task group were meeting to go over the evidence collected.

The original box, box A, was seemingly a normal business box. However, computer searches revealed no business registered under the name of Henley Enterprises, no tax number or filings under that name for local, state, or federal agencies. Therefore, the box contents were being opened and carefully analyzed by the lab before further information could be provided for action. The holder of the second key to Box A remained a mystery.

A mystery of special interest to Jordan.

The rental on that postal box dated back about eight years, which was about the same time that Jordan had suspected Henley of having linked up with Abe Damon's activities. He smelled a connection, though he didn't share that hunch yet. He personally believed the other key for Box A would be found in Damon's pocket. Conjecture, he cautioned himself. It was too big a leap to make yet without some evidence.

Another mystery was posed by one unusual item found in Box A, a black boxy object sat in a clear evidence bag on the table. It had an unknown use.

"Let's hold on to this for the moment," the federal prosecutor advised. "We've already taken the fingerprint lifts and sent digital photos of this off to the FBI lab in Quantico. We should hear back in a few days if they can identify the object."

The police would be questioning the second known holder of Box B in the next few days, after the lab had completed their work on those contents. Due to the criminal records of both box holders, and the initial highly incriminating evidence found inside, multiple lines of inquiry were already being worked by the different task force agencies.

The padded envelope inside one box had been found to contain an inner envelope with the label 'BURN' on the outside. Inside that envelope were over a dozen debit cards that were presumed to be counterfeit. Each item had to be carefully fingerprinted, and examined for trace and tool marks, before being passed on to the investigators to follow up on each trail. It was a slow but meticulous process, but clearly would lead to multiple charges and other criminal links.

As Jordan received congratulatory backslaps from the team members, and queries on how he had come up with his brainstorm, he did not admit a pretty blonde had been indirectly to blame for him stumbling on the postal keys. Feeling his face flush, he hoped they assumed his embarrassment was from their compliments, as he tried to hurry them on their way. "Seems like we have our hands full for now, and I have a deposition to take in a half-hour. Let's break for today."

The rest of the team was more than eager to leave and start following up all the new leads. Jordan sat a moment longer, thinking how quickly his luck was changing. Thinking *why* his luck was changing. He really hadn't deserved to be so lucky.

Thinking soberly about the earlier incident with his office staff, Jordan wondered when he had become such an ass. Did it really matter? He sure was one now, he admitted, realizing he needed to change a lot more than his luck, and start working on it immediately.

Grabbing the evidence bag from Box A to lock in his desk, he headed wearily back over to his office. Shelley was heading up the hall with an enormous stack of files. Files Jordan had assigned her, then hadn't given her his time to discuss.

When she noticed him looking her way, she averted her eyes, and angled sharply off toward Todd's office.

"Shelley, great," Jordan called, offering a rusty smile. "Come on in. I owe you the rest of the afternoon." He'd let Todd take the deposition, he needed to start mending some fences. He motioned her to follow him into his office.

Shelley gratefully dropped her heavy pile of files on the corner of Jordan's desk, but was still a little nervous about facing those steel-coated eyes. Easing over to drop into a chair, her eyes stayed glued to his desk, until she looked up in surprise.

"What are you doing with Chuck's camera?"

"What?"

"The juvie case. Cocky Chuck?" She motioned at the baggie on Jordan's desk. "Isn't that his camera?"

"Cocky Chuck?" Jordan's eyes narrowed, his gaze intent. "What is Chuck's real name? What case are you referring to?"

Shelley told him. Jordan made notes, but didn't answer her original question.

"Let's get started," he said, moving the evidence bag to lock in the credenza behind him, then turning back with a pen and fresh legal pad. "Go ahead." He nodded at the pile.

Shelley pulled the first folder off the top, handed him a copy of her typed summary, and proceeded to discuss the case files with him for the next two hours.

When Jordan finally finished up with Shelley, he thanked her politely for her hard work. He told her he appreciated her picking up the slack, asking her to continue picking up the new cases.

No mention was made of the earlier embarrassing incident, though Jordan was half tempted to ask where his three staffers had decided to go for lunch, but determined that was best left alone for the time being.

He did, however, immediately follow up on the information Shelley had accidentally given him, unaware her former client was involved. Jordan phoned the head of the juvenile division, then ran down the stairs to that department to chat with him in his office.

After putting their heads together on a conference call with the federal prosecutor, they decided to gather all the evidence from the juvenile case, the boxes, and the two black boxes, any fingerprint and handwriting evidence, and overnight it all to the FBI lab back east. The FBI labs would re-examine every bit of evidence.

The three local prosecutors decided to thoroughly investigate the minors, all early findings to be kept confidential until they determined if there was any linkage to the more serious felonies.

What a small world it is, Jordan thought, as he finally headed home late that evening. Of course, if it turned out Damon was involved, that's exactly what it would be, a small closed world of juveniles to do his dirty work—and take the fall for him.

As usual, what the prosecutor knew, and what he could prove, still had a big gap, yet he could sense it closing. Jordan didn't want to put away kids; he wanted to put them under pressure so that they gave up Abe Damon. The man poisoning his community.

In the face of Ms. Rhonda Sayles obvious enthusiasm at making his acquaintance, Jordan's resources were fully occupied trying to maintain a gracious diplomacy. When he stood to greet her, she'd taken not only the hand he offered, but stepped into his handshake. Grasping his elbow with her other hand, she trapped him closely to her side in a chummy technique commonly employed by politicians, especially in front of news cameras. Jordan was not at all prepared to be drawn so intimately against the sleek brunette that wafted a sophisticated, seductive scent.

As he looked down into dark lashed, vivid blue eyes gazing adoringly up at him, he had to steel himself against his natural reaction.

Fury.

Flight.

Attempting to smile politely through clenched jaws, Jordan willed himself to let his arm remain in the woman's grasp, staying the reflex to yank his hand away and flee to safety behind his desk. Incredibly, he kept from growling at her, managing a tight "Ms. Sayles," in greeting instead. The restraint had more to do with lack of oxygen, however, than courtesy; Jordan was holding his breath to avoid inviting her scent into his nose.

Todd watched in breathless amazement, waiting for his boss to explode. After ten tortuous seconds had passed, Todd rushed to rescue his boss—more out of greed than charity. Grasping Rhonda's arm, he steered her neatly to a chair before Jordan's desk, freeing his boss to take refuge on the other side of the steel and wood barricade.

Todd was impressed with Jordan's fortitude, but slightly disappointed at the same time. After Jordan's self-imposed fine for lack of courtesy to the female race, Todd, Elsa, and Shelley had looked forward to this day. They calculated they could clear anywhere from five hundred to a thousand dollars just on this interview alone. Todd had come up with the higher estimate. Having prior experience of the lovely Rhonda, he insisted a thousand dollars of 'rude charm' fines was not an unreasonable target to expect in a thirty minute session.

Taking the chair closest to Rhonda, Todd relaxed. Only one of those minutes had passed so far, and already Jordan's brows had draw down in a most promising scowl. Jordan continued that silent frown through most of the interview, which Todd was left to conduct. Jordan tilted back in a chair, secure and watchful behind his desk.

"First, Ms. Sayles … Rhonda," Todd corrected when he saw her pout. "We would like to thank you for the release your lawyer provided for your confidential business and personal accounts. That was very considerate and extremely helpful."

Extremely helpful, Todd mentally repeated to himself. Three very important facts had come to light during the examination. They had been able to assure themselves, from other sources, that Ms. Sayles had no known financial relationship with Henley or Honest Abe Damon, but a few intriguing issues remained.

Jordan, aware of most of the issues Todd planned to cover, sat back in watchful silence monitoring the interview and observing Rhonda's reactions to Todd's questions. The source of the frown that creased his forehead was not, however, as Todd suspected, but the result of his intense concentration. A faint sense that the tall brunette was vaguely familiar was nagging at Jordan's brain. So far he had only been able to pin down that he had seen her at a distance before, but he couldn't imagine where or why it would have been significant enough to continue to plague him now. He concentrated on the elusive memory while Todd continued his questioning.

"A curious item we were able to note from those records, Rhonda," Todd eased his way gently around to his question. "I happened to notice that you haven't ever used the cash machine at night before, for either your business, or personal accounts. Curious, don't you think?" Todd asked with a pleasant smile.

"How so … Todd?" Rhonda gave his smile back with only a slight hesitation, the tightly framed corners of her smile indicated the slight tension his casual question had created.

"Oh, well, you know when we chatted at your place the other day, I guess I misunderstood. I was under the impression that night withdrawals were a common occurrence for you. I guess they're not, huh?"

"I guess not, Todd." Rhonda's smile remained in place, but was definitely beginning to freeze on her face as she recognized that, despite his boyish charm and face, Todd was a more skilled adversary than her initial estimate. Rhonda was going to make him work for every word, volunteering nothing.

"No, I guess not," Todd continued cheerfully, "so that's when I realized that it was I who had misunderstood." Expecting her questioning look as all the response he would get, Todd rambled on. "You know, it's funny. In my experience, when you do the same thing all the time, it all just kind of blurs together, you know? I can't ever remember the routine things I do, the same way, all the time. Have you ever had the experience Rhonda of locking your car door, say, and walking off, and then trying to remember if you locked it?"

Rhonda waited.

"Yes, of course you have! Just normal human behavior. It's also normal that, just as we can't recall doing things the same way all the time, we easily recall something unusual. Something that only happens once, a special occasion, right?"

Such a pity, Todd thought, noting the icy-frost that was starting to coat the semi-smiling blue eyes. He was sure she had been rather fond of his charming ways before. Giving her his most apologetic grin, "So, I guess my notes were wrong when I asked you why you withdrew cash that night. Would you mind repeating for me again why you went to the cash machine for that special occasion, on that special night?"

Jordan was baffled, totally in the dark on what issue Todd was pursuing now.

Rhonda, however, was pretty sure she knew *exactly* where Todd was going.

"No, of course not, Todd," Rhonda stalled for time. She decided sticking to her original story was still her safest bet. "I told you I didn't recall."

The phrase had worked for lots of politicians, why shouldn't she give it a try? How could they prove whether she remembered something or not? She flashed Todd her warmest and friendliest smile.

Well, no big deal. Todd was more interested in *if* she would answer his question, not how. He already knew what Rhonda had spent the bulk of her cash on the following day. His curiosity came from why she was bothering to conceal such an unforgettable and easy answer. Or was there an easy answer?

Todd hadn't filled Jordan in on everything yet, he wanted Jordan's impartial opinion on Rhonda's reactions. Especially on this topic, to see if Jordan saw the same reticence he saw, to guide their investigation.

"Now Rhonda, you said there wasn't a car pulling out from the bank machine when you arrived that night?"

"That's right. There wasn't," she responded firmly.

"I don't believe I asked you before … Were there any *other* cars parked anywhere else in the bank lot?"

"Not that I recall," she answered quickly. Too quickly to consider the question first.

"I see." Todd managed to spread the three letter word out for all it was worth. "And you say that your car is a dark green BMW, and that's what you drove that night?"

"Yes."

"We have a witness, Rhonda, that recalls seeing a car similar to yours that night, but at the back, behind the bank, not in front..."

"I may have parked in back," Rhonda replied before Todd had a chance to finish his question.

"You parked in the back?" His surprise caught her off guard.

"Possibly," Rhonda answered warily.

"At night? In the dark? When withdrawing a large sum of cash?" Todd was incredulous.

Oops!

"I might have. I'm not afraid of the dark you know, Todd," she added quickly, matching her words with an unconcerned shrug.

"I never expected you to be, Rhonda. But most people, male or female, might be a little more cautious about being robbed or mugged."

"If you say so." Had Rhonda said so, in an earlier interview? She hoped not, but feared she might have. Another error.

"I certainly don't mean to belabor the point, but it has come to light that your use of the cash machine that night was logged by the bank clock to be only minutes after an unauthorized and illegal withdrawal from the same machine. It's very important that you search your memory for any clue to anything that could help. The criminal would have been on the site almost simultaneously with you."

Oh, *her* criminal was there all right! Rhonda thought dryly, before the import of Todd's words hit her.

She had been so wrapped up in covering for Sam that she had gotten herself into a hole. She was pretty sure she didn't have a ladder in her purse. Was he saying the bank was robbed?

"No, I'm sorry. I don't recall anyone," she replied automatically, distracted, before remembering the other car around back.

"Ms. Sayles," Todd was too tired to play any more games. "At the same time you were at the bank there was a car not only parked, but running, only a few feet away. The person in that car was arrested only a few minutes after the time stamp of your withdrawal, on a drunken driving charge. We have a witness, and police have bank records to verify that information. Now, why are you lying to me?"

Even the harsh tone of voice was not enough to draw an answer from the woman. She sat stricken, her face white and frozen just staring back at him with startled, silent blue eyes.

"Well then, maybe you will tell me this? Do you know a Samantha Wilson, the woman that was arrested that night?"

The question was answered by the crash of Jordan's chair as he suddenly shoved forward against his desk. They had both forgotten he was even there.

"That will be enough for now, Todd. I know you have a lot of work to get on with, so I'll take over from here.

"Ms. Sayles," he asked courteously, ignoring his stunned and gaping associate, "I wonder if you'd do me the honor of having lunch? We could finish our conversation there."

Saved by the bell, so to speak.

"Why Mr. Campbell, I would just love to have you to myself for lunch. I'll just go powder my nose first, and be right back."

Rhonda rushed off to the restroom, where she could heave a private sigh of relief at her narrow escape. This was getting very complicated. Thanks so much, Sam! Angry before she remembered the luscious Jordan Campbell was her escort for lunch. Yum! Wait until he discovered what she had planned for dessert! She forgave Sam on the spot.

"Damn women!" Jordan growled the moment Rhonda left.

"But," Todd stuttered, still in shock.

"I know, I know," Jordan angrily pulled a hundred dollars from his wallet and threw it on the desk.

"But, that's not what I meant ..." Todd was interrupted once again.

"Yes, I know, I told you not to leave. I changed my mind. Go."

"But..."

"Now!" Jordan roared.

Todd grabbed the cash off the desk and ran.

Todd had saved the drunken woman as a surprise – but *not* for Jordan.

Now his boss wouldn't even give him the chance to tell him that Rhonda not only knew her, but had used the cash withdrawal to pay her bail! Well, he'd just have to fill his boss in after lunch—if he *returned* from lunch today.

Jordan had already made his own connection between the women. The moment Todd had mentioned Samantha Wilson's name, it came back in a flash. He remembered this woman hugging the tiny blonde that had just defiantly sentenced herself to jail that day. He'd cut Todd off, issued the luncheon invitation on some strange impulse that he barely understood.

He wanted to talk to someone that knew Samantha. Alone. He had an irresistible urge to find out more about her. This would give him the excuse, and if he had to take that damn flirty brunette out to lunch to find out, well … he'd survive. Maybe he'd find out something that would help their case? Regardless, he had to learn more about the tantalizing face that had persisted in haunting his thoughts.

Jordan escorted Rhonda out past an openly staring office staff.

chapter seventeen

Jordan walked Ms. Sayles to a popular luncheon spot, a block from the courthouse. He selected the place because it had excellent atmosphere, excellent food, but was not what anyone would consider an intimate setting.

While amused at the public setting, Rhonda was much too experienced to let it upset her plans. She was more than capable of creating her own intimate atmosphere with a seductive smile, or the gaze in her cobalt eyes.

Jordan gritted his teeth a few times during the mechanics of settling and placing their food and drink orders. As uncomfortable as he was with her not so subtle signals, he had to appreciate that Ms. Sayles played the game with a sporting sense of humor, not taking herself too seriously. Jordan actually had to restrain an outright laugh when, as he removed his jacket and loosened his tie to relax, he caught the amused scrutiny his newly exposed parts were receiving from this female wolf. As he rolled crisp white cuffs up, he was so conscious of her interest in his casual actions, he felt as if he was peeling the shirt off his arms to the beat of a stripper's song.

Ducking his head momentarily to hide his amused, but embarrassed smile, Jordan leaned on the table, placing his lean, bronzed forearms along the edge, his hands clasped before him. He gave Rhonda a direct, but serious gaze, as he began to speak calmly but firmly.

"Ms. Sayles, Rhonda, you are a stunningly attractive, seductive woman. I'm sure you realize that and have been complimented by a great many men. You're also a very intelligent woman. I won't insult that intelligence by attempting to manipulate this situation. I would prefer to give you the respect of being completely honest with you, I hope you appreciate that. Because lovely as you are, you are *not* my type, Rhonda. Most beautiful women aren't. My sole interest in you is to find out everything you know about Samantha Wilson, who is, I suspect, a very important person to you."

Jordan was relieved when she responded with a good-natured laugh.

"Why Jordan, what woman would rather have a man desire her for her beauty above her intelligence? We prefer that respect any day, thank you." Adding with a teasing chuckle, "That is as long as you preface your blows with an acknowledgement of our physical charms."

Now it was Rhonda's turn to lean forward, brace her slender folded arms, manicured hands as elegant but purposeful as her tailored business suit. Rhonda's teasing blue eyes were also serious now. There was no hint of the flirt in the confident business woman that addressed Jordan.

"Samantha Wilson is my best friend and has been for a very long time. Your assessment that she is very near and dear to me is correct. As such close friends we share many secrets and confidences. I would be glad to tell you all about my wonderful friend, but, let me return the respect of total honesty, Jordan. I do *not* intend on betraying any of those confidences. Period. I don't care who you are."

They were a well matched pair. Gray eyes met cobalt in a silent, solemn assessment, identifying in the other many of their own traits. Both of them were adept at sweeping aside surface issues and getting down directly to the bottom line. They would get along well now that the game was called and the rules were set.

Jordan reached a hand out to seal the understanding. Rhonda paused until he added, "I see and I accept that she has loyal friends," acknowledging their conditions, before she gave Jordan's hand a firm shake.

"And here I thought you were just another pretty face," Rhonda teased.

Jordan recognized it as the compliment to his directness and honesty that it was.

Lunch was served and Rhonda began to talk fondly of her friend.

"You want to know about Sam? Samantha Wilson is a saint," Rhonda Sayles stated firmly. The hard look in her bright blue eyes challenged him to laugh only if he had an immediate death wish.

Tightening his lips and spreading open his palms in self-defense, Jordan Campbell said as reasonably as possible, "Yet, she *is* in jail right now. Is she not?"

Rhonda's eyes narrowed. If only she could tell him the truth. Tell him that even in prison coveralls, her dear friend was still a saint. A sweet, caring woman, a dedicated mother . . .

"Maybe," he interrupted her thoughts, "you could tell me a little about your friend?" His voice held no sarcasm or disdain. "Help me understand *why* she is so special?"

"It would take a hell of a lot longer than a lunch hour to list all the ways."

"There is no limit on our time today. Tell me everything you know about Ms. Wilson."

Wary, she studied his face searching for clues to his sincerity. His handsomeness was a distraction, but he let her look without trying to charm her with a smile. Finally, Rhonda gave him a wide and slightly wicked smile, thinking that since he had asked for it, she would let him have it—both barrels.

"As you should know, as we are of an age—though you *are* male and were probably oblivious—we grew up in a time where the social order dictated that a woman's place was in the home. But it was also a time of transition and women were starting to get a voice for the right to make a choice. Both Sam and I made our choices. I chose a new direction, college and career.

"Sam chose the traditional path of marrying young, right out of school. She was pleased that her new husband did not *want* her to work—*outside* the home. Sam saw her job as working hard to create a pleasant home and to greet her husband home at night with a smile, a kiss, and a well-cooked nutritious meal. With her sweet, caring nature, Sam was truly in her element. She joyfully looked forward to the the birth of each of her two children, Penny and Paul." Her soft smile, as she spoke their names, told of her affection.

Pausing to take a bite of her salad, when Rhonda continued, her smile had faded. "But," she gave a heavy sigh, shaking her head, "after she'd had the children, Sam found she *really* had her hands full."

Glancing up as she took another bite, and a sip of her wine. She was surprised to see Jordan waiting, watching, intent on her next words when she would have thought him bored by now. Yet some hard to define emotion lurked in his eyes that seemed almost . . . Wistful? Probably not, she mentally shrugged. The man was notorious for not having soft feelings for women—to put it mildly! Well, she'd tell her story her way until he became impatient and interrupted her.

"Everything was fine, of course, while hubby had Sam's undivided attention," the sneer in her voice matched the curl of her lips. "But the man was way too emotionally immature to share ..."

"Is that what she told you?" He inserted the question mildly, without accusation, a seasoned prosecutor getting the facts pinned down.

"That is what I saw." Her voice was as hard as her jaw. "I've known Sam since schooldays. So as he got worse and more demanding, sweet Sam the romantic just tried harder, thinking somehow it was her fault that the damned man was *jealous* of his *own* children! It was like she had three kids on her hands." Rhonda snatched her wine glass from the table and took a large gulp then a few deep breaths trying to calm the ugly memories.

"I finally told her." She said almost defiantly. "I hated to hurt her, but she had to know. Everyone else thought they were protecting her by not saying anything. Idiots."

Campbell stiffened, seeming to sense what was coming. With a grimace he looked like he was swallowing down bile that had risen in his throat. She recalled rumors about what had caused his venomous attitude toward women.

"Samantha's husband was jealous of all the attention she lavished on their offspring complaining that it interfered with her 'real job'—to nurture and care for him first! He continually tested her loyalties, creating situations where she had to choose, just like another two-year old. So I told her. He'd been having affairs."

Dropping her head down, she shifted the food around her plate with her fork for a minute, then looked back up, anguish mixed with anger in those startling blue eyes. "And you know what the asshole said when she confronted him? That it was *her* fault; she had not paid enough attention to him!

"Sam was appalled. She's just the sort to believe in her better-or-worse vows and might have forgiven him. His infidelity was one thing, but being blamed for it was over the top! And she had young children to raise. The adult would have to grown up, or not, on his own. So thankfully, Sam moved out for good and left him to it. She was a mother; her children were her prime responsibility. Sam raised her kids with the love and constant support and guidance she'd had as a child. It was a hard job, with no pay, and, as it turned out, no financial support from her ex.

"So, Sam had to find a way to feed, clothe, and shelter them. She hated having to desert them to daycare while she worked, but there was no other way. It was a tremendous shock for her to find that women, especially single mothers, were considered highly undesirable as important employees. She was pitifully naïve about the world of business and opportunities for women, no matter how smart, reliable or diligent they were, even in those changing times. A college degree, not children, was the entry fee—for women. One hiring manager even told Sam it wasn't right for him to give her a job that a hard working man with a family to support needed, as if that was commonly understood practice—unfortunately it was back then."

She glanced up and noted the look of surprise on the prosecutor's face, as if he had forgotten, or never knew what is like back then. But his parents had been wealthy, she knew, so he was probably clueless anyway. Since he didn't stop her, she shared a few more harsh realities of her friend's past.

"Sam had worked five times as hard as most of the men in the office, who golfed their way to success while she had responsibilities at home. Her hard work had earned a lot of praise, but few promotions from bosses that took the credit for the success of their departments for themselves. She wasn't in a position to complain with her children's welfare contingent on her steady uninterrupted employment.

"At least her positions slowly become better and higher paying since her bosses took her along as their 'assistant' to insure their continued success. Sam could easily have run the department without them—but then she didn't play golf." She arched her eyebrows at a man she knew had a country-club membership—in his past if not now.

"Luckily, her kids were almost grown and through school when the financial markets collapsed, taking her company, and long slow climb to a decent wage away," Rhonda finished, picking up her fork and enjoyed her seafood luncheon salad while she let the man contemplate all she had told him.

"Those of us that love her, call her Sam, by the way, not Samantha," she advised as she filled him in on more of the details of Sam's life.

Jordan listened quietly. He watched the loving glow, the tender voice when Rhonda spoke of Sam and described her life, her wonderful children, her special parents, and the relationships that bonded them all.

The meal came and went. The other diners left, and still Jordan listened, content, as Rhonda described all the values and strengths of the friend she so dearly loved.

Rhonda left her long lunch with Jordan to return directly to the office.

She knew she had rambled on and on about Sam, but she missed her intensely, she had needed to reminisce. Jordan's quietly attentive attitude, and encouraging prompts, told her that he was interested in everything that she was willing to say about Sam. He didn't bring up any questions from the recent interview, or push Rhonda to speak on any topics she would have resisted, so she was able to speak freely, without betrayal of current circumstances.

By the time the waiter had come to ask if they wished dessert, Rhonda had become relaxed enough with Jordan to tease him that *he* had been *her* intended dessert. He had laughed good naturedly, then encouraged her to tell him more about Sam

Rhonda had been amazed at how considerate and friendly he was after the horror stories she'd heard about the woman-hating man. The sources had been many and reliable, so she knew they must be true. He admitted himself beautiful women weren't his type, but she had found him pleasant and polite. Maybe he had changed his views? Or maybe his intense and unusual interest in Sam had overridden his normal attitude. But why so interested?

She first thought it was the bank investigation, and the link Todd had made between the women. Jordan hadn't questioned her on that though. He actually seemed more interested in other details of Sam's life.

Why? Rhonda supposed it might just be part of his methodical, thorough investigative technique, a know thy enemy approach. If so, she couldn't see how she'd said anything damaging about Sam. Could it have been just idle curiosity?

Jordan had met Sam in person, at their prison interview. Did it have to do with something that came out of that? He hadn't mentioned that visit to Rhonda. He had, however, made one comment that had taken her by surprise as she spoke of how close the two friends were.

"Yes, I remember you hugging her after she was sentenced," Jordan recalled thoughtfully. "You were crying ... and she was smiling."

Now why would he have noted and remembered something like that?

Well, regardless of why he was so interested, she better get up to see Sam as soon as possible. Instead of waiting another week, she'd get up there tomorrow. She better fill her friend in on all the attention they were getting from the prosecutor's office because of this other crime. Damn! What rotten luck! Two crimes at once in the exact same place? Who could have expected that?

For all his sweet boyish looks, Rhonda was certain that Todd suspected *them* of both! Maybe now Sam would realize it was time to give up and let the kids get her out. This was getting much too weird for Rhonda's comfort zone.

When he returned from lunch, an hour and a half late, Jordan was much too occupied with his own thoughts to notice the heads that raised and stared pointedly at the clock. And the fact that he also strolled in whistling some unrecognizable tune through his teeth sealed the mouths that were about to tease that there must have been something other than lunch to delay him. With his sleeves rolled up, his tie askew, and his jacket draped casually over his shoulder, the relaxed, whistling man looked every inch the truant, returning to work with the pleasant memory of a woman on his mind.

Jordan waltzed right by Elsa, not even stopping to check for messages. She shook her head wondering what her boy had been up to. Any other man ... but Jordan? He was acting so out of character lately, she was beginning to wonder if the guy showing up for work each day was the same man. Maybe she should sneak his coffee mug to the gang at the lab, see if the prints matched? Her excuse for the test? What? That he was acting like a normal man, instead of himself? Maybe even like a normal man that was falling in love? Jordan? Maybe she would get those prints checked after all. And some DNA.

"Is he in?" Todd asked as he breezed by Elsa's desk.

"Who? There *is* a man in there, but—" She found herself muttering to Todd's back as he barged into Jordan's office.

Shelley had spotted Jordan returning and alerted Todd that he was back—and what he looked like he was back from. Todd thought Shelley's impression highly unlikely knowing his boss, though Jordan *was* a thorough researcher. Maybe he had felt the need to sacrifice himself to the lovely Rhonda, for the cause. Todd didn't care how Jordan discovered the links between Rhonda, Samantha, and the bank crime, as long a the job was done.

"So Jordan, I suppose you've discovered by now that Rhonda used the cash withdrawal to bail Samantha Wilson out. So how does it all fit?" Todd pulled a chair up to Jordan's desk.

"What cash?" Jordan asked blankly.

Todd stared at Jordan a moment, wondering if he'd been asleep during the pre-lunch interview, instead of just silent.

"O-okay, let's start from scratch. Samantha Wilson's car is at the bank, parked and running. She makes an illegal withdrawal from the cash machine moments before her friend Rhonda pulls her car into a dark area behind the bank, comes around to the front, sees her friend Samantha at ..."

"Sam," Jordan interjected. "Rhonda calls her Sam."

"Sure, so she sees *Sam* there up to no good. Her friend is drunk as a skunk. Rhonda makes her own withdrawal, an unusual and large night time cash withdrawal. Goes home. Meanwhile, Saman—, Sam, passes out in her car, face on the horn, and the police pick her up as a drunk moments later. The next morning, without a phone call from the jail I might add, Rhonda is there at Sam's bail hearing and uses her cash to bail her friend out.

"So what's up? Are they in it together? Did Samantha pass her the cash? Or did Rhonda not realize what her friend was up to until later?" Todd seemed to have finally captured Jordan's wandering attention.

"You mean you think *Sam* stole the money?"

"Of course. I just don't know whether Rhonda is just covering for her friend, or whether she was part of the plan."

"Absolutely not!" Jordan's response was fervent. "She didn't do it!"

"Hey, Jordan, I know you just had a pleasant visit with the lady," Todd emphasized the word 'visit', "but don't let it cloud your judgment. I admit I don't think it's probable that Rhonda was in on the plan, but she is definitely covering for her friend."

"Rhonda? I meant Sam. Sam did not do it. I'm sure of that. Rhonda is protective of Sam, but it doesn't have anything to do with that."

"But, Jordan..."

"Todd, I'm sure! Did Sam have that amount of money on her when the police picked her up?"

"No, she had fifteen dollars and change."

"Did Rhonda pay out more cash than she withdrew from her account?"

"Well, no, not that we can find." Todd admitted.

"Didn't you tell me Rhonda didn't need money?"

"Well, yes, Mallory did, but she might..."

"Fine. So where is this cash? You are barking up the wrong tree, Todd. It's a coincidence, nothing more, I know it in my gut. Start over and find a new lead. The women aren't connected."

Jordan obviously wasn't in a logical mood for Todd to attempt to discuss the issue further, so he gave up and left. Personally sure the women were in collusion on the bank job, Todd would just follow that up on his own, as Jordan seemed blinded now by his own delusions.

Unless Todd missed his bet, Rhonda would high-tail it out to see her friend the first chance she had. He wished he could eavesdrop on that conversation! He called the prison and gave them his private office fax number and requested all past and future updates of visitor logs for Ms. Wilson.

Todd had been kind enough to leave Jordan's door open during their discussion, so she had heard some of the exchanges. Elsa waited about ten minutes after Todd left Jordan's office shaking his head, before taking in the messages Jordan had forgotten to pick up. One was marked 'Important". She placed that one on top and placed the stack in the center of his desk.

She watched him glance over distracted and read the message aloud to himself.

"Cocky Chuck is Boxy (Box A?) Chuck.
Fingerprints just entered. Call!"

That did it!
Elsa watched the gray eyes sharpen and the body tense. There's my boy! She sighed, relieved.
"Get him for me!"
"Now!" Jordan added when he looked up to see Elsa still standing there smiling.
"Welcome back, Jordan." She left to place his return call to the federal prosecutor.

chapter eighteen

D amn! She was speeding again!

Why make such a nice flat road then make people crawl along it at a mere sixty? She had to hurry.

Rhonda tried to ease her foot off the pedal, gripping the wheel tightly, muttering tensely to herself.

"Use both hands, ten and two, check the rear view mirror!" She couldn't afford to get a ticket now. But, this was an emergency!

Rhonda was rushing to the women's prison. She was worried. Worried! Hah! Big time stressed! Again, she eased her tense foot back off the gas.

"Calm down, just get there."

Whoa! She'd just about slammed into the back of that idiot driving in front of her! Careful. She flipped him off as she sped around him. If he wanted to drive in her lane, he could have just signaled and asked nicely, asshole! Just popped in front of her!

The maniacs on the roads these days.

Oops! Ten miles over the limit again, better slow down, you just couldn't trust these other drivers. She would leap into the car pool lane for a little while and get past some of these Sunday drivers. Didn't they know it was Thursday? There, she zoomed past about twenty cars, slipped back into the proper lane.

No cops. Good.

"Oh thank god, I'm here."

It was a good half hour before Rhonda was through the gates, through the visitor waiting room lines, through more guards. Finally, put in a tiny room, a glass partition booth this time.

The minute she saw the door open to admit Sam, Rhonda snatched up the phone they would use to talk. Dropped it, grabbed it again. Too jittery. Fumbling to get the receiver to her ear, she scanned Sam's face as she approached the partition.

Sam was surprised, but pleased, to see Ronnie again so soon, but never even got a chance to greet her. Ronnie was totally stressed out.

"Boy, are we in trouble! You may just get a lot longer time than you planned in jail, sweetheart! Just what exactly happened between you and Mr. Handsome Prosecutor when he visited you here?"

"Nothing!" Sam responded guiltily, before thinking to ask, "Why, what happened?"

"You first. Answer my question." Ronnie was firm.

"Okay…" Sam tried to concentrate on what had happened. It wasn't that she hadn't thought much about the visit. She had a hard time thinking about much else! But the memories she constantly reinforced had more to do with the man's body; for some reason she had trouble remembering his words. "Really, just what I told you before. It was only a couple of minute meeting, I guess." How could anyone, Sam wondered, have turned her mind so upside down in such a short span of time?

"Yes?" Rhonda reminded her that she was still waiting.

"Oh, yes. Just a few minutes. He wanted to know if anyone was with me at the bank that night. I told him no. Then he wanted to know why I was there so late and I told him some dumb thing like I was dropping off my check reorder form, or something like that. Then he told me not to try and play innocent, and, of course, I told him I'd *never* do that! Then he got mad at me and left. That's it. Just like I said before." Sam raised her hands then dropped them back in her lap with a shrug.

Well, that *was* it as far as what had really happened, Sam reminded herself. The fantasies were something else. She wasn't about to confess those to Ronnie!

"That's all? Are you *sure* that's all he said, Sam?"

"Yes." *With his mouth. Sam wasn't sure what his eyes had been saying.* "I take it you figured out why he came."

"Sam, you will never believe what's happened since then! I have been interviewed at home by a detective, then the prosecutor's assistant, then again by him and his boss, the luscious Mr. Campbell, in his office.

"Apparently someone was rude enough to rob that bank machine almost at the same moment that we were committing our crime there." Ronnie continued, indignant, "You'd think they would have the decency to pick a different bank, or at least a different time, but no, they had to use ours. So the police have taken all kinds of reports and witnesses and added two plus three and come up with seven.

"And *We* are seven!"

"What do you mean 'we are seven'? What are you saying, Ronnie?"

"Withdrawals from that cash machine are time stamped. Moments after an illegal withdrawal, my withdrawal was clocked. Moments after that the police booked you. There is also a witness that saw your car there, and someone saw mine leaving from the back of the bank.

"They also know that I know you, and asked me to release my banking records to the prosecutor's office, which I did in the interest of being cooperative while trying to figure out why they were looking at us. I didn't find out it was a bank robbery until just yesterday. I think they might even know by now that I used my cash to bail you out the next morning. So I'm sure they think we pulled off that crime. Bank Robbery! *And* I can't tell them the truth to get them off our back, though my attorney asked me to.

"They know I'm lying because when they first interviewed me I stuck with the story, said I was positive no one else was in the bank parking lot, when they knew your car was sitting right there running and kind of hard to miss! And since someone had to be there at that time to commit the crime, that only leaves us!" Rhonda concluded, so agitated she didn't even hear Sam's soft whisper at first.

"What did you say?"

"Except the boy, of course."

Rhonda just gaped at Sam a moment before yelling, "What boy?"

"The one that was playing with the machine," Sam replied patiently.

Rhonda's eyes narrowed, "Sam there wasn't any boy playing with the machine."

"Yes, there was." Sam wished her friend would calm down. "Maybe he saw the person that robbed the bank?" she suggested helpfully.

"Sam, I don't believe you. Nothing personal, but you were so damn drunk you could barely sit up! There wasn't any boy. You were hallucinating if you thought you saw one. Besides, the car was parked facing away from the bank, don't you remember? You could only have seen the road."

"Yes, I remember," Sam said patiently. "I was very drunk, the car faced away, and the boy was playing with the cash machine."

Her friend had such a lovely fragile neck, Rhonda thought, eyeing Sam's with an urge to strangle on her mind.

"Sam, no one was at the bank, honey. I knew I shouldn't have mixed you so many drinks, it's a wonder you didn't get alcohol poisoning." Rhonda sighed, starting to feel guilty again.

"Wait. Ronnie, you told me I had to wait until you were done before I could sleep. I waited and my eyes were rolling so badly it seemed like I would have to wait forever! After what seemed like a very, very long time, I looked in the rear view mirror to see if I could sleep yet. I saw the boy playing with the cash machine, I didn't see you. I turned around and looked and saw him, then saw you still by the back of the car, digging in your purse. Then you started walking really slow and the boy saw you coming and ran off. I was really mad!"

"Why? Because I was so slow?"

"No, of course not. Well, yes, of course, I did want to sleep. But I was mad that his parents let a young boy like that run around alone, late at night! He could have been hurt, or kidnapped!"

"Right," Rhonda nodded thoughtfully. "Sam, how did you know it was a young boy?"

"He was short, he wore dark baggy shorts and t-shirt, but he had little, skinny knobby arms and legs sticking out. His face still had the rounded nose and cheeks of the baby face it takes a while to outgrow. He was at least nine, but maybe twelve, too young for a teen."

"Incredible!" Rhonda had started taking notes, "Can you remember anything else?"

"You know how kids will check phone coin boxes, or anywhere they think they can find forgotten change? Well, that's what it looked like he was doing, or just playing with the buttons on the machine. He had a dark baseball cap on backwards, you know?

That's why I could see how round his face was from the side. I couldn't tell his hair color, or exact color clothes, they were just dark against white skin. That's about all I can remember. He ran off too fast, and I was getting very sleepy waiting for you."

"Are you really sure about all this?"

"Yes. When I first saw him I blinked, thinking it was a blur, but when I realized it was a young child out that late, my anger kind of cleared my head for a moment. Mom adrenaline, I guess. Anyway, I'm sure about him, but it's honestly one of the only things I do remember clearly about that night."

"I wonder if there is some way this could help? How would they ever find the boy? How do we explain how we saw him, well, how you saw him? You're not going to be a reliable witness – especially as a suspect! Well, I'll think on it, but Sam, I'm warning you, if they arrest me for bank robbery you are going to have to confess your innocence!"

"Of course, but not yet, unless, did the prosecutor threaten you?"

"No, not yet. He's actually kind of nice." Seeing Sam's questioning look, she added, "Oh, forgot to tell you. Wait until you hear this! I had lunch with him the other day. Such a delicious man; I'd planned on sampling him for dessert. But he very politely told me I'm not his type. That all he wanted from me was for me to tell him all about you!"

"Me?"

"You."

"What about me? You didn't..."

"I told him nothing at all about you in the last six months. So don't worry."

"Oh good. I mean, I knew you wouldn't, but ... What *did* you tell him?"

"Everything that ever happened to you from the day you were born up until six months ago, of course."

"RHONDA!"

"Sorry, honey, times up. I've gotta run," and she did, literally, tossing a "Bye, Sam. Love you," over her shoulder as she was let out the door.

"I'LL KILL HER!" Sam howled, before realizing that the guards were giving her very wary looks as they closed in carefully to get her back to her cell.

It didn't take long for word to get back to Todd that the prisoner he was interested in had threatened to murder Ms. Sayles.

When he arrived in his office the next morning the log of Wilson's visitors, along with the report of the threat, were on his desk with two other items.

Jordan had dashed off a memo to Todd early that morning before his task group meeting. Jordan's meeting had been in session before office hours commenced. The special gathering, that now also included some of the juvenile division prosecutors, indicated things must be moving rapidly on the Henley-Postal Box case.

Todd scanned Jordan's memo and breathed a deep sigh of relief. Apparently his boss had come to his senses over the weekend. The memo instructed Todd to get together with Detective Mallory and update him and pursue the following inquiries:

1) Verify if S. Wilson had accounts at County Bank in question,

2) verify withdrawals & deposits her accounts from date of robbery,

3) verify last check reorder date for S. Wilson.

Todd didn't understand what the third item had to do with their case, but wasn't about to question Jordan now when he'd finally come out of his daze and realized that Samantha Wilson was a viable suspect – probably the *best* suspect. Especially once he had an opportunity to show Jordan a copy of the prison threat report.

The third item on Todd's desk that morning was addressed anonymously to the office. Elsa had routed it to him as Jordan was tied up with the task group. He took the letter, typed on cheap copy paper, and read:

TO WHOM IT MAY CONCERN,

A YOUNG BOY WAS SEEN PLAYING WITH THE CASH MACHINE AT THE COUNTY BANK LATE ON NIGHT OF JUNE 12. HE WAS 9-12 YEARS, WHITE, SHORT, THIN, WEARING DARK BAGGY SHORTS AND SHIRT WITH DARK BALL CAP REVERSED. ROUND FACE PROFILE AND

*ROUNDED NOSE, COLOR OF HAIR & EYES
UNKNOWN. I HAVE REASON TO BELIEVE THIS
INFO MAY BE HELPFUL.*

SIGNED, CONCERNED CITIZEN

Well, well, well, Todd thought, now isn't this interesting! He rocked back in his chair with a satisfied smile. It had been less than twenty-four hours since Ms. Sayles—Rhonda, he corrected himself with a chuckle—had run to see Ms. Wilson at the prison.

Todd had never bothered to mention to Rhonda that the crime at the County Bank had never been published in the papers, and only the bank officials and law enforcement working on the investigation, along with a very few bank clients, knew of it. Todd didn't feel there was any point in telling Rhonda right away that he was on to her, maybe his anonymous investigator would come up with more leads!

He chuckled at her attempts at subterfuge, but he appreciated the attempt to help. It would probably lead nowhere—a kid, after all! Oh, well, he would check anything that might help. Maybe the kid saw someone?

Todd dropped forward in his chair suddenly, grabbing up the letter. Maybe the kid saw Ms. Wilson? Was that what this was about?

He recalled his wish to be able to eavesdrop on Rhonda's visit with her little prison friend. Maybe he had his wish, in a way? What if Rhonda had gone to ask her friend to come forth with information, to confess and get her off the hot seat, but Ms. Wilson had refused?

Would Rhonda threaten to tell the police? Or would she provide another witness that could identify Ms. Wilson, but keep her out of it? So she could get clear of her criminal friend without it seeming like she turned her in? Maybe because the prisoner had threatened to kill her if she did?

That may very well have been the scenario. He decided to hold off a bit on bringing Rhonda back in, give her a break while they followed up this new lead first, and Jordan's inquiries. They'd let her stay anonymous a little longer, see what developed.

Picking up the phone, Todd got through to Detective Mallory.

"Hey, do you still have that County bank video on hand? I'd like to drop over and take another look. I've got a few other leads for you to pursue, also. Okay, I'll be there within the hour."

Jordan leaned back from the conference table, took a gulp from his mug and almost gagged. His stomach was an acid brew from too much bitter caffeine, too much adrenaline, and too little sleep. The weekend had been torture on a variety of levels.

The information received on the case late Friday had put him on an adrenaline high. Unfortunately, it came in too late to coerce the task group away from their weekend plans with their families, having to settle instead for meeting early this Monday morning.

Able to sleep only a few hours the night he got the news, Jordan found himself pacing Saturday morning before deciding a long run would be a better option. Then trying to relax Saturday afternoon with a great book and a beer, he rested his body but his mind wandered. He found himself rereading the same page over and over again. He would have denied he had anything but the Henley case on his mind, but every female in his book, no matter how characterized, became a reminder of a tiny blonde with golden brown eyes.

Disgusted with himself, he'd finally tossed the book down and surveyed his back yard. All the new trees and shrubs had taken away the sterile look; the landscape now rich with multiple hues, textures, and shapes of leafy greens rustling in the breeze. He liked the woodsy look but soon realized that all his flowering trees and shrubs had quit blooming. His lush greenery had only the muted earthy browns to set them off.

Damn! He'd run out of colors again!

Jumping from his chair, he grabbed his keys and headed out whistling a tune softly through his teeth, glad to have an excuse to move and not think. Swinging into a drive-thru for a burger, he'd headed off to his favorite garden center.

This time he insisted on flowers that he could count on to bloom all summer long without quitting on him. "But no... "

"I know," his favorite garden lady said, "no pale pink. As long as you'll take some rose, corals, and reds, we should be okay."

Loading up with plants, soil, and more planters, he returned home and dug in plants until well after dusk, determined to awake with color in his life. Showering off dirt and sweat, the heat massaging the muscles that ached all over his body, he was convinced he would be able to sleep well that night.

He was wrong.

He crashed hard for four hours waking in the early hours of Sunday stiff and sore—and with his thoughts locked on Samantha.

Wrenching himself from bed as if the act could yank her from his mind, he stumbled in to start his first of many pots of coffee that day. He'd finally succeeded in torturing his body into submission; he had no energy left to run, dig, or even pace. But by midday Sunday he could no longer hold at bay, or deny time had come, to deal with the problem of Sam. Jordan had to squarely face his conflicting emotions and his conflicting interests.

On a personal level, he'd been attracted to Sam from the start. Her integrity in court, demanding to take responsibility for her crime, had impressed him. When he saw her again at the prison he was stunned by her impact when they faced each other in close proximity for the first time. She seemed so fragile in her prison clothes, much too soft for the harder souls they usually enclosed. Those huge eyes had grabbed a hold of him, and still held him, haunting his dreams.

He'd only become more enchanted listening to Rhonda's stories that fleshed out a special woman with old-fashioned values and a deep love and loyalty to her children, her parents, and her friends. Everything he saw in her, heard from her lips or her friend's, everything his gut told him about her was good and true.

But, as a professional, he had to reconcile all that with unemotional facts. She was in jail. She'd admitted her guilt. She was a drunken driver, just like his mother and father, he thought gritting his teeth. Todd was telling him the evidence clearly pointed to her being the only viable suspect in the county bank robbery, unless Rhonda had helped, being the only people on site at the clocked, witnessed, and verified time. Which put her determination to rush to jail on a D.U.I. charge in a different light.

How could he possibly ignore those facts as a prosecutor?

He couldn't, though his every instinct told him the evidence was pointing the wrong direction. He personally could not believe Sam or Rhonda was involved in that crime. But, he reminded himself, he hadn't been such a hot judge of a woman's character in the past, now had he?

He needed to be objective. He wasn't.

Still the job had to be done and Jordan finally admitted in the dark hours of Sunday night that he didn't have the judgment or impartiality to handle it.

He'd assigned Todd to pursue the investigation of Sam, Ms. Wilson. Jordan had no other choice. Todd would do it professionally.

Scrubbing burning eyes with both palms, Jordan realized he had completely lost track of the discussion around the conference table when he heard them teasing him about having zoned out.

"Sorry about that," he grinned sheepishly, an expression on *his* face completely unfamiliar for his colleagues. They were still staring when he added, "We've been at this for hours. Let's order in food and break for early lunch. I don't know about you guys, but I need something besides caffeine in me if I want to get my brain functional again."

chapter nineteen

Todd showed up at Detective Mallory's desk with a bag full of Starbucks coffee.

"What, no doughnuts, Blake?" Mallory grinned.

"Didn't want to spoil the lunch I'll buy you later. Besides, my wife will kill me if I come home with the smell of doughnuts on my breath, and chocolate sprinkles on my collar!" He joked with the detective. Both were married men and getting on the rounder side of lean, they shared a knowing laugh over that one.

Todd decided on the way over how he'd handle what he thought of as Jordan's 'issues' with the County Bank case. Certain it was just a temporary aberration of his boss's, now he had assigned him the case, Todd decided to protect Jordan's privacy. The 'they call her Sam' episode wasn't anything he felt he needed to share with Mallory for the time being.

"We're going to be working together more for awhile, so I guess we better set some good habits," Todd smiled. "Jordan has a case that's gone hot and he's buried in team meetings for the foreseeable future, so this one's mostly up to the two of us to work. We just need to give him regular updates on what we are up to.

"We finally made some progress with Ms. Sayles, as you requested," Todd continued. "It turns out she's tight as a tick with that other woman, the drunk that was picked up at the scene, so your instincts were dead on. We think she's either in collusion with the main suspect, the drunk, Ms. Samantha Wilson, or an unwilling witness. Ms. Wilson is currently serving a sentence at the Women's Center for the DUI charge." Todd paused to hand a paper over to Mallory. "Jordan wants this info on Ms. Wilson checked out ASAP!

"Now, let me fill you in on what we learned directly from Ms. Sayles." Todd covered the dark green BMW and other details, then pulled out the evidence bag with the anonymous letter in it and passed it to Mallory, telling him he suspected Rhonda wrote it after running to see her friend in jail. A friend that, Todd finished with the prison report, showed her loyalty by threatening to kill Rhonda Sayles!

Mallory absorbed it all with a growing grin. Then crowed, "Whooee! I am one damn smart detective!"

"That you are!" Todd agreed cheerfully. "Which is why I owe you lunch, anywhere you want!"

They decided to get together a photo layout of dark cars, including the green BMW, and carefully re-interview the witness together, before they had lunch or reviewed the bank video tape. They were especially interested in any memories she might have about a small boy in a baseball cap that night.

Jordan's task group meeting resumed as the last chips were crunched and the last takeout boxes cleared from the table.

The big excitement of the morning had been the revelations regarding Box A—one of two post office boxes full of other people's mail, bank statements, and the like.

After Shelley had accidentally seen and misidentified the black object as Cocky Chuck's, they had matched his fingerprints to it and an envelope. Chuck was one of the unknown senders of the stolen mail. The other, listed only as Bob, was still unidentified.

The FBI was able to identify the two black boxes as sophisticated scanners that could take pictures of debit cards and capture the PIN numbers as they were entered in cash machines. They were still decoding the info on the scanners, but they clearly weren't for taking juvenile bathroom porn flicks, as Cocky Chuck had claimed.

Refreshed after lunch, they'd all had a chance to check their messages, and had some further updates on the various investigations to offer.

The Chief of Police was the first to take the floor.

"Just to focus you, this is regarding the second box holder of Box B, the one with the 'Burn' envelope and the counterfeit ATM cards, probably made from those little black things, I guess. The other postbox holder is a Robert Fountain." He held a hand up to forestall them, "but, he goes by Rob, not Bob. That's not the good news, bear with me. So, Fountain has a sheet similar to Henley's, but Rob isn't currently sitting in jail where he is easy to find. In fact, the bad news is we haven't been able to find him *yet* to interview him.

"But ... and here's the good stuff coming..., since he wasn't at home or work, we decided to run background on family and friends to track him down. Turns out he is divorced and has two sons by that marriage. The wife remarried and has custody of both boys, but only one lives with her. The older one. She shoved the younger one back on Rob when she got remarried. Her husband had two young daughters about the same age as young Timmy, who is a hellion and a bad influence, just like his older brother. The stepdad adopted the older boy as a compromise with the mother, probably figuring he'd get his sorry ass out of the house sooner, or spend his time in juvie away from the ten and twelve year old daughters.

"The older boy's name is Chuck Simpson, but his real dad is Rob Fountain, also known now as... Cocky Chuck's dad!" He finished with glee, to a round of cheers and applause. "So I agree we should leave young Chuck out on bail and put a loose tail on him and watch where he goes."

"That's great. But too bad the dad goes by Rob, not Bob," commented one of team. "Are you sure he isn't the sender of that envelope with the scanner, the 'Bob' one? Or do I just want it too easy?"

"Not sure, but Rob is in CODIS, so if his prints were on that envelope, I'm sure we would have known long before now," replied the Chief reasonably.

The juvenile prosecutor, new to the team, made a cautious suggestion.

"This is probably out in left field, but when Chuck was picked up he was with two of his buddies. Wasn't one of them called Bob?" He queried the case officer.

"Oh, yeah, that's right. He's close with a kid named Bob. Bob was there, also a Craig," the officer confirmed. "Anybody need a Craig?" He joked, looking around for someone to yell 'Bingo'!

The group adjourned tired but exhilarated.

They had three now—Henley, Rob Fountain, and his son, Cocky Chuck. All tightly linked, all in trouble with the law, all convictable on the evidence they'd uncovered. An ideal situation to play them and see what they'd cough up in return. The prosecutors didn't have to settle for a deal unless they really needed what was offered.

What kind of mess had she gotten them into?

Sam brooded over Rhonda's visit. Had her selfish desire to maintain her guilt caused serious legal consequences for Ronnie? Bank robbery? They couldn't be serious!

She winced as she realized she had bitten down on a spot she was wearing raw on her lip, but it was the sick feeling at the pit of her stomach, the ache over the harm she might be causing her best friend, which forced her to act.

Sam had to convince the authorities that Ronnie was blameless.

She had to make sure they knew Rhonda didn't commit a crime, didn't obstruct justice, or be an accessory to whatever fancy legal term they might use to hurt her friend. She had to find a way Ronnie wasn't involved anymore. She'd tell them about the boy. She'd take all the blame for anything they thought Ronnie might have done.

She'd do anything, including, if there was no other choice, sign a confession of innocence of the crime she was jailed for. Sam hoped she could avoid that, but ... How exactly did the fifth amendment work, anyway, when you wanted to not *un*-incriminate yourself? Time to ponder that later; time to act now.

Sam wrote a brief note asking the prosecutor to come see her as soon as he could; she had information for him. She put it in an envelope and sent it out in the Saturday afternoon prison mail, before she could think about it too much and lose her courage.

After she sent it she'd have plenty of time to think about what the right thing to do was, the right words to say, and ... consider whether the only reason she wanted to see the prosecutor again was just to set things right for a friend.

It was this note that arrived on Elsa's desk Monday afternoon while Jordan was still in meetings.

Elsa opened the envelope and read the note; mail from prisoners to prosecutors was not considered private, but part of her duties. With her protective maternal instincts for Jordan—that Elsa's husband always teased her about—she would have read it regardless. She recognized the name of inmate S. Wilson. She'd heard Jordan's voice soften when he'd told Todd 'they call her Sam'.

Elsa drummed her fingers on the desk, conflicted. She stared at the letter as if it would tell her more about a woman that could soften her boss's voice and head. She wanted Jordan to find some happiness, a fuller life, but, with a prisoner? One she didn't know? Hadn't checked out first? Elsa was half tempted to run out to the prison herself and get a look at this woman. She had *plenty* of questions for S. Wilson!

The letter was addressed to Jordan but, after his defense of the suspect late Friday, she knew he had come in this morning, looking like hell, and stepped away from the case, assigning it to Todd.

Elsa had already placed Jordan's memo and an anonymous tip that had come after he was in conference on Todd's desk. She had Todd's fax response to the memo now. What to do?

She should put the note on Todd's desk; it was his case now. But … Todd had left word that he and Mallory were delayed reaching the witness they were seeing; he would be out with Mallory the rest of the day. He also planned to go straight to the precinct tomorrow. They would spend all day going over bank videos frame by frame. So Todd was out of the office for two days, that was a good enough excuse for Elsa to rationalize she really didn't have any other choice.

Sighing, she got up from her desk and did what she knew she had to do for everyone's sake. She took Todd's fax and the Wilson letter and set them in the center of Jordan's desk along with the message that Todd would be out for two days.

Let the man decide himself what he needed, or wanted, to do.

When Jordan finally returned to his office after the task group broke up, he saw the note first. As exhausted as he was, he felt a nervous thrill shoot through him as he picked it up.

She wanted to see him.

Note in hand, he swiveled his chair to the window, trying to keep his smile from turning into a foolish grin. The note was only two sentences long but he stared at her handwriting, absorbing it as if it were calligraphic art.

She wanted to see him as soon as possible!

All he could think of was how much he wanted to see her. His daydream ended when the words about having information for him finally sunk in.

This was business. What the hell was the matter with him acting like she'd sent him a Valentine!

His face tightened, his lips a grim line. Turning back to his desk, he reminded himself this was Todd's case now, he should give the note, *his note*, to Todd. Reluctantly setting it down, he scanned the rest of the items Elsa had left on his desk. When he saw that Todd was out for two days, he started to change his mind. Maybe he should ... no.

When he read the faxed answers to his memo he saw that Sam had *not* reordered checks for over a year. He read it again, just to be sure, as his blood pressure began to rise. He felt wounded, but that reaction quickly changed to anger.

She lied to me.

She looked me right in the face with those big brown innocent eyes and lied to me! Check reorder, my ass! That does it. It wasn't Todd she lied to, but me, this is personal now. She's going to look *ME* in the face and tell me why she lied to me!

Grabbing his jacket, the notes from their prior interview, and Sam's 'valentine', he stormed out of his office, leaving a terse note on Elsa's desk telling her that he wouldn't be in tomorrow morning.

Sam hadn't lied to herself about her reasons for sending the note. It was vital she clear Ronnie's name. She *had* denied, however, the whole truth. Just as she had omitted the fact that she hadn't *actually* been driving, while drunk, earlier. And look how well that lie was turning out?

Clearly a lifetime of honesty was not the best preparation for the skill set she currently needed; because she wasn't very good at lying to herself, or others. She did not have enough experience to foresee the potential traps and pitfalls, and had gotten in a much deeper tangle than planned.

Well, she'd fix that. *And once this was all over, never attempt to lie ever again!.*

And the other reason Sam was in self-denial? Okay, the whole truth? She wanted to see Jordan again. She needed to see him again.

She'd built a fantasy that she was convinced would not stand up with the real man. She needed to see that he was *not* the dream man she had created.

It wasn't like her to have these ridiculous erotic thoughts or to long for a man. It was, in fact, downright embarrassing. This was not like her. Sam was a mom. Moms did not spend their time having wild thoughts about strange men! Of course, she *was* a mom with an empty nest. She really didn't need to protect her kids from strange men, especially if she was only thinking about them—but such un-mom-like thoughts! Goodness!

Sam's only excuse was that Ronnie's advice that she practice visualizing each man she saw as a romantic, sexy male character must be corrupting her. That combined with her complete isolation here must be the reason her imagination and emotions had spun so out of control with the first man she'd come in contact with.

Well, almost first man, she snickered, recalling the disastrous, laughing gas induced dental visit. Okay, so the first male specimen without hair sprouting out his nose!

Suggestion and isolation were surely to blame.

Isolation. Starvation of the senses. The removal of things so taken for granted every day. Barely noticed, unappreciated, then gone and suddenly they became a need—a desperate need. All the un-watched sunsets. Waking to a medley of birdsong, without listening. The exhilaration of fresh, outdoor piney scents and gusty breezes, that you never breathed deeply, or captured as cool, soothing breaths upon your neck. The sight and scent, and nerve tingling awareness of a handsome, virile male. All you might have to wait to experience for twelve long months ...

Sam swallowed the lump clogging her throat and dabbed moisture from the corners of her eyes. Maybe, subconsciously, she wanted out and regretted her decision.

Had that been another factor in sending the note? She didn't believe that, but she wasn't sure she really trusted any of her thoughts anymore. Something was happening to her here that she didn't understand or recognize. Her calm, steady purpose and reason had deserted her. She was emotional, teary, and—thinking of her shameful fantasies—out of control.

Sam saw herself as mother, not a sensual lover. Her situation had changed. She no longer needed to restrain other desires; desires she hadn't wanted before.

She had observed the lives and relationships of other couples and lovers for almost thirty years, mostly from the sidelines. She was comfortable being that person, an observer. The sidelines were safe. She was afraid of plunging into the emotional chaos, that uncertain cauldron she had been in as a young woman when everything hurt too much, mattered too much, and she was never sure what her future held. Now?

Logically, Sam knew she was at another transition point in her life, but accepting that was scary. As an adult—a mature, unencumbered adult—she should be able to plan and control her own blank future. She'd already started chasing her other dreams and tapping buried female desires. But she had never meant to do more than just peek under the lid of *that* sensual Pandora's box. Apparently that box had a leak in it—or her hormone balance did!

Sam needed to plug the leak with some discipline.

It was Monday. Her note should have reached the prosecutor's office today. She didn't know how long it would be for a response—or if she'd even receive one. The guard would just come get her and stick her in a room for whoever was there to see her, if she did. Just the same, she needed to be prepared.

Sam fretted about what tomorrow might bring. If they did come. If *he* came.

She'd already decided what she would say to get Ronnie off the hook without compromising herself. If the discussion stayed on track as Sam planned that should work. If there were other questions that strayed into areas she wasn't comfortable with, she could just stonewall, ask for a lawyer to help her before getting herself in further hot water. That should work. Sam liked to have things neatly planned out in advance.

She also had to consider that if things didn't go well, it might restrict her ability to complete her project. Not good. It was the whole reason she was here in the first place; she could not bear to have it all unravel now.

Except, if necessary to protect her best friend.

Leaning back on her cot, she tucked a stray blonde strand behind her ear, her brown eyes solemn as she'd tried to prepare without worrying herself sick.

Finding her humor, Sam realized she had one less worry preparing for *this* meeting.

What to wear.

As the hours wore on and Sam waited, she tried to read a book to keep herself calm. The classic story of a man and woman that met and spent time exploring their attraction to each other, finding common interests and values. It made her realize just how foolish all her feelings were about the stranger she had met only for a few moments.

They would never, could never, have time to spend together and get to know one another. Even if he were ever as attracted to her as she was to him. Her chances with him were impossible. She did not know why she couldn't get him off her mind, stop thinking of him as a lover.

The saying, 'only in your dreams' certainly applied to Sam.

They had nothing to share or in common...

Laughing at herself, Sam realized they *did* share one thing in common.

Crime!

Funny, but hardly valid from opposite sides of the jail house bars. That division went way beyond the barriers that separated her from him. A criminal and a prosecutor? Never! Not even in a book could love successfully cross that barricade. But she wasn't thinking about him personally. Seriously. Permanently.

Was she?

So why did his face intrude every time she tried to visualize a perfect romance? True, she didn't have an abundance of role models here, and he *was* the perfect image of a handsome, sexy man that she could build her fantasies around, but her honesty made her admit those were just her excuses—not the real reason. He was not just a role model. An equivalent substitute would not do.

Sam wanted to see *him* again, see if she'd made him up into someone he wasn't. Only Campbell had ever triggered such a response from her—and in such unlikely circumstances. Obviously for now, for Sam personally, the idea of romance—not to mention lust—only seemed to equal one man. Jordan Campbell.

Why? She didn't know him, wouldn't get the chance. There was no logic, no hope in that equation. But still … Sam dreamed—erotically, every night!

And she could not define her reaction to him solely in terms of physical chemistry. There was something else, more elusive, that made her feel like she had known him, or should have known him, without having ever met. Some natural connection seemed to exist, some unexplainable bond, almost like a magnetic current drawing them together, even though they were strangers. At least the bond existed in Sam's body and mind.

Had he felt it also?

Why had he questioned Ronnie about her personal life? Just to solve a crime? Probably. She was reading way too much into his interest, but she'd had the same thirst to know about him. The prison library had a microfilm newspaper morgue that Sam used to take a few peeks into his life, wanting to know so much more.

Ronnie had already told him Sam's whole life story! It was only fair that she would want to even the score a bit.

And speaking of scores, Ronnie was in big trouble for her loose tongue!

Lights out came and Sam set her book aside and lay down.

Yes, she's done some research on Mr. Campbell. Honest, intelligent, a brilliant legal mind, the papers wrote, saying he was as successful a prosecutor as he had been a prior criminal defense attorney.

Too bad he'd made the change, Sam thought, she could've had him for own attorney, been on the same side. Oh … yeah … except for the little fact that she had not been guilty; he would not have liked that!

Everything she'd read pointed to a great professional respect for the man, his triumphs and achievements chronicled over the years. Very little was written about his personal life, except that he was now single, childless, an athlete, and seldom seen on the social circuit in recent years. References to his wealthy East Coast, Ivy League upbringing, were numerous. The papers said his socially prominent parents had been killed a decade ago in a car accident. He must miss them terribly!

Occasionally the papers showed him at the rare social event photographed with an attractive woman on his arm, always different women. The gossip columns noted that he claimed his escorts were business associates, denying any intimate acquaintance. What was most surprising by its absence was that the society columnists never referred to him as an 'eligible bachelor'. Yet he was one of the most handsome, successful, unattached men in town.

His anti-female reputation must be widely known though never publicly printed. What columnist would chance that statement, after all, with a man so legally capable of protecting his name!

Sam still thought that his first marriage had just left him terribly hurt and defensive, not truly hateful of women—at least she hoped not. He'd been hostile to her before, but she didn't think it was personal, more a technique he used to intimidate her in order to get answers to his questions. Sam preferred to give him the benefit of the doubt. Yawning, she rolled to her side.

Sam hadn't slept well since Ronnie's visit, actually since the prosecutor's. She was exhausted. She needed to block all her worries and thoughts and just get some delicious sleep.

And it was—delicious—though not as she had intended.

As drowsy warmth stole over her relaxing her body, delicious images invaded her unguarded mind. A darkly handsome face, lips sensually curved and so close his breath brushed her face. Smokey silver eyes so compelling they sent warm trickles throughout her body, left her throat parched, her cheeks flushed.

What would it feel like to have that long, lean body stretched over her as she surrendered softly to its welcome weight? Unconsciously, she rolled to her back in her sleep, her body settling passively, receptively, as she saw his eyes just inches away, darkly intent and questioning. His mouth lowered to softly probe her lips, finding the response he sought in their eager parting. As her mouth surrendered to his demands, an ache formed deep within, warm shivers rippled down her body, followed by a trail scorched by his lips traveling down her breasts, her belly, to her ... Stretch marks!

207

Sam woke with a horrified gasp. Oh, thank god, it was dark in the room!

Still shaking from imagined sensations, she was stunned to recognize the dim confines of her solitary cell. He had been so vividly real to her that his intoxicatingly male scent still seemed to linger in her nose, the taste of his lips on hers. She'd just had an embarrassing moment, just wanted to make sure the lights were off, then she'd planned on wrapping her legs around his and letting him finish ravishing her, but … it was just a dream! Just a dream?

"No, please no." She hadn't wanted to wake up but she didn't want to need him like this. She tossed on the narrow cot finally turning to curl defensively toward the wall, trying to find some peace, some sleep, some forgetfulness.

And maybe the rest of that dream.

chapter twenty

S amantha was not alone in the sleepless night.

Jordan punched angrily at his pillow as if it, not he, were to blame for the way he clutched it tightly, embracing it unconsciously. His mind and body betrayed him with thoughts of a certain slender blonde, sweet and pliant in his arms. He was ashamed at the weakness in himself that allowed him to be robbed of his sleep just by the thought of soft lips that invited his, the shapely body he ached to possess.

She had lied to him! Lied to his face and now she had the nerve to tempt him, to invade his senses? To make him wish and dream? How could he be such a fool?

Growling, he pummeled the pillow again before scrunching it under his head. Closing his eyes firmly, he mentally ordered his weak mind and body to sleep. He refused to acknowledge to himself that it was not just the lustful thoughts that so disturbed him, but the tender, protective timbre of those desires. After what she had done, he still wanted her, not just urgently and physically, but to hold her and savor her gently.

He desired to share something that he couldn't define with her. Not just once, but for a ... Well, for a long, long time. But if Jordan allowed himself to acknowledge that, then it meant that he would leave himself open and vulnerable to a woman again, his most fearsome nightmare.

Throughout a restless night, though separated by space and their private scars, they spent the night almost as closely entwined and bound to each other as lovers sharing and exploring one another in the same bed.

Early the next morning, Sam was taken to wait in the interview room. She was not feeling prepared with a plan. She was feeling emotional, scared; she was actually pretty freaked out. Things were getting serious.

The minute the door opened behind her, she knew it was him; knew he had come personally. She felt him, sensed him. His presence struck her like a force field, as surely as if a blast of wind had hit her back. Her ears seemed to hum louder, the closer he came. She wished she had somewhere to run. All she could do was hunch her shoulders, curl in more tightly in her chair, hands clenched, and try to keep her head down.

He slapped a file down on the table, making her jump.

She was afraid to look up.

He didn't speak. Continued silence unnerved her.

She finally tried to pull her head up only to find herself staring at hands braced low on lean hips. He was still standing. She wasn't looking him in the eye; she was locked on the front of his dark tailored slacks. That's when she forgot her fear, embarrassment taking its place. A blush stole up her face. She had spent all last night making love to this man in her dreams. This stranger! She drew in a sharp breath, her face red, her ears ringing, her eyes staring at …

Abruptly, he sat down.

The eyes that locked on hers were the bruised and stormy gray of thunderclouds. His face was harder, leaner, his cheekbones a more burnt bronze, than she recalled. He was much more handsome, larger, more dangerous, than she remembered. His impact on her was too personal, too male, too devastating.

This was worse than before. Sam felt hypnotized like prey before a cobra; she felt paralyzed knowing she wanted him—just like she'd had him the night before. Her throat dried out, her lips felt slack and parched. She tried to swallow, but couldn't; tried to moisten her lips with her tongue, then bit her lip.

His eyes flashed to her mouth briefly. His jaw tightened, his eyes hardened to steel, and he spoke, finally, his voice mocking.

"Nervous, Sam?" Coming down hard on her nickname, Jordan was reminding her that he had spoken with her buddy, Rhonda.

She licked her lips again, then got her chin up and tried to hold his eyes, as she waited silently.

She saw him bite down on his lip, look down as he opened his file, pulling out a sheet of paper.

"We spoke before, as you may recall." He glanced back up at her a moment, his voice stern. "I asked you why you were at the bank."

She waited.

"Well?" She was stabbed again by those hard gray eyes.

"Yes," she cleared her throat. "Yes, you did."

"And you said?"

"I didn't recall, I was ..."

"You said you went to reorder checks!" He shouted, stabbing his finger at the paper.

"I said I didn't recall. I might have been there for that. I didn't really recall. I *was* kind of fuzzy," she'd raised her volume a few notches.

They stared at each other silently, like wrestlers facing off, planning their next lunge.

Lowering his voice into a tight growl, "I asked if you were alone and you said ...?" He waited.

Sam opened her mouth, closed it, shifted, opened it again and started to say, "I think..."

"And you *lied* to me!" He shouted again, rising angrily to his feet to loom over her.

She flinched. She *had* lied and felt horrible about it, but she did not understand why he was taking it so personally. Surely, as a prosecutor, he was used to being lied to by inmates. "I had been drinking ..."

"You were drunk!"

"I was drunk, and ..."

"What kind of mother are you?" He yelled, suddenly. "You're nothing but a drunken sot!"

Shocked, stung, hurt, angry, Sam rose, opened her mouth to object, and realizing she couldn't, sank back in her chair. She couldn't tell him he was wrong, or that she was innocent. Angry, frustrated, fists clenched, she vented the only other way she could.

"And ... and you ... you're just a woman hater!" She yelled back in his face. "You ... You're probably one of those men who think women should just stay home in the kitchen!"

"My kitchen is the *last* place I want a woman!" He shouted back without thinking. "They should all stay at work and stay out of my house!" He spun and stalked away from her, raking his fingers through his hair. Angry that he had let her closeness affect him. Jordan had responded like a fool to her feeble attack.

He needed to keep this professional, not personal. Turning, keeping his distance from her, he demanded harshly, "And just what the hell does that have to do with anything?"

Sam had no idea why she'd thrown the first stupid thing that came into her head at him. She'd been hurt and wasn't very good at fighting, but she had obviously hit a nerve. His reply still rang in her head. Was he as embarrassed at their outburst as she was? As hurt? She sank back into her chair and kept her head lowered.

He prowled back to his chair and sat, visibly trying to calm himself as well.

"Let's get back on track here." He busied himself shuffling papers in his file before continuing firmly, but politely.

"Let's forget about what you said before, Ms. Wilson. I am asking you now. Were you alone? I want the real truth. Now."

Sam studied him quietly for a few moments. He didn't look up at her, just patiently waited her out.

"I saw a friend there who is totally innocent," Sam tried to speak very frankly and evenly. "So... I didn't mention her before. I alone am responsible for my crime. I also saw a young boy there that was playing with the cash machine.

"As far as I can rely on my memory, there were no others that I saw in the lot before the police came. Again, Rhonda is totally innocent. That is the truth. I didn't remember about the boy at all when you first questioned me, not until much later. That is my statement."

"And did Rhonda Sayles, your friend that was there, see the boy?"

Sam just shrugged silently. She didn't want to get into anything beyond the fact that she saw Ronnie there. She was trying to give truthful replies and didn't want to go anywhere near whether they had spoken to each other that night. If he delved into that, she would be in trouble. Instead, she gave him a detailed description of the boy, and why it had lingered in the back of her mind.

As Jordan listened to her describe the boy and what she had felt when she saw him, he felt his edgy tension ease away. Watching the expressions that crossed Sam's delicate face, he noticed the soft lavender shadows under her earnest brown eyes, the hollowed cheeks that spoke of tense, sleepless nights. He heard the mother's concern in her voice for the young boy alone at night, and, in its soft sadness, the echoes of Rhonda's stories of the kind of woman her friend was.

He knew she didn't have a record of drinking, so his attack on her as a mother had been a cheap shot, confusing her with his own mother in his anger.

Jordan was furious that Sam had wormed her way into his mind and his dreams, after lying to him. Lying to protect her friend, he had to remind himself.

Jordan had lashed out, fairly or not, but Sam had surprised him by getting right back in his face.

And hit her target, he admitted, though she probably didn't realize that.

He had tried to push her away with anger, so she couldn't hurt him as another woman had, and she had caught him at it. Shown him what he was up to so he couldn't hide it from himself any longer.

She had also shown him a new side of herself. She was stronger than he'd thought. Before she had seemed so soft—almost girlish—but hers was not a softness of weakness, he realized, but the gentle strength of a mature woman. While she clearly didn't like verbal disagreements; she was not intimidated by him. If needed, she would stand up and not be walked on, regardless of his size or authority. She had a soft, but solid strength to go with her soft and dainty beauty, and the combination was getting to him in a most unprofessional way.

He should have left this to Todd, as planned, but he had needed to see her again.

Wanted to see her again – especially after last night. He'd hoped to exorcise her from his life, his dreams Yet here he was, already silently plotting excuses to need to come see her again.

Leaning across the small steel table, he listened intently as she described her version of what happened that evening. An abbreviated version of the truth, had he known that. The eyes she locked on him seemed so earnest, silently begging him to listen and believe her words, exonerate her friend—the one she called Ronnie.

Her eyes seemed almost too large and lovely for him to look at so closely. It felt too intimate. Though, instead of leaning back, he found himself drawn closer. When she dipped her chin, breaking the magnetic contact of eyes momentarily, a section of silky hair escaped, falling down, partially covering one check when she raised her head again.

Without thinking, he reached out a forefinger to clear the obstruction, catching the golden strands with his fingertip, curling them back around her ear, letting his finger trail lightly down to the line of her jaw. She had such delicate bones, such soft skin.

Her sudden intake of breath had him guiltily jerking his hand away, his eyes jolting to hers. So close, such large golden brown eyes, as sweetly colored as dark honey, as liquid and warm as pools he felt himself melting into slowly, surely. He watched her pupils widen. Felt the soft, surprised breath she expelled brush his face. Something shifted inside him, breath stalling, he felt as if he was tilting, sliding toward an abyss—falling headlong into those molten pools...

She blinked.

Good God! If she hadn't closed those eyes, they would have swallowed him whole! He jerked back against his chair, scooted it a few extra inches away. Grasping the tie at his throat nervously, as if trying to pull his own leash and restrain himself, he grabbed his pen and legal pad and bowed studiously over them. Clearing his throat, without looking up, he ordered, "Go ahead." His voice sounded too rusty for the stern command he had intended.

Frowning at the pad, he waited. He didn't dare glance up. He didn't want to see that look of surprise, of awareness, on her face. That slightly open mouth with those soft sweet lips just waiting for his ... Hell!

He could not do this. Not here, not now, not with this woman. She was a mother! According to Rhonda, a good one, a loving one, not like the mother he'd had. The one that, in anger, he had accused her of being. Sam loved her kids; she even worried about strange young kids out too late at night. He didn't want to think about her compassion; it made him think about those dangerous warm eyes of hers. Eyes warm down to her soul that had almost imprisoned his.

No. She was the prisoner. That is what Jordan needed to keep in mind.

Samantha Wilson was a prisoner; he was a prosecutor; they were in a jail cell, not a bedroom. That should chill his temperature down and temper his pulse. It worked until she stretched out a tentative hand and touched his; he nearly jerked from the electric shock of the simple contact.

"You do believe me don't you?"

God, those eyes! And, she was gnawing on that bottom lip again. He wouldn't mind taking a few nibbles on it himself.

"Of course." He cleared his throat. "Then what happened?" His voice was harsh, his head bent down, pen poised to take more notes.

He sounded angry, Sam thought. She had barely touched him; maybe she shouldn't have. He'd tensed and given her a startled look like she was some dangerous criminal about to assault him. She probably wasn't supposed to make contact with him in any way, but she hadn't been able to resist reaching out to him. He'd suddenly seemed so cold and distant.

Only moments before he'd touched her, hadn't he? When he'd curled his finger around her ear, hadn't his touch lingered against her skin so gently that it had made her gasp, made warmth flush her skin and heat her eyes at the sudden, unexpected intimacy?

For a moment, they'd seemed captured in each other's eyes. A moment that had ticked out in suspended time, suspended breath, suspended awareness of everything but each other. A moment when the heat and humidity spiked suddenly before chilling, just as quickly, when he had shoved himself away from her, a distant stranger again, at the far side of the table.

Or had it all just been Sam's imagination?

Her loneliness making him the fictional man in her dreams for a moment. A long, sweet, close, heated moment that still quivered in her rapid pulse. Just her fairy tale? Or was it real?

Sam had relaxed as she'd sat across the table from Jordan. He had listened with a quiet attention that made her forget they were opponents. It seemed more like a visit with an old friend. She was able to open up and share her thoughts with him, like a friend—except for that sizzle that skittered along her nerves every time she glanced up at that hard, handsome face, those sexy silver eyes that invited her confidence.

Now the atmosphere had shifted again. He seemed angry with her ... or something. She didn't let it deter her; this was too important.

"About Ronnie, she's innocent. You do believe that, don't you?" She pressed for confirmation again.

He looked at her for a while. She didn't see animosity in his eyes, but they were too guarded for her to tell what his was thinking.

He studied her quietly, then answered carefully.

"I have spoken with Rhonda at length. I've come to understand how close and loyal you are to each other," pausing a moment before continuing. "Loyal enough to cover for each other if you felt the need. So for now, I have no choice but to reserve judgment."

"I understand, but I alone am responsible, not Rhonda." Sam declared. "Just remember that I'm the woman you want!" Then she blushed furiously, realizing how that had sounded.

Jordan couldn't help but chuckle, then promised with a wry grin, "I'll remember that." He intended to try his best to forget the truth of her statement.

After carefully going over the statement of the witness on the bank job, the only new information was that she *might* have noticed a young boy in the lot that day, but much earlier. Late afternoon, she'd thought, or before dark anyway. He'd been skateboarding on the sidewalks, jumping his board off curbs, crashing into things. His board sailing off to bang into walls making a very annoying racket. But she couldn't be sure if it had been the same day because 'those dang boys were always horsing around over there'. She was sure, however, that she hadn't heard a skateboard, or noticed a young boy late that night when it was dark. Just that woman and the drunk.

Todd and Detective Mallory had come in this morning and started working their way through the County Bank video for the day in question, laboriously going frame by frame. Todd's eyes were about crossed by early afternoon when they finally reached the frame that showed the cruise lady that had been robbed, making her withdrawal from the bank machine.

They watched it carefully several times, unable to see clearly all she was doing. She did have a habit of pulling her hand way back, pausing between each button she punched, which allowed them to get a count on the number of digits she pushed for the amount. It matched her first smaller withdrawal, one digit less than the larger withdrawal, taken later. So that seemed to fit so far with the printed records, as did the recorded time of withdrawal matching the time stamp for the camera.

"This is starting to feel like when I take my wife out to the movie theater to see a picture. I don't know why she can't just wait to get the DVD. It's a good time to take a little nap. My eyes are starting to roll."

"You sleep when you take your wife to the movies?" Todd hooted. "I'm surprised you're still married, Mallory! Tell me something. When you watch a movie at home what do you do? Fall asleep on the coach, the recliner?

"See, the reason they want to go see it at the theater," Todd continued patiently, " is they want a little romance; they want you to watch it with them. They want you to hold their hand in the scary parts, and put your arm around their shoulders in the romantic parts. Share your popcorn with them, maybe nibble their ear or neck a little in the dark. You need serious help, man. Besides, it's still cheaper than a dozen roses when you're in the doghouse. Try it sometime, you idiot!" He laughed, gave Mallory a friendly punch on the shoulder to go along with the advice.

The monotony had been getting to them. They decided to go get something to eat, and some coffee to wake their brains up before continuing. Over their meal, Todd explained to Mallory that the real trick of a happy marriage was not giving your wife what she said she wanted, but to give her the things she would never tell you that she wanted.

"Well how the hell is a guy supposed to know what they are then?" Mallory groused.

"You keep your eyes and ears open during those chick flicks is one way. I sneak the romance books my wife has finished reading into the bathroom, to read on the can. She wants what those women want in those books, so you just read them and do that."

Mallory eyed Todd, not quite sure if the guy was serious or pulling his leg. Probably wouldn't hurt to read one of those books his wife sighed over, see what kind of pointers he could pick up. He didn't have to tell anyone he'd read it. The guys at the precinct would crucify him if they found out.

It was about a hour after they'd restarted the tape where they'd left off when Mallory suddenly scooted forward in his chair, suddenly stopping and backing up the machine.

"Okay," he motioned to Todd, "look sharp, here's a kid on a skateboard. He looks just like that description you got, wouldn't you say? It's just before dusk."

chapter twenty-one

The young boy seemed to match the description given in the anonymous tip, but then so did a large percentage of all young boys in that age bracket. He did have a noticeably rounded profile, but as he was in constant, acrobatic motion, it was only occasionally captured in the background by the camera mounted on the machine. Other details were hard to distinguish.

Both men automatically ducked when, apparently as a result of a out of control stunt, the small body came flying right at the camera and seemed to crash against the machine. There was the blur of a ball cap, some arms flailing, then the small athlete bent to scoop up his board, and retired to the sidelines for the day apparently, vanishing from the screen.

That brief flurry of excitement was followed by another few hours of pictures of the empty gray sidewalk and lot. A few more customers used the machine as darkness fell, then a lot more of nothing as they watched the time clock tick towards their target.

There was a blinding flash as headlights crossed the screen briefly. A car pulling into the lot. Both men tried to focus carefully on it but, due to the distance, only the very upper part of the screen showed tires rolling down the lot. Just a small portion of the lower body of the car was visible before it pulled completely out of range, apparently parking at the far end.

They glanced at the time, it was just about right. They rewound the tape and ran it again more slowly, trying to identify the car frame, both glued to the top section of the screen. The light color and details they could make out appeared to match the car that Samantha Wilson had been arrested in. It had also been located in that position on the bank lot, as best they could tell from this angle.

"Wait! Stop the frame!" Todd had noticed a blur lower on the screen. "What the hell is that?"

Backing up the tape again, they moved it forward, this time focused on the lower part of the screen. They both saw the blur, then a blockage on the lower part of the frame, shortly after the headlights had passed. It appeared that someone on foot had slipped in from the side, braced an arm over their head to lean on, and was blocking out the camera's angle of their activity at the machine. Only a blurry light colored smudge and what looked like the top of a dark hat or cap was visible on the camera, not the transaction.

They looked at the time stamp on the footage, looked at each other, then both swore simultaneously. Someone very short seemed to be blocking and using the machine at the exact time that the larger sum of money had disappeared from the bank. Then the blur disappeared, slipping sideways off camera, towards what would be the corner of the building, without a clear image of the person being captured.

Mere seconds later, Rhonda Sayles strode up, put her card in the machine and completed her transaction. Looking briefly over her shoulder toward the direction of the parked car, she too slipped away toward the corner of the building, exiting the same direction as the earlier shadow.

"Hey," Mallory said softly, sounding puzzled.

"I noticed that also," said Todd. "She arrived and left in different directions."

"No, not that. Look at this again and see if you notice anything strange." Mallory reset the tape.

"Now, watch her hands."

"Okay, I see them. Looks like she took out the same amount as what we have logged for the transaction..."

"No, that's not it! Watch again." Detective Mallory rewound the tape once more to see if Todd could spot the same thing he had, and to be absolutely sure his own eyes hadn't tricked him.

By the time Jordan finished at the Women's Center, and contacted his office, Elsa informed him the meeting that afternoon had been rescheduled.

"They are so busy tying up loose investigative ends, the Chief promised your meeting tomorrow will be a doozy, Jordan. He said to tell you to take a break while they finish gift wrapping your present!"

"That sounds like great news, Elsa. They must really be busy today. So, what else?"

"Well, here's an interesting little side note. You have a letter here informing you of new representation for Henley, from his new attorney..."

"He changed from Carpenter's group?" Jordan wondered what it might mean that Damon's attorney was either dumping, or being dumped, by one of his lieutenants. *Alleged* lieutenant, he mentally corrected himself. Yeah, right.

"Private or public?"

"Big fat, thick, creamy, rich private attorney type of stationary. He's upgraded, Jordan."

"Hmmm. Sounds like he's about to try to save his own skin and screw Damon."

"Not only sounds like," Elsa advised. Jordan could hear paper rattling over the phone before Elsa read, "The new attorney says he wants a meet, thinks you might have quote 'mutual benefits' unquote, to discuss."

"Lovely." Jordan said in the tone that told Elsa he would have that Wolf-Licking-his-Lips smirk on his face.

"Stall him, Elsa, you know how. No way am I talking to him until I have every dirty deed of Henley's our group can get nailed down. The more I've got solid on him, the less I have to give that bastard to squeal on the big one."

"Already done, sir. You won't have any breaks in your schedule until maybe next week. They are to call back then to find out. And, since your meeting was canceled, I also mentioned you and Todd were both out of the office all day."

"Aren't you subtle?" He laughed. "So I take it you are exiling me for the day?"

"Now you wouldn't want to make a liar out of me, would you boss? I'll fax or e-mail anything you need to your home. Go home for lunch and stay there. You don't wait well, Jordan. If you come in here and pace the carpet bare the rest of the day, I'll go crazy and quit!" Elsa threatened, good naturedly.

Though he was her boss, and they were close in age, Jordan recognized she was having one of her mother-hen days. Besides, she was right. He would just pace waiting to see what the chief brought to the table the next day.

Exhausted and emotionally drained anyway, he needed to take a break and recharge his energy for that conference.

"Okay, heading home, Mom," he gave in teasingly.

Earlier that day, Detective Mallory was able to get his Chief away from the other case. When he and Todd showed him what they'd found on the bank video, the Chief nearly danced in glee. Slapping Mallory on the back with a hearty 'well done', he then assigned him to go pick up more bank tapes, rewarding the detective with even more hours of monotonous viewing. He did, however, gift him with dinner on the Chief and an invite to the task group meeting the next day.

Todd, meanwhile, left to pay a quick call on Ms. Rhonda Sayles. Straight faced, he told her that a new lead had come in from a security video tape. He then asked her to search her memory for any young boys she might have seen in front of, or around behind the bank on her way back to her vehicle.

She was very forthcoming this time, as he had expected, telling him about the party car she had seen with four youths in it.

Neither Todd nor Ms. Sayles mentioned being aware of *any* anonymous tips, but the tipster seemed greatly relieved when Todd stood to leave.

After going home for dinner and a little quality time with his wife, Todd returned to the station to spend the evening helping Detective Mallory work through the new tapes. He would report in to Jordan the next day at the task force meeting which he, also, would be attending.

Jordan had little to do at home but try to relax, to think, and to wait. He was only skilled at one of those tasks.

He had managed to find enough paperwork in his briefcase to fill part of the afternoon in his gloomy, utilitarian home office. He kept checking his fax and e-mail hoping for some new distraction sent from Elsa at the office, but nothing came. He e-mailed Shelley letting her know he was available at home in case she had any case files she wanted to run by and review. He received a curt text message back, but from Elsa, telling him Shelley had nothing that needed attention before tomorrow.

They were clearly conspiring against him to keep him home and isolated today. Jordan suspected that even if the office burned down, Elsa would only call and notify the fire department.

"Nothing you could have done, Jordan," she'd breezily tell him later. True.

His self-imposed office hours finally over with and nothing left to do, he wandered out into the kitchen, opened a cupboard, then the fridge, looking for something that looked like dinner. He tore a few hunks off a head of lettuce, put them in a bowl with some Italian dressing, and called it salad. He opened the fridge again, leaned on the open door staring at the shelves awhile. Nothing inspired him so he finally grabbed a beer, closed the door, and went to call pizza delivery.

Sitting at the bar counter by the phone, munching his lettuce loudly waiting for his dinner, his eyes scanned the room. It was functional, clean enough. All hard surfaces and edges, no color, empty counters, the break room at the office was less boring.

When the pizza came he took it over to the table in the nook instead. He sat down with his back to the kitchen, facing out the glass doors to the patio and back yard. Normally, he spent all his time outside now; he lived and ate outside whenever he could. The house was too dreary. He'd have to do something about that. Someday. Today it was raining, so he had to enjoy his meal and his yard from indoors.

It had rained hard earlier in the afternoon, but now it had settled down to a steady drizzle. Jordan reached over and cracked the door open a bit so he could enjoy the sounds and smells, along with the view.

He kind of enjoyed the rain like this. The earlier downpour had flushed all the stale air from the skies. The air that brushed into the room now was fresh and sweet with intensified watered floral and grass scents. The colors were more intense also, as the trees and shrubs welcomed the long, cool drink. The grass was so emerald it was almost florescent against the dark chocolate of dampened earth and bark. The whole yard looked healthier, happier, the floral colors more lush. The soft sound of the rain washing on the deck, the funny glunking, gurgling sounds it made as it poured down the gutters and spouts, were comforting, soothing somehow.

Jordan stretched his legs out, settled back further in his chair and enjoyed the scenery, letting his mind relax and wander. His eyes drifted down, settling on the silhouette of the empty chair across the table from him.

This morning Sam had been sitting across the table from him. One not much wider than this. The backdrop was not lush and green, but the institutional beige of painted concrete block walls.

Even in that harsh setting, Sam had been beautiful and he had wanted her.

He snorted softly, thinking of his asinine statement about not wanting any woman in his kitchen. What an idiot he was for saying that. What a fool he had been for meaning it. Sitting here now he could easily picture her across from him. Listening to the soft sounds of her voice, as soothing as the quiet rain; watching the emotions dance across her face and reflect in those eyes.

Just before he had left her this morning, she had reached across the table and lightly touched his arm. He should have had his sleeves rolled down. Even now he could feel his arm tingle as he recalled the electric charge which with just her fingertips touching his skin shot through him.

He could imagine what full body contact between them could do!

She'd reached out to touch him, those dark eyes on his, and told him how sorry she was that she lied to him. She had asked him if he was sorry for hating her, women, she'd corrected shyly. He had told him gently that he didn't hate her. Rattled by her touch, he had almost blurted that he didn't think of her as a woman.

How stupid would that have sounded?

He would have meant he didn't see her as *just* a woman, just *any* woman. She was more, she was special, she was *Sam*.

"No, I don't hate you, doll. That's the whole problem. I want you in my bed, my kitchen …," Jordan broke off when he realized he was telling this all out loud to an empty chair, in his empty house.

"Well, hell!" He scrubbed his hands across his face. What the hell was wrong with him? He was sitting here talking to himself. Well, actually that wasn't so bad. Worse was that he was sitting here talking to her! He sure didn't hate her, just the reverse, he …

Ohhh no! Hell no! No way! He was not falling for her, he ordered himself. In lust? Yeah, okay. But, ... that? No, impossible. Not a chance!

He jumped up from the table and ran from it and his thoughts as if his seat was on fire. He wasn't getting suckered into *that* kind of pain again.

Thank God Sam was in jail where he was safe from her!

chapter twenty-two

Over a week had passed since Jordan last had a moment to contemplate the world outside his windows, or his inner world-shaking feelings about a certain blonde inmate.

Everyone involved in the expanded task group, and all the linked investigative agencies, had been run off their feet. The doozy of a meeting that the Chief had promised, had been just that. There were even a few last minute surprises uncovered by Detective Mallory and Todd that had linked the County Bank job firmly to the Henley task group cases.

In their review of the bank video, they had not only been able to clear Rhonda and Sam of that crime, thank God; but also had noticed that some object on the cash machine, located between the camera and the keypad, had been removed only moments before Rhonda used the machine. At first Todd and Mallory thought that a part had broken off the machine, possibly causing a malfunction when the young skateboarder had slammed into it. When they showed and proposed this to the Chief, he immediately knew what had happened, and that it was deliberate.

A review of that and other bank tapes showed that the objects affecting the camera views were the little black magnetic scanning recorders, like the one found in Cocky Chuck's pocket. Each time the scanners were magnetically attached or removed from cash machines, young kids or teens were either skateboarding or rough housing around , and banging into or slapping the ATMs.

The scanners were then passed on through the post office box drops to the part of the organization that created the counterfeit debit cards from the account numbers and PINs recorded by the black boxes. Each duplicate debit card was used only once to raid an account before being passed back to 'burn'. This one time use delayed and frustrated the ability to block the illegal transactions.

As in the case of the little old lady at County Bank, by the time the statement arrived noting a incorrect transaction, usually a same day transaction that appeared to be an error, the crooks already had the cash and had long since burned the card that could tie it to them.

Even if one of the unlikely foot soldiers were caught? Hey, they were just kids fooling around! Not only did the minors draw less notice and suspicion, but the best guys were the quickest and shortest, which further helped to foil the security cameras.

The big, bad, bank robber that had removed the cash from the County Bank account was only four feet three inches tall, and all of ten years old! He still had the rounded remnants of a baby face, but was a demon on wheels, his best stunts targeted skateboard crashes, and quick fingers.

The way the organization was utilizing the young had made all the team members feel nauseous, thinking of their own families, and those of their friends. Not only was the organization suspected of bringing drugs into the school yards of their community, but the predatory use, abuse, and criminal training of such young boys could not be allowed to continue.

Robert "Rob" Fountain, Henley's cohort, was found and arrested on initial charges with many more to come. His son, Cocky Chuck, was recharged as an adult. His party car was impounded and his two pals, "Bob" and Craig, were also found to be part of the postal-bank scam team, stealing credit cards from mailboxes and gathering other useful data.

The most wrenching story was Chuck's little brother, Timmy Fountain. Youth Social Services would currently take custody of the young skateboarding bank robber, but the ten-year old boy's future was bleak. Even though the Fountain father was finally rolling over on respected citizen, ole' Honest Abe Damon, in return for leniency for his criminally-raised sons. Fountain was able to pin Damon to both the postal fraud scams and identify him as the one who had the black scanners turned into counterfeit debit cards, receiving the bulk of the proceeds.

Henley and his new lawyer were left with very little left to trade that the prosecutor didn't already have nailed down with hard evidence and other testimony. He admitted that Damon was the other key holder to the Henley Enterprises postal box, allowing them to pass off to each other without personal contact. Tough negotiations were still underway in the Henley plea. It appeared that Henley might be willing to give up evidence of illegal practices by the Carpenter law firm, long time defenders for Damon's group, to buy himself a little less time behind bars.

The handwritten list in Box A, the Henley Enterprises box, was found to be a list of stolen and junked vehicle serial numbers. Reports had come in from Japan and other Far Eastern countries that newer vehicles registered under the junked vehicle serial numbers were being found that matched the year and models of locally stolen vehicles. Jordan felt it was only a matter of time before Henley gave Damon up as the mastermind of the overseas shipment of stolen cars that the list indicated.

There was still a lot of work to be done rounding up all the members of the various criminal enterprises, preparing the rest of the charges, and sorting out which agencies would prosecute the various crimes. However the bulk of the task group phase of the work was done. Once the top layer of the organization was brought in, the general public would be informed, but public acclaim mattered little to Jordan. As a result of the Henley case, there was something very important to Jordan personally that he felt he needed to see to now.

Shelley was at her desk, busily organizing it and her office now that the stacks, and piles, and chairs full of files were gone from her office.

Jordan leaned against her doorjamb and tapped on the frame. She looked up, saw him and froze like a doe, a look of mild terror in her eyes. Dropping her gaze to his empty arms, she relaxed slightly.

"Shelley, there's something I'd like to ask you."

"Oh, God, Jordan. Please! Not more files? Not today!"

Jordan laughed. "Relax. I guess we never let you get completely moved in before we buried you in here, did we?" His smile was sympathetic. "No, this is something else. May I come in?"

Relieved she'd smiled back, motioning to her newly emptied chair.

"Please, as long as you leave your piles of files outside."

He sat, his face sobering.

"Hey, again, I want to thank you. You did an amazing job. Excellent work! I'm sorry we had to cut you out, but I'm sure you understand now." He looked up hopefully.

"Sure. And thanks for the thanks, it helps." Shelley had been hurt at first. It was hard being new, wanting to be part of the team and being shut out. Jordan's words and manner toward her now felt good, really good. She'd been resentful. "I'm sorry about what I said…well, about …"

Jordan held his hand up palm out to stop her, shaking his head with a small smile.

"You were right, and not the first or last to mention my … issues. That was some of the best advice I've received."

"Advice?" Shelley said the word slowly, with raised brows. If he wanted to call her behind-the-back attack on him 'advice', calling him a whiny, immature woman-hater, then who was she to argue?

He grinned at her, letting her know all was forgiven.

"Yes, advice. Excellent advice. You seem to understand difficult men well, which is one of the reasons I'm asking for your help now." Jordan paused a moment, head down, thinking about how to approach what he wanted to say to her.

"When Todd came to me and told me that he had run into you after you resigned from the Public Defender's office, he mentioned you said you needed absolution." He raised serious, questioning eyes. Seeing her nod, he leaned forward and continued, holding her eyes.

"That's part of the reason I hired you, Shelley. I understood that need. I've struggled with it myself. I think, I hope, I'm finally finding the paths to cleanse my soul, to start fresh. So I think what I have to ask you might … well, it might appeal to you.

"First, it's important that you understand that this is not a job requirement, it's completely outside of your work for me. So I won't even ask you for an answer. It's your own personal decision, understand?"

Shelley nodded, surprised at the serious turn the conversation had taken; that Jordan was sharing such personal emotions with her. She waited to see where this was headed.

"I know it was tough for you being cut out here. I know the Henley case had a special impact on your decisions, your life. He, and those he worked for, caused a lot of destruction and corruption.

They hurt a lot of kids and turned their lives in a direction from which they may never recover." He paused again, his face grim.

"But, there is one. One young boy that is still young enough, I think, to really help. He is at the preteen age where intervention now just might make all the difference. His father is going to jail. Back to jail, again. His mother will be deemed unfit or unable to raise and monitor him properly because she failed to do so with his older brother. His older brother is also going to jail, as an adult. You've met him, you call him Cocky Chuck.

"Anyway, the younger boy, Timmy, he's never really had much of a chance. You have a lot of connections with the best agencies and programs from your public defender days. You know the foster system better. And you know who the people are that really help and make a difference, and the ones that can really hurt a young boy.

"Henley and the others destroyed his childhood. I'm hoping you can, I guess, just guide or oversee his situation maybe? See that he gets into the right hands. I want him to have a chance at a different life. All I'm suggesting is that you might be able to steer him to the right people in the system.

"I can't; I have to wait. I can't get involved with him now because he is a witness and he helped commit the crimes I'm taking to trial. It's going to be a long time before I won't have trial conflicts. Too long, I'm afraid.

"Afterwards, I want to find him, hope to mentor him somehow. Be a Big Brother maybe, whatever. But my hands are tied for now. So," he rose, reaching in his pocket, "I'm just going to leave his name on your desk and leave it for you to decide if there is anything you can, or want, to do personally." He set the folded scrap of paper down, and turned to leave. "Thanks again for all the good work, Shelley."

"Jordan," she stopped him. "I know you don't want an answer from me, but you know?" She smiled and reached over to grab the scrap of paper and tuck it in her purse. "I always kind of wanted a little brother. Thanks."

Jordan's long struggle with Abe Damon was almost over; a conviction was sure. Even after realizing he had finally accomplished something in his career that he was truly proud of, it still turned out to not be enough now. Somehow.

He thought at first this lack of satisfaction was because it just hadn't sunk in yet. The sense of incompleteness should have disappeared in a few days. But the feeling lingered on, an unexplainable malaise. Jordan excused his down mood, to himself and others, by saying, "Just a let down after all the excitement … still work to be done before it's time to celebrate." But somehow it just didn't ring true in his ear.

Hell! Why was he not ecstatic? What was this restless sense of unfinished business? And what kept nagging at the back of his mind?

Sam. Sam and Rhonda.

It was hard to believe that over two weeks had flown by since his last visit to Sam, though he had shared many restless imaginary nights with her since then. He wondered if anyone had found the time to inform either one of them of the good news?

It was obvious now that neither of them had even had the remotest connection to the crime at the bank. Just a pure coincidence of time and place.

So why, Jordan asked himself, had they both acted so guilty? As if they were hiding something? What was to hide? Nothing he could see that Sam wasn't already paying for.

So why?

What *was* that all about?

"Boss, I think you better see this." Elsa gently laid an opened letter on Jordan's desk, then quietly left the room.

Jordan read the letter twice before it registered.

chapter twenty-three

"You did *this* just to write a stupid book?"

The prosecutor shouted down at her as soon as she'd been seated in the interview room.

Sam wanted to tell him she thought of it as a novel now. Not *just* a book; not now that she was filling it with people and all their hopes and dreams.

She was tempted to mention that she really hoped it wouldn't be stupid when it was done, but ... Looking up at the tight line around his mouth, braced fists on his hips, his tie yanked all askew, she decided that maybe being locked in a room with a very angry man was not the best time for humor.

She almost smiled anyway. He looked so sexy when he was all fired up, and all *loomy*, scowling down at her, pacing and passionate. Instead she looked down at the hands clasped primly in her lap and tried to compose herself. It appeared the gig was up, she sighed, she might as well confess her innocence, and let them toss her out of jail—

And that was *exactly* what he expected.

"My god, woman! This is not a prank or game. You were almost charged with bank robbery, for god's sake! I want a full and detailed confession of your innocence. And I want it *now!*"

He wanted to intimidate her into surrendering her plan. Her dream. Her goals.

Stupid book? Her dream was nothing more to him than a stupid book?

Well, it might well turn out to be that, but it was crucial she do one very important thing.

Sam had to *try*. She would never regret writing a stupid book as much as she would forever regret not even *trying* before she died. And if it failed and was indeed stupid? Then she had to try again, practice, try harder, until she got it right. But there was one thing she could not do. She could not, would not just give up and surrender because there would always be obstacles standing between her and what she hoped to accomplish.

She might choose some day to quit writing, the burning need might pass, or she might try her best and realize she was not able to create something that pleased her. But she was *not* going to surrender just because someone else thought it was a silly or stupid goal.

Looking up she saw he was busily flipping back and forth through the pages in her file, frowning he asked, "They never did a full psyche evaluation on you?"

Oh!

Sitting straight, back rigid, shoulders back and chin raised, in a tight voice, Samantha asked, "Do you have a digital recorder on you?"

Startled, "Of course." Jordan pulled his out and turned it on. He started to record the date, time, location and parties, thinking that she was going to make a statement, when her out thrust palm abruptly interrupted him.

"This statement is personal, not official. Just record it," she snapped. "Ronnie, this is a message for you. My kids ratted me out to the prosecutor trying to get me out of jail. But I am here, and I'm staying here. I pled guilty, and no one can force me to change that.

"This *man,*" she nearly spat the word, "The prosecutor needs a detailed statement of what happened the night of the crime, crimes. I'm afraid I don't recall," she slanted a defiant smile at him. "But feel free to give him a statement exonerating yourself. For that you have my permission. Oh, and I am not under any duress except that he is overbearing, insufferable, and seems to think I'm a nutcase, and I refuse to speak to him any further!"

Sam stood up and motioned for him to turn off the recorder.

"Ms. Wilson ... Samantha ... "

She just turned away, went to the door and stood rigidly facing it waiting for the guard to free her from his presence.

Jordan was bewildered. He'd been routed by the tiny blonde inmate that he *thought* he had gone to rescue!

"You did what?"

Rhonda's normally sultry phone voice had climbed to a screech when her attorney called to inform her of the action he had taken.

"How many days ago?"

"Oh god," she moaned. They already had it.

"You felt *compelled*, did you?" She snarled. "How could you... you knew..."

"Yes, I remember asking you to release my bank records to the police investigators, but ..."

"We discussed the *possibility*," she emphasized the word, "that I might be in an uncomfortable position because of that bank robbery ..."

"Yes, I know you told me to confess to helping Sam then, but it wasn't necessary ..."

"You're kidding." Rhonda shifted her phone to the other ear in case it would hear something different. "Well, I knew they were *suspicious*, but they never said I was a suspect!"

"A hostile witness? I was as sweet as sugar, how ... Oh, it means unwilling? I bet Prosecutor Campbell never said that."

"I am being serious, but..."

"I don't care what your instructions were. Sam was never in any real jeopardy, she ...'

"What? She was the main suspect? I never heard it went that far!"

"What second reason *required* you to send the letter?"

"And how exactly was there a conflict of interest with one of your other clients?"

"Sam never, ever threatened to murder me! Who told you that?"

"Well, I can guarantee you that when she learns you sent that letter to her kids she will be out for blood from both of us!"

Rhonda slammed her phone down on the desk, furious with her attorney. But she had forgotten she was on her cell phone. It just made her angrier when she saw she had just cracked the glass face and could still hear his voice after she had so dramatically hung up on him in disgust.

"Stupid smart phone!" She ripped out the battery and tossed the broken pieces in her trash can.

Rearing back in her chair, she cursed and covered her face with both hands. Rhonda could not believe her damn attorney had released Sam's letter of intent to her children without checking with anyone first.

"Compelled, my ass! A high sounding word for a dirty low down action!"

This was a complete disaster!

Sam was going to kill her. Sam's kids were going to disown her as their dear "Aunt Ronnie". Then kill her for helping their mom and hiding it from them. Sam's sweet parents would cut her off from cocoanut pound cake and family holiday dinners because she had—helped Sam sneak into jail before the grandkids could stop her—their last planned line of defense. But it wouldn't really matter anyway, because by the time Christmas rolled around Rhonda would already be dead several times over from the younger, murderous generations.

Rhonda's assistant walked in while she was still groaning and holding her head and, brushing aside a piece of broken plastic, dropped a folded, lilac-scented note on the desk then left just as silently.

Only Samantha's mother sent her handwritten lilac-scented notes. Rhonda lifted it to her face and breathed in the soothing scent. This was probably the last note she'd ever receive from the dear woman.

Breaking the wax seal on Mrs. Wilson's note she slowly opened it.

Rhonda Dear, My grandchildren have been in touch and they are quite troubled about their mother. If possible could you arrange to go up and visit with them this weekend? I know you are very busy and it is a long drive, but I would deeply appreciate it. Thank you, dear

Such a classy lady. She probably meant something more like: "You helped screw this up. Now go fix it!" But she had such an elegant, courteous way about it.

Rhonda was not about to wait for the weekend. She should leave right away.

Buzzing her assistant, Rhonda started issuing orders to cancel appointments and make travel arrangements. "And send someone out to fetch me the stupidest model of prepaid cell phone they can find. Preferably one where if you snap it closed it hangs up. And if the prosecutor calls while I am gone ..."

"Don't tell him anything," her assistant finished. "Don't worry, I'll handle the prosecutor."

And she had. Quite efficiently.

Jordan had placed a call to Rhonda Sayles next.

First on her home phone, then her cell, and leaving voicemails and text messages when he couldn't reach her. When hours had passed with no response to his urgent messages, he called her office's main number to learn Ms. Sayles was not available at the moment. When he pressed for urgency he was told she was out of the office. So he impatiently demanded to know where she was and when she was due back, informing her assistant that it was important business because he was the prosecutor.

"You're the prosecutor? Really? That handsome man that hates woman?"

Jordan had impatiently snapped a yes before hearing the next question. "No. Yes, I am the prosecutor. No, to the rest."

Why did everyone keep saying that?

"Well, then, if you *are* the prosecutor, that's different. I'd be glad to give you the confidential details of Ms. Sayles agenda", she said courteously, "just as soon as you serve me the subpoena for that information." She hung up on him.

Jordan did not hate women... But...

He had never in his life physically harmed or abused or sexually harassed a woman, and he never would. But he thought with shame of how he couldn't claim the same when it came to verbal abuse. He remembered how shocked he was when he heard Shelley speaking about him that day in the office. Shocked because she was right, and she had opened his eyes to what an ass he had become. And he was trying to do better. Trying very hard. He hadn't paid a fine in weeks.

But today he could think of three women that he was at least mentally cursing: Sam, Rhonda, and her smart mouthed assistant.

Heading for the outer office, he waited for Elsa to complete her phone call.

"I'll be out of the office the rest of today, and probably tomorrow. Message any calls to my email, please, and I'll check them later. I'm driving up the coast to meet with the Wilson children."

Then without another word he pulled three bills from his pocket and stuffed them in the fine jar on her desk and headed for the elevator. After taking four strides, he turned back, and silently stuffed another hundred dollar bill in the jar before leaving the office.

Recalling there was a son and daughter, he felt he better pay in advance just in case the daughter was anything like her stubborn mother.

Elsa waited to make sure he was gone for good before breaking out in a huge grin. Looked like her boy was having some serious woman trouble. Good. He needed it.

At first, Jordan had been dumbfounded when he read the letter Elsa placed on his desk. He had to read it again, to be sure it wasn't just a product of his wishful thinking.

If this was true ... Sam was totally innocent! She had been unjustly incarcerated! He would get her out immediately. Thinking to double check the information first with Rhonda, he paused.

"No, ... wait just one damn moment!" His growl matched the scowl forming on his face. Surely Ms. Sayles would have known that her dear friend, Sam, was innocent, he reasoned. Why had she not said a word when it was so obvious how much she cared for her?

Jordan drummed his fingers on the desk, wanting to jump up and take action immediately, but unsure of the best course to take. Something was not adding up here. He examined the letter again, including the attached envelope. No, he wouldn't talk to Rhonda yet, though she was closer. He would go up the coast ...

No, first he needed to see Samantha.

Which had gotten him nowhere with the stubborn, foolish woman. He didn't even know why she was suddenly furious with him.

Maybe the children had more common sense than their mother or their "Aunt Ronnie"? He certainly hoped someone did.

On his way up the coast, Prosecutor Campbell cast his mind over everything he'd found out about the children of Samantha Wilson.

The documents processed during her arrest and incarceration gave general information on next of kin, addresses and ages. A quick records search when she became a suspect in the bank robbery gave a little more detail on her relatives. He knew that they both lived on the coast up north near a growing city where both were employed. They had separate homes that they owned with partners, but were unmarried. They were close in age.

But it was from his luncheon with Rhonda Sayles that he had learned that Sam's children were not only close in age, but close in heart. She had spoken of Penny and Paul with deep affection and told him how talented, thoughtful, and wonderful they were. And how they were both so close to their mother. Respecting her as a parent, but also considering her a close friend. That extended to their loves and long time partners also, Paul's Brittany, and Penny's Aaron. A tight knit and loving family. Good people, just like their mom, and just like her parents.

And how lucky and proud Rhonda was to be their Honorary Aunt. She told him she took her duties seriously, and related a humorous tale about how she sat Sam down one day to discuss the "birds and the bees".

"Really, Sam, I think it would be best if you let me handle your kid's sex education," Rhonda had announced.

"You think it's time to discuss it with them, but you think I'm too naïve to handle it, Ronnie?" Sam had asked, amused.

"Naive?" Rhonda had snorted. "Sam you are *The* most naive and innocent woman I have ever known that went through childbirth twice, and probably the only one that hasn't played around since! I'm quite sure you qualify as a born-again-virgin! "

Sam eyes had flashed down, and Rhonda could just see her thoughts. *Gosh, has it really been that long?*

"So yes, and I am inviting your prim, naive little self to the classes. You're sure to learn something," Rhonda had drawled, deadpan.

"And from the way their mom's eyes kept widening and the flush of her cheeks, the kids said they thought their mom might have even learned more than they had. They are such a riot! "

Rhonda bragged of how thoughtful they were, recalling one occasion in particular.

One fun, crazy, carefree Sunday, when the kids were in high school, the four of them had gone to the park for a picnic and day of play in the sun. It had been a wonderful time for the four friends because that was the nature of Sam's relationship with her children. She respected her kids as interesting people in their own right. They were among her closest and best friends, and the kids seemed to feel the same with their mom. Rhonda had always enjoyed that relationship also, as Aunt Ronnie, she considered them very mature, balanced, fun young adults.

At some point that day, Paul had captured Sam and Rhonda together, giving the camera big, corny grins. Arms around each other's shoulders, they were carefree in their sloppy torn sweatshirts, baseball-capped heads tipped together with escaped wisps of blonde and brunette hairs blowing intermingled between their happy sun burnt faces.

It was the furthest thing from a studio portrait shot of the two imaginable. It looked more like the type pictures little kids brought back proudly from summer camp.

But when Paul had the film developed, both he and his sister, Penny, had realized it captured the special closeness, the essence of the relationship, between the two best friends. Pooling their meager allowances, they had secretly had the picture duplicated, enlarged, and framed, then visited and presented one first to Ronnie, then another to their mom with flowers, one Mother's Day.

Rhonda's eyes had watered even as she told him the story, remembering how thoughtful the gift had been. And how they had thought of her and honored her, also, on Mother's Day! She had been deeply touched.

"I cried tears of happiness for a good hour," she confessed as if to a great crime. Adding, "After the kids left, of course."

Rhonda heard from Sam later that when her kids gave their mom her picture, she had burst into tears on the spot. The kids had laughed, hugging their mom at her reaction. Penny had teased her affectionately, "We're glad you like it, mom! Aunt Ronnie loved hers also, but at least she waited 'til we left to start bawling!"

The kids had understood how overwhelmed she had been, despite her gruff "thank you."

"Such great kids! They made their mom's job so much easier, raising them alone."

"When I told you Sam was a saint, I didn't mean in a religious sense. She had a rough time as a single parent trying to give her kids the kind of loving, nurturing upbringing that she'd had, while working such long hours. But unlike many in that situation, Sam stayed sweet and sunny, never complaining, always grateful to have such great kids.

Jordan had asked what had happened when Sam had lost her job after the big market crash and following recession.

"Fortunately for Sam, the kids were mostly grown and off to college on scholarships. They are so smart and talented," The proud "aunt" added. "She had been setting aside for their college earlier, and was able to sell her house and down size and bolster the fund for the rest of their tuition, and lease a small cottage for herself." Rhonda's downturned mouth indicated she had not thought much of said cottage. "She managed to hang on until she could find a position again." Her breezy voice belied her expression.

"That must have been much easier than before when there was no affirmative action." Jordan prompted.

Rhonda had snorted. "Obviously you haven't read the studies that show that women still, decades later, aren't receiving equal pay with men. But, yes, many things have improved. Sam's thrilled for the opportunities her daughter has."

"But ....?" Rhonda hadn't said it, but he heard it in her tone.

"But, it isn't the only thing that has changed. Sam's kids grew up with technology. More comfortable with a computer keyboard than a pen and paper. Our generation is not as comfortable in the technology area unless it has been part of our daily lives all along, and it has changed drastically and rapidly. Sam never was trained much in her former jobs, and for her it is a bewildering maze with a language of its own.. She is smart enough, she just never needed it before, and was never supported with training. She is still more comfortable doing her writing with pen and paper ...," Rhonda hesitated before adding, "Writing letters I mean. She is not one for email. I don't believe she even has a computer of her own, and she claims she doesn't want a phone that is smarter then she is."

Jordan had not noticed the betraying comment at the time. Now he knew that Rhonda had slipped up. She had not meant correspondence when she spoke of writing.

"At any rate, Sam had also not applied for a job in decades, always being moved along by her boss, so she was in for a shock. Suddenly none of her talent or people skills mattered much when it came to submitting résumés. That's all filtered by computer now, you know, and if the line that reads college education is blank they are kicked out and never considered. Then there are the requirements for being experienced in the main software programs. Another reject for Sam without ever seeing a person for an interview.

"And an interesting twist, when she did get a chance to interview with a few young modern managers, she was stunned to be told they were sorry but she was "over qualified" and they were afraid she would be dissatisfied and not stay with the company long term. Ironic, isn't it?"

Rhonda gave a nasty smile and leaned forward. "Do you know what that really meant, Jordan? It meant she was an older woman and they figured she couldn't learn new tricks, they didn't want to pay her health care, and yet they were savvy enough to avoid the age and sex discrimination laws."

Is that really happening? Jordan had wondered then and now.

"But there is always one job that is relatively easy to get. Sam landed a sales job. A commission only sales job. The way that works is you can work for any amount of time for the company for free unless you sell something. Then you receive a small percentage commission. After it is delivered. After no one screws up along the line and delivers the product to the customer and they are satisfied. Sometimes months later after the item has been on order and fortunately has not been discontinued in the meantime, or damaged during shipping or delivery.

"But, I'm afraid I've talked enough. I have to get back to my office. Thank you for lunch, Jordan. It has been most enjoyable." Rhonda had left him still chewing over what she had just told him.

Yes, he'd pulled a wealth of information from Ms. Sayles about her best friend and her family when he had invited her to that lunch – except, of course, any recent history or the key incriminating confidences.

Bett Bone

chapter twenty-four

U naware of the storm that was about to burst over her
head, Samantha had been making good progress on her
novel in recent weeks, despite the threatening distractions – or
possibly because of them.

Her children had become increasingly vocal about trying to
find some way to get her out of jail. And then there had been that little
bank robbery annoyance. Fortunately, the kids did not know about
that worry! But both concerns had made Sam realize that she had to
buckle down and focus on her writing before something—or
someone—blocked her.

She'd had a good start on her work and had defined who her
female lead character was when it had dawned on her that the
romance book she was writing lacked two significant elements, a
romancer—or was that romancee—and some sex. Ending up a single
mom, Sam did not remember much about sex beyond childbirth
pains.

The childbirth pains had been worth it; she couldn't
remember if the preview was.

So Ronnie had given her some scandalous sex scene ideas,
too scandalous for Sam's dreamy ideas of the romance she wanted
to write. After all, most women wanted romantic sex, not just sex,
didn't they? Sam wasn't completely sure. She suspected she,
personally, would prefer just plain old romance over easy, hold the
wild sex. But as she did not recall having any wild sex, she might be
wrong.

But Ronnie hadn't been much help providing the kind of male
lead Sam needed. It had been amusing, though, to hear Ronnie sort
through her string of boy toys trying to decide which would make the

best sample to smuggle in for her best friend. But when she found out Sam only needed an imaginary man—instead of real live flesh—Ronnie had thrown up her hands and told Sam to put that *imagination* to work.

From the time she was a child, Sam had been a collector. A collector of thoughts, events, a million little ideas. They formed together in her mind in unusual ways triggered by her overactive imagination, and made her wish to tell that story someday.

She had hundreds of scraps of paper, tucked away in a box, where she had tried to capture those ideas before they were forgotten or lost. It had been a life-long compulsion and need to get those ideas out of her head, tucked safely away on paper, so her curious mind was clear to collect more information, create new thoughts, and explore little pieces of life and her world.

Sam thought everyone was like that until she was in her teens and some boy in her class told her she was weird. He told her people did not need to come up with their own ideas because they could just watch movies or television if they needed some new ones.

Sam thought *he* needed a new one, but she was way too polite to tell him so. But she did tease him.

"Did you catch that movie where the aliens come down in a spaceship and steal people's brains?" Sam asked him, thinking that if such a thing did happen he didn't need to worry. She'd been quite surprised when she had come across him in a store, a decade later, and he told her he'd just seen the movie she had once told him about. Someone had made her imaginary movie.

But it was time to focus ahead, not behind.

Make this all worth the cost and write until she couldn't see or think any longer.

Reaching up, she unpinned Paul's photo from the wall and spread it out on her cot. She had tried to write a chapter earlier that had a sunset beach scene in it that was disappointing. It had just seemed flat, so she had resigned herself to having to redo that section later. But then Paul had brought her the exquisite photo of her favorite beach. Now she would be able to capture it in all its depth and textures.

Settling on her bunk with Paul's picture, gazing at the glorious sunset scene, Sam closed her eyes momentarily. Purging her mind of all distractions, she sought to recapture the pleasures of her personal experiences, to infuse her mind with the scents and sounds of the setting. Then she began to people it with her characters.

The female lead was already an old and familiar friend, but now she needed to flesh out the man that would be deserving of her. What kind of man could steal a woman's heart in that magical setting.

An image appeared in her mind; Sam recognized him. She tried to deny to herself that the image she saw was that of the man that had come to see her, to question her.

Sam could picture the silhouette of her man, dark against the shimmering crimson. He would be, he was, tall, broad shouldered, and handsome, moving with male grace in his stride. His inherent sensuality and magnetism would send sparkles flickering along a woman's veins at the touch of his hand, as he enclosed hers within his strong grasp, to stroll together along the sand.

She would pause to take in the breathtaking sunset and have the last of her breath stolen away as he stood dangerously close behind her, his lips softly brushing the nape of her neck, sending shivers down her spine, and heat through her veins.

As the sun surrendered to the horizon, she would surrender to the tenderness of the lips warmly nuzzling her ear, turning into his arms. His head would lower, she'd burn with tension, then his lips would sip, then crush hers, their hunger intense.

Deepening, then softening and savoring their joining, his tongue caressing the sensitive inner tissue of her lower lip until a fiery trail blazed across her senses to rival the fire that blazed across the sunset sky.

Even a cool breeze stealing across the sands with encroaching darkness, would gain notice only in contrast to the heat of joined lips, the warmth and shelter of enclosing arms in a universe of their own, beginning and ending where their bodies molded, touched, arched, ached, and demanded.

Sam gazed at the picture. She could feel herself locked in the silhouette of that passionate embrace. She could taste salt-kissed lips, feel her chilled nose warm from heated breath, burning lips, greedy on hers. She could feel a weakness in her knees, helpless in the dizzying kiss. Her heart, her breath, caught, suspended in the spell of lips and tongue and the hard exciting contours of her lover's body, searing, softening her flesh, pressing against her belly.

Shaking, Sam returned regretfully to reality.

It was only her characters , she reminded herself, their passions, not his, not hers, in that romantic scene.

Sam did not belong there; for it was only fiction.

The bolt on her cell door startled her as it unlocked. "Inmate 48549, come with me," the guard took her down the hall.

What now? Why couldn't they just leave her alone? Though it was probably a good time to be interrupted. Sam was afraid of where her thoughts had been leading.

When the guard opened a door, there he stood.

The man from the beach, the man of her dreams.

He was waiting for her, so charged with emotion and passion that, when his eyes locked with hers, she felt that a bolt of lightning had struck her.

Knees weak, Sam had dropped into her chair only to find that all that passion was *not* the good kind, but fueled by disgust and anger.

When your mom made her decision to focus herself seriously on something she'd always wanted, it was very difficult for her. Difficult for her to even tell *me* her secret dream."

Freed from the need to keep Sam's secret, after the lawyer spilled the beans, Rhonda knew the best thing she could do for her friend was to go be with the children, and help them understand why they'd been deceived. Not only because they would be angry, but especially because they would be wounded, as they'd always been so close to their mom.

"Life long dreams are very fragile things. Many people never even attempt to make them come true. Because while you hold them they represent the future and hope. I think, in fact, that it was very hard for Sam to acknowledge even to herself that she wanted to actually write a book, instead of just dreaming about it. And that is where all a person's insecurities and doubts attack; telling you it is not possible; you aren't good enough; you're a fool for thinking about it so do *not* tell anyone.

"I know she thought you might see her desperate need to write her book as kind of silly."

There was a moment of silence while all this was absorbed before Penny replied softly. "Well, of course we don't think it's silly."

"Yeah," Paul added, "She was always writing things, poems, and stuff."

"Did you know your mom wanted to be a famous author, Paul?" Brittany asked.

"Oh, sweetie," Rhonda reached out to squeeze the young woman's arm. "Sam doesn't want to be a famous author, or bestseller, or win literary awards. She just wants to write. She has so many ideas for books she has started, she just finally wants the time and the challenge and the pleasure of seeing if she can finish one. And create something *she* would enjoy reading. She has so many stories bottled up she wants to tell, and maybe share with others like her who want to get away from the daily grind for a few moments, and relax and laugh, or travel somewhere else for a while, whether it's to a romantic story or a different land. But we all knew she liked to write down her thoughts and save them. No important piece of paper with blank areas on it was ever safe left out around Sam."

"That's for sure," Paul agreed. "I learned never to leave my school spiral notebooks out on the table overnight, Brit, or the next day when I'd be taking notes in class I'd flip a page only to find it filled with one of mom's story ideas."

"But Brittany," Rhonda added, "I doubt Sam would *object* to having a best selling book as long as it didn't take any of *her* time away from writing another one. After all, she can't keep going to jail for free room and board to support her habit."

And, as she knew it would, the reminder brought out the intense emotions and anger that needed to be vented and dealt with.

"Oh yes, my mom the crazy woman that wants to go to jail." Penny shook her head. Her voice rose in sudden anger. "I don't care how many 'good reasons' she thinks she has, it's insane. Did she honestly think I was going to just sit here and say, 'Oh sure, mom, go to jail, that makes sense to me. I'll support that decision.' Not on your life!"

Gathering volume and ammunition, she continued forcefully. "And if she thinks either Paul or I don't want her in jail because of our 'reputations', well, that's a bunch of garbage! Aunt Ronnie, you know it's mom we're worried about, not ourselves. It just proves she is off her rocker thinking we'd worry about something that petty if there was something she really wanted to do! Why didn't she tell us? Why didn't she ask us to help her?" Bursting into angry, hurt tears, Penny jumped up and tore off to the bathroom.

Paul cleared his throat, blinking rapidly, watching Aaron follow his sister to comfort her when she was ready. "I think what Pen is trying to say," he cleared his throat again. "What we're both saying is that we support her decision to write. We know how much work and time she devoted to raising us, and we both want to help her have a chance now to do something for herself. We understand *why* she wants to write, but why in such a dangerous way?" Seeing his pain, Brittany reached out to hold his hand and Paul's voice steadied when he asked, "Where on earth did she get the idea of going to jail to write a book?"

"I recall your mom mentioning Watergate when she was first trying to explain this to me. I didn't get it then, but I realize now why she brought it up." Seeing their confused looks, Rhonda explained.

"When we were young adults there was a national scandal. It started simply with some clumsy burglars breaking into opposition party campaign headquarters located in the Watergate hotel. Seemingly no big deal, right? But upon investigation, turns out the burglars had ties and a trail that led ever higher up into the ruling party re-election campaign, and then on up into federal government appointees and offices and the White House itself; leading to the resignation of President Nixon before he could be impeached. Along the way many of the President's top aides and political appointees were indicted and sent to prison," pausing a moment Ronnie gave a wry smile. "Any of this sound familiar? See kids, this is why it is important to study history; it tends to repeat itself, especially when power will always attract and corrupt.

"Anyway, long story short. Those high level officials receiving free room and board in jail wrote books and exposes of their personal experiences and sold them for a fortune. That outrage caused laws to pass making sure criminals could not financially profit from their crimes. But you can see why someone of our generation would think of jail as the perfect place to write a book rent-free."

"Especially since mom did not commit a crime," Penny reminded, returning.

"But was she really that desperate for free room and board, Ronnie?" Paul asked. "She never let on to us."

"Of course she didn't. But yes, I'm afraid business had gotten very bad at the store where she worked. Apparently your mom was working longer and longer hours trying to pull in some sales. I almost never saw her so I didn't even realize how difficult it had gotten. I guess the economic slump and the winter power bills, to heat that uninsulated shack she liked to call her "cottage", just about did her in. She finally confessed to me.

"'I feel like I'm trapped, Ronnie, already in jail, so to speak. The difference is, if I were in jail I'd have everything I don't have as a working stiff. *And* plenty of time to write!' were her exact words."

"I'm surprised you didn't invite her to stay with you, Aunt Ronnie?" Penny asked, still unhappy with her Aunt Ronnie for aiding and abetting their mother in the crazy scheme.

"Oh, please, Penny. You know I not only asked, I insisted. She refused to consider it, except for the few weeks after she moved from her place and waited for sentencing. Sam very tartly told me that it would be too distracting for her to get any work done at my place, reminding me that it was *not* a sex manual that she wanted to write!"

"Oh, low blow," Paul laughed.

Rhonda grinned, "Yes, but hard to argue. I am not much of a romantic as we all know."

"I still don't understand why she didn't tell us. We would have loved to have her stay."

"Absolutely." Aaron agreed with Penny.

"I know it hurts she didn't tell you," Rhonda said quietly, a thoughtful look in those vivid blue eyes. "As strange as it seems Sam didn't show any qualms about going to jail. She was looking forward to it, needing the isolation to focus. But your mom was terrified of telling anyone about her 'silly' dream, or you kids about her plan to achieve it." She decided not to add that Sam knew her kids would block her from going. They were dealing with enough pain already.

"Well, guys and gals, I have to be going." Rhonda stood and hugged them all. "I know you're angry with me and I can't blame you, but I had a choice between helping your mom with her crazy scheme or, determined as she was, taking the chance of what she might do on her own. So I chose to be her friend and help. I hope, now that you understand better, you'll have a long talk with your mom before you do anything drastic."

Chin high, Penny stated, "It's too late."

"We already did," Paul added, grimly.

Sam had barely been able to control the shaking of her hands, biting her bottom lip to keep it from trembling, until she had regained the privacy of her cell.

The echo of his cruel words rang in her head. Her precious novel, that she had sacrificed so much for, nothing but a *stupid book*! She couldn't let him crush her dream. She would keep going—she had to—but first she was going to write Ronnie and tell her she needed a new man for her lover! And *no*, she could *not* wait.

Imagining her friend's reaction, Sam's couldn't even release a laugh with the ache in her throat so high and tight, the burn in her eyes so painful. Crawling onto her cot, curling around her pillow, she pulled the blanket over her head. For just a while, Sam would let her grief have its way.

chapter twenty five

The children of Samantha Wilson were in anguish over not having raised their parent properly. Where had they gone wrong?

After their last visit to see their incarcerated mother, Penny had left sadly, to find her brother still pacing outside, deep in his thoughts.

Paul had left the room because he understood that his own anger was just hurting his mother more. He'd been shocked by her appearance and the dark circles under her lusterless eyes. She was probably so wan and listless looking because she knew she was surrounded by murderers and couldn't sleep at night! He wished he could just take her home right now so she wouldn't have to spend even one more night in jail.

A heated discussion had erupted between the siblings the minute they got in the car for the return trip, continuing hours after they reached Penny's home.

Penny had agonized over whether or not it was right to interfere and do something to get her mother out of jail, but Paul had been adamant. Their mom's physical health and safety was jeopardized, he insisted. They needed to contact Ronnie's attorney and press him to make and appeal, or hire their own attorney to fight to either get her out or reduce her sentence. After coming to agreement that action had to be taken immediately, they had to determine how.

It was shorty after Paul left an angry message with Ronnie's attorney that the document had come in the mail. They had discussed, then rejected, involving anyone else in their decision to take steps to free their mom. Once decided they didn't want anyone else trying to change their minds, or take the blame, unaware how closely they mirrored their mother. The decision would be theirs and any repercussions on their shoulders alone.

But they would not use the document yet. They'd try sending a simple letter to the Office of the Prosecutor, leaving out any details for now that might create more trouble for their mom or Ronnie.

> We are the children of Samantha Wilson,
> currently incarcerated at the Western State
> Women's Campus prison.
> We request her immediate release.
> She was arrested and charged with driving
> while intoxicated, but she was not operating
> the vehicle when arrested. She was only sitting
> in a parked car. There is no proof that,
> and she did not in fact, drive the car in that
> condition. Without that proof, she must be
> released, or legal action may follow.

They had hoped that the letter alone would be enough to spur the needed action. As their mother had escaped to jail before they knew of her court date, they were unaware of how adamantly she had proclaimed and defended her guilt. Proof had not been at issue.

They had not been there. But the prosecutor they mailed the letter to certainly had—for a most memorable occasion.

The letter had not been enough. They had received a call from the prosecutor's office and hinted their mom might have just gone along willingly with the verdict as it would give her time to write a book. He had scoffed at that and informed them someone from his office would be up to discuss the issue with them. They had been unable to set the time for the prior evening as they were meeting with Aunt Ronnie.

Both Paul and Penny were nervously waiting at Penny's home for the representative of the prosecutor's office to arrive this morning. They had no Idea what to expect. The lady that made the appointment sounded kind, sympathetic, but uninformative about further reaction to the letter, except that an immediate follow-up appointment was required.

Penny wondered if the woman's kindness was because she knew they were in trouble. Should they expect an unpleasant visit for threatening legal action, or withholding information, or some other breach of law? Penny's personal concern was slight though relative to her worry they might not be able to free their mother from jail without getting her in deeper trouble.

"Maybe we should have a lawyer here, Paul? What if we just create a bigger mess?"

Paul stood at the window overlooking the driveway. Someone should be arriving soon. He heard his sister, but knew her questions were just last minute frayed nerves. They had both asked themselves the same questions many times already, but had opted to just go it alone for now. Once they knew what the reaction was, they could either show the statement, or involve a lawyer.

"Oh, no..." Paul spoke unconsciously. The minute the car had pulled up, and he recognized the driver, he regretted the wisdom of trying to control the situation alone. This was not some lowly clerk, but a hard and tough man.

"What? What's wrong? Who is it?"

Penny's worried voice finally penetrated.

"Unless I'm mistaken, we're being honored with a visit from the top man himself. The prosecutor, Jordan Campbell." Paul kept his voice calm and even, trying not to upset his sister further.

"Campbell? Isn't that the man that Aunt Ronnie said was a woman-hater?"

Penny's question reminded Paul of that added worry. This was going to be worse than he thought.

"Paul, maybe you better do most of the talking."

"Yeah, okay. That's probably best." His sister was a beautiful woman. Their guest's *least* favorite kind!

Jordan had had plenty of time to think on the way up the Pacific coast.

Rhonda had told him, at their lunch meeting, some time back, that Sam had grown children. Somehow, even though he'd been told, it hadn't really sunk in that she was referring to adults until their firmly worded letter had brought that reality crashing home.

He kept picturing the petite blonde, trying to imagine her with adult kids. The image had refused to gel.

His curiosity had turned to the young adults. What would they look like? Be like? Rhonda said they were wonderful, smart, and well balanced, but what did that mean?

Jordan didn't really know much about kids, except for the toughs in trouble with the courts. Would he know what to say? How to gain their confidence, so they would talk to him? Like him? He just didn't know what to expect. He didn't think to question why it mattered to him so much that they like him.

Jordan was nervous when he pulled into the drive. He wanted to make a good impression.

When the front door opened, he gave the young man at the door a broad and friendly smile. Reaching out his hand to shake.

"Hi, I'm Jordan. You must be Sam's son Paul?"

Penny watched from the back of the hall. Despite her reservations she was completely disarmed by the incredibly handsome, charming man at the door. His use of her mother's nickname had not escaped her attention. He seemed so friendly, could Ronnie have been wrong? She stepped forward and offered her hand.

"Hello, I'm Penny. Do you know our mother? You called her Sam ..."

Seeing his face redden, Penny hesitated, remembering his reputation. She wished she hadn't said anything at all.

"Shall we go into the living room?" Paul suggested, uncomfortably.

Jordan's flush had not been caused by anger, but by embarrassment. Penny's question had made him realize that his closeness to their mother existed solely in his own mind. He had barely spoken to Sam, though he felt he knew her intimately. Too intimately!

"It's a pleasure to meet you both." he said politely, waiting for Penny to sit before seating himself. Turning friendly eyes on her, he attempted to answer her question.

"I have met your mother. I took a particular interest in her ... ah," hastily changing his errant thought process, Jordan blurted, "I wondered if you'd look like her. You're very different, but at the same time similar, like sisters. It's amazing ..."

"You *are* the prosecutor, right?" Paul's businesslike voice intervened. "You received our letter?"

"Yes, that's right." Jordan disciplined his thoughts to the business at hand. His abbreviated delivery went right to the point.

"You wrote that your mother was not driving when arrested. That is correct. She was, however, in the driver's seat of a car that had the keys in the ignition and the motor running with no other visible means of arriving there. That is sufficient to make the arrest. Proof could have been challenged in court. So let me ask you this, if she wasn't driving the car, why did she plead guilty? Why would she lie?"

Jordan settled back, awaiting the answer to his simple question, unaware that it was the least simple question of all!

Paul glanced over at Penny and saw her cautious nod, he rose, saying as he went to a desk, "I think we mentioned a book... ?"

"Yes, I gather she is writing something there in her spare time, but that doesn't explain why she would plead guilty to a crime she when she was innocent. In fact, I specifically recall her saying she needed to take responsibility ... What's this?"

Paul passed the document to the Prosecutor, then took his seat and waited while he read it.

STATEMENT OF INTENT

I, SAMANTHA WILSON, of sound body and mind, (though none of my friends and family believe that) do hereby attest that I intend to stage a crime for the express purpose of receiving a jail sentence of a minimum of at least one year, to enable me to spend that time to write a novel.

The crime I am going to stage is as follows:

I will be driven in a severely intoxicated state, in my own car, by a person who shall remain sober and nameless, to a location where I will be placed behind the wheel of my parked, running car, left to be found by the authorities. The intention being that I will be assumed to have driven in an intoxicated state. Due to the strict drunk driving laws of this state, (which I commend) I feel this will earn me a prison sentence of the necessary term required for my project.

I have no desire to endanger the lives of any citizen by actually driving in this condition, despite my desire to accomplish the objective, which is the jail term. I have therefore prevailed upon someone to drive me; they do so under duress. I take full legal responsibility for any charge of kidnapping said person, as may be required to protect said nameless individual.

This document and statement of intent has been prepared at the insistence (nagging) of those (nameless) who know I will be going to jail "innocent", so they will have a legal tool to show proof of intent to be able to have me released in the event they consider my life endangered or my safety and security jeopardized from the results of this action. This document has been prepared to forestall otherwise threatened exposure of my crime, before it has been committed.

The guardian(s) of this document pledged not to use this document to expose me, except in the above stated circumstances. They further pledge and agree that this statement will become invalid and will be destroyed, at my direction, if any of my family members appear in the courtroom, or in any hearing relating to this crime, prior to the time that I am safely lodged in prison.

I DO HEREBY ATTEST TO THE ABOVE, AND SIGN IT BEFORE WITNESSES THIS 30TH DAY OF...

"May? The thirtieth of May, but that was before— Well, I'll be damned. And she looks so honest and innocent and she is nothing but a damn..."

Paul rose suddenly, fists clenched at his side, "Watch you mouth, mister. I don't care how important you think you are. No one talks about my mother... "

"Sorry. Easy. You're right. That was just wounded ego talking. I have great respect for your mother, though she pulled a fast one in that courtroom and had everyone under her spell, including the judge. Now that I see she barred you from the courtroom it explains why you didn't object then. Did you ever see the transcript from her sentencing hearing, or learn what happened?"

"No. Pen?"

"I didn't either."

"Well, you are in for quite a surprise, as I was at the time, and am now seeing your document. I think I have a copy in my briefcase. Let me get it for you." Even as he retrieved the papers to hand the kids, he was shaking his head and a deep laugh rose out of his belly. Jordan just could not stop laughing. The joke was on himself, and the judge, and Sam's own helpless public defender. Experienced men all, they had gone down to a petite blonde with wide innocent honey-brown eyes.

Soon, after reading the transcript, despite themselves, Paul and Penny joined in. They were all laughing at the defenseless prosecutor.

"Wiping tears of laughter from his eyes, Paul told Jordan, "Our mom is generally a sweet, easy going, good natured woman ..."

Penny finished it for him, "Until she's not. Then she is a force to be reckoned with. And once she has set her mind, that's it. It easiest just to surrender at that point." Penny started to sputter, then laugh again. Pointing out to Jordan, "Just like you did."

By the time they got over the second round of laughter, they had bonded as a team with a common purpose.

"She couldn't have been so serious about just a book, could she?" The look on their faces told Jordan he had just made another blunder.

"Remember mom's "ideas" box, Paul?"

"Mom had ideas for stories all the time, but most of the time it was when she was doing something else, so she would grab anything she could reach and scribble down some notes so she wouldn't completely forget it." Paul explained to Jordan. "She had this box in the floor of one of the closets and she'd stuff her notes in there."

"Well, you know how kids are," Penny said. "You tell them 'that's mom's stuff in that box, just leave it alone, please', and of course it is forbidden and therefore irresistible and fascinating."

"What kind of stuff?" Paul mimicked the words and childish falsetto he had used long ago. They both laughed.

"Anyway, she said it was just her "Ideas" box for stories she had ideas about maybe writing about someday when she was old and gray."

"Yeah, but," Paul jumped in, "she had this bedtime story she used to tell us when we were little and it had been written on scraps of envelopes and paper, so we wanted to know if there were any good teen kid stories in there."

"That was our excuse, anyway." Penny agreed, "But we were really just curious snoopy kids that wanted to see what was in the box we were supposed to leave alone. So one time when we were teens and mom was gone grocery shopping we pulled the box out and started going through it.

"Though there were a few folders with notes, and some spiral notebooks with book idea starts, or book ideas on index cards, most of it was scratching on torn pieces of paper or on old envelopes. We had watched her when she got an idea and would scribble it on the margin of the newspaper, or an empty envelope, even a handy paper plate, then go back to dishes or laundry or whatever. Then she would think of more, so she would scribble some more and more and run out of space."

Paul took over the tale, "She had all these old bill envelopes, they didn't have recycling then, but mom had her own system. She'd start a note down the center of the clean back of an envelope, then in the corners, and when that filled up she would draw an arrow and flip it over and you'd read down to, then around the hole for the address window. Turning it around and around, there would be increasingly tiny, circular, and often incoherent notes."

"Remember the hot pink mini-novella?" Penny teased.

"Oh, yeah," Paul explained. "You know those sticky notes were invented when we were kids. They had the yellow square ones, then they had some tiny hot pink ones only an inch or so big that were great for marking pages. Well, I had a couple packs of those I had left on the table after using them to mark one of my textbooks while studying up for a test.

"I passed my test, but I never did figure out where the other pad of sticky notes went. Well, Pen and I were digging through that box of mom's and came across that tiny pad. Mom had made a note about a book idea on the top page, then another note on the next, then the writing got tinier, and then pages were folded so she could write on both sides and then the whole pad was stuck on some larger sheets of scratch paper and it was all folded up in a wad to keep it together. Mom's mini-novella. What was that about Pen, do you remember?

"I think it was like an educational kid's story. I remember the title written in blue ink on that hot-pink. It was called 'Little Coho the Salmon' and about how he grew up in a fresh gravel stream and memorized its smell as home before going off on an adventure to the ocean. Mom wrote all kinds of stuff, whatever struck her at a particular moment. She must of had hundreds of story ideas in that box!

"I, um... I kept something I found in the bottom of that box," Penny confessed. Seeing Paul's shock, she shrugged and explained. "I was about twelve I think then, and mom had written it when she was only a few years older and I wanted to, I don't know, connect to that I guess. I always kept it in my jewelry box."

"Do you still have it?" Paul asked.

"Of course." Penny jumped up and went to get an old jewelry box and carefully pulled a yellowed and folded sheet of lined school paper out and carefully smoothed it out.

The first few lines were neat notations of homework assignments, then a slash across the page divided it from the hurried scrawl below.

Title: dabbling in babbling /or the writer's disease

what is this muse that makes me dabble
in the self abuse of constant babble
is there any use for the endless scrabble
for paper loose to hold my prattle?

Is it just an obsession
that all my thoughts
must find confession
on all the sheets
in my possession
until I finally,
mercifully,
run
out
of
ink?

by Samantha Wilson, age 15

"We got caught, of course," Paul said with a wry smile. "We got the 'It's-not-polite-to-invade-another-person's-privacy-when-they-have-asked-you-not-to' lecture. Then we asked her why she never finished one of her books. She just laughed and said she would someday when she had more time."

A sudden silence fell.

Their mom's 'writer's disease' had become a chronic condition. She'd always managed to find scraps of paper and ink, but she must have run out of time and high hopes long ago.

Penny and Paul just looked in each other's eyes, realizing that 'someday' chance had never come for their mom.

Until now. In jail.

"You asked if our mom was serious enough to go to jail for 'just' a book? No, it was just for a dream," Penny's voice waivered.

Jordan felt as if a splinter had torn through his heart.

It had ached unbearably as he watched the loving way the two talked about their mom, a depth of care and closeness he had never known or felt or wanted with his parents. But seeing the desolation in their eyes, on facing how desperate their mom had been to pursue a dream they had always seen, but never knew as her secret need, shattered the knot in his chest where there should no longer be anything but cold, hard scar tissue.

"We will," Jordan had to stop and cough and clear his throat. "We will work it out. But I have to warn you, she has already turned down my first offer to help her after I spoke with you." He grimaced. Knowing his offer had been shouting at her about a 'stupid book'. He would have trouble recovering from that error, but even if she still hated him, he had to help this family that cared so much about each other—and had already captured him also.

"I'll try another tack and update you by email. You'll be visiting this week?" At their nod, "Then let's meet in town afterward and work out a strategy, maybe get her buddy Rhonda involved."

"And our grandparents. We can meet there, but it will be on the weekend...?"

"Just call my cell or email me the time and place." Jordan gave them a business card and inked his private cell and emails numbers on the reverse.

After the prosecutor drove off, Penny was standing, arms crossed over her chest, lips pursed and a thoughtful look on her face as she gazed out the window at the driveway.

"What?" Her brother asked. "I thought he was a great guy. Especially after the horror stories I heard about him."

"Did you notice how he calls her Sam instead of Ms. Wilson?"

"Of course, but he's interviewed Ronnie several times, so that's not surprising."

"Did you notice how his voice and eyes softened each time he said 'Sam'?"

"They did? I guess I didn't notice, but now you mention it, I did feel that he truly cared about helping our mother. Which is surprising when she made an ass out of him in court." Paul laughed. "Fortunately the guy has a sense of humor.

Penny nodded a few times, then announced.

"I think he has the hots for mom!"

"Maybe so. But that can only help us right now."

chapter twenty-six

Sam was not truly surprised that her kids had reached their breaking point; she had been near her own on their prior visit. She thought she had put up a good front, but emotions *had* been stretched thin and ragged all around. And she knew they only ratted her out because they loved her. But she did wonder how they found out. But the prior visit was the why, she could see that looking back.

Though utterly exhausted from her latest series of sleepless nights, Sam had struggled valiantly to put a bright and cheery smile on her face for Penny and Paul's visit. The normally simple exercise of smiling felt more like weight lifting with her facial muscles so stiff and sagging from insufficient sunlight and rest. Her children tried to hide their shock at the drastic change in their mother's appearance, so Sam had been unaware that she'd looked even worse than she felt.

Sam only noticed her children seemed quieter than usual. She tried to fill the conversational void with any amusing observations she could think of to maintain the impression that everything was going just fine. Eager to convince the two, she smiled for them to see her newly repaired teeth and shiny crown, and told them what a wonderful time she was having studying the different personalities, and wealth of characters here.

"Yes," Penny had remembered. "You told us about one woman here and promised to find out her real story and tell us. I think Rhonda said you called her The Searchlight? So tell us what you found out, mom."

Samantha just stared at her daughter, her tired mind not nimble enough to leap out of the trap she had set for herself. She'd lied to her children more in the last few months that she had most of her life; Sam could not bear any more.

"Oh, well…ahh," looking briefly to the ceiling for help, Sam dropped her gaze back down to her hands clasped in her lap. "Murder," she murmured so low it was clear Sam was trying to swallow the word as soon as it came out of her mouth.

"What did you say, mom?" Penny had asked.

"She said MURDER! Didn't you, mom?" Paul's voice was harsh. "You're in here with murderers, right mom? Not sweet, innocent victims like you would like to create, but sick, nasty, violent people that can kill without reason or conscience!"

"Paul, please." His sister's hand on his arm reminded him that he was yelling. He spun out of his chair and left them alone, as he paced off his anger.

"Pen," her mom's eyes had pleaded with her. "I knew people here committed crimes, we all knew that before I came here. It's a prison, but," Sam had attempted a smile, "I'm probably safer here from the hardened criminals than I would be at home. After all, I'm locked safely behind bars. Every night."

Seeing the miserable failure of her attempted joke, Sam had tried again. "Honey, most of the people I've seen here are not major criminals. A lot of the people here are just people who couldn't adjust to living on the outside–"

"And why are you here? When and why did you start drinking heavily, mom?" Now Penny lashed out angrily, "What is it you can't handle?" Instantly contrite for the words that came out of fear for her mother, she had tried to soften the hurt she had seen in Sam's eyes.

"Listen, mom, I'm sorry. I didn't mean that. I just…"

"No, Pen," her mother said softly, "don't apologize for being honest. I know you didn't mean to hurt me, but, maybe we should visit again later. I think we're all a little overwrought today. I love you, and tell Paul I love him, also, and thank you, honey."

"I love you too, mom. We'll come back soon."

Penny had already made two urgent calls to her brother that morning. They needed to be prepared, have a coordinated plan, before heading down to visit their mother in prison the next day.

"Do you have the list?" She jumped him the minute he stepped into her house.

"Yeah, it's right here." Paul yanked it from his back pocket and spread it open on the table.

"Okay, first item. You talked to Grandma and Grandpa. Did they have any suggestions?"

Even stressed as Penny was, she was unable to keep a hint of laughter from her voice. "Grandpa says we should just find a nice, steady man for her to settle down with. Preferably a pilot."

"That would take too long," Paul replied, tapping the pen against his lips. "Though it's the best long-term solution to her financial worries..."

His sister's eyebrows shot up. "Don't even go there! It's cute from Grandpa. His generation was different. But you! Don't you start some chauvinistic..."

"Hey, hey!" Aaron joined them, bending to give Penny a kiss to squelch her anger. "He's teasing you," he said softly. "You're too smart to be fighting with your brother when you're supposed to be a team to help your mom. Besides," he grinned, "we men can be useful to have around. See, I made fresh coffee, pass your cups."

"Thanks honey. You're right we shouldn't fight. I'm sorry for exploding like that, Paul, but..."

"But," he forestalled her, "I didn't mean it that way. I'm sorry too. So, what did Grandma say?

"She said she learned long ago that mom has a problem with brick walls."

"Meaning?"

"It does no good to warn her, to try to protect her, to tell her 'you can't', or 'you shouldn't'. It just firms her resolve to check it out herself. She has to smash into it herself, before she is convinced. Grandma says she's not sure whether it's stubbornness, or an unwillingness to let others limit her, or both, that causes her to be that way. She's learned you just have to grit your teeth, close your eyes, and let her crash and burn, and then be there to help dust her off."

"So, what's she saying? She thinks we should just go along with this?" Paul asked amazed.

"No, not at all. She thought we'd have the best chance of influencing her. She had hoped we could stop her first, but it is probably too late to use the guilt card effectively now. No one expected mom to pull a fast one on us like that and sneak into jail before we knew what was happening."

"And block her." Paul added wryly. "So now what?"

"Well, when it comes to tactics, Grandma said giving orders or making demands will just put her back up, so she thinks that applying some reverse psychology would be our best bet."

"I had no idea Grandma was so devious!" They both laughed.

Then Penny added soberly, "She's just really worried, like we are."

"Okay, so we can't marry her off, and we can't just tell her 'no', especially since it's too late for that so how do we work this?"

"Basically, we need to agree that it's a good way to achieve her goal ...," Seeing Paul's mouth open to object, his sister held up a finger. "Reverse psychology, remember? And Grandma thinks mom may be at that crashed-into-the-wall and is ready for the dusted-off phase. If she's not pressured. So if we help and support her now in mom's *own* path, she feels we'll have better results."

"Truly devious," Paul shook his head smiling. "Okay Pen, give me a pen and paper. We need to start a new list. Okay, lay out how exactly that works."

"Essentially, we just tell her the truth about how we feel, or felt, before she took this drastic step we're trying to get her to change her mind about. First off, we tell her the statement made us realize how important her writing is to *her*, and apologize for not having appreciated that before.

"Then we tell her how excited *we* are that she is finally going to be finishing one of her stories, and write that book we've bugged her to do for so long. *And* we tell her that if we had realized she was ready to take that step we could have... no, make that *would* have wanted to be involved in such an exciting project. Then we tell her the ways we would help her meet her goals, without jail, and without interference." Penny rose and looked over her brother's shoulder, to check out the list.

1) Contrite
2) Excited she's finishing story
3) Would want to be involved
4) Want to help without interfering

"Okay, good. Now we need to list things we could do to support her decision. I'll tell her I would have told her about a perfect writer's retreat, with a beach, and private room and bath, and all it costs is occasional duties when she is having writer's block... "

"Does she get that?" Paul wondered. "I can't see how she could with such a huge backlog of ideas."

Seeing Penny's raised eyebrows, he returned to the point. "Duties. We shouldn't ask her to do anything, Pen."

"You know mom. She'll refuse us if she can't see a way to pay back, and we don't want that."

"True. Okay, I'll just put down, 'Beachfront writer's retreat in return for slave labor'."

"Very funny. At any rate, by this point I'm hoping she'll be curious and interested and ask where this writer's retreat is. There is a little deck off our guest room. Aaron and I were talking about maybe adding stairs that would give her private access to the beach. Anyway, we need to work up a list of other choices."

Aaron, listening quietly asked. "By the way, where's Brittany?"

"She offered to go to the store and pick up stuff for dinner, so we could have time to talk. She should be along in awhile."

"Did Brit have any good suggestions?" Penny asked.

"She looked at our other list, said she'd try to think of some solutions, but she made an interesting observation. Brittany said she suspected that isolation from everyday routine was more important to mom than the financial issues. She said she'd be glad to get a bigger apartment, so mom can stay with us, but wonders if it's the getting away that's really the issue."

"'But why would mom want to get away from family and friends? All the people that love and support her? That doesn't make any sense, does it?" Penny wondered.

"That's what I said. Brittany said she doesn't think mom wants to say that, or hurt us, but that she really needs to be disconnected from us. The freedom to be alone for awhile, of not being a friend or parent, so she can devote her concentration full-time to her goal."

"But we wouldn't bother her!" Penny insisted. "We'd give her the privacy to do whatever she wants here. Wouldn't we, Aaron?"

"Sure," Aaron replied, but after a moment's thought, laughed.

"What?" She asked.

"No, no... I think I'll keep that thought to myself," he replied, changing the subject. "Anyone need more coffee?"

"Hold it, pal! You're not running away until you tell me what you were thinking!" Penny threatened.

"But you'll throw something at me, darling." Aaron teased. "Okay," seeing her determined look, "but give me that heavy mug first. I was just thinking of the irony. You two are getting good practice deciding to let your mom do what she wants without interference."

Aaron was out of range, and safely in the kitchen before Penny and Paul realized what he had said.

"This is different!" Penny hollered. "We're helping."

"He knows, he's teasing," Paul glanced back down at their list. "I think."

Hopefully this visit will go better than the last one. Though, considering the circumstances, Sam was doubtful. She had already known she forgave her kids for alerting the prosecutor for the reason for her presence in jail. But forgiveness for her, from them, was probably too much to hope for on this visit's agenda.

When they arrived, Sam gave her children a big smile and bigger hugs—she considered all four of them as hers now. When Penny's guy, Aaron, hugged her, he whispered to her, "I think I better warn you," he said with sympathy, "they have a list to work from."

"Uh-oh, a list, huh?" She sighed, "They get that from Ronnie."

Paul spoke first, "Mom, we received your statement of intent in the mail from the attorney recently..."

Ah, so that was how, and instantly Sam realized why it had been released. She recalled Jordan yelling that she had nearly been charged with bank robbery. That must have triggered the attorney. Sam was glad to know that neither Ronnie, nor Sam's parents, had betrayed her secret, and added this hurt to the kids.

Paul must have seen her relieved smile and misinterpreted it, he looked like her was about to tell her it was not funny, but then caught himself uttering more diplomatic words. "We'd like to have a serious discussion with you, mom."

Sam almost smiled again when she saw him slip the list from his pocket.

Samantha listened patiently to what her children had to say. When they got to the part about the perfect writer's retreat option, she just smiled and said quietly, "I suppose one of those duties would be walking the dogs on the beach?"

Penny flushed. Her mother's normally playful personality, soft looks, and gentle, easy-going manners made it easy to forget how strong she was—and how smart.

After Paul had worked his way through the rest of his list and tucked it back in his pocket, he looked to his mother for a response that did not come.

Sighing, he asked, "You have made progress, haven't you? It hasn't all been for nothing, I hope." Genuine concern shone in his eyes.

"Oh yes! I don't have much to show yet. I've been doing mostly planning: characters, plot outlines, timeframes, listing subjects I need to research. I've got a start on some of the actual writing too, so no question it's helped!" Her progress was more optimistically stated, than what she truly felt about what she'd accomplished so far, but Sam wasn't about to share that right now.

"And your photo has helped tremendously, Paul. I've been trying to set up a romantic beach scene around it." *But my male lead character is giving me too much grief – and too many impossible dreams.*

"But it is definitely worth it. Everything is coming along fine. And I am gaining so much insight." No one seemed to notice her casually holding one hand behind her back.

Her children couldn't bear to have their mom here, but she knew when they saw her happy and positive about her progress, they came away with less guilt, less fear.

Mrs. Wilson had been up early that morning baking and cooking. The young were always hungry, so she had prepared a hearty meal, ready when the kids returned from the visit to their mother. A cocoanut pound cake was already cooled, divided, and carefully wrapped for the grandkids to take home with them. A section was saved for Ronnie who was also invited early for the family dinner. There were a few things that needed to be discussed amongst them before the prosecutor arrived later.

The kids wanted to wait and report on their talk with their mom just once, when Mr. Campbell was present.

Now they wanted some answers. Their loved ones had known their mother's plan and kept it from them. The signatures, on the document they'd received, proved that. Not only Aunt Ronnie, but both their grandparents, had witnessed the signing of the document.

Setting a fresh, homegrown and homemade rhubarb pie in the center of the table, Mrs. Wilson responded to Paul's question.

"I suppose we were in much the same position as Ronnie. Though we strongly disagreed, we were left with only the choice to either help and keep quiet, or have things worse and unpredictable.

"Our daughter was adamant about not having any of us in court. Only Ronnie, to drive her and make sure everything went as planned. Your mom, as she put it, 'did not want or need the emotional stress, inevitable tears, and wrenching goodbyes to take place in public, in court' when she was sentenced to prison.

"We insisted on a way to get her released if an emergency happened with you kids, or something went wrong for her, as the condition for our silence. She'd already had the attorney draw up her will, but In addition, we wanted some document from our daughter setting out her intentions before the fact. We felt that would be the least we would need to get legal help to spring her.

"On a claim of pre-meditated innocence, so to speak." Mrs. Wilson shook her head, wearily. "She was always such a sweet, but stubborn, child. We were torn, but we felt it was the best deal we could negotiate at that point. And kids, your mother truly hoped it would be less stressful and painful for you kids if you didn't know everything."

When the prosecutor arrived he appeared tense and ruffled, but he was courteous, even charming to their grandparents, before taking his seat in their living room to hear the results of the children's visit with their mother.

Paul and Penny outlined their strategy with their mother and passed around their list, which Rhonda, at least, found amusing— though not the results of their attempts.

"Basically, she said she appreciated our support, but to bear with her a while longer. Be patient and let her think our ideas over."

Rhonda smiled wryly, "A soft 'no', in other words." She could not say she was surprised. Though it *had* been a clever and well planned effort by the kids.

Discussion and argument went around the circle, and seemed to circle hopelessly, on what actions should—or could—be taken to help Samantha in light of her continued resistance.

"We finally," Paul admitted a little sheepishly, "asked mom what *she* wanted, about *her* needs, how *she* felt. It appears that Brit was right." Turning to smile at Brittany, he motioned for her to tell them.

"I want to write," Sam had told them. "And to do that I need time and isolation.

"I want to finish at least one of my story ideas and develop it into a book, and hopefully many more after. But you find as you grow older that time just slips away unnoticed. And the older you get the faster and faster it speeds until another year zips by, and can never be recovered. It always startles me that more monthly bills are due when it seems like I just paid them yesterday," Sam admitted wryly. "I would like to accomplish more than that with my remaining time.

"And to have time, I need isolation. I need to focus only on my work. Oh, I considered an *authentic* writer's retreat," she said with a small smile, "but it would not give me enough time, and all I would isolate would be my body—not my mind. My mind would be worrying about all the rent, and bills, and job responsibilities still piling up back home. Which is not conducive to a creative frame of mind.

"And, I might a well tell you now, I had to make some drastic changes in my life anyway. My rental beggared me with heating bills last winter, so I had to make a move. And the store I'm working at is headed for trouble. Sales are slow, so they cut back expenses, including the advertising budget. I could not afford to be free labor there any longer.

"I need to be isolated from being responsible for anything or anyone—including myself. So the isolation I need is not only for concentration, but from all my own problems.

"I *have* tried to work and write at the same time. But found I can't split myself like that. I just failed at both. I'm too tired after work, there's nothing left upstairs, I'm too mentally drained. I know some people can do that, I couldn't.

"I tear up everything I *do* write. It's flat, tired. There's no sparkle to it. Too many distractions, interruptions, too little imagination left to produce something that I can take some pride in.

There's so much locked up inside me I want to write about! I can't get it out that way.

"A thought comes to me... I hear it so clearly expressed. By the time I get a chance later to sit, eager to get it on paper...it's gone. Lost, or half-remembered, too distorted to express what I heard so clearly, saw so perfectly."

Sam's soft, but earnest, voice wrung her children's hearts. They heard the frustration, and felt the passion, the longing of their mother's need to pursue her dream.

"Somehow, we have to help her find the freedom and isolation she needs," Brittany said, concluding her relating of Sam's words.

Jordan listened intently, but silently, to everything that was said before he reported that he'd had yet another fruitless interview with 'their lovely, but incredibly stubborn, mother'.

Samantha's parents had remained quiet through most of the discussion. Huddled side by side on the couch, they had only communicated silently with each other, their hands tightly clasped together.

Their daughter had refused all their offers of assistance. Now they were almost numb from shock, the reality of her plans unfolded before them. This was not one of those crazy childhood schemes that faded harmlessly, forgotten before the day had passed. Their daughter had actually gone to jail!

They had always supported her with love, encouraging her to believe in herself, to follow her dreams. However, following her dreams into jail, had them second-guessing themselves.

They had instilled their values in her, then, as she grew, given her their trust and respect as an individual, to seek her own direction, though they might have chosen differently.

Now they suffered the anguish of parents helpless to protect the grown children they deeply loved.

They had been witnesses to the signing of the document. It was the only hope of minimizing the dangerous course Samantha was set on taking. Her father curled his arm around his wife shoulders, as they settled back on the couch, listening. His eyes blinking rapidly, Mr. Wilson pulled a crisp, white handkerchief from his pocket, offering it to the woman who had so lovingly starched, pressed, and folded it for him, year after year.

Sam's mother accepted it gratefully, pretending to blow her nose gently, while using the concealing white folds, to hide a quivering chin. Neither parent was able to hide their damp eyes, or the depth of the love that caused their pain. Surely, they prayed, this will end soon!

Before he left, Jordan went to Sam's parents and thanked them and told them not to worry.

Confidently, he assured them, and the rest of the room.

"I *will* fix this!"

After Jordan had left, Mr. Wilson piped up. "He certainly seems like a nice young man, and I believe he cares about our Samantha." Adding softly, "Too bad he's not a pilot, but a handsome enough fellow."

Everyone in the room laughed knowingly, the lingering tension released. Gramps never gave up

chapter twenty seven

It was over, time for her to explain. But Sam was *not* going to apologize to this man for the choices she had made.

He'd challenged her again about how she had become an inmate.

Leaning back in the hard chair, casually crossing her legs at the ankle like a lady about to smooth her skirts at a tea party, you could almost forget Samantha was wearing a pea green prison overall. "Yes," she nodded, I did do *this*," she swept a slender hand gracefully around the stark interview room, "to write my novel, a life long dream of mine."

She was so calm, so quiet, so lovely, Jordan stopped his agitated stomping around in the space too small to pace out his anger, and gazed at her. His dark eyebrows arched up in disbelief, waiting for some kind of explanation.

Sam shrugged, continuing reasonably, "What else was I to do? I didn't have time when I worked, and couldn't pay the rent if I didn't. So," she spread her palm again, motioning toward the concrete walls, "brilliant idea. Free rent."

Jordan stared at her a moment then threw back his head in a laugh that sounded more bitter than amused.

"Do not dare laugh at me, sir," she demanded, tossing that silvered blonde ponytail, dangerous sparks brewing in her eyes.

Abruptly he stopped, his voice turning sarcastic. "Why the hell didn't you just marry someone and live off him while you did what you wanted? Like most women do. Then when you're a rich and successful writer you can just dump him, kick him to the curb when he's outlived his usefulness."

Furious at his scornful attitude toward women, and hurt at what she took as ridicule of her personally, Sam lashed back, not noticing the pain that lurked behind the anger in Jordan's gray eyes.

"I would much rather be in prison than chained to some macho jerk that's more interested in a woman as a possession, than a wife that has a purpose and life of her own!" Sam unleashed some of her own buried bitterness. "But you're just like all the other men, too self-centered to think about, or give a damn about what a woman might want, or be. You think the world revolves around your wants and needs, and women are just air-headed distractions that cause trouble and get in men's way!" Pausing a moment in her resentful stream to catch her breath, Sam noticed that he had straightened suddenly at that last assault. He stood rigid and deathly quiet.

His jaws were tightly clenched, his head cocked back like a man who had just taken a blow to the chin and was preparing to fight. He stood a long time just staring wordlessly down at her, shoulders stiff, lips clamped firmly, the skin around his mouth turning white. His eyes looked guarded, but hateful, at the same time.

But was that hatred in his eyes? Or was it pain? Sam was uncertain and uncomfortable now with the words she had blindly said in anger. Somehow her defensive counter attack on men in general, had become a very direct personal attack on Jordan. She hadn't meant for that to happen, but clearly something she'd said had struck the target.

Why was he so mad at her, anyway? What difference did it make to him? She knew he didn't care about her personally, just as she knew how very deeply she cared about him. Why else did she feel so miserable suddenly, to think her careless words had either hurt him, or made him hate her?

She'd thought she had a right to defend herself, but did it really matter now, whether she was right or wrong? The ache in her heart when she looked at him, told her it didn't matter at all. She wished she could go to him now. Cup the tightly clenched jaws in her hands and soothe away the tension in his face, but the frozen space that lay between them, his hostile, rigid stance, denied her the right to trespass.

Without another word, he strode brusquely past her and out the door, a chilly breeze brushing her as he passed.

Bett Bone

Sam had a painful ache in her stomach, an empty sense that she'd done something unforgivable; that she'd never see Jordan again. Pain rose to her chest, tightened in her throat at the thought. What had she done to make him hate her so?

She waited miserably for the guard to come and take her back. The room seemed so much colder suddenly, without his intensity to warm it. Sam huddled, wrapping her arms around her shoulders, waiting. She felt the chill descending on her body, her hopes, her future.

No, Sam corrected herself firmly. Not her hopes or her future, just her fantasies. Her hope had been to write and she would. Her future did not require him – wouldn't have included him anyway. That was just a dream, she convinced herself, visualizing, imagining the perfect man to help her create her story. She firmed her jaw and her determination and waited for the guard. She felt stronger, but colder. Ten minutes, or a lifetime passed, it didn't matter which to Sam.

When the door finally opened again, it wasn't the guard.

Jordan strode back in, set a root beer shake and a gooey maple bar on the table in front of Sam. Her favorites! But he couldn't possibly know that, or care if he did. He lifted a briefcase from under the table, pulled out his chair, tweaked his slacks, and sat down. Opening the case, he pulled out a document, placed it on the table in front of Sam and, without looking up at her, he spoke in a tightly controlled professional voice.

"Please read this then sign at the x on the bottom." He pulled a steel pen from his pocket and pushed it across.

To: Samantha Wilson @ Western State Women's
It has come to my attention, during the course of investigating another case, that there are deficiencies in the DUI case and charges against you, for which you are currently serving a sentence at the above named institution.

Whew! Sam thought. Did these legal types get paid by the word?

Jordan sat back quietly, his face a mask. He was privately congratulating himself on how cleverly he had avoided implicating Penny and Paul, as promised.

Further, there are grave concerns that you may not have received the vigorous defense of your court appointed attorney, representation that each citizen deserves, and has a right to by law.

Under these conditions, we do not feel that it would be either appropriate or legally defensible to continue your sentence and incarceration.

In a desire to see justice upheld in your case, a determination has been made by my office that you should be released forthwith, while you file an appeal of these charges, and request a pardon of the sentence incorrectly imposed.

Attached is a form for you to sign so that, in the interest of justice, this office can petition for your release.

Respectfully, Jordan Campbell
Chief Prosecutor
Office of the Prosecutor

"Thanks, but, no thanks!" Sam answered defiantly. She shoved the papers back across the table, pulled the shake and pastry closer, protectively circling them with an arm, just in case they were a quid-pro-whatever that she'd lose for defaulting on the deal.

Jordan clamped down on his tongue and control. He should charge her with perjury, malicious mischief, obstructing his sense of justice! But it would probably just tickle her pink if he did. She'd get that little smile, and ask him how much more time that would give her to finish her damn book! Crazy, irritating, woman!

"I could throw you out of jail, you know!" He threatened. His anger and frustration boiling out again, in spite of his promise to himself to stay calm and in control. He grabbed up his briefcase and stalked to the door.

"Keep the food, dammit! Eat it. You need it. You look like hell!"

And with that charming compliment, he left.

For good, Sam feared.

Driving away, Jordan had a shouting match with himself, in the privacy of his car. He needed to vent, big time. You would think he'd asked her to save *him*, rather than the reverse! He had half a mind to forcibly remove her from jail; drag her cute little ass right out of there! Damn the woman! How could someone that fragile looking be so incredibly damn stubborn?

Macho jerk, my ass, he fumed. Just because he acted like one sometimes did *not* mean he was one! *She* was a closet man-hater, that's what she was. And she'd accused *him*? The nerve.

And how dare she tar him with the same brush that she used to paint other men. Couldn't she see he was different? Well, different *now*, he meant. Couldn't she see that he had changed? That *she* had changed him? That he didn't just blame all women the same now?

He really wished he had not given that little speech about marrying men just to use them though. That really was old Jordan, not new Jordan. Maybe he could get Elsa and Shelley to write him testimonials that he had changed his ways? Well, he'd almost changed them all, he hadn't quite finished the job yet.

He *had* said those words, after all, but only because he was angry and worried about her. She looked like a ghost of the Sam he had come to know and … There was that damn L word again. It kept sneaking up on him and almost catching him.

Reaching the home of Sam's parents, Jordan drew a few deep breaths, and raked the fingers of both hands across his scalp, trying to calm himself. It was important to him to make a good impression on Samantha's parents—especially before she spoke to them again and told them what a first-class ass he was. At least her kids had seemed to warm to him when he had visited with them last week.

He hoped to learn her kids had had better luck today than he did. But as hard as it was to believe, they hadn't succeeded, either. Though they, at least, hadn't gotten an angry refusal like Jordan did.

Such kids! He never would have been able to refuse them anything. They had been in his thoughts constantly in the week since he had gone to see them. He kept telling himself it was because they were so different from the young adults he saw in the courtroom, but suspected it was much more than that.

And the feeling in that room today with the whole family? It had humbled him. He'd felt like an alien that could never belong in a family like that. But Jordan could not deny how desperately he longed for that.

I will fix this! He'd told them. Wanting to help. Wanting to belong. Wanting to stop the pain of their worry.

He didn't know how, but he would—he had to.

Pulling into his driveway at home, Jordan jumped from the car and shot straight through the house out to the deck to pace off his frustration. Tired of not being able to get a good stride going with all the furniture and grill in the way, he managed to hurl himself, instead of them, into the yard.

Stalking along beside his landscaped beds, he continued his argument with himself. He'd changed. He wasn't that man anymore. He didn't deserve her blame and scorn. Didn't she realized she'd changed him? More than a few paces elapsed before the echo of his own thoughts settled into his consciousness. Wait ... when did *he* realize she'd changed him?

Well, I will be damned, he muttered to himself, unsure whether what he felt was more amusement or horror. Probably a good dose of each. He tried to pin down when his heart had turned from stone to cornmeal mush, but didn't have an answer. But it had happened, he couldn't deny that was true.

But how could he have these feelings? He hadn't even had sex with the woman yet, he'd never kissed her, except in his dreams. Of course, men had fallen for women for centuries without ever having tested the goods. Just a blind leap of faith based on a pretty face. Maybe it was better that way. Maybe it made you look more at character, values, things that really mattered.

Jordan felt like a character in some old classic black and white movie, getting hooked on a woman this way. Maybe he should ask Cary Grant's ghost for some advice. Sure, Jordan had believed in romance once, when he was *very* young, but he'd learned the hard way, become a cynic, a realist. An idiot, maybe.

He spotted a few weeds and gave them hell for trespassing in his yard. Realizing he was just making himself sweaty, without it helping, he turned back toward the house to get a cold beer.

As he entered he had a brainstorm.

That's it! He knew the answer! Rushing into his office he rummaged through files before he found a blank of the form he wanted. Locking up, he tore back out to his car, determined this time.

Now what?

Sam just wanted to be left alone to be miserable, but a guard came to take her from her cell again, only a few hours after she had returned. She scrubbed her hands across her cheeks, blew her nose, and splashed some cold water on her red and swollen eyes, before going with the guard. She tried futilely to hide the tears that had flowed so painfully after her final meeting with Jordan.

Why did he have to be the one to hate her so? And if he thought she looked like hell before, she was glad he couldn't see her now! He'd probably scream, or shudder—if not both.

She must be a fool to think she'd be left alone, that things could go on as they had before. Jordan was probably carrying out his threats, charging her with even more crimes for screwing around with the justice system. She was probably either being dragged to the warden, or punished by being sent to solitary without even a piece of paper or a pencil. It wouldn't matter if they only fed her bread and water there, but she *had* to have some way to write, or it would be pure torture.

Sam was shocked when they seated her at the same table, in the same room.

With *him* again!

She couldn't stop her heart from doing a tap dance, just to see him once more, foolishly taking it as a sign he didn't hate her. Embarrassment soon followed, but he'd never notice her blush on her ravaged, red, and tear stained face. Could this day get any worse?

Apparently, it could.

Mr. Jordan Campbell, top prosecutor, stood before her all handsome and proud, holding up a piece of paper.

"House Arrest!"

He stated it firmly, like he had said 'checkmate!' With a Cheshire Cat grin on his face, he folded his arms across his chest, and rocked back slightly on his heels. He looked like a man extremely pleased with himself.

Sam hated to burst his bubble, he looked so darn ... perfect. But with a sigh of frustration, she realized she was just right back where she started.

"I don't have a house," she said in a small voice. Glancing down at the document he had dropped on the table, she added wearily, "I won't sign it."

"Not a problem," he replied confidently. "I already signed it. Your signature is not required." He gave her a toothy grin.

"But I don't have a house, I thought I told you that already." She didn't have the strength to go through this all with him again. Or the heart.

"But I do." Jordan stated, as if that settled the matter.

How nice for him, Sam thought hopelessly. She had not forgotten what he'd said about his kitchen—and the appointments he did and did *not* want in it. Shifting in her chair, she tried to duck her head down and get her hair to cover some of her tear bloated face. Maybe he hadn't noticed?

"You will be transferred in a few days, as soon as the final arrangements go through," he proclaimed, undaunted. Looking at her slumped in her chair, he realized that he was sounding a little too bossy, too *old* Jordan. To get her to respond, he needed to show her the new Jordan. Convince, not order her. Once she spent some time with him she'd soon see he wasn't a macho jerk—anymore.

"There are certain restrictions, requirements of course." Adding in what he hoped sounded nonchalant, "I have a house I hardly ever use. You need to be somewhere like that," he assured either her, or himself. If he felt a little shaky, he plunged on encouragingly.

"It will give you a quiet, secure place to write while you are under house arrest." Seeing a strange look on her face and taking it as a reluctant frown, he added. "I'm hardly ever there, anyway."

He clearly needed a new approach, she didn't seem to be responding. He thought about her, at his house, then asked suddenly, "Do you like pink?"

"Pardon?" Sam blinked

"Pink. You know, like pink flowers, pink?"

"It's okay ... I guess," Sam answered confused. Was he trying to be nice now? "Yes, I like flowers," she answered hastily, just in case he got the wrong idea. Should she tell him she liked chocolates too?

"Great! I have flowers. Lots and lots of flowers!" He saw her glance at his empty arms and around the bare room, totally baffled.

"My house! My house has flowers, I mean. You can sit in the flowers ... on a chair. I have chairs, also, ... and write." Inspired. "No pink though. Unless... well, I guess if you need them," he wound down feeling like a gawky teen. "But, there is a table outside. To write!" he brightened, smiling like a puppy eager for a treat.

His nervousness touched Sam. He's offering his house with flowers? How sweet, she thought, with a little sigh of anticipation.

"But...Will I have a guard?" A chaperone, Sam privately thought, but more to protect him from her, if he was this sweet and sexy.

Jordan had been watching the play of emotions across her face (which *was* quite a mess!). They'd need to get the lady some good food and sleep, and get those pretty pink cheeks back.

Roses came in pink, didn't they? Maybe she'd settle for the yellow ones that had pink edges? He could picture her in his yard, surrounded by those roses, with her golden yellow hair flirting with a breeze, her normally velvet skin rose-scented, her pale cheeks—currently mostly gray and mottled-red—all pink tinged to match the petals.

Samantha was a lovely woman, with her delicate bone structure and those big warm honey-brown eyes that glowed from an inner light that captivated. Even now she was a delicate flower only slightly bruised from a passing rainstorm. She would be more beautiful returned to her health and her gold and cream and pink freshness.

Hell, Jordan thought gazing at her, he would even get the brightest, shocking pink flowers he could find if that was what Sam wanted; if that's what it took!

His thoughts led him to finally answer her question, softly, "I'll watch over you and guard you, Sam. You'll only need me." He hoped.

He watched as some of that pink came back to her face. Her brown eyes glowed gold, trapping him. No, he corrected himself, he did *not* feel trapped, he felt invited by her eyes to share something together, something very special.

That was an extremely important distinction to the new Jordan. And he realized that, while not trapped, he was well and truly caught. A dazed grin slowly lit up his face. Sure, it was a little ... terrifying. But in a good way.

Sam had been on an emotional roller coaster all day, and this was just too much!

There was something surreal about this conversation that her mind was just too tired to grasp. She thought maybe, with all the stress, her battered brain had finally cracked. Was this some kind of daytime fantasy? Something she had mentally created, and imagined so she could make the day turn out the way she'd dreamed? What else would explain this unlikely transition?

This morning he had raged at her, his eyes gray points of steel, his face stern, hard, coldly bitter. Now he seemed to be grinning at her like a fool! He acted a little nervous, looked kind of goofy, spoke deep and soft to charm her, if he wasn't still so dreadfully handsome, Sam might not have recognized him.

Look at those gray eyes gazing so fondly into hers. Eyes that had warmed to the soft color of her favorite quiet seas, lapping at her so calm, steady, soothingly hypnotic. Not a chance this was real!

Sam pinched a little skin on her arm. It hurt, but she was still convinced she was trapped in some lovely mind dream—with pink flowers and a smiling hunk to guard her. Why fight that? She might as well play along. Tomorrow she could wake up and find this was all just some fairy tale she had written down on her notepad.

Hardly able to marshal her thoughts, Sam tried to recall where they were in this dream. Oh, yes, the house, of course.

"Ah, how many bedrooms does it have?" she asked, trying to maintain her lines in this dream scene.

"Too many," Jordan answered without thinking. His eyes, still locked on hers, noticed hers go wide. "I mean two! Two bedrooms and an office. Too many for me alone. Two bathrooms. One for you alone."

"Well," she responded, softly expelling a breath. Looking down at the table she asked, "Do you really think this house arrest is necessary? It sounds so ... unusual, dramatic." Read, not real. "I mean can I think about this first?"

"Yes, sure." Jordan sat down, folded his arms, and waited.

"Alone?"

"Oh, right," he jumped back up, edging to the door. "I'll ... I'll just go get..."

"A *day*, at least?"
"Um. I'll be back tomorrow, then. Early." He finished briskly.

Jordan exited, feeling a little foolish, but excited at the idea she might actually agree. He knew it wasn't a real house arrest. Just a technical means to pry her out of this place—and better yet—get her securely in his personal custody.

He was sure her kids wouldn't mind him all but kidnapping her like this. But he wasn't going to tell Sam that's what he was about.

She *had* mislead him, after all. He'd tell her the truth. Later. Much sooner than she had confessed to him!

All is fair after all, in L-L-L-Love and war. There. He'd said it! Silently.

Jordan wiped a little sweat off his forehead.

chapter twenty-eight

Jordan didn't waste the rest of the day. Once he made a firm decision, he was a man of action.

Stopping at the courthouse, he immediately filed the Transfer to House Arrest documents, using his address and sponsorship for the record. Then employing a dazzling smile, and all the charm he could muster, he convinced the overwhelmed female court clerk to stamp, file and record the transfer immediately, despite the fact it was mere ticks of the clock away from the end of the work day. The procedure, that usually took several days to process, was rushed ahead of the line in mere minutes. Jordan realized he should smile more often—though his face muscles ached a bit.

Next on his list? He would need a good solid handcuff to transfer Sam to his custody. He knew just where to find what he needed, laughing with sudden joy at his own cleverness.

That task completed to his satisfaction, he stopped at a department store to prepare her cell.

In the electronics department, he purchased a printer and a laptop with word processing software. In the stationary area, he stocked up on paper, pens and ink, adding a hanging file folder cart. There was already a small desk in the room.

In the women's clothing department, he stood baffled, scratching the back of his neck, frowning. Whipping out his cell phone, he found the entry for Sam's daughter he had made before traveling up to her house the other day. He left a message for Penny to call him at home that evening.

Relieved to have escaped that task, he headed off to the housewares department. Along the way he snagged a prepackaged basket of scented soaps, lotions, and other girly stuff, off a table. The bed in the guest room was queen size, which seemed appropriate. Despite his fantasies, he knew his little queen would sleep there. Alone. He wanted her to feel safe and secure in his home, to have her own private space. As he had hoped, he was able to find a bag that had all the bedding needed for a queen so he didn't have to try and match all the stuff. *Not* his forte. The bag he found looked like a flower garden. That should work; it was pretty like Sam. He bought that, a couple of down pillows, and a stack of soft, thick towels for her bathroom. To wrap her soft, damp, naked skin ...

Thank God the doors already had locks on them, Jordan thought as he left. He wouldn't have to stop at a hardware store but could just head straight home and take a long cold shower.

After his shower and a long phone conversation with Penny making arrangements, Jordan carried in his purchases and set up Sam's 'cell'.

Finished making her bed, he sat down on the edge of it, and appraised the results. It still looked a little bare in this room, but Sam would want to fill it with her own things. He'd found a low bookcase, emptied it, and brought it in ready for her. Penny and Paul would be bringing down boxes of Sam's stored books and clothes and personal things.

He put a vase of fresh-cut flowers on top of the bookcase, to make her room—cell—more welcoming. He smiled slightly at that touch, proud he had grown and cut the flowers himself. He looked down at the bed, running his hand across the cheerful looking new comforter.

He hoped she liked it.

Jordan had a moment's panic. He hoped he was doing the right thing. He needed to be absolutely sure before taking this next step. There was no question that he needed to get Sam out of jail immediately; he would bring her here tomorrow. The rest of the legal details could be worked out later with Sam's family and lawyer, once he had her safe.

What Jordan needed to be sure of was himself. Was he committed to the rest of his plan, before he shared it with Sam? Could he trust his judgment? He had been a poor judge of a woman once before. That had ended disastrously—at least for him.

Jordan sat back and tried to face the pain that misjudgment had caused him in the past. He had made a decision on shallow values, his parents' values, which he wasn't sure, even then, he respected. But he was young and still desperate for approval. Finally, realizing his mistake, he had cut her loose. Too late. He had ended it. But it was like firing someone that had already quit and left the company. The only thing he really ended was her right to his profits and property—and his naive innocent faith in wedding vows.

But had he really ended it?

For her, sure. But had he just fooled himself, thinking he was free and unchained? Jordan thought of all the cycles of depression and repression he had gone through, because of her—his ex-wife. The anger he had used as a sword to keep women from his door. But had he gone through all that, suffered all that because of her? Or was he his own jailor?

When he'd heard Shelley's words, behind his back in the office, he'd begun to see what he had become.

A first class asshole!

He was working on that. Jordan knew his life was lacking something, but he was unsure what, or how to fix it.

Until Samantha Wilson became a bank robbery suspect, maybe even, subconsciously, before that when even as an irritant or opponent, she had drawn his attention and attraction.

The attention of a man who had no time or desire for any beautiful woman any longer, feeling only aversion. Jordan did not believe in fate; however he had been wrong before. It certainly seemed clear to him that this time he must be wrong in all the right ways.

He could not deny that he had found the desire to change after Sam appeared in his life; and he could not deny that Sam was essential to his future contentment. Existing just for his work, or finding some some few pleasures were not enough anymore. He'd found what he did not know he had needed. She was the water in the desert of his life. He would challenge himself, go to whatever lengths required to deserve that and deserve her. A new Jordan, for Sam.

And because of her, Jordan was seeing clearly for the first time what the core of his problem was—that he had done it to himself!

Why had he cut his wife loose, but not himself? Why had he let her own him all these years, poisoning his life, making him fear relationships for the misery they might bring, not seeing the joy they might hold? He thought that he had freed himself by divorcing his wife, but he had chained himself to the misery of that one youthful mistake.

She'd won, he'd even done it for her!

He had chosen to let her own his life since then. He hadn't freed himself, but locked himself in a self-restrictive, tormenting prison. What a godawful waste. Her hold on him was gone now, he was finally free. Free to be happy, free to be comfortable with his life, and especially, free to love one very special woman.

So did he really know Sam? Enough to place his life and future in her slender, delicate hands? That was what he needed to focus on. He didn't need to worry he would make the same mistake. He could never be blamed for letting social status blind him this time. Sam was in jail, not a debutant at a ball, but more adorable, more admirable that any he ever saw. So did he know her well enough? That is where he needed to concentrate, mentally cataloging every moment he had spent with Sam, everything he knew of her as portrayed through the eyes of those that knew her best.

He pictured the first time he had seen her, standing up against herself in court. What a gutsy woman, he recalled smiling. Though now that he knew all the details, he still had to chuckle at her grit in making her dream come true, regardless of the lunacy of her mission.

'How much time is that?' she had asked. *Then hearing her sentence, 'Okay, I guess that's enough.'* What a character! She would never bore him, that was for sure!

It was just a fluke that Jordan had even been there that day—or a benevolent fate. What if he hadn't? He knew she had grabbed his subconscious, even back then. But was that right? Something very faint nagged at his mind. It wasn't the sense of having known her before that tugged at him. That was something he still just accepted, as some connection of souls he might never understand.

But a haunting memory of a fresh spring breeze, cheerful smile, vibrant form, a melodic voice echoed somewhere in the past. Had that been in one of his endless dreams of her?

Mrs. Appleberry! Jordan slammed his hand on the desk. Unbelievable! He remembered wondering who had made the sour librarian turn up sweet, long ago. He had looked up, and yes, that had been Sam! He had noticed her and then immediately hoped she didn't bother him. Jordan groaned in self-loathing, even while he recognized that the time had not been right back then for him to open to her. Well, hell! But, making that librarian smile, that was a huge plus on Sam's list.

Physically, sexually, Sam had knocked Jordan for a loop on his first visit to the jail, without ever trying. He recalled how he cut the meeting short, embarrassed by his physical reaction. If it hadn't been for Sam, would he ever have thought about Henley's keys, and unwound those crimes? Scary thought. Sam had changed his life for the better, continually, unknowingly.

Then Rhonda—Ronnie, her pal—had portrayed a loyal, dedicated, caring, honest woman. A family woman, who set aside men, for the important things—her children.

'Prim', that's what Rhonda had complained about. Prim, but passionate, from what she told him.

Jordan had gone back to the prison, even when he knew he shouldn't. Unable to stay away from her, hurt by her lies to him. But she *had* lied in a good cause, protecting an innocent friend. Even as she had become a suspect in a bank robbery, she had kept her potency for Jordan. She had not let him intimidate her, she had done her best to help his investigation.

Then Jordan had received the letter, and traveled up to see her kids. That had been the meeting that completely tipped his emotions over the cliff. He had really liked them, impressed by how mature and well balanced they were. They finally seemed to warm to him, also, when they saw he was there to help their mother.

It was Jordan's respect for them, and the open way they discussed their concerns for Sam, and showed their love, that made him finally ask them, in anger and frustration, "Why the hell did you guys let her do it in the first place?"

They hadn't taken offense. It was Penny that patiently explained to him.

"There is something you need understand, Jordan. We love our mother, as a parent, and a friend. When we have gone through troubles, made mistakes, she didn't punish or judge us first. First she held our hand, helped us to understand and find the good lessons. To help us grow, and build ourselves within."

"Then she grounded us." Paul interrupted with a grin.

Penny smiled. "Discipline is an essential part of a parent's love and guidance of her children," she quoted her mother. She continued seriously, "Mom also shared all her own mistakes and flaws growing up with us, and the ones she was still making. It was a way of showing us that just as we loved her despite those, she would always love us just as we are. We didn't need to be perfect to be loved. And she showed us that even as adults, we would make mistakes, and needed to move forward, continually learning from them and growing better and wiser.

"We don't agree with what she chose to do, but after the way she has always been there to love and support us, how can we withdraw ours from her now?

"She never gave us a chance to stop her, or we would have. And maybe someday we will be glad she didn't, so we don't have any regrets. But not until she is home safe again. With her book."

There was a long silence in the room after Penny finished.

Jordan was speechless, in awe of this amazing family and its bonds.

"We're miserable about using the letter now." That misery was clear in Penny's voice. "But she looks terrible! She isn't well. We have to do this for her sake, even if she hates us!"

Jordan cleared his throat, trying to swallow the lump lodged there. "It doesn't sound to me like your mother could ever hate you for anything, no matter what. Just keep that official letter sealed and locked away for now. I'll look into it, and see if I can get her out another way, so you kids don't need to feel any guilt. You're doing the right thing. I'll do everything to help you get her out." Jordan promised quietly.

"We appreciate the offer, and we do want you to help us get her out, but there have been too many secrets already. It's time to get back to the openness our family is used to sharing. We want our mother to know that you came because we received the document. She will be relieved to know that we know now, though we don't expect her to admit or show that for some time," Paul's mouth quirked up in a small smile.

"If you're sure?" Jordan saw Penny's nod of agreement with what her brother had requested. "Okay, but I will still try to resolve the issue through the prosecutor's office, so I can take the heat and try to take the need for you kids to take any other legal action off your shoulders. You kids reason with her and convince, and I'll," Jordan paused, then let loose a bark of laughter. "I'll probably try threatening her with 'impersonating a criminal' or something. Hard to be very intimidating when your target *wants* to go to jail. But I'll think of something. The important thing for you guys to remember is not to worry. I'm on your side in this."

And not just because of his physical attraction to their mother, because it had become so much more than that as he saw her through the eyes of her best friend and her children.

Jordan would have been surprised to know, after that first meeting with Sam's kids, that Penny was well aware that he was on their mother's side—and why.

He had come to know Sam through the eyes of those closest to her. He wanted to belong to that magic circle of family and friends he so admired. He wanted to belong to Sam.

So he knew her; he *was* sure.

Sam was the one he wanted and needed in his life. He was committed to that. He was sure of himself.

Now all he had to do was pick Sam up from jail, and convince *her.*

That would be the tricky part.

chapter twenty-nine

Jordan entered the Women's Compound unsure of what his reception would be, but determined this time. He had called ahead and discussed the transfer with the warden, so a guard led him directly to Sam's cell. Seeing the prosecutor hesitate at the door, the guard told him it was unlocked, and to come find her at her station, with the prisoner's paperwork, when they were ready to leave.

He stood outside and looked in the window at the figure slumped on the stool at the small table she'd set up as a desk. Though her back was partially turned towards him, he could see from her lifeless profile that she wasn't writing. Probably concentrating over her words, Jordan assumed, before realizing she didn't even have a pen in her hand to capture any of her thoughts. The slump in her shoulders told him they were not happy or inspired ones. In fact, she just seemed to be staring at her blank notepad, a little dazed.

Maybe this meant she was resigned to the change. He'd planned, at first, to make this quick and painless—for him, anyway. He was reluctant to expose himself so soon, time enough, he had rationalized, to do that later.

But as Jordan placed his hand on the door to enter, he felt the excitement build in him. He knew he would not be able to wait, not the way she looked just now. He needed a reason, a right to touch her, to hold her. He wiped his palms on his slacks, straightened his tie, checked his pocket, then entered.

Hearing the sound of the door opening, Sam turned an uncomprehending stare on him, before her eyes widened, seeing her thoughts materialized into flesh. The impact of those wide, warm brown eyes made Jordan's throat go dry. She was so close, so lovely, so small. Trying to clear his throat, he awkwardly launched his planned approach.

"I've come to transfer you to house arrest. Please rise and place your hands in front of you to be cuffed." Too nervous to remember what to say, Jordan had decided to try to joke his way through until he recovered. He didn't realize how tight his nerves made his face, how gruff his voice.

Sam rose silently, intimidated and overwhelmed by his sudden close presence. She meekly brought her hands together in front of her, staring up at him like a trapped rabbit.

Jordan reached out and clasped both of her hands in his. A bolt of heat and awareness flashed between them at the bare skin-to-skin bond—so often dreamt, so long withheld.

Jordan held her eyes locked with his as he reached one hand back to his pocket, then brought it forward to encircle her hand.

Sam, was so lost in the strange intimate intensity of eyes she just stared up at him, hardly noticing the metal cuff that circled only her left hand, third finger.

Jordan waited, his gray eyes patient and amused, watching hers as awareness dawned.

Sam gasped, surprised, then pulled her hands free, and looked down. "But…that's…"

"Routine procedure ma'am when I place a women under arrest in my house." Jordan tried to keep a straight face, but could feel his lips twitching.

"But, this is a ring. It looks like …"

"A color coded cuff," Jordan corrected. "Golden-brown topaz encased in sparkly diamonds to match the inmates eyes."

Jordan couldn't help himself now, he laughed at the expression on Sam's face. He didn't know if she would throw the cuff back at him, or not, but the sheer joy of seeing his ring on her slender finger could not be contained.

Sam stared at her splayed fingers, gave her head a clearing shake, and stumbling, backed up and sat down hard on her cot. Her legs couldn't hold her up any longer. Her brain would not function. Staring up at him like he was some kind of alien, she tried to speak again, "But this looks like an …?"

"Engagement ring." Jordan stated firmly, helping her, nodding his head in confirmation.

"You'd do this just to get me out of jail?"

Weren't they supposed to say 'yes' or 'no' when a man mentioned the word engagement? Off his script, Jordan reverted to humor again,

"Hell, no. I plan to imprison you at my place where I can have my wicked way with you." He laughed. She didn't.

"But, we don't even know each other." Sam whispered, still dazed.

Jordan dropped down to her level, recapturing her hands and her eyes, knowing now was the time for him to step up and give his closing argument.

"But *I* do know *you*," he told her seriously, pouring every bit of his certainty into his eyes, as he knelt before her. "I know who you are, I know what you are. I know your values, your beliefs, your dreams, your life." Pausing, he gave her a fond smile, "I even know your flaws. Your family told me; Rhonda told me. I know *you*. I know what I want. I want you." He gently squeezed the hands he held in his, then lowered his head and kissed them.

All Sam could do was think, *Oh My God!* The tenderness of his touch made her shiver. He had become so important to her – too important. He meant too much for them to rush like this, her numbed mind protested. "It's too soon," she told him wistfully. "This is so fast."

He rose to sit beside her, keeping her hands in his, not giving her any chance to remove his ring. Glancing thoughtfully around the room, trying to summon up the best words, the best way to explain to her all he felt, Jordan's gaze landed on some pieces of paper on her desk.

"We all go through life and it changes us, sometimes for the better, sometimes for the worse. It weathers us. Our experiences and journey are like those papers over there, each of our lives shown in the written lines, but especially in the torn edges, all the tears and gaps, all the ragged edges make us each unique.

"I felt like I knew you, even before I heard your life story. From those you love, I've learned what is written on your side of the page, what caused all the tears and gaps at the edges. I also have gaps and scars that I haven't always dealt with very well, though I'm trying to now.

"You don't know all my story, but I want to tell you. I want to show you who I am, who I can be. I know that you will need time. You're right that it is too soon, too fast for you. But for me it is not, I've wasted too much of my life not seeking what I needed. I let fear cripple me. I won't let it cause me to lose the one thing, the one woman I need most.

"I know I am telling you the truth when I say that I know I want you, I need you to help fill those gaps, to make me whole and that I am committed, Samantha, to helping mend any you have.

"I feel that somehow our separate lives and paths have made us like two halves of one single torn page. We were meant to find the way to weave together those ragged edges. I knew instinctively, subconsciously, from the first, that you were the rest of my life, even before I heard about the wonderful woman that you are.

"Somehow those two torn edges were meant to come together, in this time, in this place. So that once placed together, side by side, we could be joined, weaving all the edges together. Fitting perfectly, the way it was meant to turn out all along." Jordan finished passionately.

Sam gasped softly, the tender, sober words filling the corners of her heart with warmth and certainty.

"I've felt it too," she admitted shyly, "as if I knew you somehow. I don't know how or why, but I felt I ..." Embarrassed, her voice trailed off.

"I know you feel it's too fast, too soon, Sam. But not for me. I know you through your friends and family. And I confess," Jordan smiled wryly, "I'd probably marry you just to get my hands on them so I could have a family like that for myself. But I know you need time to find out if I'm right for you. If I deserve you. I will want you for forever. Need you always. You have freed me Sam, from a jail that I didn't even know I was in until I met you. Until I wanted out, so I could have you."

Before she questioned that statement, which he needed more time than he had now to fully share with her, he tried for a lighter note.

"Besides, now that you will be loose, out where all those other men can see and fall for you, I want to make damn sure I get the first chance to make my case. I want my ring on your finger. I want you cuffed to me while you get to know me, while you decide for sure if I deserve to marry you. And on those terms," he grinned, "we will take as long as you want until you are ready. I'm ready now. I'm sure now. Will you take this first step with me seriously?"

Sam gazed at him a moment. Though her face remained serious, as he had requested, there was a little glint of imp, a shimmer of joy, in her eyes.

"I think that is a wise plan," she nodded solemnly. "I do have to make very sure that my family wants you, of course."

Jordan laughed out loud, relieved and charmed. He scooped Sam up and pulled her into his lap, cuddling her in close, burying his face in her hair, suggesting in her ear, "Should we shake lips on that deal?"

His lips brushed across her cheek, eagerly seeking her mouth. He almost groaned in pleasure at his first taste of her, the first capture of those soft lips, their sweet warmth. He sipped tenderly, raising a hand to cup her face, gazing into her eyes, before kissing them closed. The feelings, too intense, took all his restraint not to crush her lips, all his patience to wait for her mouth to rise up again and seek his own.

Through lazy lashes Sam gazed at him, curled a hand behind his neck, and pulled him down, capturing his mouth and owning it. She parted her lips, inviting him, and he plunged in, drowning her soft moan. Only his strong arms kept Sam's weakened, pliant body, from falling off into space. His mouth sent waves of passion undulating through her veins, so filled with sweet sensation, she never wanted to come up for air.

He tightened an arm around her, pressing her breasts into his chest, his mouth never leaving hers. She could feel the fast, heavy thudding of his heart, as his other hand glided softly along the curve of her waist, sculpted her hip then slid down her thigh, before wandering slowly, teasingly back up across her hip to rest just shy of the swell of her breast, as if waiting permission.

Releasing her mouth with a infinitely slow sweet suction, he dove back hungrily to capture her lower lip softly between his, before straying to the pulse in her slender throat, then to nuzzle at her ear.

He nibbled there, then whispered huskily, his breath a sensuous tickle, "You are sweeter than all my dreams of you." He claimed her lips again, as they parted in a soft sigh. She felt as if she was going to melt, or burn up in flames...

"HEY! What do you think this is?" The harsh, sudden voice of the guard startled them rudely from their rapture.

Untangling themselves, quickly and guiltily, they turned startled eyes to each other, then Jordan began to chuckle, then threw his head back and laughed in delighted abandon.

"Sorry, guard, we completely forgot where we are." He grinned shamelessly. "Oh, here is a paper for you, by the way. It's the release form for this delightful damsel," he turned and threw a rowdy wink at her.

"I've come to rescue her and carry her off into the sunset like any self-respecting romantic knight," he claimed boldly.

His beaming announcement completely stunned the guard who, recognizing him, was staring in shock. Could this really be that ice-cold bastard of a prosecutor? My god! The man must be drunk!

"Are you drunk?" the guard asked suspiciously.

"Yes, maybe I am! I'm over my limit. I'm drunk on love!"

"Right," the guard noted dryly, checking the release paper again.

Sam was hopelessly dissolved in laughter, some of it from nerves. She rolled on the cot hugging herself, wallowing in sudden happiness. She didn't know if she was laughing at the craziness of it all, or the giddy thought he must really love her to proclaim it so boldly. She could not believe how wildly romantic Jordan was!

"This must be a dream!", she thought in wonder, unaware she had spoken out loud.

"No, it's not a dream," the guard replied gruffly. "More like a nightmare, if you ask me," she muttered under her breath. "Okay, you're free to go, and a good thing too if you're going to carry on like this!" Scowling, she turned to lead them out of the cell.

Sam grabbed her duffel bag and began to unceremoniously toss in all her belongings.

Jordan swept an arm across her desk, sending pencils and pens flying, a dictionary thudding into a box then, pausing a moment, he turned and roughly shook a pillow free of its case. Carefully he collected and evened the edges of the stack of written pages at the edge of the desk. Placing it inside the pillowcase gently, he wrapped and folded it into a neat bundle then shifted things aside to nestle it safely and securely at the bottom of the box.

Sam gasped. Her book! She'd almost forgotten about it! How could she have?

Hearing her startled breath, Jordan whipped around then stilled when he saw her standing there frozen, eyes wide, her mouth open as if to speak. He waited, but she just stared at him.

"Sam? You okay, honey?" At her continued silence he twisted to look down at the desk, and the floor beneath it, checking to make sure he hadn't missed a page, before turning back to her.

"I was careful with your novel. I didn't mix up the pages," Jordan promised, only to see her eyes flare wider with surprise, or was it shock? "Don't worry about the pillowcase, sweetheart. I'll return it, I promise." He saw her face seem to relax slightly at that comment, her eyes warm a little.

"Besides," he teased, "no one steals prison linens!" He knew his laugh sounded nervous, but was relieved to see a slight smile bloom slowly on her lips. "You trust me then?" It was meant as a casual question, but he saw how seriously she was studying his face, before answering.

Sam looked at the man whose presence filled the cell and felt her heart filling with him. He had called her pile of pages, that had looked so small and insubstantial but had meant such a sacrifice for her, a 'novel'. Not a book, but a novel. It had a ring to it of value, as if its completion was already assured. It had a weight she had been afraid to assign her efforts out loud; though as her characters developed and grew and lived a life of their own, it had the weight she had secretly hoped to give them someday. Now Jordan made it sound real.

'Your novel' he had said, as casually as if he'd never once called it 'a stupid book!'. He'd wrapped it as carefully as if it was something fragile and precious.

Stepping up to him, Sam put her arms around his waist, looking up at the soft silver of his eyes.

"Yes, Jordan, I *do* trust you," she whispered as she rose on her toes to brush his lips with a kiss. As his arms circled her, wrapping her in his scent and strength, she nestled her face against his chest, her cheek over the warm steady heartbeat of this man that would let her make her own dreams become real. She trusted him.

"Ahem!" The impatient guard in the hallway cleared her throat again.

Laughing, Jordan scooped up the rest of her clothes and threw them over his shoulder, and just that quickly she was gone from the cell that had been her hope and home for months.

Outside, after clearing the final formalities, they headed across the grass to his car.

"Wait a minute," Jordan stopped suddenly, remembering he had forgotten something important.

"Do you think, someday, you might be able to love me?"

Sam set her bag on the lawn and turned to him. Nerves had been chewing at her again. She looked up at the anxious gray eyes, and glanced down at the ground, unsure what to say. Spotting the cuff, glimmering on her left hand, she blushed. Trying to think of some light way to give herself some time, she asked, with a mischievous smile, "Well, I don't know. Are you always going to be so wildly romantic?"

Jordan grinned. She looked so shy, and scared, and lovely.

"You know what, Sam? I have been a very public, very unromantic fool for the last twenty years of my life, as you've noticed. How does a penance of being a wildly romantic fool for the next twenty sound?"

He dropped her belongings and swooped down grabbing her around the waist, then bent her back across his arm in a passionate dip. Grinning at her surprised giggle, he kissed the tip of her nose, looking into those heated, sparkling golden brown eyes.

"Well...one would have to love that, I'd think," Sam laughed, before his mouth stole her breath, crushed her lips in a kiss that showed her the passion he had planned for her.

Oh yeah! Sam thought, as liquid heat stole through her. Her head fell back and Jordan took advantage of her exposed throat, burying his face against her neck, nibbling sweetly along its length.

"GO HOME!" hollered the guard angrily. "We run a decent prison here!"

Laughing madly, they grabbed up Sam's belongings and raced to Jordan's car.

Shelley was helping Elsa set out bowls and platters of food on the linen draped tables set in Jordan's fragrant and colorfully blooming back yard. Setting down a bowl filled with juicy watermelon, blueberries, and pineapple, she thought the scene looked more like a wedding party than a 'welcome home' event, as the gaily strung banner declared.

"Elsa, I just don't understand. Why is this party being held here? Why not at Ms. Wilson's parents house?" She glanced over her shoulder, hoping she hadn't been overhead, but spotted Sam's parents happily chatting with their grandkids as they packed soft drinks into ice-filled coolers.

Elsa gave a mysterious smile, but answered seriously, her words belied by an amused sparkle in her eyes.

"Jordan feels he can maintain better control of the prisoner here. She is still under house arrest, you know." Her cough sounded suspiciously like a swallowed chuckle, but it was hardly noticed.

"Still, it just doesn't make sense to me." A worried frown crinkled Shelley's forehead as she slowly shook her head. "Since when do prosecutors put people under house arrest in their own homes, Elsa? He's not responsible for that! And what about a chaperone? Do you realize what this could do to his career? His reputation? What if it became known? The papers would crucify him and any possible future political career he may want."

Elsa laughed. "Oh, honey, I know you haven't known Jordan that long, or had a very pleasant time from what you did know of him." She paused to chuckle, remembering, "Did you know he told me to order you a bouquet of dead flowers once?"

"What? Why that ... wait, I don't remember..." Shelley sputtered, angry.

"Oh, never mind that now." Elsa calmed her with a pat on her shoulder. "He didn't mean it personally, it was just frustration on his part. I knew that and never ordered them. It was justice he wanted, Shelley, and you happened to be the one thwarting him at the time, at least in his mind.

"That's all Jordan's ever wanted since I've been with him. He tossed away the elite career and society's approval long ago, after it burned him and turned him into a bitter man. I've been so worried about him," Elsa sighed.

"He doesn't care about politics or the media's adulation now, though some think he does. All he cares about is right and wrong, that's all. And now, hopefully," Elsa's smile was as warm and wistful as if she was speaking of a favored child, "finally, he's starting to care about himself again, and what his own life needs. And," she grinned, "being Jordan, he has it all planned out methodically so that every detail is under his control." Especially Sam, she smiled privately.

Shelley still didn't get it, but it was clear that Elsa seemed to and heartily approved.

Brittany's frown matched the confusion of Shelley's across the lushly planted yard.

"But if she's innocent, and he knows it," Brit complained, "why is Paul's mother still under house arrest?" She glanced again toward the deck door to see if Sam had arrived with Jordan yet.

Rhonda glanced beneath her lashes in time to catch Penny and Paul quickly concealing smiles. Yes, they knew she saw, but were keeping the secret well.

"Because, darling, he tried to release Sam but the stubborn woman wouldn't go or accept his help." Aunt Ronnie enlightened Paul's girlfriend with a roll of her eyes that showed how clearly disgusted she was with Sam for rejecting such a prime hunk of a man.

"The only way he could get out of his own jail was to arrest the silly woman!" Rhonda finished cryptically, then sauntered off to find a cool glass of wine, leaving Brittany even more baffled than before.

"But.. what? He's not in .. this is *not* legal, is it? Paul, what it so damn funny?" she huffed, clearly the only one not in on some joke.

He leaned over and wrapped her up in a bear hug, trapping her arms so she couldn't take a swing at him for not telling her sooner, then whispered in her ear.

"Oh, I see, so it's not real?" She listened again, then whispered back, "Just a few days then, while the paperwork's done?" Relieved, she asked louder, "Then she's free?"

Paul turned to wink at his sister and laughed, adding in a normal voice, "I don't think he actually plans to let her go. At least not until she's finished her book."

"But," Brittany was still worried for his mother, "that could take a long time."

"Exactly!" Beamed Sam's father joining them. "Doesn't he seem like a fine man for my Samantha? She needs someone to take good care of her."

For once, Sam's kids could laugh in agreement with their dear Granddad's oft heard comment.

Sam sat quietly as Jordan negotiated the roads. Leaning dreamily against the back of her seat, she watched the outdoors pass by with a contented smile on her face, amazed at how new and green everything seemed since she had last been free. Rolling her window down a bit, she sniffed at the fresh air like a happy puppy on a drive. Jordan stayed silent, letting her alone with her thoughts, holding her hand each chance he had and casting her fond glances. It was enough for him just to get to touch her after all the imagined times he'd done so in his dreams.

Sam was letting herself absorb everything she had missed, the sights, the sounds, the smells, and being touched – by anyone – aside from a guard's hand clamped just above her elbow. Touched by someone with caring and affection, being touched by the man in her dreams, was just ....

Sam could not even come up with the words to express her feelings to have the man she'd hoped for, but never really touched, clasp her hand in his. The desire she felt was too much to even try to absorb at the moment. Or even just the wonder, the simple pleasure and warmth of having his arm wrapped around her shoulder.

To have a shoulder—his shoulder—to use for anything and everything. His warmth to lean on, to cry on, to bury her face in and feel his heart beating beneath, sure and steady—there for her and *with* her. And add to that Sam's love for him, which she had been so afraid to confess yet to him—or barely to herself.

When the car pulled to a stop, Sam stared around her in delight, hardly believing where she was. Jordan came around the car and clasped her hand, folding her fingers in his, pulling her with him over the logs and down onto the sands of her favorite beach.

Sam sighed and felt a lump rise in her throat. He does know me, she thought. Jordan had claimed he could be sure, he knew all about her. For the first time, Sam could really believe in that, trust it, as he took her directly to her favorite driftwood stump.

Climbing up into the wooden palm, Jordan reached down and lifted Sam up, then sat down and pulled her between his legs, her back against his chest. Cuddling her close against him, he folded his arms over her chest, his cheek warm against the side of her face.

Turning his head to plant a kiss on her temple, Jordan began to speak to her, his voice soft and quiet showing he respected this as Sam's sacred place.

"Sam, I wanted to be here with you, I hope you don't mind. I know it's special. I can see why. I wanted to share that and have a private moment with you before we go back to my house. Your family, your parents and kids, with Aaron & Brittany, and Rhonda are all there, setting up a welcome home party for you. "So before we get there, I wanted to talk about the ring, and my dreams for you.

"I love you Sam," his voice was soft and deep, sending a shiver down her spine. "I know that it must seem too sudden to have my ring on your finger, but I want you to understand that all it says is that you will give me a chance, give me time, get to know me. Try to love me.

"I have made my commitment to you, but you are free to take all the time you need to decide if you want me. But, I want to warn you that if you do say yes, if you marry me, it *is* forever. I won't let you go once you've accepted the wedding band that goes with it.

"Regardless of what you decide, my home is yours, your room there yours alone, you don't owe me anything you don't want to give. And the ring is yours to keep. So before we go back to the house, if you're not ready for a trial engagement, you might want to move it to another finger. It's up to you."

Not letting her speak, he rose and lifted her down to the beach. Clasping her hand in his, he urged her to stroll out with him toward where the tide receded, and together they walked as one close silhouette as the sun turned the sky violet, then red, as it set.

Sam knew he was the one for her as Jordan tenderly recreated her own romantic beach scene.

Only better than fiction.

Oh, so *much* more sweetly than Sam could ever have dreamed!

Bett Bone

epilogue

It was a tiny news item, hidden on a back page of the local news, Jordan saw to that.

Un-drunken Driver Freed From Jail—

S. Wilson, female, originally charged and sentenced four months ago, has been found to be guilty only of sitting in her car inebriated. As there is no drunken parking charge currently on the statutes, she has been released from her jail sentence. Police have decided not to charge her for falsely trying to maintain her guilt. When asked if she will seek damages, the victim smiled and stated that she thinks the prosecutor in the case deserves a life sentence, but she will not bring any charges against the department.

It would not receive much notice as the front pages of all the papers had banner headlines concerning the recent arrest of an organized crime ring that had had its far flung tentacles wrapped around much of the crime in the community for the last decade. The head of that organization was a locally prominent citizen, Abe Damon, aka Honest Abe. His corruption included using the youth of the city to commit crimes. Serious charges were being filed both locally and at the state and federal levels, all having cooperated in a task group to bring the organization down, led by local Chief Prosecutor, Jordan Campbell.

A picture of the handsome prosecutor leading the formerly prominent citizen away in handcuffs, covered half of the front page. When asked if he was disappointed that most of the charges would be prosecuted in federal court, rather than by him after years of work, he was quoted as saying, "Not at all. What is important is that we have removed this poison from our community and from damaging our youth. Remember, we are not competing against each other, but against the criminal elements, and it takes the whole law enforcement team, together with the help of the citizens, to get the job done."

The announcements page carried another photo of the man. In this one, the prosecutor's grin covered half of his face and he had a petite and beaming blonde wrapped in his embrace. The joyously happy couple wished to announce that they were engaged to be married for forever.

Sam cut out all the newspaper articles to save. Her mom did the same, so did Rhonda, and Penny, and Paul. Sam and Jordan had an extra wallet size picture made of the engagement photo, which they fondly presented to Sam's dad.

Mr. Wilson was a very happy man.

Bett Bone

About the Author

Bett lives in the beautiful Pacific Northwest near what is now known locally as the Salish Sea and just an hour—or so, depending on the ferry lines—from the Olympic National Rainforest. Just a short drive in any direction brings plenty of scenic inspiration. But, in addition to reading every chance she gets, she loves to visit the national parks of the Northwest also.

Bett has written two books of her National Park Roads Series—*Buffalo Road* and *Going to the Sun Road*, about Montana's Parks, Yellowstone and Glacier, and is working on a third book in that series.

Guilty Plot is the first book in her "Beware of Boomer" romance trilogy, a trip down memory lane for the Boomer Generation.

Contact by email : Bett@bettboneauthor.com

Coming Next

An ARTS & CRAFTS AFFAIR

A beautiful Pacific coastal town hosts their annual Arts Festival drawing artists and visitors from all over to the beautiful views both on canvas and along the rippling waters—and in the eyes of Rhonda Sayles—the backside of a handsome male potter. But why does it also draw the interest of Prosecutor Jordan Campbell's office?

Start your summer on the coast with An Arts & Crafts Affair, by Bett Bone, Book 2 in the Beware of Boomer Trilogy

Other Stories by Bett

Can't get out to a National Park lately?

Hitch a ride with the National Park Road Series by Bett Bone

Enjoy amazing scenery, ancient stories, travel, romance and laughter.

www.ingramcontent.com/pod-product-compliance
Lightning Source LLC
Chambersburg PA
CBHW032152190626
46814CB00005BA/1956